Also by Stephen Sheppard

The Four Hundred

Monte Carlo

A novel by

Stephen Sheppard

SUMMIT BOOKS
New York

Copyright © 1983 by Aphelion International Limited
All rights reserved
including the right of reproduction
in whole or in part in any form
Published by SUMMIT BOOKS
A Division of Simon & Schuster, Inc.
Simon & Schuster Building
Rockefeller Center
1230 Avenue of the Americas
New York, New York 10020
First published in Great Britain 1983 by Secker & Warburg Ltd.
SUMMIT BOOKS and colophon are trademarks of Simon & Schuster, Inc.
Manufactured in the United States of America

1 2 3 4 5 6 7 8 9 10

First American Edition
Library of Congress Cataloging in Publication Data
Sheppard, Stephen, 1945–
Monte Carlo.

1. World War, 1939-1945—Fiction.   I. Title.
PR6069.H4553M6   1983   823'.914   83-15403
ISBN 0-671-44789-0

For the two Williams in my life
My darling son – Stephen William Alexander
Who wonders
and
My dearest beloved father – Reginald William
Who now knows.

Acknowledgements

My thanks are due to the following for permission to quote from the lyrics of songs:

1. *These Foolish Things*, (music by Jack Strachey, words by Eric Maschwitz) are reproduced by kind permission of the copyright owners, Boosey & Hawkes Music Publishers Ltd.

2. *A Good Man is Hard to Find*, (music and words by Eddie Green) © 1918 Edwin H. Morris & Co. Inc. are reproduced by kind permission of Francis Day & Hunter Ltd. 138–140 Charing Cross Road, London WC2H 0LD. Copyright renewed 1945 Edwin H. Morris & Co., A Division of MPL Communications, Inc. International copyright secured. All rights reserved.

3. *Love Me or Leave Me*, (music and words by Gus Kahn) © 1928 Bregman Vocco & Conn Inc. are reproduced by kind permission of EMI Music Publishing Ltd. 138–140 Charing Cross Road, London WC2H 0LD.

4. *Mad About the Boy* by Noel Coward, copyright © 1932 by Chappell & Co., Ltd. Copyright renewed. Published in the U.S.A. by Chappell & Co., Inc. All Rights Reserved. Used by permission.

If fate has a face, it must smile often.
If fate has a voice, it would say:
   'You might get lucky if you're careful.'
In Monte Carlo, who is careful?

Prologue

A young boy came into the drawing room and crossed to the grand piano. The seated audience had gathered two deep in a semicircle facing a huge leaded window. Several sections of the opaque coloured glass were open and from the well-tended garden outside, where twilight glowed, the scent of roses in bloom drifted into the large house, reminding many amongst the expectant group of other summers which had ended more pleasantly . . .

The boy's fingers poised for a moment, then with confidence and real talent he began to play Chopin, his hands moving with great skill, the suppleness of youth and astonishing sensitivity for one who was barely eleven years old.

As the music played, tears were shed and a proud father looked at the mother of his child with the same love that had created their son.

The boy touched the last note softly, looked up and saw the faces of his parents, beaming. There was a silence, then enthusiastic applause. Adults forgot that they had been listening to a child. For a moment they had heard passions from another era.

The boy played again, a short piece by Liszt, then the lamps were lit and his mother sat down to play Brahms. Tentative at first, her performance was more delicate, but no less impressive. Then it was time for dinner.

That night the boy was allowed to stay up and dine as a man, dressed for the occasion; he was flushed and proud at the concession. 'His Excellency' Aram Pilikian – so his men had called him for many years – introduced his son to friends in the city of Baku who had previously only heard mention of the boy's skill as a pianist. Stiffly, remembering his father as an example, the son of 'his Excellency' bowed and shook hands. He even kissed the fingers of a young lady who was particularly attractive, which caused both boy and woman to blush. Aram's fatherly eyes meant to be admonishing, but instead they twinkled. Hovahannes was seated next to his mother, at the end of the long dining table, beautifully set. He was introduced to two army officers: one a general in khaki with red flashes on his collar, the other a captain. The boy was in awe – real

1

soldiers, and British! The general's name was Dunsterville. He had come to save them all from the imminent Turkish invasion just when it seemed the war would be over.

Dinner in the great house was served with style and consumed with much appreciation. When the meal was over the boy was gently told to take his leave of the dinner party, where he had drunk his first glass of wine.

The ladies retired from the dining room and the men were left with cigars and brandy and hard talk of war. An American missionary, a perspiring young man called Clarence Symes, became nervous during the conversations and drank more than a man of God should have done, but the Turks had already proved, just south of the city, that these were indeed 'ungodly times', as he repeated often that evening.

Oil had given Aram Victor Pilikian power. His treatment of those who worked for him had earned respect, and the development of new techniques in oil drilling, extraction and delivery had made him wealthy, until revolution broke out in Russia and his situation changed. A Centro-Caspian government was set up and the opposing factions began to interrupt normal living. 'His Excellency' became inwardly confused by the disruption of all that was familiar. He strengthened the defences of his already imposing home against a possible rising from the oilfield workers. Then the Turks declared war and moved against southern Russia, facing Aram Victor with an agonizing decision. Should he remain and defend everything the Pilikians had owned for a century, or evacuate his family and servants and become a refugee? At that moment fifteen hundred British soldiers – 'Dunsterforce' – arrived to help defend liberty, so 'his Excellency' stayed on, and entertained.

General Dunsterville was very confident. He reaffirmed his mission to support any resistance, which leading men in the city assured their British deliverers would be total – they would 'overwhelm' the Turks! After numerous ports and brandies had been dispensed, the reverse became unthinkable. But the first thing a man of any intelligence learns is that liquor lies. And at the end of their magnificent dinner party, at the beginning of September 1918, in that palace of a house in the best part of the suburbs of the city of Baku, where the Armenian oil magnate Aram Pilikian had held court for so many years, alcohol fooled them all.

Flames engulfed the Armenian quarter in the city of Baku on the Caspian Sea. During the night the outlying oilfields of Balakhani and Sabunchi-Ramani had been set ablaze by artillery fire, so by midday a thick pall of black smoke blotted out even the distant, shimmering horizon. Fifteen thousand men of the Ottoman first army waited patiently on heights above the city that gave them an excellent view of the destruction and panic within the walls. Several officers checked their watches whilst

2

most of the men sat in the broiling sun, lazily gossiping or picking their teeth after a meagre issue of bread and potatoes. Horses whinnied, unslung rifles were stripped and oiled, bayonets were honed on soft rock. The ammunition carrier, pulled by two exhausted mules, moved from group to group distributing shells of assorted calibres to the numerous field guns. Water boys followed, leaping out of range as Turkish soldiers invited them closer with extended fingers. Coarse laughter and yelled invective spluttered and died in the heat. By 3 in the afternoon even the insects were silent.

Sweat rolled down the faces of two divisions, dripped from the chins of three hundred officers and glistened on the brow of Enver Bey. His eyes squinted beneath thick brows. There was no pity in his expression, as there was none in his heart. He watched carefully through field glasses as the first wave of recruited irregulars, his 'Bashibazooks', excited to fever pitch, succeeded in forcing open the distant city gates. Then they poured through into Baku itself to make it a hell on earth.

Enver lowered his binoculars slowly and leaned back in a wicker chair set beneath a canvas awning. For a moment he surveyed the surrounding barren hillsides where the might of the Ottoman Empire sprawled awaiting his orders. Enver's regular soldiers were ready at all times to serve as he commanded. They had fleets of empty carts to transport their loot, their loins were always susceptible to the pleasures of the flesh, however acquired, and their weapons were the tools of cruel, soulless bodies. To them all, conscience was a word for the weak and had no bearing on the work to be done that day.

At 4 o'clock on 15 September 1918, in the southern Caucasus province of Azerbaijan, outside the Russian seaport city of Baku, bugles sounded from all over the hillsides occupied by mud-green-uniformed soldiers. Within moments they were on their feet and alert. The orders of the day were bellowed loudly – the instructions unashamedly clear. Seen from below in the surrounded city, the hillsides themselves seemed suddenly to move, lurching forward and down towards the houses clustered inside the walls of Baku, slowly gaining a horrific momentum. As tangible as the fear and panic in the eyes of those few who watched the movement of this great army was the malicious excitement and terrifying expectancy of the soldiers as they advanced in close order to the steady beat of drums.

In the city, the great bell of the Armenian church began to toll ominously. It sounded out the all too clear warning that the bringers of indiscriminate destruction and violent death had broken through the gates.

The harbour of Baku was a scene of frantic confusion and fear. Terror had driven a large part of the city's population to the quaysides in a desperate attempt to get out. There were few boats remaining and fewer still that would put in to accept refugees. The Turkish irregulars were fighting towards the centre of the city and the hastily constructed defences bounding the Armenian quarter. Half the defenders were desperately trying to control fires burning fiercely from the battles waged during the night. Now, from the surrounding hillsides, like distant thunder, the drums came nearer, beating out their message of hate and vengeance.

Throughout the Ottoman Empire, every year of the great world war, 'Kesab taburi' butcher battalions had been sent by the ruling government against Armenians justifiably opposed to deportations; their orders – to deprive, humiliate and slaughter. Eventually, they had decimated an entire population. Now, almost at the war's end, many of the refugees from this barbarism, given shelter by their fellow Armenians in a foreign country, were trapped by the Turkish invasion of southern Russia in a city at the mercy of a merciless enemy.

Clarence Symes heard the city gates splinter then collapse, even from the centre of the old town, where he occupied the garret of a ramshackle house beside the mission building. The roar of triumph from the Muslim invaders carried into the stifling air, sounding like some giant predator come to kill and feed.

Clarence's plump face glistened in the suffocating heat of his dark, cramped rooms. Fear forced him to nervous, clumsy action. Wiping the sweat from his forehead and cheeks, he hastily gathered up the papers on his desk, searched wildly around the small room for anything else he could carry, ran into the bedroom and flung everything towards his open suitcase lying on the unmade bed. He took down a picture of Christ above a table then stuffed into the case what clothes were at hand and secured both catches on his worldly possessions. He was about to leave when he saw the wall where the picture had been. In a momentary calm, he knelt down to pray. Four streets away, screams of terror came again from the throats of a horrified population: animal sounds, until now unimaginable from human voices, rising from the dust of Baku's alleyways into the innocent air.

'Dear Lord, in heaven,' he began.

Three streets away and four rickety floors below, the city was in bloody tumult as the Turkish irregulars thrust deeper into Baku's heart. Beyond the walls, the sound of approaching drums was louder.

'I've got faith, dear Lord,' Clarence finished, 'but sometimes I get the feeling it's not worth a damn!' The young man of moderate education, only twenty-six years old was a long way from Hartford. The night battle had been bad enough, the British soldiers' hasty departure worse, but this final assault and the inevitable massacres – almost inconceivable.

With fifteen thousand Turks slowly closing in on Baku, General

Dunsterville had discovered that the different factions of the Caspian city were united only in sheer terror. After first skirmishes on the outskirts to test the might of the army massed against him, he had acted decisively. 'No power on earth can save Baku from the Turks,' he stated, and during the night of 14 September 1918 he pulled out his troops and, despite desperate pleas at the harbourside, sailed back across the Caspian to Enzeli.

The missionary crossed himself quickly, seized the suitcase, and stumbled from the small rooms which had been home for several years. He negotiated the narrow wooden stairway, past other residents, who, even though panic-stricken, still dragged at their belongings. Some of his neighbours spat at him, others recognized and grasped the young man, weeping, pleading as if his often declared link with God could answer their own prayers and the horrific nightmare would cease.

Clarence burst out into the street, which felt like an oven. He gasped for breath and fell back against a wall. Donkeys, mules, horses, carts, cars and lorries pressed through wailing crowds surging towards the sea away from the onslaught. He pushed through these refugees on Surkuhanskoi Street, making for Treasury Lane. Suddenly six or seven Armenians armed to the teeth appeared before him. One of them leapt on to the running board of a battered, open car, knocked the driver aside and turned the wheel hard over. The car smashed into the facing wall of a corner building in a shower of plaster and brick chippings, effectively blocking the lane. The owner, yelling hysterically, was silenced by one of the Armenians who swung his rifle butt to crack the man's jaw, felling him instantly.

Clarence Symes shouted, and jumped on to the stationary car. He was about to protest to the Armenian militiamen when bullets smacked sickeningly into the wall to one side, then several more whined off the car's chassis. The Armenians began to reply in volleys. Clarence remained rigid, staring at the horror before his eyes, and at that moment in Baku that September afternoon he doubted there was a God.

Tears streaming from his eyes, a barrage of bullets whistling all around, he was dragged from the line of fire by one of the Armenians. He began to struggle with the strength of hysteria but received a blow which gave him blessed unconsciousness.

The Bashibazooks had penetrated the city, forming a crescent around its centre. The descendants of Genghis Khan and Tamburlane kicked open doors and shattered windows, then dragged all those sheltering within the maze of burning terraces out into the streets. Helpless children, the old and the infirm were thrown to the ground and hacked at with steel bayonets, axes and sabres until they writhed in agony and their throats were cut. Women were stripped naked, their legs spread apart, pressed against a wall and raped by groups of irregulars until they bled

5

too much for pleasure, when they were bayoneted between the thighs up into the womb and ripped open to the bone. Others were held by one captor who raped her whilst a jealous companion sliced off her breasts. Only when the screams became irritating would they sever her windpipe and jugular vein. Children not more than nine or ten simply cowered near their mothers and grandparents, wailing until a Muslim knife incised that most delicate of wounds beneath their soft, unformed chins, or an Ottoman bayonet thrust into the sensitive skin of a small protruding belly. But dumdum bullets, scored across their blunt noses, were more effective. Once they had entered they exploded from within, destroying all that God had created from the love of Armenian parents.

Soon the boredom of inventive slaughter, spent sperm and exhausted loins forced the irregular Turkish battalions to more orthodox killing. As they stormed over the barricades and into the Armenian quarter, victims were merely butchered like animals in an abattoir.

Clarence Symes regained consciousness as he was dragged from beneath the car. He staggered to his feet, still clutching his battered suitcase. The Armenians were falling back, so Clarence began running. He hurried down Surkuhanskoi Street, threading his way through the crowds, into Telephone Street. Ahead, militiamen were racing for the intersection into Tamarian Road, where the Armenians had come to a halt under heavy fire. Bodies of the dead littered the pavement and the dirt road, but Clarence ignored them and turned left, then right and across the burning square. He narrowly avoided falling beams from overhead balconies on Suruskoi Avenue, where people were running in all directions, and came finally to the corner of the newly named Lenin Walk. At the end of the cobbled street, a hundred yards away, was the great walled house of Aram Pilikian. Sweat poured from Symes as he pressed himself into the shadows of an alleyway to catch his breath. Above the sound of his own heavy breathing he heard the blood-chilling noises of massacre from the breached barricades of the Armenian defences and, beyond, the terrifying drums of the Ottoman regulars of Enver Bey.

Holding his battered suitcase tightly, Clarence Symes stepped from the shadows onto the hot cobbles of the dusty street. He took a deep breath and ran the last hundred yards to the huge metal double gates, which were barred and bolted from within. There he began banging wildly with his fist.

'Mr Pilikian!' he shouted. 'Your Excellency, please! Please!' Behind locked doors of the other houses there were the sounds of whimpering children and wailing women, and the prayers of those few who still believed in God.

Two streets away, there was a mighty explosion. Screams rent the air. Rifle fire became almost continuous as smoke billowed between the houses.

'For God's sake!' pleaded Clarence, as if he were being rejected from the very gates of heaven. 'Please! Let me in!' They heard him in the end.

Aram Pilikian grasped his son's shoulders and, leaning forward from a chair in his panelled study, stared for a long time into innocent grey eyes. 'Hovahannes,' he said tenderly. 'His Excellency' had a strong face and, at fifty years old, a fine head of grey hair. His thick moustache was dark and his jaw firm. He was a big man with a strong heart, but there were tears in his eyes, not of self-pity but of love for his son, who instead of the future he had been promised now faced a terrible fate.

'Remember me,' said the father, not to the eleven-year-old boy but to the spirit of the man he would become. 'Remember all that you have learned. Never forget who you are or from where you come.' The father saw puzzlement in the boy and hugged him to his chest. Embarrassed at first, the boy struggled, then was still. 'One day my spirit will give you courage,' said the father.

Outside, an explosion sounded from nearby and made the boy jump. Now he clung willingly to his father.

'It's all right, boy,' said the man, 'it's all right,' and knew it was not.

The father pushed the son gently away from him and smiled. The boy was fighting tears. Aram Pilikian loosened his tie, unbuttoned his collar and took a gold chain and cross from around his neck. On the back of the crucifix was inscribed his own name and that of his wife, Mary. He placed the chain over young Hovahannes' head. Boy and man looked at each other in silence for a long time. Outside, in the distance, a fusillade of rifle fire began and someone started banging on the huge gates in the outer wall. Aram Pilikian ignored everything but his son. He knotted his tie and buttoned his shirt.

'That look right, boy?' he asked. Hovahannes nodded, his eyes wet. The father stood up tall and strong. 'We must be brave.' He placed a hand on his son's head. 'Our whole family is depending on us both.' The boy straightened his back proudly.

'Come,' said Aram, 'and let us pray for a miracle.' He and Hovahannes stepped forward together.

Then everything became confusion and noise and guns and death. The young boy Hovahannes ran up narrow steps at the top of the great house and jumped onto the roof terrace. The sun was low and huge clouds had begun to build in the sky as the day's heat waned. The orange light was becoming red and the faces that turned towards him glowed as if part of some strange nightmare.

'Hovahannes, come!' shouted Mikayel, the gardener.

Uncle Levon was lying on the roof tiles, moaning. His shirt was undone, exposing the torn flesh of his chest. Hovahannes' grandfather,

7

Abraham, was already pulling at a tarpaulin in one corner of the terrace. Hovahannes ran to Mikayel and together they helped Abraham lift the heavy sheet to reveal five bee-hives. Gabriel, one of the servants, lying just below the spine of the roof, grinned over his shoulder.

'We corked 'em up,' he said to the astonished Hovahannes.

'Quickly!' said Mikayel. The two men and the boy lifted the first of the hives onto the tiles and pushed it carefully towards Gabriel. The buzzing from within sounded loud and menacing.

'I think they're angry enough,' said old Abraham, laughing to himself. Gabriel peered over the roof.

'They're in the garden, by the gates!' he exclaimed.

About sixty Bashibazooks – Turkish for 'wild heads', men without discipline – had gathered on either side of the gravel drive and began chanting in blood-curdling voices.

'Wait!' Mikayel said. He was leaning against the hive poised on the tiles. Abraham and Hovahannes had already begun rolling another towards the roof. A great shout went up from below.

'They're rushing us!' shouted Gabriel and pulled hard at the conical home of thousands of bees. Mikayel pushed and the hive went over the edge and rolled off the roof.

As the Turkish irregulars ran up the steps to the entrance of Pilikian's house, the hive burst open on the marble. Aggression turned to fear as the killers hesitated, suddenly engulfed by swarms of bees bent on vengeance for the destruction of their home.

'Another!' shouted Mikayel, and a second hive was pushed off the roof. Below, there was chaos. The men were no longer a group, but individuals suffering an attack against which they had no defence. As a third hive exploded in their midst, the confusion was complete.

Aram Pilikian reached the roof terrace, ran across to his comrades and began directing their fire accurately into the screaming masses. The Turks were standing, running, falling down, hitting each other and themselves, firing their guns wildly, driven mad by the bees' stings.

The Armenians began to take revenge. Even Hovahannes, crouched on the roof, arm extended, pistol aimed into the garden, fired again and again with the others. Aram watched his son's cool courage and, as he reloaded for him, marvelled at the fearless determination in the boy's face. Only a sudden organized return of fire from beyond the walls forced their heads down and stopped the slaughter. The shooting ceased. Aram Pilikian was puzzled for a moment, until a bugle's sound confirmed his worst fears.

He peered over the roof. The streets beyond his property were no longer filled with undisciplined bloodthirsty mobs, but with lines of uniformed soldiers, the Turkish regular divisions, sunset glinting on

8

their bayonets. Aram lay back against the tiles and stared up at the sky of early evening.

'What is it, father?' asked Hovahannes, clambering across to lie beside him.

'God has been unable to provide a miracle.'

A commanding Turkish voice rang out in the sudden stillness of the evening. Aram Pilikian peered over the roof once more. There was a shout and a tremendous volley of rifle fire ripped at the tiles about him. He slithered down the terrace, gashing his face.

More commands were given from below. Gabriel clambered back up the roof.

'They're running,' he said.

'Where?' asked Pilikian, urgently, trying to stem the flow of blood on his cheek.

'To both sides,' whispered Gabriel.

The high wall to one side of the entrance had been blown in and the bolts pulled on the heavy metal gates which had impeded the irregulars. Turkish regulars were running through and dispersing amidst the trees and bushes.

'What's happening now?' asked Abraham excitedly.

Gabriel was puzzled. 'Nothing,' he answered. The sound of sporadic rifle fire came from the back of the house, then an answering volley from the servants below who were protecting the women. Aram Pilikian looked at Mikayel, who shook his head, frowning. Silence from the many troops in front was ominous. Now even the hum of bees was less angry.

'We are to be given no quarter,' stated Aram simply.

Bashibazooks lay on the lawn in the front garden. Many were corpses, some whimpered, others attempted to crawl, badly wounded, trailing blood and broken limbs; but from the regular soldiers there was silence. Three lines of them were alternately kneeling, crouched or standing, all with their rifles aimed at the roof.

'Smoke!' said Gabriel suddenly. Kerosene had ignited the dry vegetation. Aram Pilikian gritted his teeth.

'Of course,' said Mikayel.

'The wind is from the west,' said Pilikian quietly, and what breeze there was indeed came from the sunset, where gigantic clouds piled angrily upon each other. All the men on the roof began to smell smoke.

'The bees will die,' said Abraham softly.

A single voice chanted a slogan from the street and a great cry went up from the assembled ranks of soldiers as they answered it. A second voice called out what sounded like a challenge; a second chorus, louder than the first one, answered.

The men on the roof of the Pilikian house clambered from the tiles and began to make their way to the stairway which led to the top floor.

Inside the house, followed closely by his son, Aram Pilikian ran down the huge marble staircase to find his chauffeur Daniel, whose eyes were alight with determination and hate. The two men peered out of the window between the broken slats of the shutters and what they saw was terrifying. The entire street was full of soldiers with lighted torches, moving under the archway of the broken gate into the gardens, to surround the house. The dancing flames amidst the pall of smoke looked like spring fireflies in the early mist of a pre-summer twilight. There were no voices, only the distant rattle of equipment.

'My God!' said Daniel in awe. He crossed himself.

'What is it, father?' asked young Hovahannes, trying to peer out.

A command sounded loudly. Both Pilikian and Daniel understood – their features indistinct, lit by the fading sunlight between strips of shadows through the shutters.

Aram Pilikian turned to Daniel. 'Take the boy, Mary and Symes,' he whispered. 'We'll cover you. Drive west to Wolfsgate. If you get that far, they'll think you are turning south towards Baladjari, but go on the coast road through Bailov to Bibi Eibat. The missionary will get you aboard a Persian freighter the Americans have been using. It's moored offshore.'

'But your Excellency . . .' Daniel began, 'you . . .'

Pilikian glanced at Hovahannes and immediately tears came to his eyes. 'Go to your mother,' he said. 'I will be along.' Hovahannes nodded and ran off. Aram's gaze followed him for a moment then he turned again to the chauffeur. 'We are finished – you must know that. But the boy . . .' he paused, heartbroken. 'Make for Tehran,' he commanded, 'then it will be easy to buy your way to the Mediterranean coast. There's gold in the car.'

'I cannot leave you, sir,' said Daniel hoarsely.

Aram Pilikian grasped the man firmly and there was a madness in his eyes. 'You will do it, Daniel!' The chauffeur lowered his head and tried to control his sobs. Pilikian shook him. 'Do it for us all,' he said. 'There are many on this earth who do not even know what the word Armenian means, and believe our country to be a myth; someone must live!'

A great roar went up from the gardens outside as scores of torches were hurled against the house. That was when the horror began for Hovahannes. There were screams from the women, fearful shouts from the men, but above the clamour the commanding authority of his father as he thrust the boy along the corridor. Then the firing began.

Bullets ripped into the ground floor from so many guns and with such force that it seemed the house would be cut from its foundations. Acrid smells came from burning furniture, panelled walls and the very fabric of the building. Grenades exploded, splintering wood, tearing metal. The front doors were forced, then barricaded rooms were broken into and as the fire spread rapidly, the occupants of the great house were overwhelmed.

Pilikian, with Mary, his wife, Symes and the boy, led by Daniel, ran to the back of the house and down the stairway to the small courtyard beside the rose garden. Here they ran across to the garage next to the stables, where horses whinnied and plunged.

Daniel leapt into the Rolls Royce Silver Ghost and started the motor, which turned over slowly. Pilikian opened doors facing a short drive at the back wall where double gates – yet to be forced – had kept out the irregulars. Apparently they had decided to leave the dangerous assault to the regular soldiers of the Turkish army.

Mary, who was crying hysterically, had to be dragged bodily into the car by Symes. Hovahannes jumped in beside his mother.

'Can you drive, missionary?' shouted Daniel. Symes shook his head. 'Then use a gun!' Daniel threw him a revolver, before turning on the headlights, sidelights and twin spotlights either side of the windscreen. Pilikian leapt on to the running board as the car moved forward and out into the courtyard. Suddenly, directly above them, there was what sounded like an explosion even louder than the noise coming from the house, where the servants and remaining family were putting up an heroic defence. Several drops of rain fell, and in a moment became a deluge. Seconds later the group in the open car were soaked to the skin. The Silver Ghost continued to rumble over the cobbles towards the back gates. Aram Pilikian leapt from the running board and ran across to pull the bolts and lift the bar. Several of Enver's Bashibazooks, alerted by the commotion within, had climbed the outside wall and saw the open car below them through the pouring rain.

Pilikian, even though grasping his pistols, undid the bolts then pushed up the bar with the palms of his hands. He lay against the gates a moment longer then turned into the headlights. Mary was standing in the car, screaming hysterically as Symes vainly attempted to pull her down. Pilikian dropped the bar and the gates began to swing open. He ran back and jumped on to the running board again. Several bullets smacked into the chassis. Symes, waving his gun wildly, ducked immediately, but Pilikian aimed and fired twice. One man fell from the wall and crashed onto the cobbles. Outside the gates, the street seemed alive with armed Turks caught in the headlights. A bullet passed through the windscreen and hit Daniel, who shouted then slumped back in the seat, screaming obscenities.

'Come with us, Aram!' Mary screamed, and seized her husband's arm. The car began to move forward, gathering momentum.

'Down!' bellowed Pilikian. He pushed at his wife, pressing her down

11

on the seat. With his free hand holding a pistol, arm fully extended, he was firing accurately into the group ahead. Turks fell one after the other. Another great crack of thunder sounded as the rain intensified and lightning flashed in the sky.

'Drive, Daniel, drive!' yelled Pilikian. Rivulets of water were pouring down his face and he raised a hand quickly to wipe his eyes exactly as Daniel accelerated. The jolt made him lose his footing, and when Mary saw her husband fall heavily onto the cobbles, she stood up screaming in the back of the Silver Ghost, arms outstretched. In a second Pilikian was on his feet, both pistols pointed towards the open gates. The volley of rifle fire that came from beyond the gates hit Mary Pilikian knocking her out of the car, over the trunk and onto the rain-soaked cobbles.

The car roared away, slamming into several of the irregulars, thrusting them aside. Pilikian had taken three paces towards the broken body of his wife when a second fusillade tore into his chest, felling him to the ground. For a moment he lay on his back, then he pulled himself to his knees and watched the rear lights of the car disappearing into the teeming rain and darkness. His vision began to blur and for the first and last time in his life he began to fire his pistols inaccurately towards the mass of figures descending upon him. His last memory was of his wife's face, her open eyes and moist mouth seeming to beg for a kiss. He sank down to the cobbles, only inches away from her, and as his eyes closed to greet the darkness of eternity, he was sure that their lips met.

Daniel died of his wounds in Tehran, where Symes and the boy were delayed, but the gold eventually allowed them to obtain passage west. They left Haifa two months later on an American merchantman, soon after the Armistice had been announced to the world. The steady rhythm of ship's engines became the background to Hovahannes' life as he tried to forget the horror and accept that he would have a future. He remembered one early evening on deck with Mr Symes. He had pointed to a great rock towering from the sea to starboard.

'That is the tip of Europe, and on the port side is North Africa.' They looked across the deck and towards the Jebel mountains of Morocco. The missionary went on: 'In ancient times, the two sides of this narrow strait were known as the Pillars of Hercules. To go beyond this point was to enter the unknown.'

Hovahannes, wide-eyed, looked towards the western horizon.

'Is that where you're taking me?' he asked.

Symes smiled. 'I'm taking you to America. It is my country.'

'But it is not mine.'

'It will be.'

'I am Armenian,' said the boy quietly and proudly.

'And you will become American.'

Hovahannes stared at the missionary.

'But I am a refugee.'

'Who told you that?'

'A sailor,' answered Hovahannes.

Clarence Symes shook his head and marvelled at the resilience of children. The boy had been through hell and faced death, yet already he had regained his confidence, as he had certainly retained his pride.

'The United States is a land of refugees.' The boy gazed steadily at Symes and said nothing. 'There are many different kinds of people in America. People forced out of their own countries by political or economic pressures.'

'And war?'

'That too.'

Hovahannes Pilikian thought for a moment. 'Why do they let those people in?' he asked.

'Because they want to become Americans; because they think they will like it there.' For a moment Clarence Symes found it impossible to describe the love he had for his country. 'It is better . . .' he finished weakly.

'Will I like it, Mr Symes?'

'You have a very big heart and an excellent mind. You will like it very much.' The missionary put his hand on Hovahannes' head, but the boy drew away.

'Is it like Baku?'

'No.' Symes paused as the word brought back memories whose horrific clarity had only just begun to fade during their time at sea. 'No,' he repeated, 'nothing will ever again be like Baku.'

'Where are we going to live?'

'I'm taking you to a big city. It's called New York.'

Dusk was gathering to the west as a light wind of evening ruffled the hair on the heads of both man and boy. Clarence Symes began to tell Hovahannes about America and its wonders as the freighter *White Cross* out of Wilmington, Delaware, under a growing panoply of stars, passed between the mythical pillars of legend, out of the Mediterranean and into the greatest unknown of all – the future.

Chapter 1

In the magnificent weather the Mediterranean sparkled from shore to horizon, where azure sea became cerulean sky and white cumulus clouds moved slowly to far off destinations. Sunlight dappled through the tall trees which bordered the Basse Corniche roadway leading eastwards all along the French Riviera into the morning mist. An unmistakable pine sap aroma wafted on a light breeze softly whispering dark secrets from another millennium.

The driver of the two-tone automobile, his senses seduced, turned the convertible expertly into each bend, accelerating out of sharp curves with the confidence of practice. Steep mountain foothills on the one side, sheer cliffs on the other and a narrow coastal road to negotiate were all familiar. The yellow and black car raced up the rise above the bay of Villefranche, turned again into the morning sun overlooking Cap Ferrat, took a hard right then, as the driver changed down and indicated left, quickly descended the slip road beside the Hotel Bristol to avoid the main town.

Wind whipped the young man's dark hair as he accelerated the two-door Phantom sports towards an incline, took a calculated risk that his left would be clear, and continued at speed straight across the fork back onto the Corniche. In front of him great coastal bluffs towered high towards the hanging village of Eze. Ahead appeared the long straight which ran beside the railway; road and rails now continued together almost all the way to the not too distant Italian border town of Ventimiglia. To his right the harbour of Beaulieu was already stirring with fishing boats unloading the morning's catch.

Harry Pilikian inhaled a salt smell of the sea and was enveloped with a feeling of euphoria. He had come a long way. The poor boy from downtown Manhattan emerged to remind this now sophisticated American exactly how fortune had smiled upon him and how lucky he had become. For a moment he was blinded by the sun rising above mist on the horizon, forcing his grey eyes to squint, illuminating his tanned, unshaven face and pale silk shirt which matched the magnolia leather interior of the car.

14

Suddenly, behind him, the sound of a powerful railway engine obliterated the rush of wind and the almost silent horsepower of his Rolls Royce. Here was a first glimpse of the South of France to many of the waking passengers who had travelled through the night from Paris on the famous Blue Train. Running parallel only for a moment, the scything wheels of the locomotive slowly edged the train ahead of the Rolls. Harry grinned and pressed harder on the accelerator, raising a hand high to wave. Blinds began to snap up in the wagon-lits as the coaches hurtled along the rails and several people started to wave back through their half-open windows, but, with a warning whistle, the train plunged into a tunnel. Harry changed down to take a shallow rise. In front, approaching fast, was the long curve leading to Cap Estel. He glanced beside him to the passenger seat where he had thrown his jacket and tie, dispensed with after a late dinner.

He had emerged from La Pyramide, a restaurant in the town of Vienne, south of Lyons, to take coffee and cognac on the terrace beneath tall plane trees whose new foliage almost obscured the night sky. His friends had agreed that dinner had been magnificent as they grouped around a large trestle table to drink old brandy. The owner, François Point himself, had gently taken the bottle from his *sommelier*, Louis Thomasi, and poured generous measures. The roses blooming in the *jardin fleuri* scented the air as the group raised their glasses. French bravado increased with each toast until all fear of the Nazi threat was dispelled. Laughter turned to patriotism and the group stood up stiffly to bellow the Marseillaise.

Harry fondled the three large white Pyrenean dogs before shaking hands with Monsieur Point, joking about his sizeable girth and complimenting him on his remarkable cuisine. With a parting bow to Madame Point he told the group that he had decided to drive south through the night. Everyone expressed alarm, called him foolhardy and said it was madness, but Harry was adamant.

Their cars were parked outside the walled garden. Harry remembered that he had left the hood of his convertible down, and when they all stepped out onto the road he decided not to close it but to travel with only the heavens above him. The car's strong headlight beams were officially illegal and had been commented on during dinner. The *drôle de guerre*, or Phoney War as it was called, made the blackout necessary by law. The majority of Frenchmen had become quite exasperated by the inconveniences this caused when nothing was happening. Eight months after war had been declared, a chorus of political blusterings in Paris, Berlin and London was all that seemed to have happened. Even the police had begun to turn a blind eye to what they considered the more petty of their official duties.

With a wave to his friends and a promise to run over every German he

15

saw on his way south, Harry Pilikian, under a sky encrusted with stars, had driven off bound for the Côte d'Azur and dawn.

Roaring from the dark tunnel, the Blue Train began thundering through sleepy coastal village stations towards its destination on the Mediterranean seashore that early May morning, as if it were a dignitary in haste, ignoring servants in a crowd. And aboard the coaches there were certainly a number of dignified, especially affluent passengers hoping for at least one last summer of comparative peace. Paris, for them all, had been a strain – on the one hand pooh-poohing the very idea that the Teutonic horde was again a threat, and on the other, more privately, worried sick.

As car and train came parallel once more, Harry began to fall behind; he was five wagon-lit carriages from the end. The sleeping cars were really blue, thought Harry, and the faces staring out towards him through the many windows really were so pale. His tanned face smiled, then he laughed with pure exhilaration as a long moaning whistle sounded from the steaming locomotive. In answer, his hand hit the steering column for his twin horns to wail a reply. Here he was having the time of his life . . . Harry pressed the brakes hard, swerving into the centre of the road. He swore as an unsteady cyclist tottered back against the kerb, shaking his fist at the Rolls.

With the sea appearing in flashes between houses to his right, Harry started down the long winding slope five hundred yards before the fork that would take the Rolls off the Corniche, out of France and into another world. At the border, he brought his yellow and black sports car to a stop, showed his papers and received a salute from the smart policeman; only then was he allowed entry through the road barrier from France into the Principality. He slowly negotiated the run down into the harbour area, still partly in shadow, watching the train from Paris, now far to his left, throw clouds of steam and smoke into the bright morning air as it passed beneath the Hermitage Hotel making for the green girders and glass of the Belle Epoque railway station.

Harry Pilikian took the incline north of the harbour at speed. In the tranquil water below, beautiful yachts, motor cruisers and small boats were crowded at their berths beside the quays. Beyond was the deep shadow of a sheer rock face, topped by old buildings which caught the sun and showed their Venetian colours of magenta, cream, ochre and rose, like icing on a cake.

Harry changed up and began to coast into the square; to his right, first the ornate theatre entrance, then the Casino façade adorned with Stecchi sculptures. At the centre of the square was a circular lawn and tall palm trees, swaying in the light warm breeze, where gardeners were hosing the foliage and flowers. Cleaners had begun to sweep the steps of the adjacent buildings, early risers were already seated at the café tables outside, waiting for steaming French coffee and croissants. The Rolls Royce Phantom sports rounded the square and came to a halt in front of the Hotel de Paris. Harry yawned deeply and turned off the softly murmuring engine. Peace. Home. Monte Carlo.

On the morning of 10 May 1940, communiqués conveyed urgent information to the world. The headline in one of the many newspapers being anxiously scanned around the square read:

Adolf Hitler Follows Schlieffen Plan

In the early hours of this morning, the German army began a thrust through Holland and Belgium that is developing in two directions. It follows the famous battle concept of 1914, an enveloping sweep on the right flank. The objective is the North Sea, and the Wehrmacht plan to reach it near the Dutch coast at Walcheren. Then the strategic idea of the German thrust must be to turn south, always holding the North Sea on the flank of the advancing armies. If Hitler is checked in his tumultuous outbursts to the west, if he can be held anywhere east of the French frontier and if severe losses can be inflicted on him, it is unlikely that the battle now being waged will be as decisive as the Battle of the Marne. One word in conclusion. The bombing of Lyons indicates that Hitler may be launching an attack on the whole front, from the North Sea to the Alps, even into France. We shall see in a few days, even a few hours.

'Bonjour Michel.'

The doorman was deeply involved in the morning's news, and the open newspaper almost concealed his face, until he looked up.

'Pardon, Monsieur Harry, mais c'est finie, la drôle de guerre.'

'What?' questioned Harry.

'The war – she is begun for real.'

For a moment Harry froze, then the tiredness in his body and limbs evaporated as the implications struck home, and he snapped awake and leaned over Michel's shoulder. When he saw the word 'Lyons' coupled with 'bombing', he began to move.

'Park the car!' he shouted and raced up the marble steps at the entrance of the Hotel de Paris. He spun through the revolving doors and ran across the huge baroque lobby and into the packed bar. Everyone seemed to be drinking champagne. Some people were dressed, others still in night clothes.

He pressed his way through the crowd until the barman, Louis, saw him and instantly shouted a greeting. The explosion of smiles, felicitations and arms thrown around shoulders across the bar top cleared a small area for Louis to put the telephone which Harry asked for. He dialled the operator, and asked desperately for Lyons. Static crackled on the line. One hand over his ear, Harry was forced to shout.

'*Ils ne répondent pas? C'est pas possible!*' he protested. Now he was staring into the still eyes of Louis the barman. 'I had dinner with them last night. They live in the city.'

'Try later,' said Louis. Harry replaced the receiver and Louis took the phone. 'Champagne?' he asked. 'The Boches are on the move again, this time we'll really have to teach them a lesson.' He poured two glasses and Harry slowly absorbed the atmosphere of the crowded room full of laughter and heated conversation.

'They're very confident,' he said.

'They are French.'

'And you are not?'

'I am Monégasque,' said Louis, smiling, spreading his arms.

'You are a very wise man,' said Harry and raised his glass. '*Santé!*'

Two men clambered down from the Blue Train and began arguing as they stepped onto the platform beneath the girder and glass station of Monte Carlo. Both men were overdressed for the already warm morning. The younger, Bobby Avery, slipped off his overcoat, taking a cue from the crowds disembarking from the train, many of them already carrying jackets and in shirt sleeves with loosened ties. Some had even taken off their hats. A number of women looked garish in the light of day with their pancake makeup, rouged cheeks and ruby lipstick. Although it was officially spring, the smell of summer came from the almost tropical vegetation surrounding the Casino.

The older man peered about imperiously.

'Get a *fiacre!*'

'Horses and carriages *might* be difficult,' replied the young man.

'Sarcasm will not move me a metre.'

'Don't be a bitch!' hissed Bobby Avery.

The older man undid his overcoat slowly as a first concession to the Riviera. 'I'm just telling you that if this' – his eye indicated his luggage – 'is not moved, then I do not budge.'

'You're quite capable of carrying at least one piece.'

'You, my dear, may have youth and beauty, but I have to preserve what remains, and these delicate fingers have much better uses than grasping the worn leather of a dirty and very heavy suitcase.' Hugh Sullivan rose to his full height of five foot eight, set his generous mouth defiantly and allowed twinkling Irish-American eyes to emphasize the fact that he would not leave unless his baggage was carried.

'Dear Bobby,' he went on with a smile, 'if this is civilization there must be a porter in some urinal or other.'

The plump young man gave a sigh. 'Hostilities have begun and they

18

may not be available, Hugh. It's the porters of the world who fight wars. We just become the playthings of the victors.'

Sullivan stubbornly spread his legs beneath a full girth and folded his arms. 'I am already a plaything,' he stated.

Many of the passengers leaving the train and crowding on to the platform showed equal consternation, shouting for porters and the *fiacre* horse carriages. For some it was the first time in the South of France, although others obviously knew Monaco from before the war. Ben Harrison had done it all regularly. He knew most of the best watering holes in the Mediterranean, from Tangier to Oran, Tripoli to Alexandria, Beirut to old Constantinople, Athens to the island of Capri, but if for no other reason than that it had become a pleasant habit, Ben always came to the Riviera some time in the late spring or early summer.

He lit an oval cigarette and coughed once to welcome the first draught of smoke. At fifty, he was still lithe. His English accent was reminiscent of Cary Grant – if that was possible for anyone but Archie Leach – and his face could best be described as rugged, with clear eyes of a hue between shamrock and gunmetal glinting from beneath fleshy lids and dark eyebrows. All this was complemented by thick greying hair which provided him naturally with the distinguished appearance he had worked so hard to achieve in his youth. When not in his London-tailored Anderson and Sheppard suits, he wore pale worsted trousers and a tweed jacket, or a dark-blue blazer with cream flannels, and always starched light blue or white shirts with school or military ties. These combinations, as he knew quite well, made Benjamin William Harrison a very presentable fellow.

He stepped from the train and, in the absence of porters, walked quickly against the crowd, back in the direction of the luggage van. Quietly, with the help of a guard and several French francs, he carried his portmanteau into the left luggage office. He smiled at being recognized, dispensed several more francs, then, loosening his tie, walked leisurely through the employees' entrance to climb the deserted narrow lane in front of the Opera, taking the short cut up to the Casino Square and the entrance of the Hotel de Paris.

Maggie Lawrence adjusted her wide-brimmed, soft felt hat, stuck a pin through the crown to secure it in her blond hair, and, pouting into the long mirror, surveyed herself a moment longer. She was certainly striking, with her slim body voluptuous only in the right places. If her face had been less like a gypsy's and more voguishly soft, she might indeed have married a prince. Instead, she was internationally and discreetly acknowledged by discerning clients as one of the great and therefore very expensive ladies of a rich man's leisure. She smoothed her carefully fashioned cream silk dress then stepped out of the mahogany-panelled wagon-lit compartment into another season. Two porters ran across to her. She smiled sweetly and indicated the carriage.

'Everything's inside, boys.'

Some women walk in a straight line, one foot before the other, thighs squeezing together, some women walk as if they've just come off a yacht and move from side to side from ankle to neck. Others have developed peculiar quirks. Many are self-conscious and throw their hips far to the left and right, swinging to a degree that makes them the object of unkind attention. Others slouch, some scuff, but seldom do you find an ungainly walk in a truly beautiful woman.

Maggie Lawrence moved in a way that drew every male eye. Her passage through a crowd was always marked by a succession of turning heads which had seen self-supporting breasts jostling lightly above almost no waist at all, then watched the flesh of her buttocks tense and relax as long legs, fine calves and perfect ankles transported 'the goods', as she often privately described herself, to a steady rhythm of clicking high heels.

'I'm at the Paree Hotel, boys,' she said to motionless porters. 'I'll make it worth your while.'

Sullivan recognized the attractive woman and nodded with a slight smile.

'I'll bet she had no trouble,' said Bobby, referring to the luggage.

'She never does, dear,' replied Sullivan icily, then cast a quick glance over his shoulder in time to catch Maggie as she disappeared into the crowd. 'If she could do all that just standing still, she would provide me with better accompaniment than four marimba players drunk on cheap tequila.'

'When did you see her last?' asked Bobby.

'That was in Buenos Aires, Mr Avery, whilst you were nowhere to be found.'

Bobby smiled. 'It was only a tiff,' he said, languorous eyes softening the older man's heart.

Sullivan sighed. 'Well, don't let's have one here.' He tapped a lust-struck porter on the shoulder, smiled grandly and indicated the luggage.

'Have you heard the news, Monsieur?' asked the porter, bending to the bags.

'Clark Gable just married Bette Davis?' suggested Sullivan.

'No, Monsieur.'

'Worse?' he asked.

The porter nodded, 'Hitler has invaded.'

Sullivan stared at his young companion, who was genuinely shocked. He made a grimace. 'Well,' he said, 'it looks like we'll have to revamp some of the German numbers, dear.'

Louis pushed quickly through the crowd in the American Bar of the Hotel de Paris and put two glasses of champagne on top of the piano. He remained standing there with Jean-Pierre, a fellow barman with black curly hair and a big grin. Harry Pilikian was poised at the keyboard. He looked up to see Maggie Lawrence.

'Hi, Harry. How're you keeping?'

He smiled. 'Just fine, Maggie.'

She nodded. 'You look good. You gonna play?'

'Sure,' said Harry.

An English voice called for the Noël Coward song, 'Something Fishy About the French', but was shouted down by several others, at which point Harry began a fast rendition of 'We're Going to Hang Out Our Washing on the Siegfried Line'. Those who knew the words, as Harry did not, sang them as he played faster.

The song finished amidst much hilarity and 'Dutch courage', while in the north the Wehrmacht was systematically punching through the crumbling defences of Holland and Belgium, crossing the unblown bridges, encircling regiments, defeating armies and thrusting ever nearer the English Channel.

Harry stood up from the piano to a chorus of disappointment. He held out a hand and pointed towards the entrance. There, in dark hat and formal suit, overcoat on his shoulders, stood Hugh Sullivan, with Bobby Avery hovering behind.

'Is it in tune?' asked the Irish-American.

'It makes a noise,' said Harry.

'Good,' said Sullivan, 'then all I have left to do is create an atmosphere.'

Harry moved away from the piano. 'This morning I think the Germans have done that,' he said.

'Let us drink,' said Louis quickly, 'to a swift victory.' He thrust two glasses of champagne at Sullivan and Bobby Avery.

'To a swift victory!' said everyone.

Faces glowed, eyes shone and lips spoke the words with confidence. Only Hugh Sullivan soured the toast for those few about him who understood him as he muttered: 'They didn't say for whom.'

Chapter 2

Venetian blinds at the french windows of the high-ceilinged bedroom had been left half-open overnight to let in fresh air. Morning sunlight streamed into the room, patterning the wall, creating diagonal, parallel shadows.

In a large bed, a copy of a seventeenth-century Sicilian marriage four-poster, a woman in a satin nightgown stirred. She was of medium size and perfectly proportioned, with symmetrical doll-like features, red hair and green eyes, all of which she had discovered at a tender age appealed to most men; and it had taken only a short time more to realize that in most cases it was older men who had the money. Many of them had been to bed with her, but very few had been allowed to see her wake at this hour. Youth, which for her had stopped four years ago at twenty-five, she had replaced with mystery.

She sat up in bed, pressed the buzzer on the side table, then watched her hand hover over the telephone for a moment before she changed her mind. Breakfast would arrive soon, and she decided to use these quiet moments to think private thoughts.

She swung her legs out of bed and crossed to the open french windows, pulling up the entire centre section of venetian blinds to step out onto the balcony and lean on the rail. Below her was the lush garden of the ornate Italian villa, in front the shimmering sea horizon of a beautiful day. To her right the town of Monte Carlo and the Rock of Monaco. It was all so idyllic that she felt she should want to cry, and would have done so had she been in public.

The celebrated Miss Evelyn Martineye had been born Alice Hover-strom, a dirt farmer's daughter in the Midwest. Where her tenacity, ambition and intelligence came from was one of Evelyn's true mysteries. How she used them to elevate herself was already part of her history, though in the main unknown.

She had changed her name, divorced her first husband and was on the road in Hollywood as Evelyn Martineye when Thomas Curtis, a Southern gentleman forty years her senior, had happened along. A brief sojourn in Los Angeles had given her experience, and the certain knowledge that what exceptional talents she possessed lay not between her ears and on a sound stage, but between her legs and in bed.

A honeymoon in Europe cemented the happy couple's love match, confirming for Evelyn that Curtis wasn't up to it. Twenty-seven days after returning to America, he collapsed with a massive coronary in the restaurant of the St Regis, and died on the way to a New York hospital.

The will, as Evelyn had once informed her husband, was as important to a marriage as a contract is to a star. She got the lot.

As a youthful widow, Evelyn's inherited fortune ostentatiously displayed had bought discreet silence and guaranteed privacy. Otherwise spiteful tongues became obsequious in the face of her calculated generosity. She enjoyed travelling for many years and soon had been most places, seen what had been touted loudest, enjoyed offered distractions and indulged in exclusive pleasures. She also discovered, as new money does, that there is an emptiness in life without a struggle. But beneath the superficial woman Evelyn had created there really was something she valued – her ambition. She desperately wanted the only thing denied her, to truly arrive in society.

The door of Evelyn's bedroom opened and the maid came in with a tray of breakfast. Evelyn moved not a muscle. She missed her old house on Cap Ferrat, but what with France declaring war and all, she thought whimsically, Monte Carlo was just as pleasant.

'Madame, the concierge of the Paris Hotel informs you that Monsieur Harry is returned,' said the maid. She curtsied and left.

Evelyn sat down alone to her breakfast for two. She glanced at the bedside clock, then at the telephone. 'If he can't keep a promise,' she muttered to herself, 'he might at least let me know.' She poured coffee and picked up the newspaper exactly as the phone began ringing.

Evelyn resisted the impulse to race across the room and pick it up immediately. It rang six times before Danielle answered in one of the downstairs rooms. Evelyn counted the seconds it would take her maid to climb the stairs. She missed Harry. He had gone to Geneva to sign papers for his own account and a transfer of cash she had promised him. His promise to Evelyn had been a rendezvous for breakfast at 9 am on the tenth of May.

There was a knock on the door and Danielle entered. Evelyn played out the scene to perfection, slowly replacing her coffee cup before accepting the phone, which Danielle brought over from the bedside table on a long lead.

'Where are you?' she asked harshly.

'Back,' came Harry's voice.

Evelyn became impatient. 'Why can't you be pleasant like anybody else?'

Harry said nothing. Evelyn used the pause. 'I've missed you.' She didn't often say things like that, and he had to admit her timing was improving. It hit him right where it hurt most, in his little sack of cynicism, buried somewhere deep, which was expanding all the time.

'Is the coffee hot?' he asked.

Harry and Evelyn had taken up together after a chance meeting during an audition for a New York musical. Evelyn had become confused in Europe's aristocratic society and fled back to America, where she became involved with an old flame, a director from Hollywood who had graduated to Broadway. It was a late spring morning when she crept into the theatre and took a seat in the rear stalls to one side of the centre aisle. A fight developed between her old flame and a young writer employed only for rewrites, as Evelyn gathered from the heated conversation. Things eventually calmed down and the dark-haired, attractive young man slumped back into his seat, took out a cigarette and began to search for matches.

'This sort of thing happens in movies too,' said Evelyn with a comforting smile, and leaned across the aisle with her lighter. The young man reached over to take it as a young girl up front began the current favourite, 'There's a Gold Mine in the Sky'.

So Harry Pilikian met Evelyn Martineye and entered the world of the rich. In the winter of '38 they went to Europe, where she showed him the sights, then on to Africa to shoot game, Mexico to fish and the Far East, where Harry remembered many dismal sunsets. They took a Zeppelin from Rio back to Europe, landing in Germany, and crossed the Atlantic yet again for the rehearsals of Harry's first musical, called *Love and Laughter*, written and produced with Evelyn's financial help. It was a moderate success, with the semblance of a hit song, 'Laugh It Off'.

When war broke out in Europe, whilst it provided a measure of excitement, to all who enjoyed the South of France, and who voiced their opinions without reserve, the hostilities had quickly become merely a boring hindrance to pleasure. Harry Pilikian's respect for the international society to which he was introduced through Evelyn diminished with familiarity. He retired to a suite in the Hotel de Paris which he declared an office and started to work on his next musical. He also attempted some serious writing in the light of world events, privately toying with the idea of becoming a war correspondent. Harry's salad days were fast coming to a close, as was his love affair with glamour and excessive wealth.

When he arrived at the villa, they began an argument over breakfast, which was not unusual, but he was tired and Evelyn, in thin satin, wearing a delicious perfume, was persuasive, merely by the attention she began to shower upon him. It would be unfair to say that Harry was lured back into bed, or that what took place between the sheets was entirely from her prompting – after all, as Harry would always acknowledge, sexually Evelyn was a very attractive proposition. They remained in bed well into the afternoon.

The day passed. The sun set. Early evening hilarity faded quickly and most people decided they wished to be private, with family and loved ones. Monte Carlo that night lost its glitter. Most people fell asleep with forebodings, and their dreams were of evil and darkness.

In the early hours of the morning, Harry Pilikian walked across the almost deserted Casino Square into the Hotel de Paris and took the stairs up to his rooms. He stepped to the open french windows, lit a cigarette and stared out into the night. What would they be doing in Manhattan now? Sitting down for dinner, listening to the wireless news. Hearing of a war far away, in distant countries – as strange to them as America had been to Harry when first he had arrived, almost a quarter of a century before, as a boy, a refugee from a country that now existed only in the imagination of those who had lived there. Armenia. Where was Armenia on the map? He had been asked that so many times at school, and had pointed to where Russia, Turkey and Persia met. Children had laughed because children are cruel and Hovahannes Pilikian, as he was then called, discovered isolation and self-pity and began his search for strength and love.

The missionary pointed to a steep wooden stairway and the young boy went ahead, negotiating the steps carefully. When they reached the narrow landing above, a door was opened by an old man and Clarence Symes ushered the boy into two little rooms on Great Jones Street, off downtown New York's Second Avenue. Full of the old man's memories and mementoes from Armenia and southern Russia, to the child it was an Aladdin's cave; to the missionary it resembled a hovel.

'Your father's brother,' Symes had said, beaming at the small boy. It had been a exhaustive search via the Armenian church, but would certainly relieve the Mission of a responsibility which Symes obviously no longer wanted.

'This is your nephew,' said Symes.

The old man seemed bowed by time, the city, poverty. He moved about making tea, staring at the boy. 'Can he do anything?' he finally asked.

'He plays the piano very well,' Symes answered, 'and we can continue to pay a small consideration . . .'

'How much?'

'Two dollars, for five evenings a week – the twilight service we like to call it.'

'For drunks,' the uncle grunted.

'They are souls as we all are,' said Clarence piously.

25

'Drunks,' Uncle Krikor repeated, and poured the tea.

'He is receiving further education at the Mission's school and from myself, privately. It is a consideration I promised his father. He is very bright.'

The old man was not interested. 'Can he count?'

'Of course,' answered Clarence, affronted, 'He has been my pupil not only in English but in everything that is essential to make a young gentleman.' He sipped his tea.

'Useless if he works with me.'

'At what, may I ask?'

'Hardware.'

'In the Bowery?'

'Where else?' The old man tugged at his grey beard and looked directly at the child. 'Why is he here?'

'It was in the letter I sent you,' Clarence reminded him hesitantly, almost chiding. 'He is – a refugee.' The missionary glanced at Hovahannes, embarrassed at the word. 'We both escaped together from . . .' Clarence hesitated, '*your* country.'

The old man fixed Clarence with a disparaging look. 'My country no longer exists.'

The missionary became confused. 'But,' he touched the small boy's head, 'your nephew does . . . and you are family, Mr Pilikian . . . his father . . .'

'A brother of the blood, that's all,' interrupted the old Armenian.

'You were not close?'

'That's right,' answered Uncle Krikor, grinning to reveal yellow teeth.

'My given name is Hovahannes,' said the boy, and stared at his uncle as he had done throughout the meeting. 'I am of the family Pilikian.'

'So, the boy's got a tongue.'

'They call him Harry at the mission,' Clarence explained. 'We find it more familiar.'

Krikor looked into the boy's steady gaze. 'He's got his father's eyes,' the old man said and reached out a hand to touch the boy's cheek.

'Yes,' agreed Clarence, weakly.

'And his mother's skin.' The old man's face softened.

'You knew her?' asked Clarence, surprised.

'I was at the wedding. She came from Lake Van.' His voice hardened. 'Which is now in Turkey. She was very beautiful, as I remember her.' He glanced across the gloomy little room at a wall where there might well have been a photograph. Anyway it was unnecessary as an aid to recollection – just looking at the boy he was already in a different land, young again in Armenian pastures.

Clarence coughed. 'Your whole family originally came from Turkish Armenia, I believe?'

'We did,' said Krikor softly. His eyes had clouded and he noticed that the boy's lips were trembling.

'My mother is dead.'

'Yes boy, I know,' said Krikor and took him gently by the shoulders.

'And my father.' The boy's eyes misted. 'He was a hero.'

Krikor nodded. Hovahannes was desperately trying to control tears. 'Mr Symes has told me everything,' said Krikor, and glanced at Clarence, who swallowed mightily.

'Now I am to live with you?' asked Hovahannes, wiping his eyes, angry at himself.

'I am your Uncle Krikor.' The old man was also finding it difficult to check emotion, but what family character remained in him gave his voice an authoritative ring. 'Mr Symes, I think it is best you leave us.'

'Of course, of course.' He stood up quickly. 'There is still the question of a small amount of gold entrusted to me for the boy's welfare that . . .'

'Not now,' said Krikor.

'Of course not, of course not,' repeated Clarence. He took his hat. 'If there is anything . . .'

'Leave us!'

'Goodbye.' Clarence paused at the door. 'Goodbye, Harry.'

The boy looked briefly at Symes then burst into uncontrollable tears and fell into his uncle's arms. Krikor began talking softly in Armenian. Clarence quietly left the room.

Harry Pilikian grew up, and protected his sensitivity with a cavalier attitude. He cried alone occasionally, but only behind a locked door. Desperation and despair had become his travelling companions, but he did not have to like them. His sessions in the Mission, playing for Clarence Symes's lost sheep, brought home to him the fact that no matter how bad things got they could get worse. He practised the piano alone when he could and began to nurture the idea of becoming a composer and lyricist in musicals.

Before his agile fingers found him a niche in life as a newspaper compositor, Harry had lived through a variety of jobs. In a country with more than ten million unemployed, he was happy with anything he could get. It is difficult to become a gentleman sharing the same bedroom as an ageing and distant relative. Uncle Krikor's fading dreams were so much more to do with daily survival than planned ambition. At least it was better than the Hooverville shanties on Riverside Drive and in Central Park, where the destitute existed in appalling conditions.

One winter, Harry had been the skinniest Father Christmas outside Macy's on that or perhaps any other Yuletide. Ten days' work, standing in the snow with a bowl of hot soup every five hours and other people enjoying everything that he was denied – it was here that the bite of real ambition took hold of Harry, here in the street, on the outside.

Chapter 3

Harry Pilikian woke up in the late hours of a beautiful Riviera morning. He remained in bed listening to the sounds of the day unfolding outside in Monte Carlo's Casino Square. The night before, he had finished dinner with Evelyn soon after 11. He had left her asleep in the early hours and walked back to his room at the Hotel de Paris, his only freedom from the attentions and possessiveness of his mistress.

Harry watched reflected sunlight play on the ceiling and remembered the previous evening, when he had glimpsed himself in a mirror on one of the huge pillars in the lobby. With shock, he had realized that the stranger he saw there was himself. White suit, lavender shirt, pale tie, hat, highly polished shoes – a groomed appearance, the Riviera man on his way to dine. He had stared at the reflection and in those moments understood that in this world he had found – a world he had only dreamed of in downtown Manhattan poverty – he was already lost.

He rolled out of bed and went to his desk in the lounge of his suite to re-read the lyrics of the song he had written in the early hours. It had something. He yawned. 'What the hell,' he said aloud. Here he was, another day dawned, there was a war on and it was almost time for morning cocktails.

Louis had brought a wireless into the bar and from that moment was never short of customers. Hourly bulletins were issued via Radio Monte Carlo, whose huge masts above La Turbie dominated the great heights directly behind the Principality.

Day after day, mornings began in the American Bar with coffee, champagne and croissants. A babble of conversation greeted the end of each news bulletin, as silence anticipated the next. The listeners knew that part of a huge French army and the British Expeditionary Force had moved into the Low Countries to meet the Wehrmacht.

To the veterans assembled, clutching their drinks with excitement, the speed at which the war in the north was being conducted was certainly an astonishing change of pace from their experiences in the First World War. The French constantly anticipated Hitler's defeat, but his increasing momentum had become threatening news. France had assumed that the Maginot Line was protecting its Eastern frontier. France was wrong.

On 14 May, from a small bridgehead established at Sedan, in the northeast, General von Kleist's Panzers broke out westwards with a directive to move northwestwards to the English Channel, thus, in a gigantic pincer movement, entrapping the majority of the opposing forces. By 20 May there were three-quarters of a million allied soldiers isolated and the German Panzers had reached Abbeville, near the Channel coast. The French news had become more strident, panicked by the course of events. Claims were made that were obviously inaccurate, causing many arguments and heated exchanges.

Each night, in the bar, Sullivan sat at the piano and delicately reminded the clientele, most of them partially drunk, that there was a world elsewhere. 'I've Got You Under My Skin', 'Anything Goes', 'I'll Follow My Secret Heart', 'September in the Rain', even 'Deep Purple', and when Sullivan was in a semi-haze after midnight, occasionally 'On the Good Ship Lollipop', in an appalling attempt to be both endearing and funny.

After the Wehrmacht's pincers had closed in the north and even the French had been forced to admit, on the night of the 21st, that there was indeed an emergency, the entire bar sang 'South of the Border', which Sullivan played with gusto. They drank some more, became sentimental with 'Wish Me Luck As You Wave Me Goodbye', and listened to Sullivan's emotional rendition of 'We'll Meet Again'. Many of the British residents were poring over a large map of the action spread on the bar top, and several fingers found the port of Dunkirk.

The mood in Monte Carlo became one of gloom and a despair generated from shock and sheer astonishment at the lightning German victories. Life had taken on a pace over which there was no longer any control. The small government of Prince Louis could only hope they would be able to preserve their neutrality.

The days were passed, listening to the wireless. What had been hastily conceived by Louis, in the American Bar of the Hotel de Paris, as a public service to friends and customers, became the norm. People would greet each other with a familiarity reminiscent of a well-run office, the increasingly dangerous news creating amongst them all that unique bond which arises from common fears. Correspondents unable to travel north, or briefed to remain where they were, wrote their pieces over expense account drinks, picking up a deal of gossip from refugees who had been allowed into the Principality.

As spring became summer, the British forces were trapped on the beaches at Dunkirk. By the 2nd of June, the majority of England's army

29

had been evacuated. When this news began the morning bulletin on the 3rd, there was silence – and such silence – as if the entire Western world held its breath. Static crackled briefly and drowned out the 'Marseillaise' until Louis switched off the wireless.

France was alone. With this disaster, the daily banter became less jolly and nervous anticipation was the underpinning of most conversations. The talk was much the same over lunch at the Beach Club, where international society was able to bathe in the large saltwater pool, or indeed the sea itself. Harry would swim far out beyond the buoys where, under the clear summer sky in the warm swell of the Mediterranean, all these man-made problems seemed a strange way to go about living life. He would lie on his back listening to the distant shouts of children on the beach, seagulls wheeling in the breeze and laughter rising occasionally from the crowd at the open restaurant. How could there be a war, with all this? he asked himself at the end of that first week of glorious June weather.

A wave splashed into Harry's face and he started treading water. There, in front of him, in the distance was Ventimiglia and Italy. 'Thank God,' thought Harry, as he churned into a fast crawl, 'they at least, even under Mussolini, have had the sense to stay out of it!'

On the morning of 10 June, with dawn at his back, Harry Pilikian came in from the balcony of his suite at the Hotel de Paris. He took the ashtray beside his typewriter, now full of cigarette butts, and emptied them into the bin already full of discarded words on paper. At that moment there was a huge flash in the sky, and a noise began which initially seemed like rumbling thunder, except that the quality was more penetrating. Harry had heard it before, as a child. He recognized heavy artillery fire and guessed immediately what was happening.

He ran through the bedroom to the other balcony, overlooking the Casino Square and beyond, to Italy. Smoke was rising from the town of Menton, built on a very narrow coastal strip behind which rose sheer coastal bluffs several thousand feet high.

More flashes, and the crack-crack sound that artillery makes. Then the explosions, heavy-calibre shells.

'I don't believe it,' said Harry to himself. 'Not now – Jesus Christ!'

The phone started to ring and he did not have to guess who it was. In the half-light of dawn, lights began to go on all over the Principality as the shock waves carried even to the slumbering population. Then, almost as quickly, those lights went off, indicating that the majority of Monégasques did not perhaps believe that their declared neutrality was sacrosanct.

The telephone continued to ring. Harry went into the room and picked up the receiver. He listened for several moments. Here was Europe coming apart at the seams and the essence of what Evelyn was saying was simply: why are they bothering us? Harry shook his head in wonder. More explosions sounded and there was a little cry of fear on the line from Evelyn.

'I think Mussolini wants to get to the Casino before Hitler,' said Harry soberly, as artillery flashes again ripped the sky silently and glittered in his eyes before their sound travelled the distance to Monte Carlo. He put the receiver down. This was serious. He owed himself some private moments to consider the possible consequences.

If the morale of the French army had collapsed under the shock from the speed and force of the arms of Germany's Panzer divisions in the north, it was in no way impaired by the Italian onslaught in the south. The French had little respect for Mussolini's boasted might, and soon proved, with merely six divisions, to be a formidable foe against Italy's thirty-two. Amost before they moved, Mussolini's troops came to a standstill, trapped in the French Alps, unable to penetrate the passes, completely blocked on the Mediterranean shore, where the actual negotiable terrain was barely half a kilometre wide.

So the days passed and there was much noise but no movement.

More and more German stations had been appearing on the frequencies used in France, relayed to the hotel bar via the transmitter on the heights of Monte Carlo, but the most powerful station was Paris, and the news bulletins had continued to be broadcast during crisis after crisis in French. Now, on 13 June, there was a German voice speaking.

'Tune it!' said Louis urgently, and Jean-Pierre began to turn the station selector again. There was a hush in the bar, a moment of frustration as German martial music blared out from the speaker. Jean-Pierre stood erect and with something like awe in his voice said: 'It *is* tuned!'

No one spoke. The strident music finished. A French voice began with forced enthusiasm to describe the many columns of combat troops marching in good order towards the Arc de Triomphe, where General von Bock was giving the salute to a conquering army.

The bar was frozen, as if preparing for an old plate photograph. Explosions again sounded to the east. Someone came in chattering, sensed an atmosphere and began whispering questions until he too picked up the significance of the broadcast. The German band had begun playing in the background as the announcer went on talking. A rumble of drums sounded, static crackled and there was a volley of rifle fire. The announcer stopped speaking. The music finished and only the heavy tread of marching German feet could be heard.

Louis was facing away from the bar, staring at the wall of bottled liquors. He reached slowly towards the noise and turned off the wireless. There was a moment when nothing happened; most people were staring fixedly ahead as if they could clearly see before them France's capital. Everyone has a different Paris – it is that sort of city. A place even for strangers. At that moment, Paris had entered into the American Bar in Monte Carlo: a gentle ghost with sad secrets, she touched each of those assembled. To some the voice they heard was saying goodbye, for they would never see Paris again.

The crowded bar emptied slowly as Frenchmen went out seeking somewhere to be alone.

Harry looked at his friend with compassion. 'Louis?' he said. But the barman was as separate as any man can be from another, caught in the past, at a café table outside the Deux Magots on the Boulevard St Germain, laughing with a young girl he had eventually married in a small church not far from Notre Dame.

On 18 June, Colonel Charles de Gaulle broadcast from the BBC in London that France had not lost the war, but only a battle. Brave words, but at that moment France had certainly lost something else – her pride, her liberty and her heart.

On the summer day of 21 June, at Compiègne, where Germany had ignominiously surrendered in 1918, Hitler convened a meeting. He demanded that it should be on the exact spot where the previous armistice had been signed. The Germans even insisted upon the same panelled railway car, taken from a museum, where a wall was demolished to remove it. Leaders from both sides met, once again. At 6.50 pm the following day, the armistice was signed for the French by General Huntziger. Peace was was to come into effect at 1.35 am on 25 June. For France, at least, after only forty-six days of fighting, the conflict would be all over.

In the early hours after midnight that morning, in the bar of the Hotel de Paris, Jean-Pierre switched on the wireless. A silence enveloped the room. Throughout Europe millions of radios were tuned in to the various stations that would relay the final information of the fall of France. As a halting voice began a whispered commentary, Jean-Pierre turned off all the lights.

To herald the armistice, four buglers stationed in a small village which was the temporary headquarters of the Führer of Greater Germany, and now Dictator of France, began to proclaim the ceasefire; the plaintive, penetrating sounds might have come from another world.

The German buglers finished. Their still triumphant notes faded with an echo into the night forest of the north, and it was over.

The silence in the American Bar remained absolute, as it was throughout Europe.

'So,' whispered someone, 'it is finished.'

Chapter 4

There was once no station in the world quite like Grand Central in New York City. Transcontinental trains arriving and others preparing to depart amidst the noise, smoke, steam and echoing announcements familiar to any terminal created a sense of anxiety, feelings of excitement, urgency.

In the late morning of Sunday, 24 December 1933, Alexandra Cunningham, waiting for Harry Pilikian in the centre of the great marble lobby beneath the four-sided clock that hung from the roof, glanced around her at the many strange faces. Sunlight streamed through the huge windows, momentarily illuminating the bustling passengers before they plunged back into shadow.

Alex sighed nervously. She was dressed in a simple pink suit and a hat to match with an oval brim and shades of grey around the sides and crown. Her high heels and gloves reflected the subtle colours. None of the clothes were expensive, but all were chosen with obvious taste.

At five minutes to eleven, Alex decided to drink a coffee. She picked up her heavy cases and was immediately helped by a sailor who took her through the milling crowds, up a stairway to a small bar. She sat with a view of the throngs below in the great marble lobby, and could see her rendezvous beneath the suspended clock. Her train was leaving for the west at noon. Alex shivered and her stomach turned over at the sudden terrifying prospect of having to go alone, but she was determined, no matter what, to be on that train. It would be the beginning of everything new for them both.

At 11 o'clock that Christmas Eve morning, Harry Pilikian was already thirty minutes late.

Alexandra Cunningham's parents had come over from England in the early Twenties, wealthy enough to set up house in Manhattan on Park Avenue. Her father, George Leonard Cunningham, came from a good family, and had prospered in London as a successful broker on the stock market. In New York, he joined the Exchange and immediately made the first of several killings. Many more followed and his reputation grew.

33

But in October 1929, like others in America, the Cunningham fortunes changed. The crash left George with nothing but his wife and daughter, and when that proved insufficient, he shot himself. So Alex lost her father whilst her mother lost not only her husband but her hope for the future. The two of them were plunged into the unfamiliar world of poverty.

At twenty, Alex was fashionably slender but with rounded breasts and hips: she appealed more to instincts than to vogue. Her face, framed by long, thick, Titian hair, was unforgettable – firm contours, cherry lips which needed only the hint of lipstick, sculpted nose and long black lashes accentuating her eyes, which were a canvas of colours, grey, green, blue, hazel, changeable as the sea, moods dictating intensity. Although a refined English temper controlled her actions, her eyes behaved with complete emotional disregard of her commands. It was this, and the terribly English accent, that had intrigued Harry Pilikian.

Alex had been sent to the best schools before she was forced out of Vassar by her father's death and the resulting complications. She and her mother, accompanied at first by a loyal maid, moved to a small apartment on Second and Twenty-Third, then when the block was torn down to build a new skyscraper they arrived in Great Jones Street with only a Siamese cat, two heavy suitcases and very little joy. All their own friends had been very understanding, but no one had really wanted to help – taint by association. It was all very embarrassing, but it was a fact. Alex faced it. Her mother wanted to hide, which was why they had been seen simply to disappear.

Alex's job as a waitress from early morning until 4 pm enabled her to supervise the move downtown. She argued with the taxi driver who tried to charge the English accent rather than the cool and knowing eyes. As a result, she was left stranded on the street, with cherished books of poetry in her pockets and her life in a suitcase.

The sight of a young girl attempting to lug cases up the steps in front of 9 Great Jones Street brought out all Harry Pilikian's chivalrous instincts, and he assisted.

'Need any help?'

'No, I'm doing this for exercise.' Alex went on pulling at the two cases.

'Let me.' Harry took one of the heavy pieces of luggage. 'Jesus, what have you got in here?'

'My mother.'

Harry flashed Alex a glance. 'So what are *you* carrying?'

'My life.'

He put down the one suitcase and picked up Alex's. 'You weigh heavy.' At that moment the Siamese cat emerged between the railings from the basement area where it had been exploring . . .

'Edison,' said Alex proudly.

'Why?'

'Because his eyes glow at night.'

'So do mine.'

'Is that a line?' asked Alex.

'No, but it could be a discovery.'

'What's your name?'

'Harry Pilikian, ma'am.' He grinned roguishly.

'Just carry the cases, Harry.' Alex's eyes twinkled.

They negotiated the steps, followed slowly by the cat. By the time Harry was on the second floor, he had broken out in a sweat.

'Are you all right?' asked Alex, knowing how heavy the suitcases were.

'I work out,' said Harry between his teeth.

'Then I'm sure you'll manage,' said Alex, and began running up the stairs.

'Which floor?' shouted Harry.

'The top!'

Alex was out of sight. The cat crept past, pausing a moment, seeming to survey Harry's condition.

'Glows in the night!' he muttered, and seized the luggage with a surge of energy.

'What's your name?' he bellowed up the stairway.

'Alex,' called an almost ethereal voice. 'Alexandra Cunningham.'

'You're English,' Harry shouted again.

'Why not?' came the reply, and a door on the top floor was opened, then closed with a bang.

The rooms were furnished badly. Alex fed the cat then made some tea, and the two young people sat together and looked out into the fading day over the jumble of rooftops, exchanging quips, a few ideas and snippets of information.

When Alex's mother arrived from work with a man, well after the cocktail hour and certainly the worse for wear, she requested a 'little privacy'. Harry took Alex for coffee, and they talked some more of the inconsequential. But other forces were at work already. He said goodbye an hour later, and that night was late for work. Alex had entered his life and he had decided to save her. It was not very practical, as even he admitted, but it was extremely romantic – as Alex appreciated.

They made love, clumsily at first: nervous, passionate love in the later afternoons during the long hot summer of 1933, at the Cunninghams' or Pilikian's residence, as Harry referred to their sleazy rented rooms. His experience was limited to unwilling girls at a Midwest university, hers to a long-protected virginity. Their lives changed, and they began hoping, knowing instinctively that there must be something better for them both, as they lay beside each other, smoking the right cigarettes and saying what they thought were the correct things, after sex.

Alex knew this other world that Harry described and wanted so badly; but she had adapted to her new reality. What had once been unimaginable was now daily living, and as she admitted to herself, it was only Harry's ambition that now kept her alive. She had fallen in love.

Months passed. Someone stole the cat, and Alex captured the heart of Harry Pilikian. They became inseparable, rushing to meet each other whenever it was possible. They vowed to be together always, promised nothing would ever change, swore fidelity, declared their passion as lovers do. If only time was a willing accomplice.

One late afternoon, at the end of that year, ensconced in the plush décor of the Plaza Hotel, Harry found himself wondering if he had enough money to pay for tea.

'One lump or two?' asked Alex.

Harry held up one finger. She poured the tea and handed him a full cup. He put out his cigarette and took the saucer, stared around him a moment, then took a sip.

'Amazing,' he said quietly and sipped again.

'Indian,' said Alex. The music stopped and light applause spattered the room. A peal of raucous laughter, forced, without humour, rang out from a corner table full of bright young things.

Alex began to dream, eyes wide, thoughts distant. Harry enjoyed her beautiful face for a moment.

'Need any help?'

'No, I'm doing this for exercise,' Alex replied without changing her expression, then glanced at him with a quick half-smile. Their first exchange had become an affectionate code to explore each other's feelings.

The musicians began a sentimental waltz. Harry waited for Alex to speak.

'I have to leave,' she said finally.

Harry was thrown into a panic. 'What do you mean?' he questioned. 'I thought you'd like this – you said you came here regularly with your mother and . . .'

Alex looked tenderly into his eyes. 'Away, Harry,' she said. 'West.'

Harry stared.

'Where?'

Alex's gaze became cool and penetrating. 'I'll tell you on the train.' The violins started up once more. They sounded as exhausted as the old musicians. 'I used to watch you,' Alex began, 'walking out of your doorway, down those steps – going – I didn't know where, out into the rain . . .'

'Romantic,' said Harry, his throat tight.

'It always seemed to be raining when I saw you.'

'People usually remember sunlight.'

'I remember rain falling softly from a night sky – on you.'

'And you felt sorry?'

'No, I – fell in love.'

'The lady from Vassar reads too much poetry . . .'

'. . . which is bad equipment for life . . . yes, you've said that before.'

Harry's face hardened. 'Night work on a newspaper, putting together words written by someone else, read by others, might not be life, but it is a living. And it gives me – time.'

'For what?' she asked simply. Harry became confused. The violins played on. 'If you want to live,' said Alex, 'you must reach out and seize it. Do you think working as a waitress, thinking of Keats and Shelley, Byron and Donne, is uplifting to the soul?'

'It's a living.'

Alex stared and smiled. 'Now you've said it yourself,' she stated quietly. 'Your ambition is becoming more of a dream every day . . .' She leaned closer to him, compassion welling up in her, seeing Harry's obvious consternation at what seemed to be an attack on everything that he cherished. 'Harry, what do you want to be? Successful? Rich? Rewarded? For what?'

'I've told you,' he protested. 'I'm going to be a writer and make musicals!'

'Harry.' Alex was urgent now. 'I know you; you only ever see the book in your hand finished; the song being sung; the story in a magazine being read by millions. Harry, you're at the Broadway party after the first night even before you've written a word – of anything.' She stopped abruptly. She did not have to ask his reaction, she could see it on his face. 'If you are blessed to have found a vocation for all that ephemeral ambition which everyone has but few can realize, then *strive*, Harry. Work. Make yourself that someone, don't be just a dreamer.'

'Luck . . .' began Harry. Alex cut him off.

'Luck will come to the man who has the courage to court fate – I believe that . . . and I want you to believe that too. We have each other now . . .' she finished hesitantly. 'Don't we?'

Harry said nothing. Her fingers touched his hand.

'Our destiny is like a child,' Alex said tenderly. 'We can only make it together.' The music finished. 'Ask yourself: where are you going?'

Harry blew smoke into the several seconds it took to answer. 'With you,' he said.

They made a plan, counted available money and agreed on a rendezvous at the end of that week. Harry would not, as he had twice before, work almost twenty-four hours for ten days as Father Christmas till twilight and a compositor till dawn. They decided to leave on the Sunday with his Christmas holiday bonus from the newspaper. Alex would go on

37

ahead from Great Jones Street and Harry agreed to rendezvous directly from the printing works, beneath the great clock at Grand Central Station not later than 10.30. They made a pledge and became very excited. Harry almost proposed, but Alex stopped him, blushing.

'There's time enough,' she said. 'Just be there.' Harry swore on anything she wanted to name. She merely smiled and listened to Harry the songwriter talking about his idea for a musical. Then Harry the novelist and the book he would conceive, and the short stories he would write when their poverty was over. Resilient, effervescent Harry. What they would do when they got to California – where they would go. Harry on oranges. Harry about the similarities of climate between the American Pacific coast and his memories of his Armenian youth by the Caspian Sea. Harry on the longevity factor of yoghurt.

Alex listened and Alex laughed, but sitting there glowing with that insubstantial security lovers have, all she really said with glittering eyes, lips parted over beautiful teeth, responding to Harry saying this, doing that, deciding something else – all she really said was:

'Just be there.'

And that day in New York, towards the end of the last month of 1933, Harry had actually believed that he would be at their rendezvous at Grand Central Station.

Chapter 5

The dark-haired young man stepped from the subway train at the stop nearest to 187th Street and made his way quickly from the station along cold, windswept streets to the Armenian church, where the service was about to start. His suitcase held everything he owned. He left it with the woman who took care of the coats, as he filed in with the morning's congregation. It seemed an appropriate end to his time in New York. Fifteen years ago, to the day, he had arrived.

Harry Pilikian wanted reassurance or a blessing. Uncle Krikor was dead, and with him had gone everything that had reminded Harry of ancient traditions. Now, only the church which he had attended since

38

first arriving in the United States offered anything to his memory of the world he came from.

The choir began to sing and the smell of incense permeated the church. Harry knelt down.

When Uncle Krikor died, Harry had inherited the only things of value the old man possessed – an early pocket watch and some faded photographs, one of his parents' wedding, another of his father, whose youthful, handsome face had been consigned to Harry's wallet, with another revealing his mother's porcelain features. He could seldom look at them, those two pieces of photographic paper pressed close to each other against the bosom of their son. All that hope and expectation, pride and beauty, gone as if it had never been. But he often touched the gold crucifix round his neck, a last gift from his father.

For a moment, he rested his forehead on his hands, clasped against the pew in front. He thought of Alex and the life they would have together in California. More than the future, it was her trust and belief in him that was exciting. He raised his head and gazed around at the congregation. They were mostly poor. Some had been in America since the turn of the century. Many had arrived recently as refugees. It was a small community, and they were jealous of their faith and worship. It had been months since Harry had attended, and he noticed several new faces who appeared to be equally interested in the rest of the congregation. In fact, two of the men, middle-aged, were looking around almost furtively.

Harry checked Uncle Krikor's pocket watch; he intended to stay for half the service and then leave surreptitiously. That would give time enough to make the subway and placate Alex on arrival at the station.

The choir changed key as they paraded slowly around the church. The organ began its overture for the procession to come down the aisle before the service started. Archbishop Leon Tourian, followed by two deacons and a bishop, was carrying in one hand a crucifix and in the other his crozier. The procession moved in silence whilst the congregation took up a murmuring chant, counterpointed by the choir, which proceeded down the centre aisle.

Tourian paced his way confidently towards the altar. He was a man who, although born in Turkey, had become bishop for England. He had served as vicar to the American Patriarch of Constantinople. Although his soul was Armenian and he had vowed it to God, his heart, it appeared, was in Russia, where he felt the communist protection of his people was the solution to centuries of persecution by bordering countries. If Harry understood this man correctly, he had stated that there had been no recognized Armenia until the USSR had taken her population under a protective wing. He rejected the idea of self-rule and condoned the Russian occupation. During the Chicago exhibition on Independence Day that very year, the celebration had been marred for many by

Mgr Tourian's insistence that the Hammer and Sickle flag replace Armenia's on the podium from which he was to speak, and in so doing he had created enemies. Harry crossed himself and wished the archbishop as much luck as he hoped for himself.

The choir, led by an acolyte, in advance of the dignitaries behind them, was already dispersing to either side of the altar. Archbishop Tourian, moving up the nave, was just a few yards from the chancel rail when suddenly there was a swift movement in the small church, and Harry, who had continued to stare, saw everything.

From the fifth and sixth rows of pews, three men sprang up and ran out towards the moving procession. Two of them pinioned the deacons, who were so shocked that they both collapsed to the floor. The third man hit the bishop, who had raised his crucifix, and they fell against the pews. A fourth man leapt from his knees, lunged across the centre aisle and plunged a long butcher's knife into the archbishop's stomach. Leon Tourian bent almost double, mouth wide in silent agony, and the assassin pulled on the knife so that the blade cut upwards towards the prelate's breastbone, impeded by the thick robes he wore.

Harry was moving already – it was a reflex. He jumped onto the ridge of the pew in front, avoided several bent heads and leapt into the centre aisle. The first of the group of assassins, kneeling on one of the deacons, received a kick in the face from Harry Pilikian that knocked him from the prostrate body.

The man beneath Harry was like a tiger and seemed to surge to his feet against the will of gravity. He struck out and Harry received a blow on the jaw and a kick in the stomach which took all the air from his body. He sank to his knees, reaching out vainly to protect himself. The assassin hit Harry twice more then kicked him again. Harry was slammed on to the floor. The man turned and began to run towards the altar.

In the next moment, he had been pulled to the ground as several men in the small congregation seized him. In a tumble the group rolled in the aisle and fists flailed, but the man was caught. Dimly, semi-conscious, Harry heard whistles blowing outside. Groaning in pain, he tried to rise, but his head was spinning and he could not focus. Just before he lost consciousness, be became aware of a heavy weight falling onto his legs. Then he vomited, blacked out and slid sideways onto the tiled floor of the nave.

Everyone who had entered the church had come through a police cordon, as the archbishop's life had been repeatedly threatened. So the police were quick to arrive and burst into the church to see near the altar a group of men holding the still body of one of the assassins. Before them, halfway down the aisle, two deacons were propped against the pews being tended by some of the women in the congregation. The bishop had been hoisted between the fifth and sixth pews and someone was giving him smelling salts. One man in a dirty raincoat was spread-eagled in the aisle, and there was much shouting that two others had run for it through the vestry. A fifth man lay beneath the body of Archbishop Leon Tourian, which was upturned – arms outstretched – with the bloody shaft of a butcher's knife thrust deep into the centre of his torso.

'It's murder!' said one of the Irish policemen, in awe.

'It's assassination, that's what it is,' said the second. Both men had their guns pointed at the corpse of the archbishop, which was lying over the fifth assassin. This man's eyes now opened.

'Don't be thinking of movin',' rapped one of the police.

Harry Pilikian groaned, shook his head and slurred his first words to be taken down:

'I can't.'

Christmas came and went. Bleak for Harry Pilikian in a hospital bed under protective police custody. Distraught for Alex, who had travelled to California alone, had arrived in trepidation, but been received with affection. She began by staying with her aunt, who was indeed in movies. As a designer, the woman had made enough money to buy a place in Beverly Hills, and a very red-eyed Alex had already been introduced at several parties during the holiday.

After days of telephoning, eventually Alex had found Harry, who explained everything – almost.

'When can you come?' she asked, her voice singing with joy.

'Soon,' lied Harry.

'When?' She sounded like a little girl expecting a present. Harry mumbled through gritted teeth. 'I can't hear you!' she said.

'What are you doing tonight?' Harry repeated, barely intelligible.

'I'm going to a New Year's party,' said Alex quickly. 'When are you coming?' Her excitement plunged into Harry's heart, and the idea of being without her became agonizing. He mumbled again. 'Can't you speak, darling?' she asked.

'My jaw,' he said and began to laugh – which hurt. Now in his eyes were tears of frustration. Alex too, on the phone, thousands of miles away in California, was crying and laughing.

'Is it broken?'

'No,' mumbled Harry. 'I'm just talking this way to make you feel more English.' Now the laughter really hurt.

Alex's humour faded. 'Please come,' she said softly.

Harry looked about the room and tried to peer through the blinds – anything to create a diversion for his mind. There was none. Outside it was already almost dark.

'The trial,' he said.

'How long?' Static crackled on the line. Harry said nothing. 'A week?' she suggested.

'Maybe two.' He'd been told six at the earliest.

Silence. An operator cut in: 'Do you wish for more time?'

'Yes, operator,' said Harry angrily. 'Give me your number,' he asked Alex quickly.

'Six five nine eight seven five seven. Oh Harry . . .' she began, and they were cut off.

Harry tried to ring back but was told there would be delays on long distance. An hour later, Alex's incoming call was ignored by the hospital switchboard below, busy gossiping about the New Year's Eve dance they'd been invited to that night, organized by police headquarters. At 7.30 pm the plugs were pulled on all personal calls. It was a lonely entry into the New Year for Harry Pilikian, listening to police sirens coming and going outside.

He had not told his newspaper that he was leaving, so when he contacted them they had agreed to wait until he was able to return, even accept a story if he wanted to write a first-hand account – 'Witness at Assassination'. Great Jones Street still had ten days to run on the month's rent he'd paid, and the police had already informed the landlord of Pilikian's imminent return.

In the early hours of the first day of 1934, Harry sat up against the pillows and turned on the bedside light. He couldn't get Alex out of his mind, which for a young man of his emotional disposition was not unusual in the circumstances. But deep down somewhere inside, something had happened that he could not explain. Something had changed.

In the morning a delegation from the church on 187th Street arrived with fruit and flowers and thanks. They were hardly able to afford the subway fare and were dressed in threadbare clothes, meticulously cared for. They were proud people. The women cried a little; the men shook his hand.

At midday, the phone rang and it was Alex. She'd been to a wonderful party but had ushered in the New Year in tears because Harry was so far away. All the same, Harry detected in her voice that she'd had some fun too. They spoke each day. A week went by.

Alex broke the news to Harry the day before he had to leave hospital. He remembered it well, standing at the window of his room.

'I'm so excited, darling.'

'At what?' Harry had grown sullen as the days passed, perhaps because he resented Alex's happiness without him. She certainly seemed to be thriving in California.

'They're going to test me!'

'For what?'

'The movies.'

42

A chill went through Harry. Why, he did not know as yet, but there would be plenty of time to find out.

'Do you want that?'

Alex ignored the question. The wires sang for a moment. Harry pursed his lips, staring through the open blinds at the sunlit squalor of tenement roofs below. Outside it was very cold – New York cold . . .

'I'm astonished, really I am. John's been so kind. He thinks my face will be perfect for the camera. I'm so thrilled – of course we have to wait and see what happens, and I'll have to learn to go to sleep early because movie stars get up even before the dawn, John says. He . . .'

'Who's John?'

'A friend of Aunt Phyllis at the studios. He's really very nice. You'll like him a lot.'

'I'm sure I will,' said Harry.

'What's that, darling? I can't hear you.'

The sun slipped between the clouds and gusting wind threw sleet at the window. Every time Alex had rung, Harry had travelled three thousand miles for the minutes they spoke. For some reason, today, he had not left the room.

'I said, darling, I can't hear you!'

'I asked what the weather was like.'

'There's wonderful sunshine and flowers – in January, can you imagine? The palm trees and beautiful lawns. The sky is so blue!' Alex was in rapture. Harry had already heard some of it before. But there was something in her voice now, perhaps it was independence, perhaps it was the certain knowledge that she could survive without him, even for a while – after all he had managed without her.

Sleet flurries obliterated Harry's view and the window rattled.

'When?' Alex was saying. 'John is having a party next week and we're both invited. Will you be here by Friday?'

Harry decided to be honest. 'I can't leave until the trial's finished.' A hollow noise sounded on the line like the echo of the sea. It reminded them both they were three thousand miles apart.

'When?' There was unexplored fear in Alex's voice.

'Four, perhaps six, weeks.' The sea on the telephone line seemed to thunder in over many exposed rocks.

Their long-distance relationship had acquired a third party, who never failed to join them. She would cut in with the confidence of Ethel Merman making her first entrance into stage history.

'Do you wish for further time?' said the voice of the operator. Only the seashell roared on the line. In California Alex was unable to speak. In New York, Harry said nothing.

'Your party has disconnected.' Harry was about to speak but no words came. The line went dead. He put down the phone.

43

Harry went back to Great Jones Street and to work. Alex was tested and several studio executives who saw the celluloid marvelled at her emotional range and especially her ability to cry. Someone said: 'Garbo.' Someone else murmured: 'Better.' And she was bought and sold.

The intensity of feeling that had given Harry's life so much colour and excitement had begun to slip away and no matter how he tried to readjust his thoughts, it was beyond his control.

He put on his old trenchcoat, which had been cleaned twice to remove the bloodstains, and walked until he found himself outside the Plaza Hotel, just after dusk. There he sat on a bench and watched the fountain. He did not see the horses and carriages, or the automobiles, that rattled and roared by. Just the light playing on the always moving water.

The following day, the trial began. Harry gave evidence and received a commendation from the police. In three days, the trial was over and so was Harry Pilikian's affair with Alex Cunningham. It was inconceivable to Harry to be standing in inches of snow on the courtroom steps, now free to go where he wished, and yet not instantly to race off to California.

He had been given a week's leave of absence from work, and that night began drinking heavily. He telephoned Alex from an almost snowbound booth around 11 o'clock with a pocket full of quarters.

'It's over,' he said.

'You're drunk,' said Alex.

'Sure I'm drunk, wouldn't you be?'

'I'm not,' she said coldly.

'Well, you damn well ought to be.'

'There's no reason for me to be drunk.'

'There's every reason.'

'Look, Harry,' said Alex quickly, 'I've got to go to dinner in a few minutes. What do you have to say?'

'It's over, don't you understand?'

'Can't we talk tomorrow?' Harry could sense Alex putting on her gloves and looking across the room – at someone else. 'I really do have to go.'

'I'm talking to you now! I'm in a telephone booth. I don't have a fancy car waiting outside or an elegant dinner to go to in some prissy white hacienda. I don't wear hundred-dollar tuxedos or crocodile shoes, custom-made for the "dear Johns" of this world. I eat cheap Italian, wear ten-dollar suits and walk most places when I can't pay for a ride. New York City . . .' Harry hiccuped, 'Great Jones Street, two up, three across, remember me, Harry Pilikian, the Armenian kid with a dream?' The old seashell on the line began ushering in the tide right on cue.

'Harry, you're drunk.'

'You already said that.'

'Look, Harry, please, it's important – tonight, I mean.'

'I'm glad you understand that,' Harry slurred.

'I'm meeting some very important people tonight, Harry, and you're going to upset me.'

Tears of anger sprang into Harry's eyes. 'What did you say?' he bellowed.

'That'll be three more dollars,' cut in the long-distance Ethel Merman. Harry searched frantically for another quarter.

'Please, Harry, you're shouting,' said Alex. 'And I have to go.'

'Of course I'm shouting – it's over! You selfish bitch. Don't you understand?'

'The trial – or us?' asked Alex.

'I said three dollars, sir,' said the operator, 'and I don't appreciate your language.' Harry shoved the coins into the box. One came out and fell onto the floor of the booth. 'I'm sorry, sir, I shall have to disconnect you.'

'No, wait a minute,' said Harry and bent drunkenly to the floor, still holding the phone. 'I've got it,' he said to no one in particular. Then he stood up clutching the quarter. He put the receiver to his ear. The line was dead.

Harry stepped out of the booth and fell headlong into a pile of snow.

And that was that. A letter arrived from Alex telling Harry even more about her experiences and, as an afterthought, asking about him. It seemed to have been written by a stranger. 'John might be able to help you,' she suggested, 'if your behaviour is better than it was when last we spoke on the telephone.' Harry wrote back a letter, composed with the inspiration of a bottle of Scotch, suggesting what John could do with his help.

Nothing from Alex for two weeks. She was never in when he telephoned. Then the first of several letters was returned unopened. Harry got the message. He sent a wire – would be arriving such and such a time and day. He actually got to Grand Central Station, and quietly watched the train pull away. Only then did he really know.

'It's over,' he said softly. But he was wrong – it was just too late.

Alex kept her secret from everyone until the last minute. Many guests at the wedding said it was obviously a marriage of love, and only a few cynically suggested the word necessity. In any event, history records that Alex Cunningham became the wife of a studio vice-president called John, and had a beautiful baby.

Chapter 6

A convoy of lorries bearing a regiment of Italian troops rumbled to a halt at the border where occupied France met the outer limits of the Principality of Monaco. Here the soldiers jumped down from their transport, formed up in columns and, led by their officers, many of whom knew Monte Carlo as well as the residents, marched what was little more than a mile along the sea road, then up the final incline and into the Casino square, by which time they were sweating profusely. Customers of the Café de Paris, crowded around tables looking on to the square, stopped to watch the representatives of Mussolini's mighty army, most of whom were unshaven, slovenly, some even hungover from the night before, turn around the square until the leading column came to a halt outside the Casino.

On the word of command, the men turned facing the palm trees, then stood at ease. The numerous officers were pleased to relinquish their authority for a while to the NCOs. Several of them ran up the steps into the Casino, but were stopped at the door. Their orders had been merely to reconnoitre and report, at the same time making a show of arms. Those on the Casino steps were old prewar customers, and coming from good families, they understood immediately what they were now asked to remember – the Casino rules, 'No uniforms, gentlemen'. Traditional rules must be adhered to, it was explained.

'After all, gentlemen,' the manager pointed out, 'Monaco has yet to enter the war on either side.'

Disappointment was assuaged with glasses of champagne that the manager insisted they should all consume in the great marble foyer. No one quite knew what to do, or even whose authority should dominate the moment, so because it was a lovely summer's day and Italians, when offered pleasure, are the most reasonable men, the assembled group sat around on hastily produced chairs and talked of the past, the present and the glorious future. Many toasts were proposed and no one was reluctant to clink glasses if both Mussolini and the Prince were mentioned in the same breath.

A precocious young colonel, whose rank and dark tan were a product of recent heroism in Abyssinia and Libya, went directly into the Hotel de Paris with three of his officers, to be greated by Louis like lost family. All of them were known to him from before the war. Jean-Pierre shook hands warmly and several of the other waiters waved hello. The men sat atop stools at the bar and began to gossip as if Mussolini had never existed. The colonel's favourite champagne was broached – Louis Roederer Cristal – and, although as yet it was difficult to imagine quite what, everyone celebrated. The colonel crossed several times to tables occupied by familiar faces. There was much clicking of heels, shaking of hands, invitations to lunch and polite refusals.

'We are just passing through,' the colonel said several times. 'Our soldiers will be nearby in case you need us.'

Several rooms had been arranged by the Italians in the Hotel de Paris, Hermitage and Metropole. Official billeting would be outside the strict limits of Monaco, adjacent to the Beach Club, where the Monte Carlo Beach Hotel annexe was to become a barracks.

And really that was it. Several phone calls were received at the switchboard of the Hotel de Paris, from the Palace. Immediately the columns of soldiers formed up and marched back in the direction from which they had come. An army staff car arrived, then a second, which was quickly filled by the now tipsy officers – and the Italians were gone.

The only immediate inconveniences to be inflicted by the new order surrounding the Principality were upon the British. A number of them already listed by the Italian Secret Service, and proven to be without either second passports or full residence permits, were given notice to pack and assemble, when they would be taken to an internment camp in the nearby hill town of Sospel. Here the authorities of Mussolini's empire hoped to gain time to find a solution to an embarrassing situation. Most of the English had lived in Monaco for many years, and were already protesting their neutrality. But it was now too late for them to go elsewhere, so there was no escaping the order.

Ben Harrison, lying on the bed in his hotel room, lit yet another cigarette and, as he digested the news that had spread around the bar in minutes, thanked his lucky stars he had acquired a Swiss passport. He had come to Monte Carlo to avoid the war, as everyone else in the Principality hoped to; he, after all, had done enough in the first, the Great War. He laughed. What would they call this one? And how long would it last? If it was going to be years . . . He began to cough. Surely they couldn't hold innocent civilians for the whole duration? Perhaps after a few months . . . He swung his legs from the bed. He had decided to go back to the bar for a drink, now that all the Italian uniforms had gone. He stood up and stretched. They'd have to let them all go eventually. After all, they had homes to keep – and they were not fighting a war in Monaco.

'Bloody Mussolini,' muttered Ben.

Wearing nothing but a black garter belt, and sitting on the edge of her large bed, Maggie Lawrence began slowly to roll on the first of a pair of Du Pont's newly created nylons; the sensation of the man-made fibre against her skin was one to which she had recently grown accustomed. She stopped momentarily and listened, to assure herself that the sound of marching feet was taking the Italian soldiers out of the Principality. With a sigh of relief, she continued to roll the fine material over her knee, ensuring that the seam was straight, until it was taut around her upper thigh. Securing the stocking top at front and back, she then carefully bent over once again to roll on the second of the pair. This she also secured front and back. She stood up, slipping her feet into high-heeled shoes, then walked over to a full-length mirror where she surveyed herself.

It was not yet midday and she had an appointment for lunch with a new customer. She was very expensive and must ensure that her client was generously appreciative.

Maggie had a golden all-over tan. Her body, slim and long-legged, was firm and curved in exactly the right places. She touched her skin delicately with fingers that knew her body well. It was not often that a man caressed her the same way. It had been depressing to discover, as her career blossomed, that the more money a man seemed to possess, the feebler were his sexual capabilities. If there was an exception, she was still waiting to meet him.

Maggie held her firm breasts and cocked her head, focused for a moment on the erect nipples. Her fingers strayed to the tips and she half-closed her eyes, then parted her lips to let her tongue play slowly over brilliant white teeth. Her hands began sliding, as if with a life of their own, past the narrow waist, across her flat belly, until they met, hesitantly, between her legs. It was here (and certainly not in the bank) that Maggie's problem lay. Although there were only a few days in the month when she did not couple with a man, she herself was seldom allowed the pleasure of an orgasm.

Her index fingers slowly negotiated the familiar route between fine pubic hairs and rested upon the delicate gatehouse which most men considered merely the entrance to her palace of delights. For the majority, the moment they were inside, paid no further thought to the guardian which gave them access, and certainly when they withdrew, tail between their legs, they were oblivious to the almost imperceptible sound of Maggie's thighs closing tightly.

'What's on your mind, honey?' some of them would ask, and she'd smile and say, honestly, what most of them did not want to believe.

'Money, sweetheart, what else?'

She groaned as her fingers became moist, and began moving them with a steady rhythm. One hand urgently sought out her breasts and, with the perfection of practice, she began to massage first one, then the other, playing with each nipple momentarily until the tingling sensation which coursed through her body began to flood her imagination. Now, suddenly, she wanted to lie down, but she remained standing, seeing in the mirror not a beautiful creature with an attractively flawed face, but some doyenne of sexuality who had come, as always, to give her joy.

She moaned with ecstasy as the building pleasure within intensified. Now she was wet, and with knees locked, she gently splayed her legs several inches wider. Knitting two fingers together she slid them into her vagina, at first tentatively, then, unable to restrain herself from an immediate reaction to that initial sensation, thrust them up deep inside, immersing them in the warm sexual juices of her excitement. She gasped and slowly withdrew her fingers. Immediately she began rubbing her clitoris with barely controlled abandon. Her breath came sharply as she approached the climax that she now so desired.

A sharp knock on the door sounded loudly. Maggie Lawrence gulped in air. She leaned forward with both hands and grasped the long mirror. The knock sounded again. She released the breath in her lungs.

'Who is it?' The handle turned on the unlocked door and it opened. A man entered. Maggie looked at him in the mirror's reflecton. Slowly she pivoted on her heels until she faced him. He remained composed and elegant.

'You're earlier than we agreed,' she said huskily.

He glanced at his watch and shook his head.

'Before lunch,' he said. 'And I never like to be late.'

'Well,' replied Maggie, cocking her head, excited at his self-assurance, 'then you'd better close the door, and lock it.'

Harry Pilikian was lying on a sofa in the lounge of his hotel suite. He had already been to the gymnasium beside the harbour to work up a sweat and freshen himself after a long night of attempted creativity, which was not going well. A light breeze off the sea came through the tall french windows into the room where the blues of the walls, carpet and patterned furniture gave a cooling effect even on the hottest day. A fragrance of fresh flowers filled the room – a luxury Harry really enjoyed. Someone, several floors below, was mowing the lawn of Monte Carlo's Casino Square. The smell of newly cut grass wafted into the air. Peace had descended once more. The Italian invasion of the morning was over.

Harry looked at his watch with a sigh. He had a date with Evelyn.

France had fallen. Monte Carlo had survived the first diplomatic skirmishes and been recognized as neutral. For the moment, it appeared that they were all to remain unmolested even by the Italians, so it was not the fact of being in Monaco that troubled Harry, but the idea of lying in bed with Evelyn all night, every night, and waking up every morning to her personal brand of tittle-tattle. It so disconcerted him that already he'd left her twice. Once in Kenya on a safari – his last vision of her had been of a screaming harridan dressed for Africa, in a white silk blouse, cravat newly pressed, riding trousers, crop and boots, telling him that he was nothing, always had been nothing and always would be nothing without her, and how the hell was he going to get back to Europe anyway? It was the dirt farmer's daughter's language that followed which had cheered him up. Then at the Villa d'Este on Lake Como, which she announced had been her 'honeymoon hotel', Harry, fully clothed, had just dived from the terrace into the water at the end of one of her social lunches for twenty people and begun swimming across to the other side of the lake. Laughter had turned to concern and eventually Evelyn had come after him in a speedboat.

They had made it up on both occasions, but the second time he had established some kind of independence. When Evelyn suggested that they move into her 'little villa' in Monte Carlo, which she'd just bought and refurbished, having relinquished Cap Ferrat, he had insisted on having a suite in the Hotel de Paris, where he could work alone. The prospect of losing Harry worried Evelyn, so she agreed.

The door bell rang. Harry rolled off the sofa, and dressed only in shirt, slacks and soft-soled shoes, ambled down the corridor and opened the door.

'If you knew I was coming, why did you keep it locked?' asked Evelyn, and walked straight past him. She was beautifully turned out, and so she should have been: most of the morning had been spent putting on four different outfits before reverting to the first, a grey suit and little trilby, with a crimson silk shirt which matched her lips perfectly. She looked, Harry imagined, fairly attractive – he was no longer sure. To him she was now just Evelyn Martineye.

She strode up the long hallway, pulling at her gloves as if bent on finding Harry in a compromising situation. Harry closed the door and took a cigarette from the silver box on the small table beneath the hall mirror.

'If you're looking for the blonde, she's on the bidet in the end bathroom.' He lit the cigarette.

'Harry, don't be coarse,' she said quickly, then stopped and looked back at him. 'We've got cocktails and lunch and you're not dressed.'

'I'm awake,' he said.

'Harry, you'll give me a headache. Sometimes I think you've got no manners at all.'

'Sometimes I think you're right,' said Harry, and ambled back up the hallway.

Evelyn put down her bag, then looked at the typewriter and Harry's piano. 'You're a very slow writer,' she began.

'I'm slow at a lot of things.'

'Then give me a kiss.' He kissed her, a long kiss. She drew her face slightly away, aroused, her lips parted. Harry looked at her beautiful face for several moments. She gave him a genuine smile, which was unusual for Evelyn.

'Why do I always get the impression,' he said, 'that whenever I'm this near to you, somewhere there's a camera focused on close-up?'

Evelyn's eyes flickered. She absorbed the remark, utterly aware of herself once again. 'Get dressed,' she said softly, then picked up the small crocodile bag which she had put on the low table with her gloves, took out a tortoise-shell compact and lipstick, and looked in the mirror. She had recently taken to using just a hint more make-up.

'You've got crimson on your collar, so change your shirt and *quickly* – I don't want to be late!' she said, as Harry went into the bedroom.

Minutes later, dressed, Harry stepped back into the lounge, wearing a white suit, shoes to match, a lavender shirt and white tie. Evelyn surveyed him critically. 'We're on the terrace of the Salle Empire and everyone's going to see us, so bring your white hat as well,' she said, and walked down the hallway.

'Do I have to take off the black band?' Harry asked mockingly, following slowly. Evelyn grimaced and turned to him.

'Harry, sometimes I wonder if you have any clothes sense at all.'

Taking his hat from its peg, Harry opened the door of the suite. 'You, darling, must remember that you bought *your* clothes sense from people who thought they were the very best.'

'You're damned right,' said Evelyn, putting her gloves back on. 'And it was worth every nickel.' She re-secured her grey trilby with a hatpin. Harry watched patiently, pity appearing in his eyes.

'What is it?' she snapped. 'Is something wrong?'

'War,' said Harry softly, 'and your three major worries are a headache that could deny you a pleasant meal, the possibility of being late for drinks, and your appearance to this residue of European society.'

Evelyn's face froze. She spoke icily. 'Let's go to cocktails.'

Beneath the yellow awning spread to protect the clientele from the sun, the Terrace Restaurant of Monte Carlo's Hotel de Paris was crowded to capacity. Dining outside the Salle Empire had always been fashionable before the war, and now it had become even more difficult to reserve a table, yet Evelyn Martineye had never been refused a reservation – she had quickly learnt how to exert the tacit pressure of reputation. She led

51

her guests to one of the best tables in the very centre of the Terrace, affording them a view on to the Casino Square over a low hedge which concealed them from passers-by who might linger to peer in at the privileged taking luncheon.

Evelyn introduced everybody, finishing breathlessly, as if it had been all effort. There was an attractive American woman in her thirties, and Maggie Lawrence, who smiled at all the men but winked at Harry.

'Harry Pilikian,' he said, and shook hands with a bright-eyed, dark-haired Irishman called Quinn, a stiffly elegant Swiss banker named de Salis and a German brought by the Irishman.

'Jürgen Pabst,' said the stranger. His eyes were startlingly blue in a face with firmly handsome features. He wore a cream-coloured jacket with a pale-blue shirt, open at the neck over a grey silk cravat. He had a light tan and fashionably slicked blond hair. He was of average height, but solid, with a skier's build. Harry found it difficult to tell his age. He could have been a well-preserved forty or a thirty-year-old beginning to show his years. Aware of his appeal to the women, the German became animated as he revealed information about himself in a studiedly self-deprecating manner. Harry watched and listened.

Heidelberg and Munich had given Jürgen Pabst an excellent, although on the face of it confused, education. He had started as a lawyer, then again as a doctor. His father, a wealthy Count and owner of a large estate, was distressed that his son wanted to work. Pabst stated disarmingly that personally he felt that in the great new Germany everyone should work. Finally, he had decided to study sociology and psychology. This, he informed the table, in reply to a question, was proving useful in his present position as a consultant to the rapidly expanding industries of the Third Reich.

'So your work must take you abroad – now – more and more,' said Harry. The German stared, no one laughed, someone coughed, and then Georges, the *maître d'hôtel*, arrived flourishing menus.

The ladies ordered first, taking their time, whilst the men drank cold, dry, white Sancerre wine from bottles in the ice buckets. Quinn ordered '*truite aux amandes, pommes vapeur et haricots verts*' whilst Guy de Salis ordered sole.

'Is it fresh from Dover?' he asked with a smile.

'The sole? But of course it is fresh,' said Georges, and wrote it down.

'How can it be fresh if it's from Dover?' asked Harry.

'I assure you . . .' began Georges, puzzled.

'Brought down by Messerschmitt,' suggested Pabst, and there was laughter from all but Harry.

'Sounds like an epitaph for a Spitfire pilot,' he said. Silence replaced the laughter. Pabst stared at Harry.

'You are from Germany, Mr Pabst?' asked Evelyn, diplomatically.

'Yes,' he said coldly.

'Then I must compliment you on your English,' she said, forcing a smile.

'Thank you,' he said. 'I spent some time in Britain – *before* the war.'

'And do you intend to spend some time there *after* the war?' asked Harry quietly.

'That, I think, is the intention of many Germans,' said Pabst slowly, his face impassive.

'Monsieur . . .' began Georges, sensing tension, 'may I suggest . . .' Harry interrupted, still gazing at the German.

'I am sure you are right, Herr Pabst . . .' he said, taking off his hat. 'The English, I believe, are building large prison camps.' He picked up his glass of wine, which sparkled in the sunlight. The others tried to laugh.

Pabst put a firm hand on Harry's arm. 'You are very outspoken, Mr Pilikian. What is your business?'

Harry removed the hand. 'None of yours,' he said, and sipped his wine.

'Gentlemen, please order,' said Evelyn. So they did, and lunch began.

Superficial conversation carried the group through the meal until the arrival of a bottle of Veuve Cliquot champagne.

'Psy-cho-logy,' said Maggie, affecting difficulty over the words – she was intrigued by this handsome German. 'My, my, that *is* interesting.' She stared at the blue eyes. 'Does that mean you can tell what I'm thinking?'

'Sometimes,' he answered as the woman giggled. 'I would have to know the conditions in which you lived – what you do – to explore your vocation in life,' Pabst finished seriously.

'My vocation!' replied Maggie putting a hand to her moist lips. 'Well, that sounds like a proposition!' All at the table laughed, except for Pabst.

'I don't think so, Miss Lawrence,' he said coldly.

Coffee was served with brandies for the men, liqueurs for the ladies. A variety of Turkish and Virginia cigarettes was taken out of cases and handbags. As smoke curled into the air, Harry asked blandly: 'And how is the war going for Germany, Herr Pabst?'

The man was sipping coffee. 'Like this meal,' he said quietly, 'it is over.'

'Really?' countered Harry. 'I thought England had just reached the finals.'

Quinn burst out laughing.

'War is not sport,' said Pabst acidly. 'The English are proving stubborn. If they have any sense they will surrender.'

'I think not, Herr Pabst,' stated de Salis. 'Not to Germany.'

'Then they will be annihilated.'

'That's a big word,' said Quinn, eyes dancing. He drew on his cigarette.

'It is a small island, Mr Quinn.' Pabst smiled.

'With a wide moat,' said Harry Pilikian, silencing the table.

Evelyn glared and stood up. 'We girls are going to the Ladies' Room.' Everyone at the table got to their feet and the men watched the women make their way across the crowded terrace.

'Evelyn is a charming hostess, Pilikian,' said Quinn.

'You are not married to her?' asked Pabst.

'I'm sure you wouldn't advise it,' replied Harry with a vicious grin. 'She's Jewish.'

'I think that's about enough, Pilikian,' said Quinn. People at nearby tables sensed trouble and cast furtive looks at the still standing men.

Pabst stared at Harry. 'And you are not – Jewish?' He had shifted his weight firmly on to both feet, and become quite still.

'I haven't bothered to look,' answered Harry. He too was solidly planted. In the distance, the head waiter moaned and began moving rapidly through the crowds.

'So you are not her . . .?' Pabst appeared to have forgotten the word.

'Husband,' said Quinn.

'No, I'm not.'

'You are not many things, it seems.'

'Exactly,' said Harry.

'But you must be something,' stated the German. Harry only grinned. Out of the corner of his eye he had seen Evelyn, who had left her powder compact, fussing back onto the terrace.

'A gigolo?' suggested Pabst.

The head waiter saw the first blow struck, and stopped dead.

Jürgen Pabst was much faster than Harry expected, and his straight left only brushed the German's moving head. Harry saw the uppercut coming a heartbeat before it would have hit his chin square-on. He turned fractionally, and took the dangerous blow against the side of his face. Pabst's ring cut the cheekbone as his fist lost its impetus, then Harry threw a perfect right cross which rocked Pabst, and again a straight left which smacked directly into the German's face. Pabst staggered. Harry stepped one pace forward. Ignoring screams from the women all around, he drove a straight right-hander with all his weight behind it, aimed at the side of Pabst's jaw. The German's reflexes were astonishing and he almost dodged the blow, but Harry's clenched fist connected – hard. The startling blue eyes glazed even in that second, and Pabst lost consciousness and balance; he fell backwards over a lunch table where five people had only just started their *crème de volaille*.

As Pabst rolled off the table into a woman's lap, which was already full of soup, one of the men scraped back his chair and ran at Harry shouting angrily. He threw a punch which Harry ducked, but was by now too steamed up to ignore. He smacked the man lightly with his fist on the side of the face and the assailant fell to the terrace floor.

Quinn grabbed Harry's arm from behind.

'That's enough!' he shouted.

'Agreed,' said Harry breathing deeply. Evelyn thrust several thousand francs at the head waiter, who had pushed through the throng.

Evelyn and Harry left the terrace together, went across the lobby into the American Bar and sat down on stools. Harry ordered glasses of champagne. Louis brought a damp cloth which Harry put to his cheek. Evelyn wanted an explanation but Harry refused to say what the fight was about. Finally, exasperated, he spoke.

'He called you a Jewish whore.'

Evelyn became indignant. 'But I'm not Jewish!' she snapped. Then the chief of police arrived. He knew them both, and kissed Evelyn's extended fingers before shaking hands with Harry Pilikian. There was a sudden drop in the level of conversation at the bar tables.

Gerard was not in uniform, but everyone in Monte Carlo knew his face. He undid the two buttons of his dark-grey suit, settled himself on a stool, stared at Harry and spoke softly.

'Scandal is not an uncommon occurrence here, as you well know, perhaps because the Principality attracts – can I say – "colourful" people. But we do feel for the benefit of all who live here that unless a major offence occurs and we cannot deny information either to the press or public, if the parties concerned can be reconciled, then it is a simple matter to do no more than to issue a private warning.'

'I don't like the word warning,' said Harry.

'Harry, please!' interrupted Evelyn. 'Gerard's just trying to help.'

Harry said nothing. The chief of police coughed. 'Evelyn, may I have a few words with Mr Pilikian alone? It is a very busy day for me. We have a concert at the Palace tomorrow evening and responsibility for security is mine.'

'I was hoping to go,' said Harry.

'Then you shall, Mr Pilikian, have no fear.'

Evelyn slipped from the bar stool. 'A few moments,' she said, glared at Harry, then strode out.

The chief of police settled back on to his bar stool. 'Well, Monsieur – Harry. Let me tell you the good news. I have spoken with everyone who might create friction in this matter, and there will be no charges.' He paused. 'Monaco is an island in a sea of war, and for the present we remain neutral.'

'Herr Pabst is German,' said Harry.

Gerard nodded. 'I am concerned that private arguments should not be aired in public, and even more so that political disagreements do not come to the attention of the police.'

'Your English has always been very good,' said Harry and ordered another brandy. Gerard smiled.

'English and American people have lived here for many years. To speak their language has become a necessity. I love them as I love their countries, as indeed they in turn who are resident here love Monte Carlo. We are all, who are fortunate enough at this moment in history to be living here, in this minute part of Europe, sheltering from turbulent times. Our neutrality is precious and must be guarded. Every day, refugees come to our border, and most must be turned away because we are such a very small country. Those who are allowed to stay must prove themselves special cases. It is not a pleasant duty to decide who may remain and who must go. You understand, I hope?'

The chief of police hesitated, then leaned closer to Harry and lowered his voice. 'I like you, Harry, so I will warn you in confidence. Herr Pabst is a major in the Gestapo. He works for a counter-espionage section directly under the command of an extremely able officer called Schellenberg. They are able to demand many . . .' he sought the correct word, 'favours – which unofficially we are obliged to grant.' Harry said nothing. Gerard leaned back on his stool. 'Germany is so very big,' he said, 'and we are not.'

Harry nodded and swallowed brandy.

'You have a quick temper, I am told,' stated Gerard.

'Sometimes,' said Harry.

'And a quick tongue?' Gerard's voice was hard. 'Guard it!' He stood up. 'Au revoir, Harry, we will, of course, meet again, but next time I hope under more pleasant circumstances.'

'You sound like Vera Lynn,' grinned Harry.

The chief of police smiled. 'She is my favourite.'

Chapter 7

Christopher Quinn swore, put his finger into his mouth and began sucking, then leaned down to read what had proved so sharp. 'Cactus Peruvianus Monstruosus'.

'Well now,' he said to himself, 'an exotic garden, is it? Then we'd better be taking a look at what they have here.' He looked at his watch again – almost 4 o'clock – turned around and stared seawards where the sparkling water and the beautiful afternoon belied even the idea of war. He had made a rendezvous after the eventful lunch and come early to survey the tropical vegetation growing amidst rocks on the outskirts of Monto Carlo.

Feeling the warmth of the sun, the young man in grey slacks and open-necked shirt, hair ruffled by the breeze, took off his light sports jacket, draped it over one arm, and paused where a wall of the exotic garden faced out beyond the Rock of Monaco towards the southern horizon.

'A wonderful day,' he murmured.

'I don't suppose you will be going back to Amsterdam for a while?' said a voice addressing the Irishman in English, with a French accent. It was familiar to Quinn.

'So the Swiss really are punctual,' he said.

'Always,' stated the man, and came to sit beside Quinn, with his back to the view.

'Even with a war on?'

'Even for lunch.'

Quinn's expression hardened as he remembered the fight.

De Salis's eyes were dark, his face pallid, and although only in his late thirties, his well barbered full head of hair was turning grey. He wore a sober black suit and a cream shirt, his single concession to being abroad – in Switzerland, it was always white. Even though the day was warm and the sun bright, his black tie was knotted against a stiff collar. There was not a bead of perspiration on his face.

'You're a cold fish,' said Quinn, and took out a handkerchief to wipe his brow.

'I would like to talk about diamonds, Christopher.'

Somewhere in the distance an aeroplane droned, circling over the border of Italy. Quinn replaced the handkerchief in his coat pocket, then slowly folded his arms.

'Whose diamonds?' he asked.

De Salis undid his jacket.

'Possession is a very interesting word, hein?' There was no reaction from Christopher Quinn. 'For a banker it is immaterial who once owned an object – it is who holds it at any given moment. *He* has possession, and if the trouble has been taken to certify to the law which is currently recognized that what he possesses is acknowledged as belonging to him, then what more is necessary? Laws change, as do governments. Borders move, sometimes this way, sometimes the other. In Switzerland we are neutral and face, yet again, the gravest problem – who owns what?'

Christopher Quinn smiled. He admired de Salis but did not like him. 'You want to talk about diamonds?' he said. De Salis nodded. 'My own diamonds are in England,' the Irishman told him.

'Ah!' said the Swiss banker. 'And the others?'

'In Amsterdam.'

De Salis swallowed, then asked softly: 'The Nazis have the diamonds?'

Christopher Quinn stood up. He was taller than de Salis and broader. 'They have all of Europe,' he said.

'But I thought the diamonds were for sale?'

'They are,' said the Irishman quietly. 'From the Gestapo.'

De Salis stared. 'But the Dutchman . . .?'

'He will be arriving tonight,' Quinn interrupted, 'and he has all the papers.'

'And samples?'

'He will bring them.' Quinn paused. 'It is all very official.'

'But the Gestapo,' began de Salis, 'the Nazis . . .' He stared at Quinn. 'I thought we were doing business direct with Amsterdam?'

'I am only the broker,' said Quinn, and grinned. 'It is my duty to establish the best deal.'

'With the Gestapo?'

'Their representative is here.'

'Does the Dutchman know?'

'Not yet.'

De Salis became nervous. 'But can you assure me he will . . .'

'He will sell to the Gestapo,' Quinn interrupted. 'On my advice, at a considerable discount. They will then do business with you – through me.'

'Can you be sure?' whispered the Swiss banker.

'He will be persuaded,' said Quinn.

'Legally?'

'Officially,' stated Quinn softly, 'by the Gestapo.'

Quinn extended his arm and the two men shook hands.

The roaring engines of a Junkers Ju 52 trimotor were gunned once more by the pilot as he taxied slowly towards a group of buildings where many lights were shining. He throttled back on the port engine and the starboard wing swung around. The runway landing lights which had guided him to a safe approach were switched off. One by one the motors were cut and, for the passengers, after hours in the night sky flying down from Paris, there was a wonderful peace. Overalled men wheeled steps to the exit door, which was opened on to the balmy air of the Riviera.

The large plump Dutchman carrying a maroon attaché case paused in the doorway and breathed deeply, tasting salt on the light sea breeze. He grunted in satisfaction – Paris had been stifling. He put on his white panama, then stepped down and made his way with the other passengers across to the small buildings of the terminal.

Van der Voors was expected. He had a special pass and was escorted through several barriers by a tall man who had signalled to him. The Dutchman had already begun to perspire because of his size and the humidity of the Mediterranean evening.

'Mynheer Quinn?' asked Van der Voors politely. 'He will be waiting?' The man in a long black coat said nothing.

A large Mercedes drew up and a porter loaded the Dutchman's luggage with the help of a chauffeur in grey uniform.

Van der Voors looked at his watch. 'Will it be the same time in Monte Carlo as Paris?'

'It will be Reich time,' was the curt reply as the car pulled away into the night.

Several minutes after midnight, still clutching the attaché case, Jan Van der Voors climbed awkwardly out of the large black Mercedes outside the Hotel de Paris. He attempted to straighten his crumpled white suit and pressed his panama on to the back of his head. Michel, the doorman, was ordered to see to the luggage, then the two men made their way up the steps into the revolving doors.

The Dutchman stood at the reception desk and registered, giving his occupation as 'merchant'. The tall man in black made a quiet request of the manager, who nodded but asked that the contents of the attaché case should be declared. Van der Voors opened the case; it was full of diamond samples. He watched the manager's reaction and smiled, then accepted a receipt as the case was carefully placed in a large safe.

'It has been a long journey from Paris,' said Van der Voors in a genial manner.

The manager coughed. 'How is Paris?' he asked.

'Occupied . . . with herself, as always,' said the Dutchman, and burst into loud coarse laughter which died when the tall man in black touched his arm.

'Perhaps, Mynheer,' said the manager sourly, 'you would like a drink at the bar?'

'I would be delighted.'

'Your bags will be taken up.'

The three men walked across the lobby and into the bar, where the notes of a piano faded away. Sullivan had just finished singing 'The Touch of Your Lips'. He acknowledged the applause, took a gulp of white wine, and with one hand indicated that the bottle was now empty.

'Now, ladies and gentlemen,' he began into the microphone, '"These Foolish Things".' Somebody cheered and there was more applause. Sullivan pouted:

'A cigarette that bears a lipstick's traces . . .
An airline ticket to romantic places . . .'

'That's Brazil,' said Bobby to his crowded table, 'he adores South America.'

'And still my heart has wings –
These foolish things remind me of you,' sang Sullivan.

'Louis!' shouted Bobby Avery. There was no one to take an order. 'Excuse me,' he said to those at his table and began to make his way to the bar.

'A tinkling piano in the next apartment,' sang Sullivan and started a thirty-second break which reminded the audience that once he had been not only fast but very good. Perspiration appeared on his brow and many of the drinkers rose to their feet and applauded.

'Those stumbling words that told you what my heart meant.'

Sullivan's eyes sought Bobby, lost for a moment in the crowd.

'And still my heart has wings . . .' he sang, peering through rising cigarette smoke. In the distance, Bobby Avery stepped under a light set in the roof of the bar. 'He looks so elegant in evening dress,' thought Sullivan. 'Even if he is a little plump, he is still young, and there is real feeling between us.' He deliberately slowed the tempo.

'These foolish things remind me of you.'

Bobby found himself beside a large man in a white suit seated on a bar stool next to a tall blond companion in black.

'You came, you saw, you conquered me . . .' came the lyrics with added energy. Jeers started from the French, who understood Sullivan's jibe at the German occupation. He raised his eyebrows and leaned quickly into the microphone.

'Well, we love them, don't we?' Someone drunkenly shouted '*Sieg Heil!*' and there was much laughter from the audience.

'And when you did that to me,
I somehow knew that it had to be.'

The Dutchman at the bar, drinking brandy, began wiping his brow with a damp silk handkerchief and glanced at Bobby Avery.

'Five double whiskies, Louis,' said the young American, 'and wine for the penis.' Louis laughed; the Dutchman moistened his lips. Bobby turned to him. 'That's Irish for piano player,' he explained affectedly.

'You are not English, I take it?' said Van der Voors, and his face widened into a smile.

'Neither are you,' said Bobby. The Dutchman's large, watery-blue eyes surveyed the young American's face, which he found instantly appealing. He liked men plump.

'Do you live here?' he asked.

'Passing through,' said Bobby.

'For how long will you stay?'

Bobby pursed his lips, staring at the Dutchman. 'My God!' he said with a grin. 'You don't play around!' He shivered; despite the man's size there was something in Van der Voors's voice and manner which he found attractive.

'What is your name?' asked the Dutchman.

'Well, if you're interested, I'm sure you'll find that out for yourself,' said Bobby. 'What's yours?'

'I only make a fair exchange.' The Dutchman's eyes offered Bobby excitement, his moist lips gave promises.

'That's good business.' The young American hesitated.

'And still the ghost of you clings,' sang Sullivan from beyond many tables across the smoke-filled bar.

'These foolish things remind me of you.'

Bobby threw back his head and looked at Van der Voors through half-closed eyes. 'You know,' he said coquettishly, 'I think you could be a real bitch.'

The words were drowned by such enthusiastic applause that Sullivan had to raise his voice. 'I'd just like to remind everybody that here, in what is still called the American Bar . . .' there was laughter from the audience, 'this is Hugh Sullivan playing to you under the influence . . .' more laughter came from the audience, 'of the magic of Monte Carlo!'

The applause continued. Jan Van der Voors's laugh began in his large belly and travelled upwards, loud and coarse. 'Very good,' he said. His blond unsmiling companion, drinking only water, said nothing.

Sullivan watched Bobby Avery return with a tray of drinks and then pour cold white wine. He accepted a glass and took a gulp before starting 'Bei Mir Bist Du Schön'. At that moment Jürgen Pabst and Christopher Quinn stepped into the entrance of the bar. The Dutchman's companion indicated that they should leave and began moving to the doors. Van der Voors finished his brandy, prised himself from the bar stool and followed quickly.

A single light illuminated the lounge of Jan Van der Voors's rooms on the fourth floor of the Hotel de Paris. Gestapo Major Pabst sat beside a low table. Behind him stood another German. They were listening to Christopher Quinn, who was leaning earnestly towards the massive figure of the Dutchman slumped in an armchair holding a glass of brandy.

'The instructions are quite clear,' said Quinn. 'I repeat, if you have brought the correct samples they will be taken to Switzerland and the sum total of what we have in our possession will be calculated.'

'I can tell you their value now,' said the Dutchman. 'You know that I . . .'

'There is a war in progress.' The Irishman hesitated. 'We must understand – values have changed.'

Van der Voors stared at Christopher Quinn. 'We?' he said. 'The diamonds are mine.' He paused, seeking polite words. 'You are only the broker.'

The Irishman sat back out of the light. His voice came from the gloom. 'You acquired the diamonds, Mynheer, as we shall now acquire them.' There was silence in the room.

Van der Voors nodded his head and glanced at Pabst. 'We,' he stated flatly. Quinn nodded. 'For what price?' asked the Dutchman.

'A business price,' Quinn replied.

The Dutchman licked lips now dry. 'So I do not sell to the Swiss?'

'No, Mynheer,' said Quinn, 'you do not.'

'How much do I lose with this, ah, business price?'

No answer came immediately, then Major Pabst leaned into the light, which threw strong shadows on his angular features. 'You will keep – your life,' he said softly. 'The diamonds belong to Germany.'

'They are mine,' the Dutchman grunted. 'I bought them.'

'From Jews, for nothing.' Pabst's eyes glittered with hate. 'They did not all get away, as you know.'

Van der Voors shook his head. 'I paid . . . I have the papers to prove it. I swear . . .' the man began to sweat. 'Everything is correct.' He looked wildly at Quinn. 'Legal. You said that in a war, values change. I just did . . .' he paused, trapped, 'good business.'

Again there was silence in the room. Pabst watched as the Dutchman gulped his brandy. 'I am pleased "we" have the papers,' he said, 'as we have the Jews – and will have the diamonds.'

Van der Voors looked at Quinn with tears in his eyes. 'Why did you bring me here?'

'To endorse the legality of the transaction,' replied the Irishman. 'What is yours will become . . .'

'Ours,' Pabst broke in. 'You have all the papers of sale?'

'Yes,' said the Dutchman.

'And they are properly signed?'

'All the papers are signed – to me.'

'You see,' said Pabst, 'the world suspects us of being criminals, but we adhere always to the letter of the law.' He snapped his fingers. 'Rudi, another brandy for Mynheer Van der Voors.' The German poured from a bottle of Courvoisier. The Dutchman sipped, Quinn coughed.

'The papers can be reassigned?'

Van der Voors nodded, wiping his moist brow. Pabst seemed to relax.

'When?' asked the Dutchman.

Pabst waved a hand. 'Soon,' he answered, 'tomorrow – the next day. On the Riviera, time stands still. You must enjoy yourself while you are here . . .'

'I will try,' said the Dutchman, quietly.

'Do you like music?'

Van der Voors nodded. 'Classical,' he replied.

'Then tomorrow, you will be my guest at the Palace.' Pabst was expansive. 'Everyone will be there.' He paused, and grinned cruelly. 'Diamonds everywhere.'

Chapter 8

At 7.30 in the evening of a soft summer night, a large black Rolls Royce pulled away quietly from the entrance of the Hotel de Paris and began driving down the Avenue Monte Carlo towards the harbour.

'You should use this more often,' said Harry as he leaned back in the rear, appreciating the beige leather interior. He took out a cigarette and pressed a lighter set into the polished walnut console.

'That would be ostentatious,' murmured Evelyn.

Harry grinned. 'If you knew what it meant.'

'Oh Harry,' said Evelyn tartly, 'that really is too much.'

'Nearly,' he smiled, and reached forward, opened the cocktail cabinet, set two crystal glasses into the insets of the fold-down walnut tray, then poured himself whisky from a decanter and began to open a bottle of vintage Taittinger which was sitting in a bucket of ice.

Evelyn was wearing a figure-hugging long white jersey evening dress, designed by Gres from the spring collection in Paris, and despite the warmth of the evening she had brought a three-quarter-length white mink jacket. Red hair tumbled onto her shoulders and her golden skin set off a Van Cleef necklace of spectacular emeralds – the largest reaching down to her cleavage – which emphasized the green of her eyes in a way calculated to induce rapture from men and jealousy in women.

The black chauffeur began to negotiate the sharp turn near the harbour.

'You know where we're going, Johnson?' shouted Harry through the glass partition.

'Don't be ridiculous,' said Evelyn.

'Not until we get there sir,' answered Johnson loudly in a throaty voice, and cackled to himself. It was a familiar exchange. The two men liked each other. Johnson was the only other real man in Evelyn's life. He was inherited from Thomas Curtis along with the car, which was a 1932 limousine, specially built by Hooper's, as its owner always proudly stated, 'right down to the luggage in the trunk'.

Harry eased out the Taittinger cork, pouring cold froth. Evelyn took the champagne, and they clinked glasses.

The 'dim-out' in Monte Carlo, unlike the total black-out in France, was never very successful. As lights were turned on in the Principality, reflections glittered in the harbour water, which was almost the same colour as the magenta sky of dusk. Great flocks of birds were wheeling and turning quickly over the house tops, chattering excitedly in the summer twilight. The Rolls Royce slowly accelerated up the well policed road which gave access to the old town and the Palace precincts built on the great Rock of Monaco.

The Palace looked like something out of a fairy tale, the inspiration of a child's toy fortress. Johnson edged the car between others already parked in the outer courtyard. He stopped in front of the entrance to the Palace; to either side was a red and white diagonally striped guard box, with guards in traditional Monégasque uniforms.

The crowds moving towards the arched entrance way were dazzling, as if arriving for a twentieth-century Cinderella's ball. Dinner jackets, or white jackets and black ties amongst the men, and myriad colours from the ladies in evening dresses, flared, frilled, diaphanous, severe, laced or beribboned. Eyes darted to pearls, jewelled necklaces, rings, tiaras. The war seemed a long way away.

Tickets were presented and checked in the light of torches which flanked the entrance and the audience went through to the inner courtyard, where ushers indicated their seats. Before them, soft lights lit a long open corridor with pillared arches and potted palms. At its centre were two wide staircases of white marble that curved to the cobbled ground in the shape of a heart. Here, a large podium had been erected with chairs and music stands set out for the orchestra. Above were the first evening stars in a clear sky where the flocks of small birds still spiralled and dived as if anticipating the music.

'Oh Harry, it's breathtaking,' whispered Evelyn.

'Yes, it is,' he agreed quietly. It was a magnificent setting for dramatic music.

64

Harry looked at the white marble staircases that curved so elegantly up to the open corridor where the ceilings were painted with frescoes depicting the labours of Hercules.

'It reminds me of home,' he murmured.

'Where?' asked Evelyn.

'A town called Baku, in southern Russia.'

'Oh.' She paused. 'But I thought you were from Armenia?'

'I would be, if it still existed.'

'What do you mean?'

'Find it on the map,' replied Harry softly. He appeared to be looking at the programme in his hands, but in fact he was far away in his childhood. For many years it had not happened to him, but the Armenian name Khachaturian, listed as composer, had stirred his memory.

At that moment, the orchestra trooped in. Evelyn removed her white gloves, to reveal sparkling gems on her fingers. 'Harry!' she nudged him. 'Clap!' The conductor made his entrance. More applause began and faded. The Prince and Princess appeared and everyone stood up. The royal anthem was played and everyone sat down again to a moment of absolute silence. Evelyn glanced at Harry and, as never before in their relationship, saw something in him of which she was afraid. His eyes appeared to be on fire and yet he looked like a man sculpted in stone.

The conductor tapped his baton and for the first time outside of Russia – since Khachaturian's First Symphony had been published in Moscow and Leningrad only the previous year – the music began: a hymn to beauty and a paean for the joy of life. The symphony depicted all that was once Armenia – the happiness of her people, the pleasure of the seasons, the relationship that the young and idealistic have with the mature wisdom of their elders. There was love, heroism and tragedy. Tumbling rhythms, soaring themes, soft melodies, exuberant dances and a falling cadence ending in deep lament. The tunes were old ones, the notes brilliantly orchestrated, reflecting an ancient culture of strong traditions.

As the last bar was played, the conductor dropped his arms and turned to face a silent audience. For seconds no one moved. Suddenly, there was an explosion of applause. Many of the audience found themselves standing. If there had been concealed tears during the music, now there was unashamed weeping from people who had forgotten what it was to cry. But now it was for joy. A surging passion had flooded over them and they were giving their appreciation to the music – while it played they had lived.

For those moments, the elegant man in evening dress who sat beside Evelyn became an eleven-year-old boy who lay huddled in the back of a speeding car on a wet night, trembling for fear of the future. She could not sense the agony of remembrance in Harry, nor feel the pain of unbidden recollection as, with horrifying clarity, images, faces, people, places from another world arose in the memory of a boy christened Hovahannes, who had sailed through the pillars of Hercules to become Harry Pilikian in the city of New York, amidst the strange sounds and unfamiliar customs of his adopted American culture.

'Harry!' insisted Evelyn. 'Everyone's applauding, clap!' She saw Harry's confusion. 'You're crying. What is it?' she asked and sat down beside him.

Harry smiled the open smile of a child, looked at her and laughed. 'The old, pure music,' he said.

Applause began to die, as the orchestra filed out and the audience followed slowly.

Outside, the two of them crossed to the car and Evelyn stepped in, but Harry hesitated. For a moment time seemed to stand still. It was as if he had felt a familiar hand touch his shoulder; he heard his name whispered, twice, in warning – 'Hovahannes,' and again, 'Hovahannes.' A chill went up his spine. It was his father's voice. He turned slowly. No one was there. Harry's blood ran cold. He touched his father's gift, the crucifix around his neck, and shivered. Thrusting his hands deep into his pockets, he threw back his head, gazing far into the night sky, but saw only stars.

'Herr Pilikian.' Harry lowered his head. Standing before him was Jürgen Pabst, with three very large men in evening dress. The German's face was still bruised, but his eyes were as bright as a barracuda's.

'Did you enjoy the music?'

'Yes,' said Harry.

'So did I,' agreed Pabst.

'Harry!' shouted Evelyn from inside the car.

'I am sorry that we shall not be friends,' said the German with the flicker of a smile.

'Are you?' asked Harry pointedly. 'Really?'

'No,' answered the Gestapo officer quietly.

'Then you are honest,' said Harry.

'As you are irritating, Mr Pilikian.' He paused. 'I do not mean to give you a second chance.'

'There are no second chances in life, Pabst,' said Harry. 'This is not the rehearsal – it's the performance. I try to make the most of it all the first time around.'

'You were lucky, Pilikian.' As Pabst stepped closer, Harry tensed. The German smiled. 'And you are the type which we – National Socialism – have developed means of dealing with most effectively.'

'Are you talking about people?'

'Certain people.'

'No minorities in the Third Reich,' said Harry. 'Is that it?'

'If we are to last a thousand years, how can there be?' Pabst's eyes were cruel.

'I'm glad you said "if",' said Harry. 'It gives us all hope.'

'Harry, come on.' came Evelyn's voice. 'We've got supper guests at home!' He grinned and stepped back, reaching for the door handle. One of the large men began to move, but was stilled instantly by a quick glance from the Gestapo officer as Harry opened the door.

'I'm surprised you liked the music,' he said. 'The composer was Armenian.'

'As you are, Herr Pilikian.' Harry nodded silently. 'We have nothing against Armenians,' Pabst continued. 'Not yet.' He grasped the door handle as Harry stepped into the car. 'Music makes it easy to forget the war don't you think?'

'No,' said Harry. Pabst grinned and slammed the door. Immediately, the black Rolls Royce pulled away and Harry's body sank into the leather darkness of the interior.

'It only makes me remember,' he whispered.

'What?' asked Evelyn. But he was no longer in the present. He could hear old, pure music from long ago . . .

Harry Pilikian stared into the face of his friend Louis, the barman, and pushed forward his empty glass.

Evelyn had dropped him outside the Hotel de Paris then driven off to preside over the supper party at her villa, infuriated that Harry wouldn't come with her. He had made his way directly to the American Bar, the sympathetic ear of Louis, and whisky. Evocations stimulated by Khachaturian's music had hit hard in Harry's memory.

'So much passion,' he whispered to Louis as if revealing a secret, and accepted another drink before reaching for the telephone on the bar. An operator gave him a line, he dialled and let it ring for several seconds.

'Hello, Danielle?'

'Yes, sir.'

'Give me Miss Martineye.'

'She's still at the supper table, sir.'

'Well then get her away!' Danielle hesitated. 'Get her!'

'Yes, sir.' The phone was put down. Harry could hear laughter and someone walking to the telephone.

'Hello?'

'Who's that?' asked Harry.

'I do not think we have met,' said the voice.

'You're damn right. Who are you?'

'Colonel Navara,' said the voice. 'You must be Harry?'

'And who the hell is Colonel Navara?' Louis, wiping glasses, winked. Harry ignored him.

'You may call me Luciano.'

'Get me Evelyn,' said Harry.

'She is busy,' said the Italian. 'Can I take a message?'

'Just get her!'

'You are not very polite, Mr Pilikian.'

'I can get worse,' said Harry.

'In which case,' said Luciano, 'I would feel it necessary to meet you.'

'What's he saying?' said a voice in the background. A hand went over the receiver in Evelyn's villa. Silence, then a sweet voice. 'What is it, Harry?'

'Who's that creep?'

'Don't talk about my guests like that,' said Evelyn sharply. There was laughter from the villa. 'Where are you?' she asked.

'Berlin,' said Harry.

'And are you enjoying yourself?'

'I always do.'

'Then so will I,' said Evelyn and replaced the receiver.

Harry slammed down the phone and swore, spinning round on his stool. The number of different nationalities he could see crowded at the small tables astonished him. Monte Carlo was becoming a sanctuary for all those in Europe on the run, or at any rate those who had money, contacts and persuasive tongues. Harry slid from his stool.

'Where are you going?' asked Louis.

'Across the road,' replied Harry.

'Give me two minutes and I'll join you. I'm not supposed to be here this evening.'

'Sure,' said Harry. 'I'll wait at the door.'

When Louis had changed and arrived beside Harry, wearing his dinner jacket, the two men stood for a moment, staring out into the bustling square, appreciating the lights in a world at war.

'Excuse me,' said a voice behind them. The men parted. A woman wearing a long grey coat with a pale grey fur collar and silk scarf over her head, its ends thrown over her shoulders, passed between them. She started quickly down the steps, but caught her heel in the long dress beneath her coat and stumbled. Harry lunged forward and gripped her arm. The woman turned and looked up at him. The scarf had fallen over her face so that Harry could only see her eyes. They smiled at him as her voice spoke huskily.

'Thank you,' she said. Harry's heart began to beat faster – he felt like an adolescent.

A large man wearing a dark hat and coat, babbling in what sounded like Hungarian, came down the steps behind them. He tapped his black cane on the marble.

'*Merci, Monsieur,*' he said curtly. Harry released the woman. The Hungarian took her other arm and looked at the Casino clock across the square.

'With luck we will be late!' he said, and began to lead her down into the square.

'Is Françoise not singing tonight?' Louis shouted at the Hungarian. The large doleful face beneath the black hat turned quickly back. 'My Liebchen,' he indicated the woman, 'is standing in for that French animal who has never been able to sing!'

'Monsieur,' said Louis, acting shocked, 'that is not a nice thing to say.'

'But it is true!' retorted the Hungarian, and the two figures were swallowed up by the crowds milling outside the Casino entrance.

'Who is she?' Harry asked Louis curiously.

'Difficult to forget, my friend,' he replied, then laughed at Harry's confused expression. He put an arm over his friend's shoulders.

'Come, let us find out.'

Low lamps, red plush and gold ornament, the interior of the Cabaret focused upon a small stage surrounded on three sides by the audience, which was able to wine and dine while watching performances, which took place at 9 and again at 1 o'clock. Between shows, they danced.

Harry Pilikian and Louis were shown to a table moments after the second show had begun. They were offered champagne but asked for a bottle of whisky, and as neither had eaten, they ordered from the menu. The two men lit cigarettes and watched the chorus prepare the ground for the acts to follow.

'They have beautiful legs,' said Harry.

'I know most of them,' said Louis.

'You're a lucky man.'

'But my friend, they are all English or American,' Louis smiled. 'Across the Channel the British are fighting to survive, and here we are ordering drinks and looking at the legs of pretty girls, so you too are a lucky man, M'sieur Harry.'

'That's because I'm careful,' said Harry. The two men chinked glasses.

The girls made a full circle, arm over arm, high-kicking until they had swung around, when they began to exit, one by one, each waving to the enthusiastic audience. Then the lights were switched off and music began an introduction. The audience became hushed.

Harry reached for the whisky. His eyes were trying to focus on a figure moving quickly towards a microphone at the centre of the stage. An announcer was saying something in the background and a drumroll started. Soft lights began to play around the microphone, where Harry could just see a statuesque figure. The announcer revealed that there was a surprise for the audience. Harry glanced at Louis, who put a finger to his lips. It was dark a moment longer, as violins soared and the drums crescendoed, then a spotlight was turned on, and there was the woman Harry had held for a moment on the steps.

'You see, my friend,' whispered Louis.

She was tall, wearing a long golden dress, with bare shoulders. Her blond hair was swept back to accentuate her face, which, sculpted by the light, was proud and finely shaped. Her pale eyes glittered as she surveyed the audience. Music was already introducing a song, and as her lips framed the first words of the lyrics, Harry Pilikian's heart stopped.

The song finished and the last note died away. Harry, along with others at the Cabaret, leapt to his feet, carried away, furiously clapping. The lyrics of the song belonged to someone else, but the way she had conveyed them to her audience was, in Harry's experience, unique. He should have listened to the words, but remembered only her voice. The applause for the woman would not stop.

'Who is she?' he shouted to Louis, who was now eating.

'You don't know her?' he replied, chewing a mouthful of steak. Harry glared. Someone was shouting 'Bravo!' The woman at the microphone said nothing, but her shining eyes smiled into the darkness beyond the spotlight.

'She is called Vondrakova,' said Louis, and reached for the whisky bottle, pouring for them both. The woman on stage allowed mystery into her smile and began a second song slowly.

'Vondrakova,' said Harry.

Chapter 9

Christopher Quinn looked at himself in the bathroom mirror. Perhaps his face had become arrogant, but those who took the trouble to see beyond the self-assured eyes discovered that there were depths to the man. He finished tying the knot on his black bow tie, which complemented the well-cut dinner jacket from Huntsman in Savile Row. Not displeased with the reflection, he smiled to reveal even, strong, white teeth, then prepared to rejoin his friends below.

They had all enjoyed the concert at the Palace and, over supper in the

Salle Empire, whilst the ladies powdered or whatever they did, he had briefly discussed further details of the coming diamond transaction with de Salis. An attractive American woman, Francie Pinkerman, was showing more than passing interest in him and he had begun toying with the possibility of an affair.

In the small lounge of his rooms, the telephone rang. He turned off the bathroom light and crossed the thick carpet to answer. It was de Salis.

'I'm on my way,' said Quinn.

'Is Maggie with you?' asked the Swiss banker.

'Of course not.'

'Well I can't get her on the line. Bring her down, will you? She's in 417. We'll be in the bar.'

'Sure,' said Quinn and put down the phone.

Maggie Lawrence had become tipsy at supper and had spilt lemon sorbet on her dress. She had retired to her room to repair and change, since they had decided to go to the Casino. She wore twin diamonds in a pretty setting hanging from a gold chain around her neck, and as she slipped out of blue crêpe-de-chine she decided that a scarlet dress would look so much better at the tables.

She put it on carefully, then examined her reflection in the long mirror as she stepped back into her high-heeled shoes.

'Well, Miss O'Hara,' she said, and giggled to herself at the connotations of the words, 'you are looking pretty as a picture!' And she was.

Her blond hair was too blond to be real, but men loved it, so she kept it that way. She touched it lightly then sensuously ran both her hands down over her body and hips. The dress clung tightly, so she had discarded her underwear. It gave her a sense of excitement to know that she would be with all those men in stuffy suits with only a millimetre of silk between her and them.

There was a knock at the door.

'Who is it?' she asked, and shook her head so that her hair cascaded down her back then fell again onto her shoulders.

'Quinn!' came a voice.

'Come in!'

Christopher Quinn entered the room. 'Well, well,' he said. 'Now that is something!'

'I'm like Cinderella,' said Maggie. 'It all turns to rags at midnight.'

'It looks pretty good to me,' said Quinn.

'You look pretty nice yourself,' said Maggie eyeing him up and down.

'Better be careful,' he said. 'You're Guy's girl.' Maggie crossed to within a pace of him and put both hands on his shoulders. She smelled of fresh flowers and her eyes were alight with champagne and the excitement of the evening.

71

'It was a lovely supper,' she said.

Quinn watched her lips moving. 'I'm glad you enjoyed it,' he replied. They stared at each other.

Outside in the Casino square, cars were moving, people were laughing and the night was becoming lively.

'I think we'd better go down,' said Quinn. 'They're waiting for us.'

'You really want to?' Quinn had also been drinking, and he breathed deeply, but said nothing. 'Guy is . . .' Maggie paused, 'so Swiss.'

Quinn smiled, sliding an arm around her waist then dropping it slowly down to the back of her thighs. He felt the uninterrupted smoothness of her dress and smiled at the discovery that she was naked underneath.

'Well now, Miss Lawrence,' he said quietly, 'that's a dangerous game.'

Maggie's lips parted. 'What exactly do you do, Mr Quinn?' she asked.

'I look for opportunities. And when they arise, if they are attractive, I seize them. Everything has a price.'

Maggie's tongue touched her glistening teeth. She bent slightly at the knees, reaching out for her small evening bag on the low table. 'That's my line of work too,' she said, 'exactly.'

She stood up slowly and took Christopher Quinn's arm.

'Shall we?'

At a table for four beneath the dividing pillar of the crowded hotel bar, Guy de Salis checked his wristwatch.

'Where are they?' he asked Francie.

'Oh don't be stuffy, Guy, you'll give the Swiss a bad reputation.' She began to laugh. 'They'll be down. Maggie wants to be spectacular tonight.'

'She's drunk too much champagne.'

'So have we all,' said Francie. 'This town is filling up. It's becoming quite a party. And I believe you are jealous.'

De Salis only grunted at the suggestion. 'There are many Maggies,' he said.

'That's not a nice thing for a gentleman to say about a lady.'

De Salis smiled sourly. 'I'm not talking about a lady.'

On the fourth floor, Christopher Quinn and Maggie Lawrence had been waiting for the lift to arrive. Now the doors were open in front of them. Maggie stepped in and Quinn followed. She turned to face him and smiled . . .

During the day and until a reasonable hour of the evening, the lift was manned, and a French voice would politely enquire: 'Which floor?' After midnight it was hoped that the majority of guests could remember for themselves.

The interior of the lift was large, its walls lined in red damask, with velvet seats on three sides. Christopher Quinn closed the doors and pressed the down button, and the lift began to move. Then it stopped.

He pressed the button twice more, the lift lurched a little, then the circuit broke and it jammed.

'Are we stuck?' asked Maggie.

'We seem to be,' said Quinn and tried again.

Maggie put her hands together and looked at the roof, where she saw a small chandelier.

'Has this ever happened to you before?' she asked.

'Never.' Quinn pressed the emergency button. Bells should have rung, but there was no sound.

'How long are we going to be stuck here?' she asked.

'Until help comes.' He pressed the button, and again there was nothing.

'Do we need help?' Maggie smiled.

'I'll try once more,' said Quinn.

Maggie put her bag on the seat and slid her hands down the side of her dress. 'We could be here all night,' she said.

'Not *all* night,' said Quinn.

'Try the other buttons,' she suggested. Quinn pressed each of the floor buttons one by one, but nothing happened.

'You missed one,' she said.

'Which?'

'Stop.' Quinn pressed it and smiled. He put out his hand. Maggie reached over and touched his fingers, then pulled him easily towards her. Quinn's knees touched hers and there was a moment of shock as if electricity had passed between them. Maggie's eyes became hungry. She slipped her hands behind his neck and slowly pulled him towards her lips. The kiss was a recognition between two people already familiar with each other's desires.

The passion of their lust leapt between them like a flame which does not merely kindle, but roars into a fire. There were no niceties or caressing. Quinn's hands cupped Maggie's breasts and squeezed them. She gasped and drew away, her head arched as his lips sought her neck and throat. Her hands, already beneath his jacket and pressing against his thighs, now slipped between his legs and moved towards his groin. Immediately her head came forward again, her blond hair falling around their faces; finding his lips, she thrust her tongue into his mouth. His hands charted the contours of her body and reached far down over her legs, almost to her knees. Maggie had begun to unbutton the front of his trousers. She tore her mouth from his and said between breaths:

'Pull it up!'

'It'll crease,' he said hoarsely.

Her hands reached into his shorts and found the stiff erection. She

73

seized it gently. Immediately Quinn began to pull either side of the scarlet silk dress until his hands were full of material. At the level of her hips it suddenly slipped up to her waist and she pressed herself away from the wall towards him. He glimpsed her long, brown, beautiful naked legs, feet in high-heeled shoes pressed firmly to the floor. Maggie moaned.

'Put it in!' she whispered.

'We mustn't . . .' began Quinn in her ear.

'I've been wet since I touched you at supper,' she murmured and her mouth brushed his lips. Quinn kissed her savagely and thrust his pelvis against yielding flesh. He bent his knees and his erection found the opening between her thighs. Moaning with anticipation, Maggie guided the shaft into her body. Even though impassioned, Quinn controlled his movement and slid into her slowly, then away, as if he would deny her what she so much wanted. She whimpered and pulled him to her. Now he thrust deeply. She gasped then let out a small cry as her arms locked around his body, and she pushed her crotch against his.

'Oh God!' she said. Quinn withdrew slightly then, appreciating Maggie's sensuous movements, he gasped and they began to fuck.

'Oui, Madame! We are coming, M'sieur, we are coming!' shouted Gastaut, who turned to the night porter.

'They are shouting, Antoine.'

'But who *are* they?'

'Who knows,' said Gastaut, and shrugged. The two men were on the fourth floor, outside the lift shaft.

'I have the box open now, Madame! Can you hear me?' He listened for a moment while looking into the emergency box which he had opened with a key. He found the circuit breaker and pulled it.

'It is done, Madame!'

'And M'sieur,' said Antoine. He pressed a button for the lift and a light went on. The floor indicator began to move, then stopped again. The two men looked at each other, eyebrows raised, then shrugged.

'M'sieur, Madame!' Gastaut shouted. 'Perhaps you would press a button, I am sure it will work now.'

In the lift, Christoper Quinn's finger was on the 'stop' button. He was lying against a red damask wall, breathing hard. With his other hand he was attempting to button his trousers. Maggie was wiping herself between the legs with his silk handkerchief, her chest still heaving. She pulled down her dress and stood shakily to her feet. She clasped Quinn, pushing the handkerchief back into his top pocket, and kissed him tenderly. The Irishman pressed the button for 'four' and the lift began to move slowly up.

'*Voilà*,' said Gastaut. '*Ils arrivent!*' The lift stopped and the doors opened. The two men stood still and gaped. Christopher Quinn smiled and thrust two hundred francs at Gastaut, then, with Maggie behind him, stepped out into the corridor. Apart from the fact that the Irishman had lipstick all over his face and shirt, it looked as if the two people had been in a fight.

'Not a word!' said Quinn.

'Mais oui, Monsieur,' said Gastaut. *'Rien.'*

Chapter 10

In the American Bar, Ben Harrison sat on a stool and listened appreciatively to Hugh Sullivan at the piano. Ben was staring into the distance where there was no distance at all, just smoke and crowded tables.

'The sun went down just like a dying ember . . .'

The audience was hushed by something in Sullivan's voice that 'sold' the song.

For a moment, the bar area seemed to clear. Hesitantly, a handsome woman made her way from the entrance to a stool in the centre of the bar and perched, turning to look at Sullivan, who had captured the room. Jean-Pierre nodded recognition, took a bottle of Cointreau, poured a measure and added ice. Ben beckoned to him.

'Who is she?' he whispered.

'Monsieur Harrison, she is a resident.'

'Really, in Monte Carlo? I've not seen her here before.'

'No, M'sieur, she does not come to the bar often.'

'What's her name?' Ben asked and sipped his whisky, glancing at the woman. She seemed familiar.

'Madame Parry,' said Jean-Pierre.

'Oh,' said Ben, finished his whisky and took another look at the woman His eyes widened. 'Good God!' he murmured. 'Agatha!'

'That September in the rain . . .' came delicately from Sullivan's lips as fingers found the chords which tugged at every heart in the room.

Feeling the gaze of curious eyes, Agatha turned her head slowly and saw a man staring at her from the end of the bar. She sipped her drink while the song finished to much applause. The middle-aged gentleman smiled and she caught that unmistakable twinkle in his eyes.

'Good Lord!' Agatha whispered. Jean-Pierre was leaning against the back of the bar watching first one, then the other. Ben Harrison stepped from his stool and walked towards Agatha Parry.

'More!' shouted someone in the audience, and the applause grew louder.

'Aggie?' asked Ben Harrison.

'Yes,' she said. 'Is that you?'

Benjamin William Harrison was born in the English county of Kent, where his father had a small farm and hotel outside the village of Sisehurst. The hotel, the Golden Fleece, provided a fair income from its twelve bedrooms, excellent restaurant and popular bar. It was *trade*, but at the same time, as landowner, through weekend hunting, Harrison senior was eventually accepted in county society, a position he was determined to pass on to both his sons.

Young Benjamin William went to a good public school and emerged with minor qualifications but major expectations. At least he mastered that particular English attitude and accent that commands, if not respect, then certainly attention. He had shown himself to be exceptional only in charm, so it was natural to want to capitalize on it. He had made many friends who enjoyed his wit and dry humour.

He failed to get into Oxford, and drifted around London in its Edwardian heyday, where Harrison's natural advantages were honed and polished in the whirl of an era later to be notorious for its frivolity and self-indulgence.

After several months dallying in town at the Café Royal and other popular haunts, he eventually found a position. A school chum interested him in the attractions of the sale rooms of London. Joining a Bond Street auction house, Harrison discovered what would become his true vocation, beautiful objects, and he spent eighteen months learning very quickly. It was a fascinating experience, but being so close to, and yet so far from, so much money he found that he was entertaining disturbing thoughts. The temptation to elevate himself into this world became almost uncontrollable.

It is difficult for a man of moderate means and soaring ambitions to be near the rich for any length of time without it becoming one of his life's goals to join them. The following year he decided to remove himself from temptation. Through a connection of his mother's brother, a position was offered to him which carried too much kudos to refuse. An uncle from the best side of the family was a regular army colonel with a substantial private purse. Benjamin William Harrison was put up for Sandhurst, where he did surprisingly well. As a successful graduate he joined a smart regiment and became an officer – an exceptional privilege for one so socially unqualified.

The life suited him, as did the uniform, which – cut to perfection and worn with a swagger on his well-proportioned body – drew many an appreciative eye from the ladies, whose admiration of the military man was at its height. He prospered. Then his father died and left him with money which he found no difficulty in spending. His younger brother took over the family businesses, which was convenient for the older son as his regiment was posted abroad. Ben Harrison began to travel widely in his country's far-flung Empire, and became a collector of objets d'art from India, the Far East and China. By July 1914, he was a major.

That life ended in late August when the world, and his regiment, went to war. Harrison's battle experiences as liaison officer to American divisions after April 1917 provided him with proof of his courage. He became a signals expert in what was then the fairly new technique of radio communication, saw a good deal of action and was twice decorated. After the November Armistice, the new year of 1919 found him no longer in the army and drinking far too heavily, recuperating from the Great War in his small, lonely flat. His sole occupation was commiserating with surviving friends on the declining quality of life and the miserable prospects for the future.

He met the girl who was to become his wife at a charity ball in the Ritz. Margaret was twenty and suffering, like many young girls, from the lack of eligible men in postwar England. They did not fall in love at first sight, but affection grew between them and became a bond greater than friendship. They were married in a fashionable church, and honeymooned in Italy with what little money Ben had remaining.

Margaret had an adequate allowance, but in the changing world of the Twenties it was not enough to maintain a prewar lifestyle. By 1926, life was tough. Ben had become a collector's consultant, with a small office in Bond Street, but business was not exactly booming, so Margaret went away one weekend to enquire discreetly whether some relations could help them financially. It turned out that their straits were equally dire, although in the country it was possible to enjoy a semblance of prewar life, so at least the trip provided a break from the general atmosphere of gloom in the capital.

She arrived back in London, went directly to the flat and opened the door on another world. There were flowers everywhere, a magnum of vintage champagne on ice, caviare on the table, fresh strawberries in a silver bowl, and Ben sitting in a corner of the drawing room with a smile of self-satisfaction on his face and a cigar in his mouth. He took out his pocket watch, uncrossed his legs and said: 'Thank God you took a taxi. I thought you'd be late for lunch.'

'What's happened?' asked Margaret in a hushed voice.

'Fortune has smiled upon us,' said Ben.

Over lunch at Pruniers in St James's, Ben explained that he had sold the last of his objets d'art to a collector who had been sufficiently impressed with his expertise to employ him on a retainer basis. Margaret was pleased and Ben's enthusiasm was infectious.

'It is a miracle,' she said, and he agreed. She vaguely wondered, the following week, why her husband had been upset and irritated when she confessed to giving thanks to God in church that Sunday. The truth was that Ben had discovered that if miracles do not come from heaven, then they must be created by man.

For three months, several nights a week, Ben Harrison spent long evenings, sometimes until the early hours of the morning, advising his rich employer. He even spent a long, long weekend away from Margaret, not returning until Wednesday, very agitated, with several cuts on his arm which Margaret noticed when he climbed into bed that night. He remained nervous for a week and then suddenly he came home beaming early one afternoon and was his old self. Small but valuable objects began to appear in the flat. Tokens of gratitude from Ben's employer, he explained, and life began to look rosy.

Margaret spent her days between Knightsbridge and St James's, sometimes having tea with friends who lived off Regent's Park. She returned one evening to cocktails with Ben when he explained that he must leave at once to see the employer she had, curiously, yet to meet. Ben normally involved her in all aspects of his life, and his elusive answers to her questions sowed the first seeds of suspicion. Society was gossiping as usual, and one subject aired in detail over tea that afternoon had terrified Margaret. She had excused herself with a forced smile and walked round the Park before returning via Bond Street to their flat behind Piccadilly.

'Sorry I can't take you with me, darling, but you know how it is with these fellows,' said Ben.

Margaret sipped her cocktail and looked directly into his eyes. For the first time in their relationship she made him uneasy. 'You went to Halesworth last week,' she stated.

'Well, you know that, darling, why do you ask?'

Margaret replied, enunciating every word: 'The robbery at Whaley's Manor. It's in all the papers. The Greshams are still away on their winter cruise, remember? I told you they were going.'

Ben looked into his wife's eyes before he replied: 'Did you?' He seemed confused. 'The Greshams?'

Margaret pressed her point. 'We've been there together.'

'Have we?'

'Twice. I went riding.'

There was a pause.

'Oh, that's right, and I didn't.' Ben took a gulp of his cocktail.

'You were with that Agatha Parry woman, alone.'

Ben coughed. 'I beg your pardon?'

'She's quite attractive,' said Margaret, her gaze unwavering.

'She's married,' he replied.

Margaret nodded. 'Or were you casing the joint, as the Americans say?'

Ben tried an explosion, but it was very weak.

'That's a hell of a thing to accuse a fella of,' he spluttered. 'Adultery? With Agatha?'

'I didn't say I was accusing you of that.'

'Then what the devil are you saying?'

'I'm stating a fact,' said Margaret. 'You were alone in a house with precious things that are no longer there.'

Outside, the early evening traffic swished by in the cold rain, while the little gas fire in the grate glowed brightly.

'Margaret . . .' began Ben, but couldn't finish. His cigar was held poised in his hand at an unnatural angle.

'You'll drop ash on the carpet,' said his wife.

Ben knocked the end off his cigar into the ashtray she held out, then settled back in his armchair and looked at Margaret, who continued to stare at the ashtray. Eventually, Ben followed her gaze, and realized with horror what she had found so fascinating.

Margaret looked at him coolly. 'If we had been able to afford a maid who could read, instead of the dunce we've grown used to, and if she had the slightest intelligence or even a penchant for detective stories, I think we would now be in a bit of a pickle.'

Seldom had Ben been in a position where there was so little to say. The silver ashtray was clearly engraved with the Gresham crest. But he still had courage. Although his face was grim there was a twinkle in his eye and he seemed to relax.

'Yes, m'dear, I do believe you're right.' He reached for the cocktail shaker and poured for them both.

Margaret's familiar face was only inches from his own as she leaned forward. 'Why didn't you tell me what you were doing?'

'It was too dangerous, my dear.'

'But darling,' she said, 'I can help.'

The marvellous thing about the Harrisons' thefts thereafter, as the papers said several times, nicknaming Ben 'the cautious cat burglar', was that they were never greedy. Selection was Ben's speciality. He took only the best when he gained entrance to the great rooms of empty manors. He had taste and a trained eye, and now Margaret to help. And she was brilliant.

Ben's contacts had given him access to several high-class fences. Through them discreet collectors added to their private acquisitions. After a final coup Ben and Margaret crossed the Channel to Europe. It was their consciences and accumulating fears that prompted their departure. There had been no scandal – society believed that an eminently respectable couple had gone abroad to economize.

They went to Paris first, then travelled up and down the Mediterranean that summer, staying with friends in exotic places. In autumn they found themselves in Switzerland, living in the library suite of the Palace Hotel, in Lausanne. It was on the sixth floor overlooking the Lake of Geneva. Here, to Ben's horror, Margaret's health began to fail. After the best doctors had seen his wife, there was nothing he could do. She had contracted tuberculosis.

He remained at her bedside night and day, sometimes talking, sometimes reading to her. War had steeled Ben for many things in life. It had hardened his heart and cauterized areas of sensitivity in him, but no experience he could recall – even the most painful during his time in the trenches under heavy bombardment or subjected to the constant fear of death – nothing had prepared him for this intense private agony.

By 5 November 1929, Margaret had become so weak that it upset even the hotel doctor, who was always on call. That evening, she seemed suddenly to rally and insisted on sitting up in bed. Ben remembered their plans to be in London and at Westminster, where the royal fireworks celebrating Guy Fawkes night had always signalled Margaret's favourite time of year, even more than Christmas.

Her breathing was laboured but controlled. She asked for champagne – Ben obliged. Caviare – it was ordered. Strawberries – they were brought.

Margaret was distraught that her appearance had suffered during her illness. She had lost weight, so that her soft features had become hard, her eyes large and hollow and her hair lack-lustre. Ben ignored her complaints and assured her that he loved her deeply.

That night there were moments when they were almost like children. Ben had bought some fireworks and let them off, to Margaret's astonishment. Out of the first empty champagne bottle he fired several rockets from the balcony, high into the night sky above Lake Geneva. The first brought a smile to Margaret's face; the second a hugh grin. Ben's enthusiasm and expertise in igniting the largest, which soared from the windows and exploded in a cascade of colours over the little port of Ouchy, below Lausanne, made her laugh without restraint – which was probably the cause of her death.

The doctor was in the bedroom within minutes of Ben's emergency call as Margaret arched her body, trying to suck air in a last desperate effort to live. A minister was quickly summoned.

Margaret Harrison died soon after midnight, locked in her husband's arms. He wept unashamedly. The following morning Ben found himself alone and sedated in the twin-bedded room of their suite. In his memory was the wasted flesh of his dearly beloved and her panic-stricken cries as she fought for life, and lost.

After Margaret's funeral, Ben returned to London and did not leave his flat for a month. People called and friends telephoned, but he remained shut away. Then, towards the end of December 1929, their last Christmas together came into his memory in detail and he felt Margaret's presence as clearly as if she were with him in the room. He decided to take his own life. He closed all the windows in the flat and turned on the gas. Looking at a photograph of them both taken during their summer in the Mediterranean, he poured himself a drink, and one for his wife.

He lifted his glass in a farewell gesture, but somewhere in his mind a voice spoke to him that he recognized as Margaret's, telling him to live. Ben turned off the gas and opened the windows. From then on he had never been really lonely. Wherever he went, he felt she was always with him.

Ben Harrison had travelled far, and had many adventures, escapades and what he described as dicey moments in the course of his career. International thief might sound like a glamorous occupation, but age and frayed nerves had all but put paid to his run of luck. He had never been caught by the authorities, and now on the Riviera he had decided to retire. Although he had been many times to Monte Carlo and in the American Bar of the Hotel de Paris, he had never run into Agatha Parry, who was now gazing into his eyes once again. He smiled as she remembered exactly where they had first met.

'Halesworth!' she said. He nodded, they laughed and left the bar together.

Ben, with Agatha on his arm, ran down the steps of the hotel, into the rain. The sleek English sports car came as a surprise to him.

'Good God, Aggie, it's an MG!'

She smiled. 'Bought it in '37. Everyone thought it was a bit racy, but I like it. It goes like the wind and is a dream to drive.'

'It suits you,' said Ben.

He ducked his head under the black canvas hood, eased his large frame into the passenger seat and stretched his legs beneath the dashboard. Aggie climbed in, turned on the ignition and windscreen wipers, let go the handbrake, engaged gear and they were off, racing down the Avenue Monte Carlo towards the harbour. She changed gear beneath the Rock of Monaco and took the slope at speed. In no time they were in the old town, where she parked the red convertible skilfully between double iron gates. A minute later Ben was sitting on the edge of an arm chair in a pretty drawing room whilst Aggie went to make tea.

'Emma's asleep,' she told Ben, referring to the maid, as they entered the villa, 'but she's out at the back, so we don't have to whisper or tiptoe or anything . . .' Embarrassment had made her pause. 'All this makes me feel quite like a girl again.'

'Mind if I smoke?' asked Ben, sinking back into his chair beside a dying fire.

'Not at all,' came the reply from a distant kitchen.

Ben leant forward and stoked the coals. Immediately flames leapt up; it was all quite like home – an English country house in the heart of Monte Carlo. He lay back, took a cigarette from his case and lit it.

'Quite something,' he murmured.

'What's that?' asked Agatha, coming in with the tea tray.

'You have a lovely house.'

'Thank you.' Agatha put down the tray on a table between them then sat on the sofa opposite. 'Is there enough light?' she asked.

'Quite enough.'

'At this hour, at our age, I do agree,' said Agatha with a wry smile, and poured the tea. 'I love it when it rains at night. Makes me feel cosy.' She sighed and looked up. 'You never did tell me where you live now.'

Ben took the porcelain tea cup, ignored the question and sipped his tea. 'Hot,' he said.

'From what you were saying, it would seem that you spend all your time travelling.'

'I'm a gypsy,' he said with a smile. 'I hope I'm not boring you?'

'When I'm bored, Mr Harrison, I show the culprit – or get myself shown – to the door!' They looked at each other: the sparkle in their eyes was unmistakable.

'I don't know how you recognized me,' said Agatha.

'How could I mistake you?' Ben spread his hands expansively.

'You haven't changed though,' she went on. 'A little more crinkly perhaps, and greyer – but not really changed.'

'Well, neither have you.'

'Of course I have.'

'A little more rounded, perhaps.'

'Exactly.'

'But then that's an improvement – you were always a skinny little thing.'

'Was I?'

'All that riding, I expect.' Ben coughed and inhaled cigarette smoke.

Agatha lay back on the sofa. 'Perhaps you're right. I always resented it if I'd had a fall and was grounded on doctor's orders!'

'I remember,' said Ben.

'Do you really? At the risk of blushing like a virgin, exactly what do you remember?'

'A very attractive young girl who seemed to develop a rather large crush . . .'

'On you?'

'Yes.'

They looked at each other in silence. Outside a rumble of thunder came from far out over the sea. Heavy rain fell from a pitch-black sky.

'You were too young to know what you were doing,' said Ben softly.

'Then why did you kiss me that day when everyone else went hunting?' Agatha's eyes were lit by flickering flames from the fire.

'Because I was afraid I would be tempted to other things if I didn't.'

Agatha's expression became perplexed. 'But you told me then that women, and especially romance, didn't interest you. I remember you making romance sound like a dirty word.'

He smiled. 'You were very persuasive.'

Agatha blushed. 'You must have thought me very forward?'

'You were . . . are . . . very attractive.' Ben hesitated.

Agatha laughed. 'The first time you said that to me was when you met me at the station in London.'

'King's Cross?'

'You remember?'

'Of course.'

'Only because you were scared stiff someone would see us.'

'Why should I have been? You came to see your aunt.'

'I came to see you, and you bloody well know it!' There was mischief in Agatha's voice.

Ben coughed. 'Well, I mean, Margaret could have . . .'

Agatha interrupted. 'I was at school with Margaret. She was my senior and friend long before she knew you. We were always close but that didn't change anything.'

'You were married too.'

'That didn't seem to stop you,' said Agatha, and sipped her tea. Ben inhaled deeply on his cigarette, then burst out laughing. 'Why is it,' he said, 'that people talk all sorts of nonsense and waste so much time covering up when they should know that at our age it will all come out in the end?'

'What do you mean, at our age?' said Agatha indignantly. 'You know, you really have become quite pompous.'

'Well, I mean wisdom,' said Ben.

Agatha pursed her lips. 'Wisdom, as you call it, is only the excuse older people have for not doing what they wish they had done gaily and without conscience a thousand times when they were young!'

The feeling in her voice gave Ben a jolt. 'You have so much passion still, Aggie. And I've lost that.'

'Did you ever have it?'

'Once I did.'

Ben seemed to shrink into himself. Agatha Parry recalled those months of what was still to her a wonderful affair. Now a little of it had been rekindled by a few hours of light conversation.

'Yes,' she said gently, 'you did, once. More tea?'

Ben opened his eyes. 'No. I'd like a brandy.'

Agatha went to the drinks tray and poured a small tot. Ben took it and touched her hand. 'You look tired,' she said softly.

'I am, Aggie. But it's not the night or the hour, it's simply a sense of emptiness, days passing without purpose.'

'You sound like an adolescent,' she said, and knelt beside him.

'No Aggie, then I was . . .' he found the word, 'expectant. Living was glorious with possibilities, so many things to see, to do. Life was an adventure. Now I'm like a buffalo with a round of water holes to visit, only I don't drink water except with whisky. I feel nothing and am close to no one . . .' His voice trailed off. A tear appeared in his eye. 'There, you see, I've only self-pity left . . .'

Agatha touched his arm with delicate fingers. 'You were not the first man I ever slept with,' she said quietly, 'but you took advantage of me.' She was recalling Ben's gentleness.

'Perhaps it was the reverse,' said Ben. 'Margaret and I were not getting along in that way.'

'She told me.'

'She did?' Ben paused. He was always astonished at women's revelations to each other. 'I loved her in the end you know, very much.' The tear ran down his cheek.

They looked at each other for a long time. Ben eventually leaned forward and kissed her moist lips. They were both surprised; it had been so many years since either of them had given any significance to a kiss. In France it was a mere social formality.

Agatha pulled away and smiled. 'Be careful of the handbrake,' she said. 'It sticks.'

Ben blinked. 'What?'

'I want you to take the car.' She put a finger to her lips. 'Drive carefully. Now you know where I am we can meet often if you stay in Monte Carlo.'

'Agatha.'

'Bring the car back tomorrow afternoon.' She stood up and took his hand, Ben got to his feet and they walked out to the hallway, where she gave him the car keys. She opened the door and they stepped out under the porch, protected from the rain.

'Do you think you can manage?' she asked.

'I think so,' he replied.

'I hope so,' said Agatha, her eyes shining. 'After all, you've already had one spin in her.'

Ben began to kiss Agatha lightly, until her lips found his in a more intimate embrace.

'Goodnight,' whispered Ben.

'Good morning,' said Agatha and stepped back inside the villa to close the door quietly.

Ben found the ignition and the car started. He changed gear hesitantly and his driving abilities slowly came back to him, although finding his way out of the old town through a maze of narrow streets took longer than he expected. But he was so light-hearted that nothing mattered. He began singing to himself, and for the first time in many years he had nothing to say to Margaret. After all, he was alive again, and she was finally buried.

Agatha Parry was brought up in the winter resort of Monte Carlo. As summer approached each year, she, her parents, two brothers, staff and dogs would return to England, and their villa on the Rock of Monaco would be closed until the late autumn when they returned. The family, and others like them, were behind the legend that the English had 'invented' the South of France.

Then the Great War started, and before it finished she had lost her father at Passchendaele and both her brothers in the battle of the Somme. Several days after the armistice, she married an English major she had nursed back to health after shell-shock and a disabling leg wound.

Agatha's mother took the death of her husband and sons hard, lost interest in life and began to fade away. She was buried one autumn afternoon in 1922 on the outskirts of Monaco. Agatha inherited the villa in Monte Carlo, which she and her husband made their winter home. In the spring they returned to his small estate in Suffolk.

The major was already a considerable drinker, but as his physical condition worsened, and with the certain knowledge that he was impotent, he became an alcoholic. By 1929 he and Agatha no longer slept in the same room and she was rumoured to be having an affair with a local landowner – seeking comfort as her life deteriorated. She was well liked locally and a regular churchgoer, so despite the coroner's open verdict, the major's death whilst cleaning his own shotgun was said to be a tragic accident and the vicar sanctioned the body's burial in holy ground.

Agatha sold up and moved permanently to Monte Carlo in an attempt to begin her life anew, but the glamour quickly tarnished and she became restless.

Early in 1933, Adolf Hitler became Chancellor of Germany and Agatha began to make discreet enquiries in London. Her upbringing had provided her with the opportunity to learn several languages. As a child born to privilege, she had been doted upon by many of her father's contemporaries who were now prominent figures behind the scenes in Whitehall. One winter afternoon that same year, she presented herself in a large, sombrely furnished office overlooking St James's Park. In the course of the following three weeks she walked from the Savoy almost every day to be examined by experts.

It seemed to Agatha that she did quite well when in a final test she confidently corrected the suspect syllables one of these experts slipped into his Württemberg dialect, saying that it sounded far more like Schweizerdeutsch than German. Her examiners were duly impressed. She had proved her potential, and once she had learnt the appropriate expertise and modified certain attitudes, it was suggested that she would make a competent agent.

Almost a year after that first interview, Agatha returned to Monte Carlo, followed not long afterwards by various furniture vans whose labels assured the customs that they came from Harrods in London. A man came with them to install the cupboards and cabinets. It took him a whole day to put in the wireless transmitter, and only at twilight did he venture up a ladder he had propped against the flagpole on the roof. The following morning it had been repainted to hide an aerial wire which extended to the very top.

That evening, as the Union Jack was unfurled, the respectful workman set off for London, and Miss Agatha Parry began working for the British government. There were many names for her new occupation, but in short she was now a spy.

Chapter 11

Vondrakova bowed to the storm of applause that filled the Cabaret. The show was over. The principals took their calls as chorus and extras remained in the background, then the musicians played a final rousing number, the stage was cleared and the lights went down.

Harry Pilikian reached for the whisky on the half-lit table. 'She's magnificent,' he said.

'*Magnifique* is a big word,' replied Louis. '*Santé!*' He lifted his glass. The two men chinked rims and drank.

'You want to meet her?' asked Louis.

Harry smiled. 'Wouldn't anyone?' And followed Louis round the auditorium towards a back-stage door.

The guard on the connecting door had given them an intimidating stare until he recognized Louis. Harry followed the barman down a labyrinth of corridors. Show girls were running around half naked, and each one received an appraising glance from both men, several a fond hello from Louis. Eventually they were guided to a door with three stars. It was half open and the room within was full of laughing, chattering people.

To one side there was a table with champagne and glasses. Louis took a bottle and poured. Sipping their drinks the two men began to push towards the focus of attention. Harry heard her first, a wonderful open rolling laugh, full of joy, then the group in front of him parted and the face of the woman who had been singing on stage turned to look at the new arrivals.

The social smile faded as her lips touched delicately. Harry and she gazed at each other in silence as the room around them dissolved and the bantering, boisterous hilarity receded.

Her eyes were as grey as his, his mouth as expectant as hers, their expressions the same combination of wonder and surprise. A shadow seemed to pass over her face then was gone. Harry smiled hesitantly and she responded tentatively. The room became hushed.

'Harry Pilikian,' he said.

'Irelena.' She pronounced her name softly and slowly,

'Vondrakova,' Harry said simply. Somewhere in the room a glass sounded against another and someone took a deep breath. Harry put out his hand in greeting and Vondrakova reached up to take it. Their fingers touched and both felt a static shock. Harry smiled, Vondrakova laughed, then people moved again and conversation began once more.

She was older than Harry had imagined. It showed in her eyes. They held knowledge, wisdom, a sparkling appreciation of life that younger women had yet to learn. Her face was tighter and more drawn than was fashionable, and even away from the spotlights her eyes shone from within as if charged by some secret source of energy created to dazzle.

'What else?' thought Harry quickly, wanting to imprint first impressions in his memory. Straight nose, wide mouth, softly etched lips.

She stood up and gave Harry a very private smile.

'I must go,' she said quietly.

'I'll take you,' Harry offered.

Vondrakova laughed. 'That could be dangerous!' Laughing, she whirled around, extending her hands to friends. The goodbyes were all theatre and Harry merely sipped champagne, listening to Louis murmuring to those he knew until the room was almost empty. Harry recognized the balding, fat Hungarian who had been talking to Louis. He was wearing a pinstripe suit with a large black camelhair overcoat draped over his shoulders.

'Ludo!' Hearing Vondrakova's voice, the man turned to her. 'Do not lose tonight,' she said and pressed a hand to her cheek, pointing a finger at him as if she were a child and he her parent.

'Liebchen,' he began, 'I play, I win. I play, I lose. I have only two women in my life – Vondrakova and Lady Luck.' The loose flesh of his face absorbed the smile on his thick lips, as bags around his eyes half hid the dull black pupils.

'Then go quickly,' Vondrakova replied. 'My rival is no more patient than I.'

Ludovic kissed her cheeks lightly. 'And you will not come?'

Vondrakova glanced at Harry then smiled at Ludovic. 'No,' she whispered, and reached up to undo her hair, which fell to her shoulders. Her dresser, who had been hovering in the background, switched off the lights on the dressing tables and put the long grey coat with its pale grey mink collar round her mistress's shoulders. Ludovic, a man of many years, twelve of them spent with his protégée, Vondrakova, shook his head, then put on his dark Homburg.

'I shall be late for the last game,' he said, and grasped his ebony cane.

'I'll come with you,' said Louis.

'Are you allowed?'

'In influential company,' replied Louis, and grinned. Ludo burst into loud, deep laughter. 'Young man,' he began to Harry, 'remember that you do not know Vondrakova . . .'

'Go!' shouted Irelena affectionately. Louis kissed her hand, waved to Harry then wandered down the corridor with the Hungarian and was gone.

'It's late,' said Vondrakova quietly.

'We both know that,' answered Harry.

'Excuse me, Madame,' said the dresser. Irelena nodded and the woman switched off the last lights in the dressing room, curtsied quickly and went.

Harry and Vondrakova were left standing in a red glow from the corridor's tinted bulbs, their faces inches from one another. Vondrakova's lips framed words that were barely audible.

'He's right,' she said, 'you don't know me.'

'He's wrong,' Harry replied softly. 'I have always known you.'

Her eyes widened. 'Harry,' she whispered slowly, for the first time. He reached out, and slipping his hands beneath the coat on her shoulders, grasped the warm flesh of her arms. The shock that passed between them was unmistakable. They stared at each other silently.

Some chorus girls ran past, chattering and giggling, excited by the prospects of their liaisons for the night. They ran through the exit door, where the guard slammed shut the iron bar and looked down the corridor.

'Madame!' called the guard respectfully from the exit. 'We must lock the doors.'

Vondrakova shivered and seized Harry's hand, squeezing it hard. 'This cannot be happening,' she whispered.

He leaned forward and slipped an arm beneath her long coat, then around her waist. 'Come,' he smiled.

Outside it was raining. Vondrakova looked up. 'There are no stars,' she said plaintively, like a child denied a promise. She put on the long grey silk scarf to protect her hair, and draped the ends over each shoulder. Harry watched her every movement with pleasure.

'Come quickly,' he said.

They ran up the slope into the square and a pool of light cast by four lamps suspended above the Casino steps. As they stood under the canopy, protected for a moment from the gently falling rain, Vondrakova seemed fascinated by the way the drops ran down the decorated ironwork. Harry held her close. She turned to stare at him, to remember the place, the time, the rain, the magic of the night. A raindrop that had been hesitating on her brow coursed down her face. A group of young people came laughing down the Casino steps, followed by more sober couples, who paused at the entrance to look for cars and chauffeurs.

Harry could smell the rain on the fur collar and soft silk scarf, lying against Vondrakova's face. Captivated, she drew away from him.

'This is madness,' she whispered.

'Fraulein,' said a voice. Vondrakova looked up. At the top of the steps to the Casino was a tall young man in a long black leather coat. He took off a dark hat to reveal blond hair, and began to walk slowly down the steps.

Harry could see one hand holding the hat, but the man's other hand was trailing amidst the folds of his black coat, where he saw a glint of metal. With sudden shock he recognized it as the barrel of a Schmeisser machine pistol, used by the German army.

'Who are you?' asked Harry roughly.

'My name is Held.'

Vondrakova pressed against Harry. Above them the young German looked gaunt in the harsh light.

'Yes, Herr Held?' said Irelena calmly.

'I have seen you many times, Fraulein,' he said, 'but I did not expect to see you here.'

Harry tensed, not knowing what to expect. Vondrakova smiled. 'I used to come before the war began.'

'I have only just arrived,' said Held.

'Then I hope you enjoy it.' Vondrakova turned to Harry and took his arm. 'I am afraid we must leave you.'

'But it is raining.'

'Then we shall get wet,' said Harry, and began to move away with the blond singer.

'Don't!' said Held, and thrust an arm at Harry, who immediately started to counter a blow then saw that the German was holding out an umbrella. He opened it and smiled.

'Held means hero in English, Harry,' said Vondrakova.

'Thank you,' he said.

Irelena Vondrakova, now firmly on Harry's arm beneath the umbrella, looked anew at the tall young German. 'Where did you see me?' she asked.

'In Munich,' he answered.

Irelena smiled. 'I loved Munich.'

'And Paris,' he went on. Harry could hear an excitement in the man's voice which was incongruous with his menacing appearance. 'And Düsseldorf, Frankfurt, Berlin, Prague, Vienna, even Venice, once . . .'

Vondrakova's eyes were wide. 'Venice,' she said softly, 'nineteen thirty-eight, Christmas.'

'I had a pass to ski in Bolzano. I went to see you instead.'

'Thank you,' she said gently.

'No,' said the German, 'it is I who thank you.'

For a moment, Harry was distracted by movement at the Casino doors. Several people had emerged and were coming down the steps. Only one figure remained in the half-lit doorway. Harry recognized him immediately. It was Pabst. The two men stared at each other as the people making for their car burst into laughter, then a door was slammed shut.

'Held,' said Pabst from above. The young German in front of Vondrakova spun round and straightened up as the car roared away into the wet darkness.

'Goodbye, Herr Held,' said Harry, and grasping Irelena's arm he walked her briskly across the square under the umbrella towards the entrance of the Hotel de Paris.

At the top of the hotel steps, Harry folded the umbrella before they spun through the revolving doors. He pointed to the wet Casino Square outside.

'Held must be quite a fan,' he said.

'I am lucky,' said Vondrakova. So both of them did what was a tradition amongst gamblers and rubbed the raised knee of the horse and rider statue that stands inside the entrance, just for luck.

They crossed the lobby beneath the great chandelier, then took the wide staircase which led to the second floor and Harry's rooms. There seemed no reason to speak, so Irelena merely smiled, her eyes trusting the man before her, knowing that his intentions would not exceed her own desires. Harry took out his key and unlocked the door.

Vondrakova's eyes were shining. She crossed to the window and saw the typewriter next to the piano.

'This is where you work?'

'Yes,' said Harry.

'A writer of musicals,' she said, smiling, and lifted some sheets of paper on the desk. 'Words. Songs.' Her voice was wistful as she tried to read the verses Harry had committed to paper.

'You sound as if you knew already.' Harry moved towards her.

'I asked Ludo to find out, after you had caught my arm on the steps.'

'Why did you do that?'

'Because Ludovic knows everything – or what he does not know he finds it easy to discover.'

'That was not the question I asked . . .' began Harry, then saw the expression in Vondrakova's eyes flicker for a moment, giving him the answer.

The sensation that passed between them as they touched, lightly, was ecstasy. For a moment there were no words. Irelena Vondrakova's lips parted, inches from Harry's face.

'What do you see, Harry?'

Harry breathed in the essence of the woman. 'I see excitement, trust, joy, love.'

Vondrakova smiled slowly. 'You really are a writer, aren't you, Harry?'

'An American writer.'

'You were born Armenian. Do you speak Russian?'

'Badly,' he answered.

Vondrakova's eyes danced as she surveyed him. 'You dress like a gigolo,' she began, watching Harry's expression change, 'but you have the face of a young warrior.' Her eyes were laughing kindly at Harry.

'I was brought up on the Caspian Sea.'

'That sounds very romantic.'

'And you?' asked Harry. Vondrakova moved her lips to his, and it was as if neither had ever kissed before. They parted reluctantly.

'That is my answer,' said Vondrakova.

Harry smiled. 'It must have been a great question.'

She laughed aloud. 'Do not ask questions, Harry.'

91

'But I know nothing about you.'

She sighed and shook her head. It was a small gesture of defiance.

'To know everything about a person and feel nothing, or to feel everything about a person and know nothing, which is better, Harry? Choose.'

'Why not a little of both?'

She shook her head again. 'We all begin so well' – an accent began to colour Vondrakova's English, as emotion betrayed her voice – 'if only we could always remain at the beginning, Harry.' There were tears in her eyes.

'I believe we can,' he said, 'if we try.'

'How?' she asked.

'I can't answer that because I don't know you.'

Her eyes clouded, momentarily perplexed, then came her infectious laugh. 'Harry, I must leave tomorrow for Marseilles.'

'Then I will come with you.

'No,' she replied. 'I have to sing, and I also have to remember what it was like before I met you. But I will come back for *you*.'

Chapter 12

Jan Van der Voors heaved his naked body across the bed and swung both legs on to the mat. His feet found slippers and he reached for the dressing gown lying on the carpet. Another body in the large bed stirred and a voice spoke.

'I need a light.'

Van der Voors switched on the bedside lamp.

'For a cigarette, dope!' said Bobby Avery, sitting up against the pillow. He dangled a cigarette from his fingers. The big Dutchman grinned and took a packet from his dressing gown pocket, struck a single match and lit the cigarette slowly, with the concentration of a man obviously drunk.

Bobby Avery inhaled deeply and blew out smoke as if he was auditioning for a Mae West movie. 'Where did you learn it all, sweetheart?' he said in a rasping voice. 'You've got a lot of action for a fat man.'

Van der Voors roared with laughter, dribbling saliva. 'I lived for years in Indonesia. The people are poor, and poverty is a great inventor.' He shuffled over to long curtains at the open window. 'It is become cold, yes?'

'I'm warm,' said Bobby Avery, squirming from the waist downwards beneath the sheets. He looked towards the upturned bottle in the champagne bucket and groaned, remembering how much he had drunk. 'Do you have a glass of water?' he asked.

Van der Voors opened the curtains. It was dark and still raining. 'Would you like room service?' he asked.

'My God, I thought I *was* room service!' said Bobby.

The Dutchman leered at the plump young man propped up in bed, and grinned wickedly. 'Then you should be given a tip, I think.' His words were slurred.

'You haven't got that kind of money,' Bobby replied.

'I am not a man "down on his uppers" – I think that is the expression, no?'

'You *were*,' emphasized the young man, blowing smoke.

'Yes,' said the Dutchman, returning unsteadily to the foot of the bed. 'I was actually – once.' His face became doleful.

Bobby was unsympathetic. 'Listen, heartbreak, I'm talking about half an hour ago.'

Van der Voors looked into the eyes of the arrogant American lying back in his bed, trying to decide what he had found so attractive. 'I have money,' intoned the Dutch accent.

'Good,' said Bobby. 'I told you, I love rich men.'

'Then you must stay in Europe. This war will make many more men rich.'

Bobby watched the man's thick lips meet, forming the shape of a large cupid's bow. Moisture advertised longing. Van der Voors sat down beside him, reached for the phone and dialled two numbers.

'You will be satisfied,' he said, and leaned towards the young man propped against the pillows, to kiss the pouting lips. Avery resisted for a second then succumbed to sensation, closing his eyes.

'*Oui, Monsieur?*' came the voice of the operator. The two men parted slowly. '*Monsieur?*' said the operator again.

'This is the fourth floor and I want the cashier, please,' said Van der Voors, carefully disciplining his thick tongue.

'If it is possible, Monsieur,' said the operator.

'It will be,' replied the Dutchman confidently. 'Or you can find the manager.'

'What are you doing?' asked Avery as a smile spread across the Dutchman's florid complexion.

'I am going to show you something you will never have seen before.'

'I can't wait,' said Avery with affected boredom.

'It will be our secret.'

'I only asked for mineral water,' said Bobby.

'This is better.'

'What is it?'

The Dutchman thought for a moment, focusing on the young man unsteadily. He found what he thought to be the correct American slang for diamonds.

'Ice,' he said.

The cashier closed the great safe door as the manager, Cornwallis, quickly signed a document releasing the hotel from all responsibility for what he now grasped firmly in his right hand. He crossed to the lift, pressed the button and waited.

The descending lift whined to a stop, but as Cornwallis opened the gates a curt voice behind him shouted: 'Halt!' It was Pabst and a companion.

'I wanted to speak with you about our – arrangements.'

'Of course, Herr Pabst.'

At that moment, Pabst's tall companion identified the maroon diamond case in the manager's hand. He whispered several words to the Gestapo officer, whose face froze.

'Where are you going?' asked Pabst dangerously.

'Up,' said the manager, and coughed. Pabst pointed to the open lift, which they all entered. The manager closed the gates awkwardly and pressed the button, feeling the weight of Pabst's attention.

'Your preparations are proceeding as instructed?'

'Yes, Herr Pabst, indeed they are.'

'It is to be an informal affair,' Pabst reminded him.

'I understand,' said Cornwallis, 'and the Beach Club is an excellent site. It was created for just such an event. We had many before . . .' he paused.

'The war,' Pabst finished for him.

Cornwallis continued hurriedly. 'The weather promises to be excellent. It has been such a magnificent summer – a little rain, of course . . . My golf at Mont Agel has suffered a little . . . but now the autumn . . .' he paused, running dry. The German made him nervous.

'Yes, it has been a magnificent summer, for Europe,' said Pabst, as the lift stopped.

Smoke curled between the two men in Van der Voors's suite. Bobby Avery inhaled and again blew into the grey, swirling fog he had created in the half-light of the bedroom.

'I would never have guessed you were Jewish,' said Bobby.

Van der Voors blinked and grinned. 'You did not guess. You

discovered.' He reached out a hand and touched the soft flesh of the young American, who shivered.

There was a knock on the door. Van der Voors finished his brandy in one gulp and put down the glass. He stood up unsteadily and tightened the belt of his dressing gown.

'Now, my little friend.' He stepped out of the light, crossed the spacious bedroom to the door and opened it with a welcoming grin.

The manager of the Hotel de Paris stared with distaste at the picture of dissolution before him, and watched the man's face change from geniality to fear. The Dutchman had recognized the two other men with Cornwallis.

'I gather you asked for your property, Mynheer,' said Cornwallis, and held out the maroon briefcase.

Van der Voors did not move as one of the men behind the manager stepped towards him.

'Take it.'

Still Van der Voors did not move.

'Take it,' repeated Pabst's voice quietly. 'It is yours.'

The Dutchman reached out and took the case.

'Thank you,' said Cornwallis brusquely, and was about to go when he noticed the sudden deathly pallor of the man before him. 'Are you all right, Mr Van der Voors?' he asked. The Dutchman nodded, slowly. 'Are you sure? We always have a doctor in attendance at the hotel. Simply dial six-one.' The manager's attempt at reassurance trailed off. 'I gather you know these gentlemen?' he said, referring to Pabst and his companion. Van der Voors nodded as if mesmerized.

'What's going on?' shouted Bobby Avery plaintively from the bedroom. Cornwallis frowned slightly and decided to ignore all the implications of the situation and retire to bed. He had done his duty.

'Goodnight,' he said, spun on his heels and strode away down the corridor.

Pabst watched the Dutchman back slowly into the room.

'For Christ's sake . . .!' came Bobby Avery's voice from the bed. Pabst smiled viciously. 'Six-one,' he said, and stepped into the dark room. The tall German beside him followed quickly, then closed and locked the door.

Some men can take physical punishment, others discover that they cannot. Proof is not pleasant, as it is sure to require considerable pain. Pabst stood squarely in front of Van der Voors, who was mouthing silent pleas in German.

Bobby Avery began to climb from the bed. Pabst snapped his fingers and Van der Voors followed the swift movement across the room.

'Who the hell . . .?' began Bobby Avery, his plump, naked body

95

pale and vulnerable in the light of the small lamp. The large German seized the young American by the throat.

'Get your fucking hand . . .!' Bobby tried to move his knee towards the man's groin but pain exploded in his head, accompanied by a great burst of light, and he felt warm blood in his mouth, then there was only darkness. Van der Voors winced as he watched the brutal blow connect and saw Bobby fall heavily to the floor, blood flowing between his lips and from his nose and ears.

'Oh, my God!' whispered the Dutchman in terror, as his body, composed predominantly of excess flesh, began to tremble. Pabst reached out slowly and touched him on the cheek. The Dutchman's eyes closed and he almost fainted. Pabst dropped his hand and carefully took the briefcase from Van der Voors.

'I only want to ask you some questions,' he said softly, 'to which you will supply the answers – yes?'

The Dutchman nodded.

'Sit down,' said Pabst, aware of the man's alcoholic stupor. Van der Voors lowered himself slowly into an armchair, beads of sweat appearing on his brow where the hair was receding. Pabst seated himself opposite and put the briefcase on a small table between them.

'In this case are the samples of the diamonds now being held in Amsterdam, yes?'

'Yes,' whispered Van der Voors, and glanced quickly at the body of the young American. A pool of blood was spreading on the carpet around his face. Pabst's silent companion sat on the edge of the bed near the low lamp, unconcerned, patient, watching.

'Good,' said Pabst. He smiled. 'Now you see the case on the table before us?' Van der Voors nodded slowly. Pabst stared at the Dutchman and spoke deliberately: 'Why is it here?'

The open window allowed cool air into the room. A car passed below in the rain. Someone shouted and the night was still again. The Dutchman heard a soft moan from the young American on the floor.

'I wanted . . . to show . . .' he bit his lip.

Bobby Avery moaned again, moved his head, then coughed blood. Pabst stood up.

'He knows nothing,' whispered the Dutchman. Pabst waited for silence.

'You have elected to cooperate with the Gestapo.' The Dutchman said nothing. 'With the Third Reich.' Still he remained silent. 'And you are a Jew! Did you hear me?'

'Yes.'

Pabst took a step towards Van der Voors, who froze as the Gestapo major's hand reached out to his pocket, and took from it a handkerchief, then offered it.

'You do not look well, Mynheer,' he said.

The Dutchman accepted the silk square and began to wipe his face. Pabst's eyes flashed a command to his subordinate, who crossed to the table and picked up the briefcase. This will be returned to the safe,' he paused.

'Your friend appears to have had an accident,' said Pabst. 'Be sure that *he* understands it.' He stepped to the door, and the next moment the two Germans were gone.

Van der Voors began to tremble and was unable to move as he watched the young man on the floor regain consciousness.

'Oh fuck!' said Bobby Avery, tasting his own blood, and vomited into the carpet.

Hugh Sullivan lay on his back in his room, staring at the ceiling. He was fully dressed and there was a bad taste in his mouth from the wine he had been drinking all night. The french windows were open and he had not bothered to pull the curtains. The rain outside conjured up images of the past, from dirty tenements to Park Avenue apartments, and liaisons of the night spread over many years.

He lit another cigarette before sinking back on the pillow and reaching for a glass of white wine, poured from a bottle which he always had waiting for him in an ice bucket. At his age it helped. Sleep was no longer easy; his years kept him awake, which was why, at this hour, he always needed company, needed someone, wanted – Bobby.

The door in the adjoining room opened and was slammed shut. Sullivan peered at his watch but could see nothing. He swung himself from the bed, took off his jacket, undid his tie, and in shirt sleeves and waistcoat crossed to the connecting door. It was not locked. He smiled, retraced his steps, and picked up the bucket, table napkin, white wine and two glasses. Then, acting the part of a waiter, he bustled in to Bobby's room with forgiveness in his heart.

Finding it dark inside, he moved gingerly until he located the bedside light. He switched it on, then put down the bucket and glasses.

Sullivan stared at the congealed blood around the boy's nose, mouth, chin and ears. Deep black and purple bruises stained the plump face from temple to jaw on the right side. Tears began to fall from Bobby Avery's eyes as soundlessly, helpless, he reached up with his arms and clung to Sullivan. He smelled of vomit.

'It's burning,' he said hoarsely.

Sullivan grasped the napkin, gathered some ice in it and gently began to apply the improvised pack to the inflamed cheek. Thoughts that had tormented him during the past hours now disappeared. He felt like a father to his prodigal son, and clasped the boy to his bosom, lightly kissing the damaged face, murmuring, as a lover does, words of comfort and solace.

'I love you,' he said, tears of pity in his eyes. 'I love you.'

Hugh Sullivan had been playing for a month at the fashionable St Regis when he first bumped into Bobby Avery, outside Ruben's off Fifth Avenue in New York City. It was one of those clear cold winter days that, when they happen, make New York magical. Both of them were guests and discovered that they were to make up a table of four at lunch.

Hugh wore a fawn camelhair coat with an astrakhan collar, Bobby a dark astrakhan coat with a hat to match. As Hugh watched Bobby shed his apparel he could not resist a comment: 'Now that, my dear, is style!'

Bobby Avery grinned. 'Some people say ostentatious.'

'Some people have no appreciation of taste.'

'I don't think we've been introduced,' said Bobby.

Sullivan smiled, fluttering his eyes. 'We will be, sweetheart,' he said, and with a spring in his step strode into the main dining room.

Bobby was with a promoter of Broadway shows, and sat with his back against the wall where photographs of many stars hung. The central heating was too efficient, and by the time the main course arrived he was suffering inside his tight collar, suit and tie. Sullivan glanced across the table at Bobby's glistening forehead as the young man began a pompous monologue on the merits of risk in theatre for the sake of art, then paused and took a sip of cold white wine.

'Is it the wrong time of the month?' asked Sullivan.

'I beg your pardon?' young Avery replied.

'Sullivan, don't embarrass the kid,' said the promoter protectively.

Sullivan smiled and said nothing. His companion, also a musician, and composer, and recently involved in a hit show, coughed.

Over coffee the semblance of a deal was hatched between the musician/composer and the promoter. Cigars were produced as Bobby Avery finished his double portion of strawberry cheesecake.

'You've got quite an appetite,' said Sullivan.

'I'm healthy,' replied Avery. He swallowed and licked his mouth slowly, looking directly into the Irish-American's eyes.

Sullivan reached across the table and extended a finger towards Bobby Avery's face. 'May I?' he asked, and wiped a piece of cheesecake from the young man's lips then brought it back to his own mouth.

'Thank you,' said Bobby Avery.

Sullivan put the morsel of dessert on his tongue and swallowed. 'Delicious,'

Avery's eyes half-closed.

'One has to be so careful in public these days,' said Sullivan wickedly.

'Being considerably older than I am,' stated the young American, 'you obviously know so much more.'

'Then that gives you so much more time to learn.'

Bobby's eyes grew large. 'I've always had a very good relationship with my teachers.'

'Bobby was at Harvard,' announced the promoter, and blew cigar smoke across the table.

'Where did you study, Mr Sullivan?' asked Bobby Avery.

'I'm a graduate from the School of Life, young man.'

'With *honours*,' said Sullivan's companion.

'Interesting?' suggested Bobby.

'No, my boy, *painful*,' replied Sullivan.

Lunch finished. The Broadway promoter paid the bill and all four men left the crowded restaurant for the clear air and cold streets of late afternoon in mid-Manhattan.

After that it was only a question of time. On Sullivan's midweek night off, Bobby took him to see Eugene O'Neill's *Mourning Becomes Electra*, where they both became very emotional; then on to the Rainbow Room, where they both got smashed on Zombies, a diabolical combination of rums. They staggered to the elevator, arm in arm, and their first kiss in the rapidly descending isolation of an Otis Express was something neither of them regretted. As the doors opened on the ground floor they quickly separated, and were almost inundated by a Baptist group from the Midwest bent on breaking a few vows more than sixty floors up.

'You're a very risky person to be with,' said Bobby, giggling, as they watched the elevator doors close.

'We're allowed to get drunk in public,' the pianist replied, 'but anything else we want must be done in private, and then it's strictly illegal.' He was slurring his words.

'Is that a proposition?' asked Bobby.

'No, it's an indictment,' replied Sullivan. They went outside and flagged down a cab.

Bobby Avery had money, Hugh Sullivan mileage. In his apartment on West Central Park, rented for the season, the Irish-American taught the young man some of the advantages that age brings to any relationship, however transient.

That had been in 1937. By the time Sullivan was completing a lucrative contract in Atlanta before Christmas 1939, the two were firm friends and passionate lovers. They had travelled widely and fought publicly in exotic places, but discovered a relationship that worked. Sullivan, after a major altercation with his agent, suggested that Mr Avery be his manager. There was no contract but an agreement was arrived at. The two men decided to celebrate at the first opportunity, and they spent a self-indulgent Christmas at the Miami Biltmore, revelling in the balmy weather.

Early in January, they journeyed back to New York then, ignoring the U-boat threat, embarked for Europe and arrived in Paris in time to see the first of the spring fashions. Despite what everybody agreed was only a phoney war, beneath the forced gaiety lay tension. Sullivan played in the American Bar of the Bristol while Bobby cavorted a little too much in society. When the news began to reach Europe that in the north, Scandinavia was being overrun by both the Germans and the Russians, the older man was wise enough to suggest an early departure.

'We'll have to leave some time,' said Sullivan. 'The contract is up at the beginning of May.'

'Well, where d'you wanna go?' was Bobby's reply.

Sullivan shrugged. They were having fun, but the pleasure seeking was becoming frenetic and the atmosphere increasingly unreal. He thought for a moment.

'Let's go back to Monte Carlo.'

Doctor Solomon crossed the lobby of the Hotel de Paris as cleaners finished their morning tasks and the florist completed a huge flower arrangement under the great chandelier. Sometimes his calling was distasteful, and it seemed to offer less satisfaction as he got older. He had even begun thinking about his own liver recently, and suspected that the pains he felt were not altogether normal.

The young American he had treated in the early hours might well have sustained permanent injury. He knew that he had not merely fallen: the blow had been expert and brutal. Perhaps the inner ear had been damaged; certainly the cheekbone was cracked, and he had apparently bitten his tongue at the moment of impact. As for the other one, well, he had know Sullivan for a number of years and the fact that he had lasted this long indicated that his organs might survive the litres of wine they endured every night, but he doubted if the heart muscle could hold out much longer.

Dr Solomon pushed his way through the revolving doors of the hotel and stood at the top of the steps. It was a glorious day and already November.

At midday, a black Mercedes drew up outside the Hotel de Paris. Van der Voors, who had been waiting for several minutes in the lobby, with the maroon briefcase held tightly in his grip, was ushered into the car by one of Pabst's tall Aryans. The doorman watched as the car drew away, apparently making for the harbour.

Had he been able to observe the car further, he would have noted that it took the Rue Grimaldi, made a left turn through the Place d'Armes, then went up the slope of the Avenue de la Porte Neuve until it reached the Avenue St Martin, on Monaco's Rock. The car stopped in a private area near the Oceanographical Museum, beside another Mercedes.

The two passengers went down some steps to what was officially the prison of Monte Carlo, built into the rock, facing south over the sea. A section of the prison was occupied by the Gestapo, and the steps led directly to the upper level of old cells now used as quarters and offices.

Christopher Quinn greeted the Dutchman with forced cordiality. Major Pabst shook hands briefly, amused at the Dutchman's obvious dislike of him. Then they entered and the formal meeting began. Van der Voors opened the briefcase, revealing numerous sachets, each one labelled according to the weight and quality of the diamonds they contained. Guy de Salis, the banker from Switzerland, was seated next to two gentlemen who themselves could have been Swiss. These men minutely examined each of the diamonds presented to them. At 3.30 they asked to speak to de Salis privately. At 3.45 the three men emerged from an adjoining room and agreed in general terms that the proposed transaction should take place, provided Mynheer Van der Voors was willing, first, to reassign the papers to a Monaco holding company created by Quinn for Pabst and his cronies, and second, to accept Quinn's price. With no choice, the Dutchman agreed. Champagne was broached, sparkling defiantly in the grim confines of the converted prison.

In a moment of cordiality at the end of the meeting, Pabst invited them all to what he hoped would be a particularly spectacular gathering at the Monte Carlo Beach Club. No one was quite sure exactly who, or how many would be there, but with names like Vogler, Flick, Kloeckner, Zangen, Roland, Kierdoff, and representatives of Krupp, I. G. Farben and Savoia-Marchetti, it sounded interesting.

Van der Voors was sweating by the time he had mounted the steps to the road. He lay back in the rear seat of the Mercedes as, once again, the tall German climbed in next to the driver. Immediately the car began to rumble away down the Avenue St Martin.

He wiped his brow, thanking God that his ordeal was over.

Chapter 13

Ben Harrison changed down to accelerate at speed up the Avenue de la Porte Neuve. He braked slightly, coasted around the turn, narrowly missing a black Mercedes, revved up into the Avenue St Martin and drove past the Oceanographical Museum. On his right was a line of villas with spectacular views of the southern horizon. He drove through an open gate and parked the MG. By the time he had eased his long legs from beneath the dashboard, stepped out and stretched, Agatha Parry was standing at the front door.

'Bloody good little beast,' he said. She smiled and made a small gesture with her hands that drew attention to her clothes.

'That's a lovely dress you're wearing, Aggie,' said Ben.

'I didn't think you'd notice.'

He placed a kiss on her cheek, then lit a cigarette. 'Yes you did,' he said.

Aggie smiled. 'Come in, you old water buffalo, and have some tea.' She introduced Ben to several guests, among them a pleasant middle-aged woman called Eva Trenchard, who told Ben that she came from Edinburgh. The others began to laugh, gossip and sip tea. The atmosphere of the room, bathed in afternoon sunlight, was bright and gay. An attractive American woman, introduced as Francie Pinkerman, came in, sporting a large beige hat, and announced that she was 'trapped in Paradise for the duration'.

Agatha was talking to a plump woman with a bright print dress and dark-rimmed glasses which were the main focus of a pale face. This was Jenny Cornwallis, married to the manager of the Hotel de Paris.

'Do tell us about this party,' Agatha said enthusiastically. 'Why does he want to go down to the Monte Carlo Beach?'

'Who's this?' asked Ben.

'The German, Pabst,' Miss Trenchard said.

Jenny played with her mousy hair until she had everyone's attention, then said in a loud whisper: 'Well, he told Robert that it's something to do with security.'

'It's not actually in Monte Carlo, is it?' asked Agatha.

'Actually, that seems to be the point,' Jenny answered. 'We've always used it ever since Elsa got permission from the Prince to give us all a place to bathe. It's very pretty, of course, but a little too American for my taste. Palm trees and an Olympic pool have always confused the French. They prefer the sea, which is so near – and free.'

'But so much colder,' Agatha broke in. 'I've swum in the pool every year since it was built, and I think the whole place is rather delightful. Miss Maxwell has excellent taste.'

'Does she still live here?' asked Ben.

'She has a house further up the coast,' replied Agatha, 'but she's gone now that it's become Vichy France.'

'Well then,' asked Francie Pinkerman, 'where exactly is the Monte Carlo Beach?'

'It *was* France,' Agatha explained.

'It looks pretty Italian to me now,' said Jenny Cornwallis. 'They have troops in dormitories – well, I should say barracks. It used to be the Beach Hotel's annexe.'

'So it's actually occupied territory?'

Agatha nodded. Francie took out her compact and began powdering her nose. 'How exciting!' she said.

'Not if you're French,' said Ben.

Jenny Cornwallis began playing with her dark-rimmed glasses. 'This Pabst fellow insisted on the Beach place because it can be sealed off. Apparently most of the guests are from Germany and Italy.'

'Really?' said Agatha.

'I suppose I shouldn't tell you, but I do know the Krupp people, terribly polite, a very old family business . . .'

'They make guns,' said Ben quietly.

'. . . They're all coming over from San Remo. There's some big meeting . . . I don't know the details, I'm not really interested, but I have seen the guest list.'

'But why should they want to come here?' asked Agatha.

'Doesn't everyone?' smiled Francie Pinkerman, adjusting her hat. 'I mean, Monte Carlo's so lovely, even though this horrible old war is not quite finished.'

'Lunch on Sunday.' Jenny was the centre of attention, and enjoying it. 'Open air, in the sun for almost eight hundred people, then most of the VIPs are supposed to be coming up to the Casino. Can you imagine? I think it will be quite fun.'

'Will we be invited?' asked Francie Pinkerman.

Jenny ground out her cigarette in the ashtray, embarrassed for a moment. 'That's awkward,' she said. 'Some are, some aren't. I mean Robert and I are Monégasques now, and the Americans, of course . . .' her voice trailed off. 'It's the war you see. The English . . .'

Francie interrupted: '. . . Are trapped in Paradise – didn't I say?'
Agatha smiled. 'More tea?'

It was twilight before everyone had gone, leaving an almost exhausted silence in the pleasant room, now subtly lit for evening. Ben had taken Eva Trenchard back to her house. He would be returning later at Agatha's invitation for an early dinner. Now she was alone. She sat in a corner of the sofa staring at the lighted fire, dreaming not of the past and of old loves, but of a huge and hitherto secret convention of the major Axis industrialists. The guest list would be most revealing. Agatha picked up the telephone and dialled.

'Eva?' she said. 'I'd like you to deliver whatever you can round up for me tonight.' She paused. 'Even if it seems stale.' She listened to a discreet question and smiled. 'I'll make sure Ben's gone by eleven.' She nodded to herself, hearing Eva's quiet voice. 'Yes, anything you can get,' she answered, 'I want to feed it to the birds.' She listened for confirmation, thanked the proprietress of the Scotch Tea House, who specialized in cakes, then replaced the receiver, sat back on the sofa and drew on her cigarette.

The war was changing. England had survived one battle and was now enduring the might of the Luftwaffe as they began their blitz on Britain. Hitler must be stopped, she knew that, but there seemed no way to contain his ambitions. She was merely one person in a haven temporarily protected by a dubious neutrality.

She ground out her cigarette, stood up quickly and brushed down her skirt, then made her way downstairs. She wanted to be sure that the transmitter was working. The message she would have to send later that night would be long, and she was already afraid of the possible consequences.

Saturday evening was dance night at the West Country RAF base which was Air Commodore Maynard's centre of Western Command. For many servicemen stationed there, it was also their last night in England. The atmosphere in the dance hall was warm and muggy.

Outside the weather was filthy. Parked beside a long runway, under camouflage nets, twelve brand-new Beaufighters were lashed by the driving rain. Only the sentries, huddled in the improvised shelters, 'volunteered' for extra guard duty by their sergeants, cursed the large and deadly-looking silhouettes, hoping to God that the weather would clear for the morning and these new aircraft would be off the ground and gone. That way they might be able to get a pint at the pub in the village the following day. Saturday night was already ruined.

'Bastards!' said several of them during their long hours of duty as the rain soaked deeper into their skins, referring to the aircraft as if they were alive. But the Beaufighters stood silent. They too were waiting for that Sunday morning in early November 1940. They were going elsewhere.

Shortly before dawn, Squadron Leader Danny Morgan kissed his wife Miranda goodbye and drove his Jaguar the short distance back to base. There he went directly into the Ops room to wait for a weather report and final briefing. It was raining heavily.

The conditions had still not improved several hours later. He found a jeep and driver and drove across the airfield to his Beaufighter. The camouflage nets had been removed. He spotted his mechanic, wearing a helmet and cape, sheltering beneath the starboard wing, and ran over to him.

'Everything OK, Stan?' he asked. His voice had the trace of a Boston accent, although four years with an English wife had removed its edge.

'Yes, sir, should perform like a treat.' Stan sat down on his tool box.

Danny leaned against the fuselage. Both men watched the pouring rain in glum silence.

Tall, solidly built, Danny Morgan looked exactly what he was – an exceptional athlete. His black hair and clean-cut features were accentuated by dark brows and the clear eyes of a pilot. His New England family, based in Boston and Newport, Rhode Island, had been shocked and frightened by his early taste for flying, which had been an obsession since the age of seventeen. Taught by a veteran barnstormer – the two of them had travelled throughout the Midwest in the late Twenties – his excitement had been whetted, and his love of the air became a paramount part of his life.

During the Thirties Danny had been dubbed an international playboy and had pursued everything mechanical or physical that was 'fast', until he met a beautiful English girl and married well. She had tempered his behaviour without destroying his essential qualities. The match had been encouraged by his father, who had married a similar Englishwoman a generation before. History was repeating itself.

When Great Britain went to war against Germany, Danny immediately volunteered for the RAF. His obvious ability and natural ease of command gave him experience and promotion, and although privately some of his pilots continued to call him 'the Yank' he was held in great respect.

'Don't worry, sir, she'll look after you,' said Stan, jerking his thumb at the Beaufighter. 'Been all over her this morning. Bit like a woman, sir, if you'll pardon my saying so. Keep her fully serviced and she'll do anything for you.'

Half an hour later the rain stopped.

The voices of the congregation packed into the Anglican church just behind Monte Carlo's Rue de Courtier rose with both religious and patriotic fervour, soaring towards the vaulted roof. The Sunday morning service had started soon after 10, and the doors were open to welcome any nationality. There were a few Italians and a number of French. The rest who were not Monégasque seemed to be Protestant refugees drawn from all over Europe. They were singing, if not in perfect English, at least in time to the organ.

The hymn reached a crescendo and finished. The English vicar waited for a moment's calm, then signalled to the organist, who began a soft introduction.

'And now,' he said, 'as is the custom on foreign shores, despite the prevailing conditions upon our unsettled earth, I would like you all to remain standing. This has always been an English church in which we praise God. To complete the service we ask of God his salvation for our Monarch.'

The organ began playing the national anthem of Great Britain. The women in the congregation stood straight and still; the men, almost without exception, were standing to attention.

> 'Send him victorious, happy and glorious,
> Long to reign over us, God save the King!'

The Monte Carlo Beach had been created in the early Thirties, when Elsa Maxwell persuaded the Palace that with a seaside resort area, Monaco's season would extend through the summer. The idea was attractive, and it offered increased revenue for the Principality, so she was given permission to go ahead. Utilizing ideas from America, together with a strong flavour of French and Italian taste, she created something that was designed to last as long as the Principality itself. It worked, as did most things to which Miss Maxwell applied herself, whether it was a dinner party for twelve or a social event for five hundred.

A pool of Olympic dimensions; palm trees planted at intervals; changing areas; small shops for beach attire; and above the seashore itself, in elegant lines fringing the white pebbled beach, white and green striped tents with deckchairs, loungers and tables where the hot Mediterranean summer days could be spent in select privacy. Above, cut into the hills directly behind the beach area, she added the red clay tennis courts of the Country Club. Perhaps it did all have a touch of Beverly Hills by the sea, but after the first season, the whole operation was unanimously declared a success. Large yachts and motor cruisers would moor off the beach in magnificent weather. Rich, tanned, beautifully preserved bodies plunged into the sea and swam to the shore, escorted by mahogany and brass Riva speedboats driven by crewmen in white uniforms. Sumptuous lunches of white wine and Mediterranean fish were eaten at packed tables in open-air restaurants. The men dripped with sweat, their women with diamonds. All in all it was a pleasant way to pass the time: the only requirements were time itself and money. The beach became a summer Mecca for rich celebrities, film stars, playboys and industrialists.

Then the war came. Elsa Maxwell, further down the Riviera, was standing on her terrace one night at the very beginning of September 1939 when she saw, as she described, it 'all the lights along the coast go out as if a giant hand was sweeping them away'. She left soon after, although others stayed until, with the fall of France, they too were gone, or had removed themselves to Monte Carlo.

The beach, leased by Monaco from France and protected by Italian soldiers, became the hub of a new society – those who were prepared to live with the conquerors, continuing to enjoy themselves despite the privations inflicted on the rest of Europe. But it remained as always an exclusive place. Admission was granted only to the select few, who were offered complete relaxation in guaranteed security.

Chapter 14

Twin 1,400 horse-power Bristol Hercules engines pulled each of the twelve fully loaded Beaufighters into a climb at 1,800 feet a minute, taking them 14,000 feet above towering cumulus clouds, piled high over southern England. As they levelled off, Danny Morgan, in the lead aircraft, glanced about him from the large enclosed cockpit and spoke on the intercom to his sergeant, Duffy Kelly, whose position was halfway down the slim fuselage, beneath an observation dome.

'Duffy, are you all right back there?'

'Yes, sir, but Johnny looks as though he's swinging out too wide again.'

In the forward cockpit, Danny Morgan turned his head quickly and snapped on the RT:

'Johnny, pull yourself up, I don't want you lagging when we go down over the coast.'

'Oh Danny boy, the pipes, the pipes are calling . . .' Flight Lieutenant Johnny Turnbull had a sense of humour which sometimes palled.

'Thank you, Turnbull, that will do.'

'Well, it's these bloody tanks,' said Turnbull, referring to the specially fitted long-range fuel canisters they carried beneath the wings. 'Feel like a damned slug up here.'

'Look like it too,' said another voice on the RT.

'That's enough, Jacko,' said Danny Morgan.

Most of the pilots were in their early twenties. Danny at twenty-nine was referred to by some of them as 'Grandpa'. Now their Squadron Leader decided that it was time to call a halt to this release of nervous energy. They were nearing the coastline of occupied France.

'Right, gentlemen,' he said, in a voice of command. 'I want radio silence unless there's an absolute emergency, certainly until we reach the Med. Thank you. Over and out.'

The twelve aircraft closed up in formation and almost together the pitch of the engines changed. To port, through the clouds, they could see the Channel Islands of Alderney and Guernsey. The fact that the sea was almost clear of shipping, in what was normally the busiest sea lane in the world, was the only way to tell there was a war on.

The Beaufighter squadron veered southwest, and in a shallow dive began losing altitude until they could see the Brittany coast quite clearly to port. There were clouds all about them as they dropped to sea level.

Now that they had bypassed the Gulf of St Malo and the crack German fighter squadrons stationed outside Dinard, the plan hereafter was simple. They would turn south at the tip of the peninsula beyond the German naval base at Brest to give the impression they were flying on the regular route to Gibraltar. The Freya radar or coastal observers would pick them up and the Beaufighters might have to avoid a few potshots, but they would be long gone – and with luck forgotten. Only then, out of sight of land over the Bay of Biscay, would they veer southeast and begin their run in over Germany's newly acquired territory.

Danny Morgan checked the bearing. He knew about KG 40 and their four-engined Kondors, long-range Focke-Wulf 200 reconnaissance planes based outside Bordeaux. They would be no threat. What he hoped desperately was that there were no fighter squadrons at Royan, where the estuary narrowed at the mouth of the Gironde. With their long-range fuel tanks, his Beaufighters were too heavy to engage in combat with the faster Messerschmitts. He looked at his watch. It was almost 12 o'clock on Sunday morning.

The first puffs of anti-aircraft fire appeared ahead and there was the Pointe de Grave and the coast, right on time. They were approaching rapidly at zero height. Danny spotted what looked like several German destroyers anchored beyond the breakwaters of Royan harbour. He swore and prayed to God that his squadron would be too quick for them.

The twelve aircraft were suddenly over the estuary and enemy country. The destroyers were taken by surprise and the shore flak was inaccurate. He could clearly see the running sailors and the ack-ack guns traversing, but too late. The speed of the Bristol Beaufighters gave them an advantage – they were no sooner spotted than they were lost, roaring into the hinterland, barely one hundred feet above the soil of occupied France. The squadron stayed low to escape radar detection and maintain surprise even as it passed over towns, villages and startled livestock in the vast meadows of southwestern Vichy France.

Just before 1 o'clock, they could see the Mediterranean. They crossed the coast over the great flats of Sète. Here, where the oyster beds stretched far out in a shallow sea, they began to turn and climb, exactly on schedule. Danny could see several fishing boats in deeper water and the crews all waving wildly at him. He reflected for a moment on the dilemma of the French and their split loyalties. Half their country under a grim occupation, the other half ruled by a pro-Nazi puppet government at Vichy. He shook his head – not the France he knew at all, or the people he loved. Danny grinned, waved back to the fishermen below, then checked the gauges on the instrument panel. He broke RT silence.

'Okay, Johnny, take your flight away. Any fuel problems?' No one answered. 'Right,' he ordered, 'drop tanks.'

The formation opened out and as he pulled his release lever he could see the drained long-range fuel tanks on the other aircraft falling away.

'Breaking off, skipper,' said Turnbull. 'Don't be late. Remember we'll be waiting for you with tea.'

'Make sure the petrol pumps are working,' said Danny into his mouthpiece. 'I want to be in and out quickly.'

'Will do,' crackled Turnbull's voice. 'If you're on time, I'll buy you cocktails tonight.'

'Who's paying?' Jacko broke in.

'We'll discuss it.'

'Tight Turnbull,' said Sergeant White, and all the pilots laughed.

'Drive carefully!' shouted Danny against the static.

'Ever known me not to?' Turnbull's flight of six aircraft had already split from the formation, dividing it in two. He was flying straight on to Malta to refuel at the RAF base of Hal Far before continuing to their final destination of Egypt.

'Goodbye, Grandpa,' he said, 'and good luck!' Danny clicked his radio microphone twice.

Within ten minutes the two flights had lost sight of each other. The weather had changed. The day was everything people dream about when thinking of the Mediterranean – crystal-clear, no cloud. Danny's mouth tightened. If there was trouble that meant there was nowhere to hide. The glittering water below looked very inviting. Often, at this time of the year, Danny had been out in his father's yacht, surging along in bright sunlight under full sail. Now there were only occasional small boats, limited by the wartime restrictions. Danny reached out to the throttle controls and increased power. Jacko and the others behind him followed suit. They retrimmed and the Beaufighters gathered speed as they approached Marseilles.

'Ack-ack ahead, sir!' snapped Jacko.

'I see it.' Flashes appeared along the coast, and the next moment there were puffs of anti-aircraft fire all around. This port and Toulon were the great southern bases of what remained of the Vichy navy in France.

'When we get to the target, remember, follow me in and put everything you've got into the one spot.'

Danny was becoming nervous now, his blood infused with adrenalin.

'Right, gentlemen,' he said on the RT, 'test your guns.' Each of the pilots released the safety catch at the top of their half-wheel joystick and pressed their thumbs on the buttons for a short burst of machinegun and cannon fire. Tracer arced away in front of the aircraft in a devastating display of power. Each of the Beaufighters immediately lost forward momentum, and the pilots had to pull back on the stick to correct the nose as it dropped.

Danny spoke to his sergeant observer on the intercom. 'Are you OK, Duffy?'

'Yes sir,' replied the crewman. 'Bloody lovely view, sir.'

Danny felt his palms beginning to sweat inside his flight gloves. It was just after 1 o'clock. The aircraft crew had glimpsed Saint Raphael and the shore, and were now on a slow curve moving closer towards the coast, where the pilots could see the rising cliffs, hills and mountains.

Danny had been told the importance of the mission, but he also knew that they would have only minutes over the target before their fuel situation became critical. For a moment there was a pang in his heart at the thought of what they were about to do. He looked out of the cockpit at the French Riviera.

'It's all so damn beautiful,' he muttered to himself.

In prewar years, the South of France had been his playground, as it was his father's. As a boy he had spent winters at a Lycée in Nice to learn the language. As a youth he had summered on the Côte d'Azur and discovered girls. As a man he had married a beautiful English girl and honeymooned in their first house, a rented villa in the hills above Menton.

Seeing it all before him again, he felt as if he were coming home.

Immediately beyond the port wing, hardly a mile away, was first Cannes, then Antibes and the Hotel du Cap, with its beautiful restaurant, Eden Rock. 'A whole bunch of people swimming off the steps,' he murmured to himself with pleasure – some of them waved to him. Then Nice appeared, and the long seashore in the middle of which he could make out the twin cupolas of the old Negresco Hotel. 'Now probably full of Nazis,' he thought, and hoped not.

The sensation of speed was heightened as Danny took his flight lower. Almost at wave-top, they passed beside the tip of Cap Ferrat and there were the towering bluffs above Beaulieu. Danny could clearly see the Basse Corniche running parallel to the railway line and remembered how often he had driven that road. Then there was Cap Estel and the aircraft were rushing over the sparkling Mediterranean, innocent and peaceful. The last-minute instructions Danny had received for his flight had astonished him, but this was war and here was the enemy and, finally, there was the target.

Danny swallowed and snapped on the RT.

'Good luck, boys,' he said. 'Here we go!'

Agatha Parry began to fidget nervously with her wristwatch. She had attended the church service, come directly home and sent Ben to pick up Eva Trenchard in the car. They would soon be outside.

From the Scotch Tea House, Agatha had received incredible information. One of Miss Trenchard's Italian boys had managed to steal a copy of the Beach Club guest list. Agatha had been trembling with excitement as she radioed the details to her chief in Whitehall, stating her intention to glean what further information she could about the local guests by watching the party through binoculars. No instructions or advice had come in on her regular 8 am schedule. Perhaps atmospheric interference had blanked out the transmission? She had no idea of the impact her revelations had made in London.

She immediately recognized the horn of her MG sports as an impatient Ben Harrison pulled up outside her villa. Agatha looked into the small room secreted behind a panelled wall of the downstairs library, to make sure that the set was switched off. Then she pulled the door shut and turned to go. That was the priority: to see the VIPs and guests arrive at the Beach Club party. A friend's balcony would get her near enough. She was already dressed, so only moments later Agatha was closing the door to her villa.

'There you are,' said Ben with pleasure. 'I thought perhaps you'd already gone ahead.'

'How?' asked Agatha smiling like a girl. 'When you've been tootling around in my baby all morning?'

Ben kissed her quickly.

'Not now, Mr Harrison,' she said brusquely. 'Where's Eva?'

'I dropped her at the market,' Ben told her. 'I gather you want to take a look at what's going on at the Club? Isn't that dangerous?'

'It's important to know who the local collaborators are.'

'Why?'

Agatha ignored the question. 'Let's go and pick up Eva,' she said. 'We'll squeeze her in somehow.'

'This could be fun,' Ben laughed, and the MG roared away. At that moment, London was trying to raise its agent in Monte Carlo, but there was no answer. They listened for her call sign regularly at 1 and 11.30 pm but she only stood by for messages from them at 8 am.

The message they wanted to send was short: 'Imperative stay clear of party.' But Agatha had gone and the receiver was dead.

That Sunday in November 1940, the parking area at the Monte Carlo beach seemed to belie the existence of a state of war in Europe. The vehicles were predominantly Mercedes or Italian staff cars, many flying regimental colours. As the weather was superb, some were open – Hispano Suizas, Bugattis, even Jaguars, Daimlers and Rolls Royces.

By 12.30 almost all of the guests had arrived, many from the church services in Monte Carlo, the majority from across the Italian border and their accommodation in San Remo.

Long tables were covered in white tablecloths. Behind them waiters supervised by Louis and Jean-Pierre of the Hotel de Paris served the combinations of fruit juices and alcohol that titillate the palate before lunch.

By ten minutes to one, attitudes had loosened. After days of serious discussions on top-secret affairs, the various German and Italian industrialists, many of whom knew the resort from before the war, were glad to relax and to mix with Monte Carlo society.

By ten past one, the atmosphere had become aggressively happy. Louis was dispensing even more champagne and cocktails. No one had fallen into the large swimming pool yet, but he knew from many years' experience that there would be drunken bodies thrashing about in the water come 4 o'clock.

He winked at Jean-Pierre, who was taking a long time to serve an attractive French girl giggling on the arm of a large Italian. Six months before it would have meant nothing, now she was a collaborator. Louis shook his head and sighed. War, he thought. Thank God they were out of it all. He looked above the gathering crowds where several miles distant, across the glittering bay, was the Rock of Monaco, standing out in shimmering silhouette against the horizon. It was a wonderful day and Louis felt glad to be alive.

To one side of him, there was old Doctor Solomon, well into the bottle

112

of wine he had appropriated from the bar. The large white-suited Dutchman, Van der Voors, was already perspiring from a pink face and kept glancing at the piano and Sullivan's accompanying trio. Maybe he had something to do with the bruised face of the pianist's queer little friend – who knew? Then someone ordered another drink and Louis became once more the broadly smiling barman who was everybody's friend.

By 1.30, the voices were louder, the laughter longer, and everyone seemed to be telling stories at the same time. Lunch was late. Robert Cornwallis was both nervous and angry, but as his temperamental chefs were explaining, food served outside takes longer to prepare, and they had both their reputations to protect and his standards to maintain. Cornwallis had spoken several times to Herr Pabst, who seemed pleased with the way his important guests were enjoying themselves. He adopted a professional smile and began inching his way through the groups pressing round the bar tables.

Christopher Quinn was sprawled on a deckchair in one of the little green-striped tents, away from the main crowd. Next to him was the shapely body of Maggie Lawrence, lying back with her feet crossed. Beside them was a bucket of ice and a bottle of champagne.

In the past few days, Quinn had discovered something in Maggie which she had not revealed to many people. As she began to talk, he had been surprised, then pleased, to find that the girl had more than a heart – she had a mind. Now she appeared to be giving, for nothing but the pleasure of his company, in and out of bed, everything for which she had previously been paid handsomely.

They could not ignore the noise of the large party, but in front of them the sea was the focus of their attention. Within the coolness of the tent, they had created their own peace, privacy and comfortable silence.

'So peaceful,' murmured Maggie.

Quinn leaned across and kissed her on the lips. 'Let's go to lunch,' he said softly. Maggie Lawrence and Christopher Quinn stood up, but neither of them ever made it to the table.

The moment Bobby Avery realized that people had begun to sit down at the long tables spaced out around the swimming pool, he remembered that his bladder was full. He slurred an 'excuse me' to a princess and nodded at Sullivan, playing with the trio, who was already worried about the condition of his young American lover. Bobby was not a pretty sight. He had insisted on attending the party, but as he began to make his way unsteadily through the moving crowds, dishevelled and drunk, the alcohol in his system heightening the colour of his damaged face, Sullivan became positively alarmed.

Mynheer Van der Voors's eyes followed the battered young man. The Dutchman was drinking far too much champagne, but could still assess

113

the calibre of those with whom he was consorting. Here, around this large swimming pool, in a millionaire's environment, were the minds and suppliers behind the armoured fist of Hitler's Third Reich and Mussolini's Fascist Italy, the men who produced the raw steel and roaring horsepower of an all-conquering war machine. And here he was, Jan Van der Voors, a little Dutch Jewish boy, brought up in Haarlem and Rotterdam, competing for his share of the spoils. He found himself discussing the war effort generally, and specifically Hitler's phenomenal success both in peacetime Germany and now conquered Europe. Already there were guarded rumours that the Führer's attention had turned east, to Russia. Every one of these industrialists talked as if England was already defeated. Van der Voors refrained from comment. He knew the English and disagreed: in his experience, they always seemed to pack a punch when least expected. He decided to relieve himself and apologize to the young American.

Harry Pilikian stood on the edge of the steps above the beach and stared out at the Mediterranean. Evelyn was somewhere amongst the crowd and he was glad to be alone. Here he was, once again, part of a wealthy society oblivious of anything but its own pleasures. Out there, past the shimmering silhouette of the Rock of Monte Carlo, was the real world and war.

A gong sounded, calling everyone for lunch. Harry lit a cigarette and was about to turn and go when suddenly his eyes narrowed and he saw them. Like barracudas homing in on their prey, caught in the refracted light of a clear ocean, sunlight glinting on their wings, low over the waves the aircraft began to turn for their approach. Only then did the increasing roar of their engines suggest, to those who had begun searching for the source of the noise, that here was not friend but *foe*.

Ben parked the MG at the market on the outskirts of Monte Carlo, and he and Agatha climbed out and began to look for Eva Trenchard. She had seen them and appeared immediately.

'The gypsies only come here on Sundays,' she said, smiling. 'Did you get the cakes, Agatha? I'm afraid they might have been a little stale but I did my best.'

Agatha nodded. 'Thank you for taking the trouble,' she said.

Eva glanced at Ben then back at Agatha. 'I hope the birds enjoyed them.'

Agatha's expression was noncommittal, and Eva frowned.

'What have you bought?' asked Agatha.

'I love old china,' Eva told Ben, and showed him two beautiful cups with dark blue decoration. Ben grunted his appreciation. Eva smiled.

'Are you coming?' asked Agatha bluntly.

Eva shook her head. 'I don't think it's a good idea,' she said.

'Why?' asked Agatha.

Eva's smile widened. 'Because we can wander round the stalls instead. They seem to have everything that's getting short.'

'Boot black and silver polish, instead of a champagne lunch at the beach? Really, Eva!'

'Agatha,' Eva rejoined, 'I do not want to cavort with Nazis – is that plain enough?'

'I couldn't give a damn,' Ben said. 'I'll buy you both lunch.'

Agatha Parry turned her gaze to the sea whilst Ben looked at the Italian armoured car beside the road, a reminder that Monaco's freedom was fragile.

Exactly as Agatha began to smile there was a shout from the Italian commander in the armoured car. He was pointing over the crowded stalls, where people were buying everything from vegetables to bric-à-brac. In the distance he had seen a flash of metal above the waves. His driver started the engine. The officer was staring fixedly out to sea and began counting in Italian, then everyone heard the noise he had detected and turned to look. Someone screamed in alarm.

'Oh my God!' said Agatha. 'Please no!'

'Aircraft,' said Ben slowly, his sharp eyes peering to see first one then a second and third. On the sunlit wing of the fourth he saw quite clearly a British roundel. 'How the devil . . .?' he began, but never finished. Events moved too quickly.

'They mustn't,' Agatha whispered.

Realizing what was about to happen, Eva grasped her friend, who was in tears.

'They will,' she said softly.

Agatha tore free. 'They can't!' she cried, and started to run for the parked MG. Ben shouted to her, then Eva was moving too, and so was the armoured car – but faster.

The commander was only doing his duty. He had correctly recognized enemy aircraft and was already in radio communication with his army detachment at the harbour. He had given the order to proceed at speed. The woman who appeared in front of the vehicle apparently making for her own car did not give the driver a chance. The man running behind her was screaming: 'Agatha!' Momentarily she turned and her eyes found Ben Harrison, but it was too late. The armoured car driver braked hard but hit Agatha Parry head-on.

115

Chapter 15

Enveloped in the noise of twelve huge, powerful engines, the six Beaufighter pilots now changed formation into line ahead and the roaring became a crescendo as their throttles were pressed through the gate to maximum thrust. Not a hundred yards from their port wings was the great Rock of Monaco, and atop it the Prince's palace. The Beaufighters were now barely ten feet above the sea. One by one they turned fast around the Rock, and immediately to the left was the entrance to the harbour of the Principality.

Danny Morgan could see people running along the sea walls, and suddenly there it was, directly in front of them – their target, where Danny had moored so often before the war, to swim with his friends and have a wonderful time. Then his mind blanked out all other thoughts to become the steel and nerve of a warrior who entertains no morals, merely obeys orders. He sympathized with anyone who was looking down from the Casino Square as he himself had done so often. It would be an astonishing sight – and they had the grandstand view of what was about to take place. Then Danny forgot all else but the attack. In front of his guns, as the Beaufighters rushed over the waves, one thousand yards out and closing, were the palm trees, trestle tables, Olympic pool and packed crowds at the Monte Carlo Beach Club.

His thumbs moved to the firing buttons, and with a shock he realized that the bay was not entirely empty: to either side of him were what appeared to be an Italian cruiser and several destroyers.

'Jesus Christ!' he swore to himself. They'd been told there would be no opposition, but now it was too late.

He pressed the firing button hard. Six machineguns and four cannons spoke instantly and the Beaufighter shook with power. Now in front of him the tracer bullets were a fiery hail of jacketed steel pouring towards the target in the centre of his gunsight. All hell broke loose.

In the top-floor restaurant of the Hotel de Paris, 'Le Grill', with its panorama over the harbour and Rock of Monaco, several of those eating Sunday lunch were driven to their feet by the roar of so many aircraft.

As the first Beaufighter rounded the Rock just beyond the entrance to the harbour, rushing across the water so close to the surface that it merged with its own shadow, restaurant customers dropped knives, forks and napkins, pointed and gaped. Their immediate reaction was that this was a display organized by the Italians and Germans to enhance the grand party taking place on the outskirts of the Principality. Then, as a second and third aircraft appeared below in line ahead, someone shouted the word 'British' as he spotted the blue and red roundels on the aircraft wings. There was pandemonium. Tables were overturned, chairs knocked to the floor, everyone seemed to be screaming and shouting at the same time. They ran out through the tall open glass doors onto the terrace, some leaning dangerously over the edge of the balustrade, straining to follow the course of the aircraft. Now the last aeroplane appeared, and already there was the sound of heavy gunfire.

'Six!' shouted someone. People gasped in horror and excitement.

All heads turned east, straining to see across the top of the Casino, where tracer was arcing towards its target. The bullets struck amongst the packed crowds at the Beach Club. The first aircraft pulled up steeply then, standing on its wingtip, turned sharply out to sea and began a long curve back towards the Rock. One by one, the others followed, but now the Italian warships had recovered from their surprise. Flashes and explosions of black smoke engulfed the small bay.

From the upstairs restaurant terrace the crowd of mixed nationalities could see the whole attack. The third aircraft passed over its target, almost stalling on its starboard wing to avoid the sheer hillside rising directly above the shore.

'The beach!' shouted a waiter, above the noise. 'They are blowing up the Club!'

Danny's eyes stayed locked on the centre of his gunsight. His hands were clenched on the aircraft's controls, giving a base from which both thumbs had detached themselves to press hard on the red buttons operating all four 20 mm. Hispano cannons and six .303 Browning machineguns situated outboard of the oil cooler ducts. He was almost upon his target, fighting to hold the nose of his twin-engined plane steady.

People were running everywhere. He saw the two flags, both huge, one with a Nazi swastika, the other with the Fascist emblem. There was a troop of Italian soldiers behind the long trestle tables beside the pool. The civilian guests, predominantly men, in dark suits, were falling beneath his guns. Then Danny was over the target and for a split second feared that his aircraft would not climb and he would crash directly into the long magenta-coloured annexe of the Beach Hotel.

Suddenly, obediently, as his thumbs released the red buttons, silencing the guns, the nose of the Beaufighter lifted and he turned the aircraft on its starboard wingtip. Above the screaming engines, Danny heard his crewman Duffy bellowing obscenities into the intercom from sheer tension. Then they were over the narrow peninsula, past the house above the beach, and droning out to sea. Immediately Danny dropped again to wave height as black puffs of anti-aircraft fire burst all around. He could see the flight following his course straight into the Monte Carlo Beach, between the Italian warships.

'Talk about the bloody valley of death!' shouted Duffy. Danny Morgan was too intent watching the aircraft in their approach to reply.

'Do we have to do that again?' asked Duffy nervously.

'Well, we've come a long way, sergeant,' said Squadron Leader Danny Morgan calmly, above the roar of the twin Hercules. 'It would be a shame not to.'

'I don't think those Eyeties like this one little bit,' said Duffy quickly.

'Neither do I,' said Danny Morgan.

'No, sir!' snapped Duffy Kelly, then shouted: 'Jock's got the flag!' As a fourth Beaufighter passed over the target, the great red flag with its black swastika on a white circle could be seen billowing down over the tables below. Part of it fell into the swimming pool.

As a fifth aircraft raced over the waves between the Italian warships, it seemed to get caught in a grid, almost a web of enemy tracer. Smoke appeared from one of its engines.

'They've hit Sergeant White!' screamed Danny Morgan's observer.

Danny snapped on the RT. 'Snowy!' he bellowed, 'Snowy!'

'Just coming!' shouted Sergeant White. In his voice was the laughter of nervous excitement. It was cut off instantly. Danny watched thunderstruck as Italian crewmen found their target. The Beaufighter exploded in a terrible ball of fire.

The last aircraft passed right through the billowing smoke and falling wreckage, then flattened out low over the sea as Danny Morgan turned again beyond the Rock of Monaco. The pilots were shouting into their RTS.

'Snap to!' commanded Danny. 'Here we go again!'

Standing on the steps above the beach with a clear view out to sea, Harry Pilikian's first reflex when he saw the sun flash on the distant moving objects and identified approaching aircraft had been to think of them as an Italian or German display.

They were coming directly towards him between several warships moored offshore. One mile out, its silhouette dark and looming against the sun, Harry saw an Italian cruiser, her upperworks sleek and ominous. Further in, eight hundred yards off the beach, were several Italian destroyers with rakish lines. The aircraft were dangerously low for a mere fly-past.

Out of the corner of his eye, he could see Maggie Lawrence and Christopher Quinn walking along the pathway leading in his direction. Louder every second, the drone of the aircraft increased to a whine, then a roar. People behind him had begun to shout. For several moments Harry was paralysed until he saw light flickering from beneath the fuselage of the first onrushing aircraft and along the leading edges of each wing. He threw himself headlong off the steps onto the white pebbles six feet below. Immediately above his head passed what sounded like a train rattling deafeningly at full speed down Manhattan's west side.

The fall almost knocked him out, but Harry rolled over in time to catch a glimpse of the pale-blue underside of the first aircraft, then it was gone and a second aeroplane was approaching, huge, sinister and deadly. He spread himself out flat, pressing on his knees and elbows, fighting the shifting pebbles, crawling quickly towards the sea. He was bruised and bleeding from the fall and gritted his teeth at the pain; nothing mattered but to make it into the water and survive.

Sullivan had been waiting impatiently for the band to finish playing. He was about to strike up himself when he glanced casually towards the sea, and the head-on silhouette of a roaring aeroplane dictated to sheer instinct that even if this was part of the fun and games prepared as an Axis cabaret, he would take no chances. He dropped from his stool at the piano with a scream. His last thought was for his lover, Bobby Avery.

Sullivan was lucky. The upright piano was lacerated by .303 machinegun fire, and several bullets passed right through its heavy bulk, ripping into the fabric of the seat where he had been sitting only seconds before. The Beaufighter's four 20 mm. Hispano cannons scythed into the musicians, churned across the swimming pool into the military band and traced their way through parallel tables into a line of Italian soldiers standing in front of the Beach Hotel annexe.

One of a group of Italian officers in the small lobby of the Beach Hotel heard the roaring engines outside, and through the large windows opening on to the terrace he saw the first aircraft, dark, swift and menacing, as it opened fire. He threw Evelyn Martineye to the carpet and lay on top of her as glass shattered all about them. They too were luckier than most of those outside.

Louis spotted flickering light from the approaching machine just in time, screamed to Jean-Pierre and jumped straight into the Olympic swimming pool. As he came to the surface and began thrashing about, two bodies fell on top of him. The sound of machineguns reverberated everywhere, and tracer from the cannon fire passed directly over his head. Then there was a huge rush of air and a black shadow roared above the Monte Carlo beach. The whole place was a shambles of broken bodies and screams of terror.

Bobby Avery had been accosted in a brief confrontation with Van der Voors outside the toilet. He was drunk, and the sudden noise confused him, but he had all the luck of the Irish that Sullivan wished for him when with bullets whistling all around he actually survived the first pass. Then the second aircraft was upon them. Sullivan yelled at the top of his voice: 'Down, boy! Down!!' and Bobby actually began to bend at the waist, instinctively reacting to his lover's voice, but it was too late, he was literally cut in half by cannon shells. The whole thing happened so fast he didn't even scream.

For Sullivan the horror was too much. He lost all sense of self-preservation and, shaking his head in disbelief, began to get up. Again he was lucky. The piano was hit a second time by a fusillade of bullets which lifted it into the air to land with stunning force on top of him.

As the first aircraft passed in front of Quinn and Maggie, they fell flat on the path. Only as the third aircraft began to spray fire at the tents directly behind them did Quinn see Pilikian crawling towards the comparative safety of the sea and decide to do the same.

'Run!' he screamed to Maggie. They leapt to their feet, jumped from the pathway onto the beach several feet below, and began to stumble across the large white pebbles towards the calm waters where now there were swirls of foam from the cannon and machinegun fire. The fourth aircraft had begun its run in through a barrage of flak; the sky filled with great puffs of black smoke. Maggie screamed. She had broken both high heels off her shoes and fell awkwardly to her knees.

'Come on!' bellowed Quinn, and dragged her to the shoreline. The aircraft began firing. Huge pillars of white foaming water appeared, rising and cascading as shells and bullets cut a path to their target.

Maggie rolled onto her back screaming, her hand slipped from Quinn's and he fell away from her into the waves. In panic Maggie staggered to her feet. Immediately four bullets passed through her legs, one entered her left arm, and another hit her in the shoulder with such force that she was spun around then hurled backwards to lie half in and half out of the churning water.

Beside the pool was an extraordinary scene of carnage. The German and Italian industrialists at the main tables facing directly towards the Rock of Monaco had mostly been killed outright. Others who moved and crawled continued to be hit again and again. The huge Nazi flag was torn from its pole and billowed down over the bodies into the swimming pool.

In the car park, chauffeurs hid beneath their cars as bullet holes appeared all round, penetrating the crafted chassis. Hispano Suizas, Mercedes and Bugattis were punctured in a hundred places. A large old Peugeot shuddered then blew up.

Making its approach ten feet above the sea, the fifth Beaufighter was surrounded by black puffs of smoke from the anti-aircraft guns of the

Italian warships. The pilot ignored them and began firing, two hundred yards out from the beach. A long line of running Italian soldiers, silhouetted perfectly in front of the hotel annexe, gave Snowy White a perfect target. The soldiers were knocked down like pipes in a sideshow. Then the aircraft was hit and, trailing smoke, passed over the swimming pool to make its wingtip turn above the house on the beach peninsula, where it was almost obliterated by the deadly flak. For a split second, it seemed to stop still, hanging helpless as the Italians found their mark with shell after shell; the next moment the Beaufighter exploded with deafening force and pieces of wreckage fell away from black smoke which curled round the edges of yellow and white flame.

Doctor Solomon, sprawled close to an overturned table beside the pool, just had time to pray for continued good fortune before his large frame jumped mightily and he squeezed his eyes tight as the explosion sounded directly above.

Robert Cornwallis and his wife pressed themselves to the tiled floor of the open-air restaurant. Jenny Cornwallis's sharp nails dug deep, through her husband's suit and shirt, while she screamed into his ear. Oblivious to her, he lay curled, knees tucked against his chest, head between his elbows.

Major Pabst was spreadeagled behind a pillar, part of an arcade which decorated one side of the annexe. His eyes blazed. He was a soldier of the Third Reich and somebody had betrayed him. This was now *total* war, and if the British wanted it that way, they would have it.

The screams of the mortally hit and groans of the wounded mingled with shouts and pleas for help. German, Italian and French voices made blood-curdling sounds which travelled from the pit of the stomach. Pabst glanced at de Salis the banker, prone and trembling beside him as bullets smacked sickeningly into the stucco wall behind. Erich Held, lying next to the Swiss, was as calm as Pabst, his eyes staring above, straining to follow the British aircrafts' course as they roared overhead. For the moment, here below, they were helpless, and it was not a pleasant experience. His lips were pressed tight but his face was impassive. A soldier, like Pabst, he watched and waited for it to finish. The American woman, Francie Pinkerman, was cut down directly in front of them as the fifth aircraft started firing.

Then both men saw Jan Van der Voors. Pabst instantly began to move but was stopped by Held.

'No,' hissed Pabst then screamed: 'No!' His voice was lost as the fifth aircraft began firing. The Dutchman, who had been trying to run for the safety of the arcade, was riddled with bullets then carried off his feet by the impact of the cannon shells. Like a broken puppet, his white suit staining with blood, he hit the tiled terrace and crumpled into a heap.

Pabst glanced again at de Salis, who, frozen with fear, saw nothing.

That was the moment the Beaufighter exploded with an ear-splitting sound right above them, exactly as the last approaching plane began firing. Pabst saw the bright ball of flame which destroyed an enemy pilot but could only think of diamonds and began to curse.

The sixth aircraft passed directly through the falling wreckage above the house on the peninsula and the sound of its engines merged with other distant droning and the frightening barrage coming from the Italian warships' guns as they followed the five remaining aircraft in their arc out to sea towards the Rock Monaco.

A voice screamed: '*Sie kommen zurück!*' The survivors of the attack, moving unsteadily, warily, from their prone positions or hiding places, saw sunlight glinting again on the Beaufighters' wings low over the surface of the sea in the distance, as they began to turn for a second pass.

In the street beside Monte Carlo's market, Ben Harrison cradled Agatha Parry in his arms. The armoured car had backed up and rapidly driven off after shouts of alarm and abuse from the Italian commander. Eva had taken the MG to get an ambulance directly from the hospital, knowing that shortly it would be impossible. Ben was in anguish, whispering to Agatha as she stared silently into his eyes. In the distance the sounds of battle were unmistakable.

Tears were streaming down the Englishwoman's face. Her breathing was shallow and blood was seeping through her pretty pink frock. Her mouth began opening and closing, trying to speak. Reading her lips, Ben thought she was repeating: 'It was me. It was me.'

An explosion came from across the water and Ben turned his head to where the crowds were still running to see the spectacle. He could hear the continuing pom-pom-pom of Italian ack-ack, the roaring engines and machineguns of the British planes which went on and on, then finally a droning noise which left only a whining in his ears.

'It was me, Ben,' whispered Agatha hoarsely, and he heard the words clearly before an approaching ambulance siren blotted out all sound.

'There, there,' he mouthed, 'everything will be all right now,' and kissed her softly on the forehead.

The second pass of the five Beaufighters completed the destruction. Danny Morgan estimated that more than half of the guests at the Beach Club were dead. At least the Axis would realize now that no matter where they were, even in the comparative safety of southern Europe, supposedly out of range, the RAF was still in evidence, and far from finished. The scene below and the strong smell of cordite in the cockpit was proof of that. Danny smiled grimly and led the five Beaufighters into a climb to pass over the harbour as the full weight of the Italian warships' gunfire vectored on to the formation. In the next moment Danny's aircraft was flung from his control and he found himself upside-down, staring directly at the sea only a thousand feet below. There was no time to move before another gigantic force seemed to slam into the Beaufighter with a series of hammering crashes. Smoke appeared in the cockpit. The aircraft had been raked by Italian 30 mm cannons.

'Skipper, get out!' someone shouted on the RT.

'I can't see . . . can't see!' Danny Morgan heard himself screaming, then his hands found the controls, gave the throttles everything they had and threw the aircraft into a tight spiral which took him up a thousand feet. Air rushed into the cockpit through several holes in the side panels, and as the smoke cleared he saw that his port engine was on fire. Then the starboard engine seized altogether, the nose dropped and the plane began to glide. He knew that at this height he only had seconds to react and it would all be reflex. The barnstorming stunt pilot had done his work well; he had taught Danny many things in a sturdy manoeuvrable biplane. But here was no stunt machine, and without power he knew that if he made an error he would be dead.

The instrument panel was no longer functioning. He was losing height rapidly.

'Duffy, Duffy!' he shouted over the intercom. There was no reply. To starboard he could see his flight circling as their voices erupted on his RT.

'Skipper, get out, get out!'

'You go!' yelled Danny Morgan. 'Jacko, you take them out of here! Go! I'm ditching!' All around him were bursts of flak.

Manipulating ailerons and rudder, Danny fought to keep the plane level as, with increasing speed, he passed over the Rock of Monaco. He glimpsed the other four aircraft, which had dropped once again towards the sea and were beginning a run in to the Italian warships. He knew they were trying to save him.

'Bastards!' he said to himself, then on the RT: 'Jacko, I said get out of here!'

Danny could hear Jacko singing loudly, ignoring him.

'I love coffee, I love tea, but my little Arab Mustapha has got it in for me . . .'

As Danny began to glide towards the waves almost directly in front of the Casino of Monte Carlo, he could see tracer bullets zipping across the water from Jacko's Beaufighter at the Italian cruiser, and immediately black puffs of anti-aircraft fire all around him disappeared. The gunners were changing their target. One by one the other aircraft in the flight followed Jacko, roaring in against the Italian navy. Danny blessed them all, then concentrated on the difficulties of crash-landing into the sea.

Flames from the port engine began to lick along the wing towards him. Danny brought the aircraft down, keeping it straight and level, horizontal to the surface until the last moment. 'Brace yourself!' he shouted to his crewman, then there was no time for anything but life or death. The Beaufighter bounced once amidst a spray of foam. He dropped the tail, which ploughed into the water like a drag anchor. He grimaced – one for the textbook. He was unaware that the starboard undercarriage had dropped out of its engine nacelle. As the punctured wheel and broken struts touched, the Beaufighter seemed to leap to one side, thrusting the port wing deep into the waves. Travelling at over one hundred miles an hour, there was nothing he could do. The Beaufighter cartwheeled, plunging forward on to its nose. Instantly the flames were doused in the port engine, but the tail flipped up and over and with the forward speed suddenly contained by the density of the sea, the aircraft fell straight onto its back and immediately began to settle.

Upside-down, the sea rushing into the aircraft, Danny fought to free his straps. When they were finally released he fell headlong into the flooding cockpit. He scrambled to his hands and knees on the roof of the aircraft and crawled through the swirling water back towards his observer's compartment. There beneath him on the floor, now above, was the escape hatch – the only way to freedom from drowning.

The Beaufighter sank deeper into the water, the weight of its engines pulling its nose down. Danny was in a nightmare as pouring water filled the stricken plane with horrifying speed. His hands found Duffy Kelly's chest and the straps that still held him upside-down. There was blood eddying all about his body. Danny ducked his head, found the release catches of the safety harness, undid them, pulled with all his strength and Duffy came free, though his eyes were closed and his face white.

The plane was tilting further as he dragged his sergeant the few feet to the escape hatch. There he lay on his back, submerged in the water, and kicked out as hard as he could till the hatch broke open. Danny thrust Kelly's body out, then squeezed after his crewman, inflated first the sergeant's lifejacket then his own, and pushed away from the aeroplane out into the Mediterranean Sea.

Holding Kelly with one arm, he swam frantically with the other to clear the Beaufighter and the suction as it began to sink. He distinctly felt the pull as it went down. Then they were free and floating, directly in front of the Casino. He could hear the noise of a cutter approaching fast.

Danny blinked several times in the strong sunlight. Small waves smacked him in the face. Suddenly above there was a roaring sound. He craned his neck, staring up into the sky. One by one, despite continuing sporadic gunfire from the now damaged Italian warships, the four remaining Beaufighters of Danny Morgan's flight passed overhead, waggling their wings. He waved back at them wildly, then suddenly the aircraft turned and raced out over the sea, chasing each other to the distant horizon until they were gone and it was over.

Chapter 16

'Just ten minutes,' said the nurse brusquely, and ushered the Englishman into the hospital room, closing the door.

When Agatha Parry opened her eyes, the first thing she saw was Ben Harrison. He smiled.

'Hello, old girl,' he said.

'What time is it?' she whispered.

'Almost midday, Friday.'

'I've been dreaming.'

'You have to sleep a lot – they told you that.' Ben moved from his seat and sat on the edge of the bed, looking into her eyes. 'The doctors are very pleased with you. I told them you were a fighter.'

Ben swallowed and thought of Agatha's injuries, which had been explained to him and would be revealed to her, in time. He stood up to hide his feelings, and looked out of the window. There was the Mediterranean and a crisp blue winter sky. The sun was warm, everything looked bright and friendly. Below, Ben could see the small hospital garden and beyond it the Rue Pasteur. The land fell away sharply after that towards the sea. It had been terraced by the authorities to provide more ground for burial.

'Can you see the cemetery from here?' asked Agatha.

'Yes,' answered Ben. In the distance, amidst a group of figures in black, he made out what looked like a service well under way. The casket was being lowered.

Agatha tried to laugh, but it was difficult, and obviously hurt. 'My mother's buried there. I've often visited this hospital, and I used to look out just as you are doing now, and quietly wish her well.'

'You're going to be all right, you know,' said Ben. 'Really.'

'Am I?' Agatha's eyes were wide, searching his face for the truth.

'Do you remember what happened?' he asked.

'I was stupid.'

'Careless.' He sat down on the edge of the bed once more and the two of them looked at each other in silence.

Agatha spoke eventually.

'And the Beach Club?'

'Most of the survivors have been taken back to San Remo. Those aircraft came right out of the blue and caused havoc. If that's the way this war's going to be fought, I'd dearly like to stay out of it. I thought we were far enough away down here, but it looks as if nowhere's safe.'

'Nowhere,' said Agatha softly.

She looked around the private hospital room, where flowers gave colour to the stark white walls. There was a knock and a nurse opened the door.

'Five more minutes, Mr Harrison.'

Ben nodded and the door closed.

'What are they doing to me?' asked Agatha, and tears appeared in her eyes.

Ben took her hand. 'They've kept you partially sedated since they operated on Sunday, that's all. You've broken quite a few bones, but they assure me you're very lucky.'

'But I still don't feel anything,' said Agatha. 'No pain.'

'You will, eventually. They've given you morphine.'

Agatha turned her head away. As she began to gather her strength and spirit she had time to think. The ruthless logic of the raid emphasized her own responsibilities. She had learned that there were no easy moral answers to the dilemmas created by war.

Ben had visited the hospital as often as he was allowed, several times with Eva Trenchard. Days had elapsed since the accident and air attack. Only now, with her condition improving, did he feel that Agatha might answer what had been troubling him.

'Listen, old girl,' he said, lowering his voice and leaning towards her. 'Before you passed out you kept repeating "It was me."'

She was silent for a moment.

'I only made a report. Decisions were made by others.'

'What others?' asked Ben.

'People in London.'

'By God, Aggie, how did you get mixed up in anything like that?'

She smiled and touched his cheek gently. 'Don't you love England?'

Ben became agitated. She was putting him on the spot, and he didn't like it.

'Weather's bloody awful.'

'And everything she stands for?'

'The working classes are getting too bloody cocky for my liking.'

'Could you imagine German uniforms in Piccadilly, Ben? Nazis in Westminster, Hitler in Parliament?'

'You know the answer to that,' said Ben angrily. 'What do you want me to do? Pick up a broom and beat back a regiment of Panzers with bloody bristles?'

Agatha touched his chin with delicate fingers. 'You look like an old dog,' she began to laugh. 'Where was it you lived in London?'

Ben ran a hand through his grey hair. 'You came there once,' he said, 'when you were staying at the Savoy. Do you remember?'

'Yes I do. In Jermyn Street,' said Agatha.

'Only ever there a couple of months of the year now,' said Ben. 'My brother uses it mostly, when he comes up to town. Spend most of my time travelling – well, you know that. But I suppose the flat is still home.'

'Do you own it?'

'Yes.'

'Could you describe the interior in detail?'

'My mind's not quite gone addled yet, Aggie.'

'Well, that's a start,' she sighed. 'And you'll need a code name.' She paused and smiled. 'Do you remember a young girl with great expectations, running towards you on a station platform?' Ben nodded. 'I was breathless,' said Agatha, 'and in love.'

Ben became embarrassed. 'King's Cross,' he said. She nodded. 'What are you getting at?' He spoke bluntly to conceal his shyness.

'You told me you were a signals expert in the army.'

'That's right.'

'I want you to do something for me.'

'You know I'll do anything, Aggie.'

There was a knock on the door, and the nurse reappeared.

'Come tomorrow. I'll tell you then,' whispered Agatha. He stood up. 'It's not for me, Ben. Remember that. It's for all of us. Everything we ever believed in: our country, your home, England.'

'Irish eyes,' said Maggie Lawrence.

Christopher Quinn was sitting on the edge of her hospital bed.

'My father had eyes like yours,' said Maggie, and her face clouded at the memory. Quinn grasped her hand and squeezed it tenderly as Maggie's eyes filled with tears.

The young Irishman had only grazed his temple during the attack, although he had suffered some loss of vision, which a specialist had already diagnosed as temporary. Maggie Lawrence had been badly wounded and had needed immediate surgery, followed by two days in intensive care, before she was given a private room and allowed guests. Only Christopher Quinn had come, and the doctors noticed a marked improvement in her condition after his daily visits.

'My father was Mexican,' Maggie said. 'He played the guitar.'

'Don't all Mexicans?' asked Quinn.

Maggie smiled: it was a standard retort. 'He was different,' she said, 'very different. He was a composer. He was a marvellous man.' Suddenly she laughed. 'I suppose every girl has a something about her father.' She reached up and touched Quinn's face.

'My father wanted to be a priest.' Quinn's eyes twinkled. 'Imagine! He was a devout Catholic.'

'My father was Jewish,' said Maggie softly.

In the hospital corridor, someone wheeled a trolley past the room. Quinn looked through the window at the sparkling sea outside, waiting for the noise to subside, remembering his own father.

When it was time to leave, Christopher Quinn made sure that Maggie was comfortable, promised to return the following day, thanked the waiting nurse, then stepped out of the room. He stood for a moment in the corridor, smelling the strong antiseptic that made him abhor hospitals. At least Maggie was still alive. The British aircraft had killed so many others. 'Bastards,' he said to himself. His father had been a devout Catholic, he had told Maggie. He had not said that he had been hanged by the English in 1919. That was a story no one would be told, not even a whore who was giving more than he had anticipated and for whom he was beginning to feel more than was sensible.

Christopher Quinn walked the length of the corridor and came to the lift. He waited a few moments before the gates opened and he stepped in to join another man. Quinn recognized Ben Harrison from the bar at the Hotel de Paris and nodded an acknowledgement. They had nothing to say to each other, so when the lift reached ground level not a word had been spoken. Cigarettes had been offered but each preferred his own brand. Harrison pulled back the gates and motioned to the Irishman to go first, which he did, then turned to ask for a light. Ben flicked his lighter again, and stared into the Irish eyes.

Quinn smiled. 'Thank you,' he said, as the two men began walking towards the outer door. 'Ever been to Ireland, Mr . . .?'

'Harrison,' said Ben.

'Quinn,' said the Irishman.

'Yes,' answered Ben, his voice hard. 'As a soldier.'

Quinn's eyes narrowed. He stopped and opened the door. Ben murmured politely, the Irishman grunted a reply and the two men left the hospital to go their separate ways. One had an appointment with Scotch whisky in an American Bar; the other with a German major on a Mediterranean shore.

Sullivan threw a handful of earth onto Bobby Avery's coffin, and with it went the best part of his life. They had sewn the body together then fitted out the coffin for burial. Before the lid was screwed down, Sullivan had taken a long look at the face of his lover. The song which Noël Coward had written eight years before came into his mind.

'I know it's stupid to be mad about the boy,
I'm so ashamed of it,
But must admit
The sleepless nights I've had about the boy.'

Words came to him in snatches as the grave diggers began shovelling dirt.

'In some strange way I'm glad about the boy. . .
If I could employ
A little magic
That could finally destroy
This dream that pains me and enchains me,
But I can't because I'm mad about the boy.'

Sullivan wept unashamedly. Bobby had loved him in his own way and he knew that nothing would ever be the same again.

The Catholic priest requested a minute of silent meditation, and heads were bowed. Perhaps things were made worse because it was such a beautiful day. Harry Pilikian stood apart, observing. Faces, tears beneath the veils, hands clasping tightly, skin stretched over the knuckles.

Someone coughed and a man's life was over. The group began to leave. Harry watched earth filling the hole in the ground, then understood that Sullivan wanted to remain, so he quietly walked away.

The pianist saw nothing through his tears, only the bright coquettish face of his youthful companion. The affection, the longing, the pain of love, gone with the sound of shovels biting into loose soil.

Harry drove from the cemetery to lunch. As he went up in the lift to his rendezvous in the Grill Restaurant of the Hotel de Paris, his mind continued to dwell upon death and he smiled sourly. Perhaps Evelyn had it licked: she didn't even give it a thought.

Evelyn Martineye had remained in bed for three days after the raid. Harry went to see her several times, but no matter what was said she quickly burst into tears and began describing her personal suffering, as if showering glass had been the worst of the attack.

Harry had seen the Italian colonel, Navara – Evelyn's saviour – several times. He guessed that Navara's attentions were more than casual and it didn't upset him. Harry had already started a countdown to the end of his relationship with Evelyn.

She had told him that she intended to leave for Lisbon as soon as possible, and from there fly to America. For an hour she pleaded with him to come with her.

'You'll get killed if you stay here. Please, please come back with me. It can be the way it was before, if we go back.'

'When the time comes to go, Evelyn, I'll know, but not yet.' Harry stood up and helped the reluctant woman to her feet.

'But I want you with me,' she said plaintively.

He watched Evelyn wiping away her tears with a silk handkerchief and saw her as if for the first time.

'You know, I think you really are lovely.'

Harry's smile was genuine, but her face hardened. 'No, Harry,' she snapped back, 'you think I'm convenient. You always have and I hate you for it.' She turned on her heel and strode ahead of him to the lift, where he caught up as she spun around.

'What are you going to do without me?' she asked angrily.

'Live, work, watch what happens.'

'And what do you expect me to do?'

'What you always do,' he replied. 'Seek pleasure.'

She tried to slap him, but he was too quick; he caught her hand and began to laugh.

'You really seem to take this war as a personal inconvenience.'

The lift came and the two of them stepped in.

The guests waiting below in the lobby were astonished as the lift doors opened. Harry's hand stayed firmly over Evelyn's mouth as she continued to squirm. He met the stares of the amazed group who watched him drag her upright and frogmarch her out to the car.

'What do you have?' Evelyn screamed hysterically, as he released her. 'You haven't a nickel. How will you pay your bills?'

'I have enough,' said Harry quietly. A crowd began to collect around the entrance of the hotel, obviously fascinated, as the woman stepped into the car then leaned out of the open window.

'Without my money what are you?' snapped Evelyn.

Harry smiled. 'Without it, what are *you*?'

She breathed deeply, her lips curling. 'I hate you!'

'You already said that,' Harry reminded her.

The car moved rapidly away around the Casino Square and the gathered crowd began to clap. Harry watched until it was out of sight. He sucked the fingers Evelyn had bitten, and wondered, as he tasted the intermingling of his blood and her saliva, if that would be the last memory he would have of her.

Just before her departure they had one brief telephone conversation. Evelyn, now calm, acknowledged Harry's pride but offered to pay all his bills, 'for old times' sake'. Harry refused, but privately she left a sum of money with the manager of the hotel to cover any problems Mr Pilikian might have – a guarantee for him, and for her the possibility of gratitude in the future. Evelyn always liked to keep her options open.

She left Harry the yellow and black Rolls Royce as a gift, stored the larger car, closed the villa and took Johnson and Danielle with her.

Colonel Navara, who had arranged the necessary passes, took them all the way to the airport at Marseilles, where there was a flight to Madrid and Lisbon. A short note, signed with a flourish was delivered to Harry's rooms, declaring her intention to return when the war was all over, and Evelyn Martineye had gone.

Sullivan took a last look around his hotel room as his luggage was wheeled out into the corridor. From the open windows he looked down onto the Casino Square, where the day continued as usual for everyone else.

Gently he pushed open the connecting door into what had once been Bobby's room. For almost a minute he stared at the bed and knew that life would no longer be the same for him. No one saw the tears he shed, standing there alone with fading memories.

In the American Bar, Sullivan stood in the doorway and made his farewells.

'But, Sullivan, you cannot say goodbye!'

'I said only *au revoir*, Louis,' the pianist replied, and kissed the barman on both cheeks. He shook hands with Jean-Pierre, pulling his dark coat with the astrakhan collar closer to his shoulders.

'But where are you going, Monsieur?' asked Louis.

Sullivan smiled.

'To Casablanca.'

Major Jürgen Pabst and Christopher Quinn walked slowly along the terrace in front of the Casino of Monte Carlo, conversing quietly. To an observer it would have seemed they were two friends enjoying an after-lunch stroll. They were not.

The Dutchman, Van der Voors, had been killed during the British air attack on the Beach Club without assigning the diamonds he owned to the company set up by Quinn. This fact made a sale to the Swiss unacceptable, as Guy de Salis had explained. Quinn was desperately trying to save his business deal before the banker left for Geneva.

'The responsibility is now yours,' Pabst was saying. 'You must understand,' he went on, 'that with the information you now have about the Gestapo you must solve our problem quickly.'

'But what can I do?' hissed Quinn, exasperated after many fruitless meetings with de Salis.

Pabst smiled dangerously. 'You must find a solution or suffer the consequences.'

Chapter 17

The huge engine pulled slowly into Monte Carlo's railway station, billowing smoke and steam. Harry Pilikian took several minutes before he could make out the bulk of Ludovic among the disembarking passengers, then he saw the slender figure and proud walk of Irelena Vondrakova approaching. She stopped inches from him.

'Hello, Harry.' The crowd surged past them.

Ludovic was impatient. 'Do not forget, Liebchen, we must leave tonight.' Grumbling, he walked on, shouting for porters to deal with their luggage.

Somebody bumped into Irelena, which caused Harry to take her arm. Both felt the excitement and smiled. Vondrakova's trembling lips met his, and the sensation dispelled the fears that arise between two people falling in love when they spend too long apart.

The chattering crowd started to thin out. People had boarded the train, and a whistle sounded from the engine warning of departure. The train began to move out of the station.

'I must be in Salzburg for a concert, Harry,' whispered Vondrakova. 'I promised.' She kissed him again quickly. 'We do not leave until late tonight. We have the entire day together.'

'You can't leave,' said Harry.

'I must,' she said softly.

Harry stared, holding her arms firmly in his grasp, as if compelling her to remain. She turned her head. He pulled her to him, feeling the warm body yielding in his embrace.

She kissed him tenderly on the cheek. 'It is a promise,' she murmured.

'Break it.'

'Do not ask that,' said Vondrakova.

Harry took the woman's face gently between his hands, searching her eyes, learning from her. She spoke quietly.

'You must let me go.'

'No,' he said, 'I won't do that.' She was about to speak again, when Harry put a finger to her lips and said: 'I'll do better – I'll take you.'

The rest of the day belonged to the two lovers. They discussed, argued, made plans, decisions, arrangements, and then changed them. Ludovic was determined to enjoy what comforts there were in travelling by train. They saw the large man to the station, bundled him into a dimly lit first class compartment to sit beside the huge hamper prepared for him by the chefs of the Hotel de Paris, and watched him wave mournfully as the train disappeared into the night. Afterwards they walked briskly from the station, holding each other as close as possible, and all the way back to the Hotel de Paris they kissed like children who have just discovered the pleasures of each other's lips.

That night they slept in Harry's suite, and at dawn they had a hurried breakfast on the balcony gazing out over the Mediterranean Sea. What was necessary for the journey, packed neatly by the maids, was taken down to the yellow and black Rolls Royce. The mild morning and bright day persuaded them to leave the hood down.

Harry had an American flag, given him by the hotel staff, pasted on the windshield. His neutral passport was only one of the documents necessary for travelling in Axis and occupied territories. Other papers had been obtained by Mauro at the concierge's desk; although Monégasque, he was born Italian, and knew the right people.

Vondrakova had a special pass from the office of the Reich minister for transport which would allow them to buy petrol. Armed with all this they drove out of Monte Carlo and Harry entered the real world, the world at war.

They crossed the border at Ventimiglia and stayed on the coast to Genoa, where Harry turned northeast. With their backs to the sea they began the long climb over the hills behind the great port that would take them onto the plain past Novara and into Milan. The winter sun lingered until mid-afternoon. All around them was the history of other centuries, plains on which knights in armour had battled with lance and pike; where great armies had fought with pageantry amidst the slaughter, becoming the inspiration of Uccello's masterworks. But here was a country now at war of a different kind, far from myth and legend.

Vondrakova sensed Harry's mood and against the rush of wind, the purring of the motor and the noise of the spinning wheels, the lovely woman swathed in thick furs remained silent, in awe of the images created by the magic of the countryside.

They broke their journey for only an hour, to drink local wine and eat a lunch prepared for them in Monte Carlo. Near Milan, they were stopped and diverted round the industrial outskirts of the city. With the sun setting in a bloody glow, darkness fell quickly and Harry turned north towards Chiasso, making for Cernobbio, on Lake Como, where they could stay the night at the Villa d'Este.

It was dark when they arrived. He drove past the guards at the gatehouse, along the curving drive to the great villa, once a palace, now a magnificent hotel.

The reception manager led them to the second floor, up the wide stairway which turned around tall marble pillars. Halfway down a long corridor he opened a pale green door into a suite overlooking the lake, where the water was sparkling in the moonlight.

'It looks like you have half the Italian army here,' said Harry, referring to the uniforms he had seen in the lobby.

The manager shrugged. 'It is war, Signore, at least for us.'

'Have they commandeered the wine cellar?' asked Harry, leaning on the balcony, gazing out across the lake.

'But no, Signore, that would not be permitted.' Accepting several American dollars from Harry, the manager bowed, glanced at Vondrakova, who was entranced by the view, and stepped to the door.

'Keep the dollars safe,' said Harry. 'You may need them some day.'

The manager smiled. 'My brother, Signore, has lived in New York since he was a boy. Perhaps I too should have gone. Now he is in the American army.'

'Then I hope you get the chance to see him soon,' said Harry.

'I would like that,' said the manager, 'very much.' For an Italian, even the expression in his eyes at that moment was treason. He bowed again and went. Harry and Vondrakova were alone.

He rubbed the stubble on his chin, uncomfortable in clothes he had worn all day, having become used to elegant habits.

'Forgive me,' he began by way of apology, 'I feel . . .' He stopped. Vondrakova's eyes were smiling.

'You look wonderful,' she said.

They bathed separately, dressed again for dinner and because of the unusually soft air that evening, elected to dine privately, overlooking the lake. The meal was served in candlelight on the balcony of their suite. The black-out was not strictly enforced here, so across the water on the other shore where the mountains rose abruptly from a silver sheen of reflected moonlight, lights like fireflies dotted the steep, wooded hillsides, merging with the stars above.

As they drank coffee, Harry and Vondrakova looked into each other's eyes over the small table. A light breeze ruffled their hair, and for a moment the candle guttered, throwing shadows across their faces.

Below, in the hotel, violins and an accordion were playing a plaintive melody, an Italian love song, expectant and sad.

Harry stood up and drew Vondrakova to her feet, pulling gently at her hands until her arms slipped around his body. He leaned towards her lips and the excitement between them was unmistakable.

They kissed. Again. And again. Then they moved slowly towards the bedroom. The candles went out.

The covers of the bed had been folded back by the maid, and between long curtains the french windows were left open. The air had begun to turn cold, the unusual warmth of the evening becoming true harsh winter. Harry closed the windows, then crossed the room to sit beside Vondrakova lying on the bed. They began to take off each other's clothes. He unfastened her sheer silk stockings, and began to roll them down. He knelt in front of her as she slid towards him. Her fingers dug into his thick, dark hair as Harry began to kiss her slender legs. He unfastened her dress, which fell silently to the floor.

Vondrakova leaned back, breathing shallowly, her lips parted. Harry's tongue brushed the soft down of her body until his mouth touched the hardening mounds of her breasts and delicately kissed first one nipple, then the other. Vondrakova began to move slowly.

'Dushinka,' she murmured.

He lay beside her for a moment, feeling her heart beating fast, and his own pulse racing as his hand strayed over her flat stomach. She gasped as gentle fingers found the soft blond hair between her thighs, and stifled a scream as Harry followed with his lips. Slowly she turned her face towards him and found his engorged erection. Her lips slid over its head to feel the warmth, hardness and pressure in her mouth.

Harry's flickering tongue moving regularly began to increase her own hardness as his hands grasped her small buttocks, kneading them firmly. Suddenly her body arched and for a moment she was rigid, locked in a curve of ecstasy. She seized Harry's waist and he turned towards her, forcing her hips down so that his erection, wet with her saliva, touched the moist flesh between her legs. Vondrakova stretched her arms above her head until she found and seized the brass bars of the bed.

Harry's fingers ran the length of her body to her hips, then, sliding his hands beneath them, he rose up and lifted her, slipping his shoulders between her knees. She gasped as he thrust gently into her. Clasping her hands, pressing them against the pillows either side of her face, his mouth frantically seeking sanctuary with her lips, pelvis pushing against groin, their bodies began a rhythm belonging to the ages.

'Dushinka!' rasped Vondrakova. 'Oh, Harry! Dushinka!'

The climax between them was an orgasm such as neither had before experienced or would ever forget.

Chapter 18

Jürgen Pabst looked up from his desk in a makeshift office in Monaco's prison.

'Is he conscious?' he asked quietly.

'Yes, Major,' answered the tall German.

'Good.' Pabst put down his pen. 'Let's go and see him again.'

He stood up and followed the man called Rudi down the corridor to the basement. They entered a cell containing a single bench, several chairs and a trestle table. No light came through the small barred window, but two light bulbs hanging from the ceiling shone dully. Pabst seated himself behind the table and switched on the desk lamp.

Now that German-occupied territories had been declared the Greater Reich, his Gestapo counter-espionage Section IV under Schellenberg was working with the SD foreign section VIA commanded by Jost, directed by Lopper and Tobias, which gave Gestapo Major Pabst more power. Even in this small principality, which remained officially, and to Pabst inconveniently, neutral, he was able to operate with only the minor irritation of discretion. He lit a cigarette and smiled. This single constraint would be unnecessary when the war was won and victory complete.

'Bring him in,' he said, and waited.

Having given his name, rank and number, Squadron Leader Morgan had revealed his American nationality. He and his crewman had been picked up out of the sea by the Italian navy. Sergeant Kelly had died of his wounds before the cutter returned to its cruiser, where the pilot had been held as a prisoner of war until he was handed over to Pabst. The Gestapo major had cut considerable red tape to prise the RAF officer away from the Italians, but finally authority had been granted. After initial difficulties, threats from his headquarters in Berlin had achieved cooperation. Although the Monaco police disagreed, Morgan now belonged to the Gestapo.

The pilot was brought in by two guards and seated opposite Pabst, who smiled genially at the dishevelled, unshaven character before him.

'Give him a cigarette, Rudi.'

The RAF officer had been beaten many times, and his face was bruised

136

and cut, as was much of his body. He moved swollen lips as the cigarette was lit. He had eaten nothing since the Monday afternoon of his transfer from Italian to Gestapo hands, and having been given only water, had become weak.

Pabst watched Morgan draw heavily on the cigarette. It was inconceivable to him that the man knew nothing. The six aircraft had arrived so suddenly – it had all been so well timed . . . it was obvious that the RAF had been informed.

Danny's eyes showed anger and hate. Nicotine seemed to give him some kind of sustenance. 'I've told you,' he said, thickly, 'I just fly planes.'

'And know Monte Carlo very well, I gather?' said Pabst. 'I'm told your name was familiar here, before the war.'

'That's no secret.'

'But it's a reason you were chosen to lead the raid. You knew your target well.'

'Perhaps,' Danny murmured.

'Obviously!' Pabst corrected him.

The two men behind Danny Morgan moved closer, and he winced involuntarily.

'If you are afraid, Squadron Leader,' said Pabst, and smiled expansively, 'you have only to tell us more.'

'I've told you everything,' said Danny quietly.

The geniality vanished at once and Pabst slammed his fist onto the trestle table. 'You have told us nothing!' he shouted.

Danny took a last deep draw on the cigarette, knowing what was coming. Pabst nodded to the two men.

The blow from behind rocked Danny on the chair. The second, from the side, threw him to the ground, where he rolled over groaning. In front of him, Pabst was on his feet, breathing heavily. 'Hang him from his wrists in the cell,' he said. 'We will return tomorrow.'

Rudi clicked his heels and motioned to the others. They picked up the limp body of the squadron leader and took him back down the corridor into a filthy cell with a high ceiling. Pabst followed, then stood in the doorway watching them string Danny Morgan from the window bars, so that his feet were several inches above the cell floor.

Rudi murmured in Pabst's ear: 'He will get some support from the wall, sir,'

Pabst nodded. 'We must do the best we can. That is our problem here, that we are not equipped.'

'If we could get him to Berlin, sir.'

'The one thing we cannot yet do,' snapped Pabst. 'There have already been enquiries from the Red Cross in Geneva and the Palace authorities here.' He glanced at the other German. 'The Italians have the mouth and mind of a vindictive woman. They have told everyone what we are attempting to discover.'

'That is unfortunate, sir.'

'It could be, for us,' said Pabst thoughtfully. 'One day it could be.'

Danny groaned, regaining consciousness painfully. Blood dripped from his nose and his lips were split again. Pabst gazed at him for a moment longer then turned away. 'We must improvise,' he said. 'Leave him until the morning.' The men left the cell and the door was slammed shut.

A bucket of water was thrown at the figure hanging from the bars of the high window in the cell.

Squadron Leader Danny Morgan's head moved quickly from side to side as he caught his breath, then opened his eyes. He had lost most of his circulation during the night and felt as if all the blood in his body had drained into his ankles, which were swollen and throbbing.

Gestapo Major Jürgen Pabst pursed his lips and spoke clearly: 'So you can hear me now?' Dull eyes focused upon the German, watching the man approach. 'Did you sleep?' asked Pabst. Danny Morgan said nothing. 'You have only to tell us how you came by the information which brought you here and you will be allowed to leave. A prison camp will be far more attractive than a basement in Berlin. I have never liked barbaric methods, but they seem always to be so effective. Now, who briefed you?'

Danny Morgan said nothing. The interrogator saw defiance in his eyes.

'Hold him!' said Pabst, and smiled at the RAF officer. Rudi and the other men crossed to Morgan, and in a moment the Squadron Leader was pinioned. Pabst stepped forward and examined the obstinate face. Beneath the grime and stubble the features were firm, well-bred, those of a good-looking playboy who had been in many magazines before the war.

'You are a handsome man,' said Pabst.

Danny Morgan's swollen lips moved. 'The Geneva Convention clearly states, "an officer in uniform . . ." '

Pabst's fist shot out with lightning speed, breaking Morgan's nose with a noise like a chicken wishbone being snapped. His left fist buried itself in the Squadron Leader's stomach. The two men holding the body did not even wince. Morgan's mouth fell open in agony, as blood flowed on to his filthy uniform.

Pabst stepped away and stared at his handiwork, then a sound from behind him made him turn to the open cell door, where a large young man stood at attention.

'Herr Pabst . . .'

'What is it, Held?'

138

'The chief of police, sir, he is here again with signed orders from the Palace. He has with him several Vichy French police, a Red Cross representative, and two Italian officers.'

Pabst frowned. 'The Geneva Convention,' he muttered to himself. So, they had finally come for him, this criminal flyer. When he spoke again it was with pure anger.

'Clean him up!'

Danny Morgan was removed one hour later by ambulance. His old friend Gerard, the chief of police, was first upset, then incensed at the captive airman's condition. Pabst only smiled and agreed that war was a terrible thing.

Gerard looked at the tall Germans flanking Pabst on the prison steps, two Siegfrieds bathed in sunlight, the image of the Nazi ideal sold to the world before the war, and bowed his head lest his eyes should reveal his thoughts.

'I am a plain public servant,' he said. 'I care about peace, protection and the law. That is my job, at which I do my best. I am responsible to the Prince of this little country where I was born.' He looked into the eyes of the German. Here was an adversary. 'Make no mistake, Herr Pabst, we may not have such mighty problems as the Third Reich, but we are much older than you, and have lasted so long because although we are very small we love our little country and will protect it with our lives.'

Pabst grinned and snapped to attention in a gesture of mock respect. The policeman went to his car and was driven away.

The Gestapo major began to walk down the steps with his men, then stopped before entering the shadows cast by the buildings below, and surveyed the magnificent sea view. He gestured towards the seemingly limitless horizon.

'You see! We have the world before us and we are dealing with fools like this policeman in charge of a country not one tenth the size of my father's estate. He says he is Monégasque, but at heart he is like all Frenchmen, a weak romantic!'

'It is not difficult to understand, sir,' began Erich Held, hesitantly, 'when you have been to Paris.'

'I have been to Paris, Held!' snapped Pabst.

'It is a very romantic city,' said Held quietly.

Pabst's head turned slowly towards the young man cast in the image of the new Germany. 'In your heart there should be nothing stronger than National Socialism. It is the before and after, it is the reason, it is the security of life.' His smile was patronizing. 'Is there nothing you cherish above all other things?'

Held looked out at the horizon. He was reminded by the brilliant

139

sunshine and cool breeze on his face of other places and different people. 'I love the mountains . . .' he began hesitantly.

'Mountains?' repeated Pabst.

'Yes, sir.'

'Well, I too ski,' said Pabst.

'Yes sir, but I prefer to climb.'

'Exactly as National Socialism has done in Germany. We have surmounted the Alps of opposition.' Pabst laughed, pleased at the metaphor. He inclined his hand and thrust it to the ground. 'Now, it's all downhill.'

Held remained serious. 'I like to breathe the air, sir. It is different up there . . . the feelings are . . .'

'There are greater things in our existence than the mere sensual appreciation of it. Is there nothing which touches you?' The men began to move on down the steps. Pabst's humour had become almost genial.

'I like to hear a woman's voice, sir.' The moment Held had spoken, he regretted it. Pabst began to laugh. 'Singing, sir,' said the young German desperately.

'Such a small part of life, Held,' said Pabst. He took out a cigarette and lit it. 'Women.' He pronounced the word disparagingly. 'Come!' The three Gestapo men stepped into the shadows.

Chapter 19

At midday, Irelena Vondrakova and Harry Pilikian drove out of the Villa d'Este along the shore of Lake Como until they reached Tremezzo. They took the ferry boat over to Varenna and continued along the Val Tellina, heading for Merano, where Harry planned to turn north to enter Austria and the Third Reich.

The following evening, Vondrakova was booked to give a concert in Salzburg, so they wanted to be in Innsbruck for the night and within striking distance of their destination come morning. It was late afternoon and already twilight before they reached Bolzano, surrounded by mountain peaks. The car began climbing until there was thick snow

140

either side of the road, the air had become rarefied and the temperature was down to freezing.

Vondrakova began to sing, with Harry following as best he could. They drank cognac to keep warm, became tipsy and told each other stories with much laughter. The road surface became increasingly hazardous but Harry drove on in the hope that they would reach the Brenner Pass and the Austrian border.

The clear night sky clouded over shortly before midnight, and it started snowing. When Harry found a solitary inn near the Italian border, set back from the mountain road, he decided to stop. The Furkahaus was owned by an old Austrian widow. She had lost her husband in the Great War and her two sons, both soldiers, were on occupation duty in Norway. The place was almost empty, but the atmosphere was cosy and warm. After a simple meal beside the fire in a wood-panelled dining room full of Bavarian trinkets and souvenirs of the Dolomites, watching the snow building up outside against the windows, secure in the knowledge that the Rolls was safely stowed in the barn, Irelena Vondrakova and Harry Pilikian climbed the stairs, went to bed and made love until they fell into an almost dreamless sleep.

By morning, the snow had stopped, the sun was out and the sky was clear. They started early. The car slithered at first, but after they had dropped down several thousand feet along a winding road, in awe of the spectacular view all about them, the wheels began to grip firmly and they arrived at the border.

The Italians – Customs officials, soldiers and police – were courteous enough. Half a mile further, at the Austrian border station, they were taken inside and questioned. The car was examined and their luggage opened. The guards were Wehrmacht soldiers, most of them in their early twenties, and when several recognized Vondrakova they all became extremely polite, some even asking for autographs. The two travellers were allowed to leave, and Harry was able to make good speed and time down into Innsbruck.

They reached Salzburg by 4 o'clock and arrived at an old Gasthaus called the Koblenz, perched high on the Gaisberg overlooking the city. Ludovic was angry at their late arrival, but was silenced by Vondrakova's obvious happiness. She assured him that all would be well, and she was right; the concert that night was a triumph.

If there was magic in the relationship between Harry and Vondrakova, it was because above all she remained a mystery. Her sexuality was not repressed, but constrained, given a framework by the image created partly by Ludovic and partly by her many fans, who expected her always to be the way she appeared on stage, cool and desirable, volatile but sophisticated.

From Salzburg, Harry took Vondrakova twice to Munich and once to Vienna, but was unable to obtain a pass for either Berlin or Prague, where she had to travel alone. He had begun to work with inspiration at the Gasthaus Koblenz. A piano had been found and tuned. Large windows of the lounge gave on to a panorama of the long valley in which Salzburg lay.

As winter closed in, each day developed a pattern. There were few sunrises, just a diffused light which heralded the morning, then huge clouds began to billow from the west, coursing eastwards, hanging low over the city, sometimes obliterating the buildings in thick flurries of snow until late afternoon. But the sunsets were spectacular, gilding the ever-present towering storm clouds with a fiery glow; then the red ball of the sun emerged briefly beneath the cloud layers, to sink quickly beyond the horizon.

The day before Christmas, they were snowed in. Only at twilight did the sky clear and first stars appear in the night heavens. To Ludovic's annoyance, Vondrakova had cancelled the concert she should have given in Munich, using as an excuse the metre and a half of deep snow that had fallen. A sleigh came from the city below, and wrapped in furs she and Harry took this 'troika', as Vondrakova called it, back down the mountain into the old town of Salzburg.

The Gasthaus was officially closed, and there were worsening shortages caused by the war, so the old couple called Herzog were prepared to cook only basic meals, but Ludovic, used to excellent cuisine, revealed that he had once been a chef, and paid the Herzogs to buy black market goods which he declared he would cook for Christmas dinner. Mindful of this, Harry and Vondrakova urged their driver quickly across the Staats-Brücke, where they entered the old town, travelled down the Alter-Markt and arrived at Residenz-Platz in front of the great cathedral. The candlelit service of Austria's second Christmas at war began. Massed German voices soaring to God disconcerted Harry Pilikian, until he looked at the glowing face of his companion, singing with obvious devotion to the music. He started to sing 'Silent Night', following the German text from the book with some difficulty.

When the carol service finished, people seemed reluctant to leave. Holding candles, they gathered outside the cathedral in the Domplatz, where several men were playing zithers. Hesitantly at first, the carol singing began again in the snow, by candlelight under the stars. People passed schnapps to each other and the small fire made for the zither players was enlarged as the crowd grew. Ardent voices lifted hearts; beautiful songs sent the blood coursing, warming them all as their cheeks tingled with pleasure in the cold night air.

Eventually the fire began to die and the players felt the cold in their fingers. Everyone in the crowd clasped his neighbour and murmured goodbyes before slowly drifting away. Many tears had been shed in fear of what the New Year might bring. Harry Pilikian looked into the face of Irelena Vondrakova and felt the sheer excitement of being with the woman he loved. Gloved hands linked as she squeezed his fingers. He took her in his arms and they danced across the square through the snow to the waiting sleigh. With a crack of the reins, the 'troika' was on its way back up the mountain road to the Koblenz. When they arrived, almost an hour later, the two lovers sat down beside a roaring fire at a table prepared by the Herzogs and began the superb meal Ludovic had created from them all. Afterwards the candles went out and the Herzogs, Ludovic, Harry and Vondrakova sat in the firelight, looking out over the city below covered in a thick mantle of snow. Only the distant mountains were ominous: huge black silhouettes dominating the innocent valley like slumbering giants awaiting the dawn.

'Germany,' said Harry quietly.

A log crackled in the fire, sparks fell onto the hearth and the evening was over.

When Irelena Vondrakova was with Harry Pilikian at the Koblenz, they loved each other, went skiing or made long excursions, always in the troika, whose driver appeared to prefer Harry's dollars to German marks or Austrian schillings. They even went skating on one of the nearby frozen lakes. When Ludovic took Vondrakova away, the restrictions which forced Harry to remain in Salzburg also enabled him to work hard. He often walked by himself in the mountains as the roads were cleared and a weak sun temporarily melted snow on forest pathways. In the old town of Salzburg, across the Salzach, he took coffee in the many houses set off from the squares, surrounded by centuries-old buildings. Here he would conjure up the past and examine faces, utilizing the little German he was learning to engage in superficial conversation.

He had been ordered to report regularly to the local authorities, and it was only these severe uniforms and immobile faces of Nazi power that soured the world of Mozart's music Harry was creating in his imagination. Those and the swastika flags, broken black crosses on white circles against a blood-red background, belligerently imposing themselves upon the old buildings, hanging incongruously between the painted guild signs along Salzburg's narrow streets.

Sometimes Harry felt almost like a spy, and smiled at the thought. He hoped that everyone around understood that he was a neutral, that it was his intention to be nothing more than what he often called himself to them, 'a Yankee tourist with an English car'. After all, he would argue, war was only a declaration, a torn-up paper, a rescinded treaty – what did it have to do with the people? War was politicians. Old Herzog would always listen, puff on his pipe, disagree and mutter the word 'blood'.

Harry had no answer to that, so he would return to his work and remember always that he was in love.

The Herzogs' son, stationed somewhere in Poland, came to stay on a five-day pass from his unit. He was an intelligent boy who spoke English. Their daughter, a nurse working in Dresden, arrived at the house the last week in January. She was very pretty, not at all shy, and flirted enthusiastically with Harry, which he enjoyed after long nights of concentrated work. Then they were gone, 'swallowed by the state' grumbled old Ruprech Herzog, and remained in a proud silence all the way back to Gaisberg from the railway station as Harry fought to keep the car steady on icy roads.

Whenever Vondrakova returned to the Koblenz from her concerts in occupied territories, Harry became as excited as a schoolboy. Several times she arrived by Mercedes from Munich, once in a staff car lent to her by a German general, but it was usually by train, which Ludovic preferred, his large frame fitting more comfortably into the upholstery of specially reserved compartments.

At the beginning of March, she had been away more than two weeks, in Moscow. She returned pale and exhausted, her face drawn. Even Ludovic appeared sobered by their experience in Russia.

'Officially,' he explained to Harry over a glass of schnapps in their rooms at the Koblenz, 'we are brothers. *They* drink vodka, and *we*' – he held up the glass – 'drink schnapps.' A glint came into his eye. 'But . . .' he glanced at Vondrakova seated on the edge of an armchair leaning towards the flames of a roaring fire.

'You must tell me about Moscow,' said Harry.

'It is cold, Mr Pilikian, as you see,' answered Ludovic. He poured himself more schnapps and sprawled in an armchair.

'The concerts were successful?'

Ludovic shrugged. 'My Liebchen was born in Russia. They love her.'

Harry looked at Vondrakova, who appeared mesmerized by the fire. Ludovic's fleshy face attempted a patronizing smile, then the expression became almost a leer. 'But I think they do not like her German parents.'

Harry paused, hesitant. 'Trouble?'

'My dear Mr Pilikian,' said the Hungarian and leaned back, half-closing his eyes, 'should the Führer of Greater Germany and the communist Tsar of all the Russias ever chance to meet, they would fall into an embrace and pat each other on the back whilst exchanging information about all their achievements.'

'With daggers drawn,' said Harry.

Ludovic smiled and finished his schnapps. 'No, Harry, bayonets.'

Vondrakova turned her face slowly towards the two men at the table. Her eyes were vacant, far away.

'I think the time has come to leave,' said Harry.

Soon after breakfast on Monday, 10 March 1941, with tears and hugs, Harry and Irelena said their goodbyes to the Herzogs and to Ludovic, who was staying on for two days before going to Berlin via Prague to make final arrangements for the spring concerts to which he had pledged Vondrakova. Several days of strong sun shining from a clear sky had melted snow on the roads until they ran with water. The temperature had risen and Harry felt it might be possible to make Innsbruck, and if the pass was cleared to cross over the Brenner into northern Italy.

The yellow and black Rolls Royce made good time, although it was forced to pull over on several occasions to make way for Wehrmacht convoys. Long lines of military trucks full of youthful faces staring curiously from beneath coalscuttle helmets at the American flag on the windscreen of the English car. The sight sobered both Harry and Irelena; by the time they were driving into the mountains beyond Innsbruck, both had become silent, each lost in thought.

The road was icy and hard-packed snow lay all about when they reached the border, towards sunset in the late afternoon. The sky was lowering, laden with dark clouds building into a storm.

Black uniforms of the ss had replaced all others, Customs, police and Wehrmacht. The driver and passenger were both asked to get out of the car.

'*Schnell!*' barked one of the officers harshly. Harry stared into the pale cruel eyes of the tall young man in black with a silver skull on his cap.

'Harry, please be careful,' whispered Vondrakova. Inside the Customs building they were separated, stripped and fully searched. The process was obviously designed to humiliate. Harry controlled himself and managed to remain silent.

Back in the office, seated together, Harry and Vondrakova watched an ss officer surveying various papers in front of him on a desk. There were four soldiers in the room, impassive, awaiting orders.

'I'm American,' began Harry calmly. 'We are not at war. All this is unnecessary.'

The officer spoke without looking up.

'You, Herr Pilikian, are on a list.' There was a pause and silence in the room. Harry coughed.

'You have my papers and residence permit.'

The ss officer, who looked remarkably like pictures of Heinrich Himmler, took off rimless glasses and smiled. 'Monte Carlo?'

'Yes,' said Harry.

'Do you know a German national who is living there, a man called Pabst?'

The blood drained from Harry's face.

After two hours of questioning, Harry had given a complete history of his time in Salzburg and the travelling he had done. It was only the welling anger of Irelena Vondrakova and her insistence on a telephone call to Berlin, using names which the officer recognized and indeed appeared to fear, that eventually allowed them their freedom. It was late evening when they were officially released and escorted outside.

Harry pulled up the hood, securing both locks against the windscreen before climbing into the Rolls Royce, where Vondrakova, wrapped in furs, was hunched in the passenger seat, her face a blend of fear and exhaustion. Snowflakes fell upon Harry's features as he stared from the open window at the ss officer silhouetted in the darkness.

'Where will you stay tonight?' asked the officer.

'As far away as we can get,' answered Harry.

'That will not be so far.'

'For that we must thank you,' snapped Harry. He started the motor and, with wheels spinning, accelerated cautiously into the night. The snow began falling heavily.

The officer watched the red glow of the Rolls Royce's rear lights disappear into the gathering storm. He had intended to obey certain instructions regarding Herr Pilikian, but the presence of Vondrakova, who was a celebrity, had hampered any accident that might have befallen the American in Austria.

'Eicke, Dietrich, take some men and a car with snow tyres. Follow them. Be sure they do not get lost!' He turned to the young officer beside him, a cruel face lost in shadow, only the silver skull on his black cap glistening in the low light coming from the Customs building. 'If anything *should* happen to them you must report back to me.'

'*Jawohl, Herr Hauptsturmführer!*'

Despite the worsening conditions, Harry Pilikian managed to reach the Furkahaus just before midnight. The old woman presented them with hot wurst, sauerkraut, beer and schnapps, bolted the front door and retired to bed. Only then did they both relax.

A fire was burning in the small grate of the bedroom upstairs when Harry took off his clothes and climbed into bed with Irelena Vondrakova. She clung to Harry and whispered: 'Hold me, Dushinka, hold me tight!' Her soft lips brushed his hard features and she pressed close to him. Her long blond hair fell about their faces, creating a delicious closeness for the two lovers, as they sought each other's kisses. The fire was dying and the candles they had each carried to bed flickered in the draughts which coursed about the room of the old building.

The isolation of the Furkahaus was emphasized by a sheer drop that fell almost half a mile from the terrace directly into a deep gorge through which the winter wind moaned. Timbers and joists groaned, sighed and creaked a protest at the roaring blizzard, but beneath the sheets and thick blankets it was warm and secure.

He pulled the covers tightly about them, as the wind seemed to intensify, howling louder than ever.

'The devil's organ music,' he whispered, hearing a loose shutter banging below, and the same insistent noise from unsecured timber. Several more minutes passed as Harry wondered what it would be like to be at the mercy of such a raging storm.

Vondrakova's lips gently found his and he sensed her passion. Somewhere he imagined that he heard a cry for help, plaintive, borne on the wind, lost in the snow outside, but he surrendered to desire and the love between them.

The boot that smashed open the door of the small upstairs bedroom of the Furkahaus was followed by heavy feet, guttural voices from the darkness, torch beams – then violence.

Harry had actually begun to push Vondrakova from him. His entire body tensed. Every system he had developed to survive screamed warnings, but too late.

Vondrakova was dragged from beneath the covers and thrown across the room, where she fell heavily into a corner. Harry only managed to put one foot on the wooden floor before the first blow hit him on the side of his face. The force of it knocked him out of the bed and against the firegrate. A boot aimed at his groin connected with his thigh as, instinctively, he bent his knees to protect himself. A second boot kicked his ribs, then hands dragged him to his feet.

Harry tried to control his panic and lashed out. His left hand hit metal, but his right connected solidly and he felt several teeth break against his knuckles. Oblivious to the pain, he kicked and again found substance. There was a scream and what sounded like a body falling. Then he was down again, warm blood flowing from his temple and an excruciating pain in his stomach. He was winded and sucking desperately for air.

Giant shapes appeared to be moving everywhere in the room. Torch beams played like searchlights before his eyes and glinting metal reflected in the fire glow.

Suddenly from the darkness he saw a polished boot travelling towards him, which seemed bound to connect squarely with his face, but his hands got there first, knuckles cushioning the vicious kick which broke only blood vessels where otherwise it would have destroyed his nose. At the same moment, he managed to bring his knees beneath his naked body. Holding on to the boot, ignoring a blow on his back, he straightened and stepped forward, hands ramming the boot vertically upwards into the darkness. There was a shriek and the sound of ligaments ripped as at the same time, with all the energy he could muster,

Harry slammed his right knee into where he guessed to be a man's groin. His victim fell limp, but the weight took Harry by surprise, and he was again carried to the floor.

Vondrakova was screaming hysterically. Two great shadows were astride her naked body, pressing it to the bed. Her legs were stretched apart and one of the shadows began to hover over her skin. Her screaming was cut short. In the glow from the dying fire and flashes from torch beams, Harry saw a black-gloved hand on her face and another on the white flesh of her thigh. Then the shadow merged with the woman's body, leaving only the sight of the legs spread out each side, and the dark mass began to heave rhythmically as Harry heard the sound of harsh, cruel laughter.

Harry could taste the blood pouring from his nose and coursing down his face, but at least he could now breathe through his mouth. Then his right hand, its knuckles already swelling where they had crunched on teeth, found and grasped the cold metal of a pistol. Simultaneously, from the corner of the room a flashlight beam rushed towards him. Harry braced himself and fired. The light went out. Again Harry fired. There was a sudden gurgling sound and Harry was splashed with blood. A man was stumbling, falling, breaking furniture. One of the black shadows raised itself from the bed. Harry changed the direction of his aim, but too late. A boot connected with his wrist and with a shout of pain he fell to one side, but determination would not allow him to relinquish his grip.

Now the shadow became a pair of massive legs straddled over him, kicking his body with feet that felt like sledgehammers. Harry managed to thrust the barrel of the pistol upwards, and pressing it between the giant's legs, he fired twice. These were heavy bullets at point-blank range. The huge figure was hurled right across the room and into the firegrate, where screams from the writhing body became magnified as the death cries echoed up into the chimney.

Harry rolled over as another shadow fell across him and a thrown chair slammed him up against the wooden bed. He fired blindly into the darkness, then all movement stopped and, breathing heavily, he heard only the sound of iron-shod boots running down the wooden staircase. Everything that had moulded Harry Pilikian's character, had created the man from a boy who had seen his parents cut down on a cold wet night, took him down those stairs of the Furkahaus after his assailants. He jumped the last steps and saw a fleeing figure run out of the gaping front door into the swirling snow. Following, Harry stumbled over the old woman, sprawling on the steps of her own home.

He could see a black car outside, its headlamps on, creating a wall of light in the blizzard. For a moment there were two silhouettes, the driver and the running figure. Harry braced himself, arm at full stretch, and fired the remaining bullets with deadly accuracy. His father had taught him well. The ss man scrambling into the back of the Mercedes was thrown against the car, then fell backwards from the running board.

Harry Pilikian's final shot entered the driver's neck and ear, but the car lurched forward. Harry started running, naked in the roaring storm, screaming in rage lest the Mercedes get away. He aimed again and pulled the trigger, but there was only a click; he threw away the empty pistol and watched helplessly as the car accelerated into the darkness. Suddenly it turned sharply and as the body of the driver, who died in that instant, fell against the wheel, the car broke through the road barrier. For a moment it poised on its chassis in the blasting wind, as if undecided, then it tipped, slid over the edge of the gorge, and fell to destruction almost half a mile below.

Harry stumbled back through the snow and found the ss man's body lit by a faint glow from the Furkahaus. He pulled the belt off the uniform and took the pistol out of its holster. Weak hands tried vainly to stop him, but the man was already dying. Harry put the barrel of the gun into the man's mouth and fired. The figure convulsed and was still.

Harry then grasped the old woman's large body beneath the armpits and dragged her back into the inn. He slammed the door and found himself shivering not only with cold but with fear and shock, but he was armed with anger and fuelled by revenge. Grasping a candle, which flickered in its delicate glass holder, ignoring all pain and the blood dripping from his head and coursing down his body, teeth grinding with rage, he ran back up the narrow wooden stairway to the bedroom.

The candlelight showed the men to be ss, two of them still alive. He crossed to each in turn, thrust the muzzle of the Luger pistol into their mouths and pulled the trigger. When he was sure that nothing was moving in the room and the only sound was nature's ineffectual storm outside, he took Vondrakova's limp body in his arms and held her close. With a sigh of relief, he felt her heart beating, her flesh warm and her lips moving close to his. Only then did she begin to cry.

Dawn came slowly. The old woman was not dead but badly injured. They cared for her as best they could, and she told them she had a doctor friend who lived in the little town in the valley below. Laid upon her marriage bed, she whispered his name as Harry pulled blankets over the damaged body.

Outside, the storm continued, but no longer with the intensity of the night. Awkwardly, bent against the driving snow, Harry dragged the corpses of the ss men to the edge of the terrace, lifted each body over the guard rail and watched them plunge out of sight into the shadows far beneath the Furkahaus.

Then they were gone. Harry and Vondrakova drove carefully down

149

the narrow road and stopped at the town in the valley, where Vondrakova wrote an urgent note in Italian for the doctor and put it with a wad of lire notes in the mail box outside the gates of his house. The gloomy little town was still shuttered against the snow when they set off again, but several hours later the storm was behind them and the car was racing along the roads of northern Italy, under grey early morning skies, gradually turning westwards on to the plain, making for sanctuary – Monte Carlo.

Chapter 20

The fortress of La Rivière, which is built high above Monaco, near La Turbie, commands a spectacular view and was once a formidable French bastion. With the occupation, the Italians turned it into an equally grim prison for Royal Air Force officers. The barbed wire filled the mullions of the crenellated wall. If the prisoners leaned forward so that their faces pressed against the sharp barbs, they could catch a glimpse of the Rock of Monaco far below, jutting into the Mediterranean.

The Italian guards grumbled almost as much as the incarcerated RAF officers, and those who could communicate in either language were able to establish a rapport which made life in captivity a little easier.

Initially, Squadron Leader Danny Morgan was grateful for his new quarters – anything was better than being in the hands of the Gestapo. Now, after several months perched on the coastal bluffs, with a pilot's vista of sea and sky, he was getting restless. All about him was familiar territory where he had played as a child, grown up during vacations, flirted with the local girls in the high meadows under a full moon. From early years the Riviera had become as familiar as Massachusetts and Rhode Island.

A barked command sounded across the courtyard and Danny turned from the view to see a throng of British officers. Mail had arrived via the Red Cross. Danny joined the queue to watch the letters being distributed, just in case . . .

'Morgan, D., Squadron Leader!' Danny reached for the letter, disbelieving. A young flight lieutenant grinned at him.

'I hope you haven't forgotten the bet, sir? We'll meet after muster, just to make it official.'

'Good,' said Danny and walked back across the courtyard to his perch overlooking Monte Carlo.

Danny had patiently described the surrounding countryside to the Escape Committee, in order to help anyone who actually got away, but his confidence had irritated a number of the career officers, who referred to him as 'the Yank' or 'the toy soldier', and resented taking advice from a playboy. Only his courage, obvious to all who had watched the Beaufighters' attack on the Beach Club, and the rumours of his resistance to the Gestapo, tempered their behaviour. The fact that Morgan was half American from a rich family, played polo, golf and tennis, was a yachtsman, a dedicated gambler and a celebrated prewar socialite, made him the butt of jokes – humour which became increasingly irritating. Eventually, anger had provoked him to swear not only that he would escape, but that within twenty-four hours he would be gambling in Monte Carlo Casino.

So the wager had been made with real money. Various officers put up their back pay since their capture against an equivalent amount from Danny Morgan. It had been madness on his part, but it had kept everyone in conversation for several weeks past, so at least he was contributing to morale if nothing else. As word got around, a total of twenty officers joined the list to bet against Danny, and he realized that after muster there would be even more. What had been a rash boast had become a debt of honour. The current joke was that the Yank could not now afford to escape.

Danny reached the crenellated wall, peered down towards the distant Principality, and opened his first letter in captivity. It was from his wife. He could smell her perfume on the paper.

Danny read the letter through, then read it a second time. He selected certain paragraphs and re-read them and only then did the reality of the letter's contents sink home:

Oh, Danny, I want to tell you – I must tell you. I went to London to the specialist – you know, Mr Loeffler, the gynaecologist, just off Harley Street. (I stayed with my sister Dorothy, you know, the one you never liked, she's so near.) Anyway, the tests proved positive. You're going to be a father.

He was going to be a father! Miranda was going to have their baby, and the father would be on the Riviera in a prison camp.

'That's where you're goddam wrong!' muttered Danny to himself.

From that moment onwards, there was no question whatsoever that Danny Morgan was going to escape.

At the beginning of the second week in March 1941, as he was entering his fourth month in captivity, while on voluntary kitchen duty Danny Morgan found himself in a small back courtyard watching two Italians unload some garbage down a makeshift chute. It ran beneath the wall and, if he remembered correctly, directly out onto a sheer drop. He walked directly across the cobbles to a small doorway which led to an allotment sixty yards square, originally a small vegetable and fruit garden. The Italians no longer tended the soil, so it had become overgrown.

In one corner against the main outer wall, neglected fruit trees protruded above a mass of bushes and scrub. Danny searched for several moments, glancing up now and then to where several Italian soldiers stood along the walls, too far away to see exactly what he was doing. He held his breath until he found what he had almost forgotten – the grille, thirty inches across, thin rusted bars covering what once had been the top of an old Roman water conduit. As a boy, led by some gypsies and local boys from La Turbie, Danny and his friends had climbed several hundred feet up the pipe, pushed through the grille and, reeking of slime, had taken apples from the trees under the very noses of the soldiers.

Danny Morgan plunged into the scrub and for a moment was lost from sight. He remembered that the Roman conduit, a disused drain, came out above a stream. As a boy he had found difficulty in climbing into it far below where the open stonework was overgrown and slippery. The angle looked to be about forty-five degrees, so, taking a small rock, he rolled it into the darkness of the opening and waited. Half a minute later there was still no sound from below. He swore to himself, knowing now that the drain could be blocked. If only he could get to the stream he was sure he would be able to continue on down the mountain and into Monte Carlo. He knew all the backstreets and several tunnels that ran from empty houses in France and entered the Principality. Official papers would be another thing. But he would take it one step at a time and leave, if it was agreed, that very night.

As Italian voices started shouting in the courtyard outside, he stepped from the bushes and ran back across the allotment through the courtyard and into the kitchen.

Danny informed the Escape Committee soon after dinner, and although they were sceptical they decided to allow him to try. As he said, if he were caught that would be the end to it. If he got away, others could use the conduit as a chance of freedom. If he got stuck in the drain . . . Danny smiled.

'Bury the remains with a pack of cards!' he said.

He had no trouble getting to the kitchen late that evening, but a couple of Italian helpers were still there, and he had to wait for more than half an hour before he was able to cross the courtyard, go through the door to the allotment and step into deep shadows beneath the massive outer wall. The night sky was clear, the moon almost full and the temperature near to freezing. Danny's face was hidden by a scarf, and he had liberated a pair of blue kitchen overalls for extra protection inside the conduit.

The rust on the bars of the grille was not as deep as Danny hoped. It rubbed off on his fingers, and as the flakes fell away he could see solid metal. He pulled at the bars but they would not budge. He swore. If as boys, so many years before, they had been able to . . . He crouched amidst the scrub, suddenly fearful that he would be spotted by the Italian soldiers who paced the walls of the Napoleonic fortress.

He seized the rusted padlock in his hand and twisted it, applying all his strength, but the metal only cut deep into his hands. The lock was a strong one. He could hear the prisoners singing loudly in their dormitories to distract the attention of the guards.

Two of the Italian kitchen staff stepped out onto the small cobbled courtyard and crossed to the open door leading into the allotment. Danny pressed himself deeper into the scrub, listening to their conversation. They stubbed out cigarettes and went back across the courtyard and into the kitchen, bolting the door. Now there was no way back.

Danny had to risk the noise. He picked up a heavy stone and brought it down on the padlock, which broke open with a dry snap. At once he pulled open the grille and slipped his body into the dark mouth, supporting himself with his arms over the lip of the conduit. The pipe was narrower than he remembered and, despite a drastic weight loss in captivity, his shoulders were too wide.

'*Come va?*' said a voice directly above him.

'*Bene, grazie.*'

Danny moved not a muscle. He had a clear view of the two Italian soldiers who had met on the corner of the great walls. He was less than ten yards below, in the deep shadow formed by strong lights that were switched on at night. Three minutes passed as the soldiers described in lurid detail an unattractive wife and a fantasy mistress, then switched to boxing and talked of the fight between Joe Louis and the giant Primo Carnera, which cooled them down. With a '*Buona notte*', they strolled apart.

Danny clearly remembered the conversation because it stayed in his mind all the way down. As he lifted his arms above his head to find some way to negotiate the descent, his foot, which had found a narrow ledge, slipped off, and immediately he began to slide out of control. His first instinct was to raise his knees, but they would not bite on the slippery stone. He pressed his elbows out but continued to slither even faster. He started to panic and it was an effort not to scream, but he knew that the drain might act as an echo chamber and already he seemed to be making enough noise to wake the entire fortress. He smashed through several obstructions, unable to tell what they were, almost overcome with the filth, slime and smell of old effluent, his face protected by the thick folds of the woollen scarf.

In pitch darkness and the claustrophobia of a nightmare, Danny fell helplessly downwards. He made two desperate attempts to break the increasing momentum, realizing with horror that there would probably be a grille below. He was right. But one hundred and sixty pounds of bruised muscle and sinew travelling at speed hit the bars, broke the lock and smashed the grille open. Danny Morgan fell into space, plummeting into the fast-flowing, freezing stream twenty feet below.

The water was deep enough to break his fall, but his legs buckled beneath him as they touched the sandy bottom. Then he was on the surface, thrashing out, gasping for air. His body rolled into the shallows, and he clambered out onto the bank, breathing deeply. He was free.

In the darkness, it took Danny almost two hours to negotiate the steep slope which led down towards Monte Carlo. By the time his hands found the first barbed wire, his overalls had almost dried in the cold wind, but beneath his uniform he was perspiring. He hid several times from guards patrolling with torches and dogs, but remained downwind so that the dogs missed his scent. Once he crawled past an Italian guard post where all the soldiers were inside drinking wine and playing cards. Finally, he came to some buildings on the French border which he recognized. He remained in the shadows of a porch, looking across through the barbed wire into Monaco, waiting for the covering sound of an approaching car. Finally, as an army truck rattled by in the darkness, he drove his shoulder against a wooden door. It gave way all right, but the deserted building was a shell without floors, and he found himself falling, to land with a thud in the basement.

'Damn!' he spat out under his breath, and tested his body cautiously. He had bruised his side. When he got to his feet he was limping.

'Goddam!' he hissed again, pushing what seemed to be a door in front of him, but it was not. They were loose planks propped up against the opening, which collapsed loudly. He froze.

After Danny's eyes became used to the darkness, broken only by a faint shaft of light, he limped across the basement and climbed a flight of rickety wooden steps, unbolted a door and stepped out into a back yard. Candles burning in a kitchen window gave him enough light to see that there was an alley beside the house. He made his way to the road, paused in the shadow and realized he was only two streets from Monte Carlo's Scotch Tea House.

Danny Morgan had climbed the back wall to Eva Trenchard's many times as a child, in the hope of stealing buns put out to cool. There was already a familiar smell of baking, and within, working in the half-light, was Eva.

He tapped on the window. She wiped the flour off her hands and peered towards the glass. The face was a blur, but she crossed to open the door.

'Well, come in!' she said brusquely. 'Whoever you are, you obviously know your way around.'

'Hello, Miss Trenchard.'

'Good Lord,' she said, 'you look terrible. What on earth have you been doing!'

Danny slumped on a chair, realizing how exhausted he was.

'Actually, Ma'am, I've just escaped from the fortress.'

'Well,' she said, and wiped her hands once more, 'it's about time. We'd heard that the Gestapo had you. Now, would you like a cup of tea?'

Danny looked into the reassuring face of the white-haired Scotswoman and nodded.

'Unless the Casino's open,' he said. 'Then I'd take you down for some champagne.'

'Now I think you've known me, what. . .?' asked Miss Trenchard, going about the business of filling a kettle. 'It must be sixteen or seventeen years since I first tanned your hide, young man.'

'I was eleven,' said Danny.

'Well then, that's long enough for you to know I don't drink and do not approve of gambling.'

'I used to think you sold whisky here,' said Danny with a smile.

'Scotch as in buns, dear,' said the unflappable Miss Trenchard. 'Now, if you don't mind, I'd like you to remove your clothes.' Danny opened his mouth to make a joke, but thought better of it. 'You look as though you're about my brother Julian's size, God bless his soul,' she said. 'He was always a natty dresser.'

'I don't think I ever met him.'

'No,' came the vague reply from Miss Trenchard in the adjoining room, where there was a tin bath under two taps. 'He was killed at the end of the war – the last one.' She came back into the large kitchen.

Danny stepped out of his clothes. Miss Trenchard threw him a towel. 'I'm going to burn those,' she said, pointing at the discarded uniform and overalls.

'I feel like a bad boy caught by matron,' said Danny.

'Your mother's American, isn't she?'

'Father,' said Danny. He wrapped the towel about his waist.

She looked him up and down. 'They've broken your nose.' Danny said nothing, but his eyes hardened. She held out some soap. 'The Gestapo?'

'A major called Pabst.' He took the soap.

'Wash yourself thoroughly young man, you smell like a bad Roquefort cheese.'

'French drains,' said Danny, and grinned at the older woman.

'Tush!' she snapped. 'How is that little Miranda of yours? Such a pretty thing.'

'She's expecting our child,' he told her.

Miss Trenchard wiped the soap from her hands on the long white apron around her waist, looking the young squadron leader directly in the eye. 'Then you'll be wanting to go home, won't you?'

Eva Trenchard offered Danny Morgan several suits, all of them smelling of lavender, all still beautifully ironed and hung as if awaiting her brother's return. She showed Danny photographs of a serious young man, with a young bride on his arm. Beside the happy couple was the slim figure of a pretty young woman, Julian Trenchard's sister.

'It was a long time ago,' she sighed.

Danny picked out a dinner jacket, outdated in style but of excellent quality and smart enough for any evening that did not call for a white tie. A crisp white shirt, bow tie, patent leather shoes a half size too small for him, slicked-down hair, a shave, and he looked like one of the smart crowd that milled about in the Casino Square after twilight.

He spent the day inside Miss Trenchard's private rooms behind half-open blinds, staring out on to the street, which was busy in the morning, quiet during the lunch hour, then, as the pavements filled once more in the late afternoon, thronged with people strolling in the spring sunlight of the Riviera as if war were a figment of the imagination. He had finished two whole packets of cigarettes when at 6 o'clock Miss Trenchard brought in four men. One was introduced, the other three said nothing. Danny was asked to retire to the back bedroom. An hour later, Miss Trenchard came in, and he sat up, obviously impatient.

'Have they gone?'

She nodded. 'You're in luck.'

'I'm always lucky,' he said brashly.

'Don't be flippant,' she snapped. 'There is to be a pick-up tonight one mile off the Principality. The fishing boat is under a Spanish flag but actually based at Gibraltar. There will be a full moon unfortunately, and the sea may be rough' – she paused, seeing Danny's excitement. 'Can you swim?'

He nodded, inhaling cigarette smoke.

Miss Trenchard looked at him dubiously. 'A dinghy will put out from the rocks at the end of the Fontvielle beach at exactly midnight. If there are any difficulties, you will be on your own.'

'I can't imagine there will be any, Miss Trenchard,' said Danny with a grin, 'not if you're organizing things.' He swung his legs from the bed and stood up, towering over her, but Eva was not to be charmed.

156

'Then exercise your imagination,' she said coldly. 'You are being fitted into an already complicated schedule and the men going with you are . . . well, all you need to know is that they have been waiting for weeks and *they* are *very* important.'

Danny's smile began to fade.

'This is not a jaunt,' she went on. 'The fishing boat is crewed by British Navy volunteers who will have travelled almost one thousand miles in extreme danger, and if the pick-up is successful you will share that danger on the return voyage to Gibraltar.'

'I understand,' said Danny soberly.

'You are lucky only because I was able to assure them that you would not hazard their chances.' She stared at Danny, her strength no longer a mystery to him. 'You will identify yourself with two words, "King's Cross".'

The RAF officer nodded and repeated them. 'Thank you,' he said.

'You have always had a certain reputation of which I have never approved.' Eva Trenchard stared at him. Uncomfortable, Danny thrust his hands deep into his trouser pockets. 'All I ask in return for what I am doing is that you do not jeopardize this operation or the organization we are building up here.'

'Of course not,' Danny said.

'There are others involved,' said Eva. 'An agent who is the mainstay of our operations here has been . . . ill, hence the delay which has proved so lucky for you.'

'So far, so good,' smiled Danny, trying to lighten the lecture. He hesitated. 'Can I go out before . . .?'

Eva Trenchard pursed her lips, looking the young man up and down. People in the tea room below were drinking, eating cakes and babbling in a variety of languages. The noise was distracting. She closed the door, which she had left ajar in order to hear any footsteps on the stairs, opened a drawer in a bureau, took out a sheaf of papers and handed them to Danny.

'They are in the name of Etienne Brizard. How is your French?'

'As always,' grinned Danny.

'It will be completely dark shortly,' she said, 'What you do when you step out of here is not my concern, unless you are caught. The Gestapo are not your friends.' Her eyes hardened. 'Do not come back here under any circumstances, do you understand?' Danny nodded. 'Dressed as you are, you will fit perfectly into the evening crowds. Find a quiet bar – you know Monte Carlo well enough – take a corner table and wait. In a few hours you will be on your way home.'

Danny took the woman's hand then kissed her on both cheeks. 'Until after the war,' he said. Eva Trenchard stared at him a moment longer, then stepped to the door. He followed her with his eyes.

'What did you mean, if I was caught?'

Eva Trenchard turned back to him and looked at the confident expression on his face. When she spoke her voice was quite calm.

'We would have to find a way to have you killed,' she said, and went out, quietly closing the door.

Danny stopped in front of the Casino steps. If he went in he brought danger to others as well as himself. If he did not, he had lost his wager. It was more than the money. The point was that he had boasted like a crazy fool to his fellow officers, and now he found himself trapped in an impossible situation. It was his honour that was at stake . . . His thoughts were interrupted.

'*Monsieur, vous avez votre* . . .' the Casino doorman began, then gasped, recognizing him. '*Monsieur Morgan!*'

'*Etienne Brizard, Claude, s'il vous plaît.*'

The two men shook hands.

'It is dangerous, Monsieur. There is much gossip – everyone knows you have escaped from the fortress. The Italians have been searching the hills all day.' He pointed over his shoulder and lowered his voice. 'The Gestapo are inside. Wait one hour, perhaps then it will be possible.'

'Where should I go?'

Claude shrugged. 'The Hotel de Paris, perhaps?' He saw people coming out of the Casino entrance and continued hurriedly: 'Go to Louis at the bar of the hotel. Wait there, I will send a boy.' He nodded to a group of figures emerging from the Casino and went towards them.

Danny strolled across to the side entrance of the American Bar of the Hotel de Paris. It was almost 8 o'clock.

Hugh Sullivan was perched on a stool, leaning against the leather armrest of the mahogany bar. He was drunk – not a novelty, but a condition that was becoming more frequent as the days passed. He had returned from Morocco, and was describing his time there to Louis. The bar was full and had been since 7 o'clock. This was his social hour.

'Tangier is decadent, Casablanca . . .' he paused, 'delightful. But Marrakesh . . . Have you ever been to Marrakesh, Louis?'

'No, M'sieur, never,' he said, and poured more cold white wine into Sullivan's glass.

'The Atlas mountains, standing up against the winter sky, snow-capped like chalk marks on a blue board.' He could see them with his eyes half-closed. 'Bobby used to say to me that we should settle in Marrakesh, buy a palace and fill it with friends. A fountain in the courtyard, lunches in the souk and exotic nights under the desert stars. Lots of Moors in Morocco, Louis.' Sullivan tried to laugh but the sound was full of sadness.

He looked with glazed eyes at his place of work. 'Tittle-tattle, Louis. Look at them all. Tittle-tattle.'

Outside it was dark, but the glow within the bar was warm and re-assuring, as was the alcohol – which, despite the war, never seemed to be in short supply. The black market was flourishing in the Principality, and everyone concerned with it knew that there would be a fortune to be made if the war continued. Already a number of refugees from occupied Europe had turned their hands to supplying the unobtainable. Every night they came into the bar, the men loud-mouthed, their gaudy women in garish makeup, looking like survivors of a disbanded brothel. Louis smiled to himself, surveying the room through the smoke of cigarettes and cigars, and thought how few of them he would have seen in his bar before the war.

'. . . Americans are different,' Hugh Sullivan was saying. He finished his white wine and leaned towards Louis. 'We have forty-eight states all in search of a country, did you know that, Louis?'

'So what are you suggesting for the United States?' the barman asked.

Sullivan arched an eyebrow. 'There is one solution, where Roosevelt remains the only sane politician in this mad world.' He paused, focusing on his audience. 'To fight Louis, fight!'

At that moment. Danny Morgan came in, crossed to the bar and sat on a stool beside the Irish-American. Louis recognized him immediately, but Danny put a finger to his lips. Louis' eyes darted to Sullivan, and he shook his head to warn Danny of the man's condition, but it was too late. Sullivan turned and stared at the new arrival. Recognition almost sobered him.

'Be Jesus!' he said.

'No names,' said Danny Morgan quickly, and clasped the pianist about the shoulders. 'When did we last meet? Here in thirty-seven, or was it in Argentina, thirty-eight?'

'Buenos Aires,' said Sullivan, eventually.

Danny shrugged, and accepted a glass of champagne from Louis. 'Buenos Aires,' he said to the barman.

Sullivan lifted his glass. 'Buenos Aires!' Louis joined them and they drank.

'What are you doing here?' He hissed.

'Getting out.' Danny, whispered.

'Whatever happened to that beautiful wife of yours?' asked Sullivan, dribbling. He wiped his mouth.

'She's going to have a baby.'

'Oh,' said Sullivan. 'Yours, I hope?'

'Mine,' said Danny.

'Congratulations!' said Sullivan. They raised glasses again.

'Where is . . .?' began Danny hesitantly, 'that friend of yours? What was his name?' He glanced at Louis, whose eyes were frightened.

'Bobby is here,' answered Sullivan, 'in the graveyard.' He leaned aggressively towards Danny. 'You're American, aren't you?' he asked, and placed a hand on the RAF officer's shoulder.

'Partly,' answered Danny, sipping champagne.

'I wouldn't want to offend you, but those British bastards killed my Bobby!'

Danny's blood ran cold when he realized what Sullivan was saying, but Louis interrupted.

'Play us a song, Hugh, please.' Then, in a mock whisper: 'For Danny.'

Sullivan stepped off the stool and stood erect, swaying slightly. He smiled at Danny. 'I'll play for Bobby,' he said.

Hugh Sullivan threaded his way through the crowds to the piano. He turned on the light and sat down. At the bar, Louis leaned towards Danny, filling his glass, and began to whisper urgently.

'Bobby was killed at the Beach Club. Sullivan is a bitter and dangerous man who has lost his lover.'

In the distance, Sullivan waved at the bar. Both Danny and Louis waved back. The pianist began a slow introduction.

'If he discovers it was you, Danny, he will betray you. Believe me, I know him. I think you must leave quickly.'

Danny swallowed his champagne. 'After the song, Louis,' he said. The barman quickly filled his glass, while Sullivan began to sing:

'Love me or leave me and let me be lonely,
You won't believe me, and I love you only.
I'd rather be lonely than happy with somebody else.'

Sullivan's fingers played quiet chords. Out of the corner of his eye, Danny saw a boy making his way from the side entrance. This was Claude's messenger.

'Might find the night time the right time for kissing,
But night time is my time for just reminiscing.'

Sullivan leaned into the light, his eyes glittering across the room.

'Regretting instead of forgetting with somebody else.'

His sad voice began to strain through the next lines.

The boy found Danny Morgan and whispered that the Gestapo had left the Casino.

'I want your love, but I don't want to borrow,
To have it today and to give back tomorrow.'

There were tears in Sullivan's eyes.

'For my love is your love, there's no love . . .'

Sullivan paused. In his mind's eye, he could see nothing but Bobby Avery.

'. . . for nobody else.'

'Go!' hissed Louis in Danny's ear.

Applause began, then people stood up and cheered, but Danny had gone.

Claude took the man with Etienne Brizard's papers into the crowded outer room known as the kitchen, where the rich and regular gamblers were never seen. The two men went through the white salon to the open double doors of the Salle Privée. Claude nodded to the guard as Danny turned to the cashier behind the counter near the entrance.

'Good evening, Henri,' said Danny. The man looked up and his eyes widened in recognition.

'Monsieur Morgan?'

'Brizard, Henri,' said Danny. 'Etienne Brizard.'

'But Monsieur.' The cashier was in a panic. 'We heard that you were . . .' he stopped himself.

'How is my credit, Henri?' asked Danny quietly.

The cashier sighed and spread his arms. 'Monsieur, it is very difficult.'

'Before the war it was never difficult,' said Danny.

'But Monsieur,' whispered the cashier, 'now it is "during", if you will allow me to say so.'

'And after the war?' Danny's expression was hard.

'You will be welcome as always, Monsieur . . . Brizard but now it is dangerous for you here.'

'I want ten thousand francs Henri – now.'

Reluctantly the cashier riffled through a filing case and took out a card. He read the information on it while guests surged noisily through the doors into the crowded salon.

'Is the arrangement in Switzerland still valid, M'sieur?'

'Until the Nazis invade.'

Several people who had arrived after Danny were getting impatient. The cashier counted out chips.

'Ten thousand, Monsieur . . .' he stopped himself.

'Brizard, remember,' said Danny, smiling. 'Sign for me, would you?'

Henri nodded. 'Be careful,' he whispered.

'I'd rather be lucky.'

So 'Monsieur Etienne Brizard' entered the Salle Privée, counting his stake.

Chapter 21

In the American Bar of the Hotel de Paris, Sullivan sang two more songs, 'Lover' and 'Please Don't Talk About Me When I'm Gone'. When the applause died he held up a hand, saying with a wry smile that he had started too early and needed one more drink. He promised to return shortly – he had 'just been obliging a friend' – and it was Bobby he meant. He switched off the light on the piano and, seeing that Danny Morgan's bar stool was empty, grabbed Jean-Pierre by the arm.

'Where did the Morgan boy go?'

Jean-Pierre looked quickly at the bar, then whispered in Sullivan's ear: 'He has gone, M'sieur, because it is dangerous for him.'

'Dangerous?' repeated Sullivan. 'What do you mean?'

Jean-Pierre was nervous and impatient and spoke before thinking. 'He is an airman,' he whispered, 'you know, boom, boom, boom. The RAF. The Beach Club.'

He crossed himself quickly as he saw the Irish-American's expression.

'*Mon ami,*' he said earnestly, 'if you understood me, you must forget it.' He went to attend to his customers.

Tears of anger filled Sullivan's eyes. Under his breath he hissed: 'The bastard!'

Danny Morgan, elegant in his borrowed dinner jacket, wandered amongst the crowds in the Casino's Salle Privée, absorbing the familiar atmosphere. Lights were suspended from the ornately decorated ceiling, each one contained in a large shade, hanging low over a green baize table surrounded by the crowds who had come to gamble or just to watch. Wheels spun and cards were dealt continuously.

By 10 o'clock, playing roulette, Danny had come up on six numbers and four chevals. With several hundred thousand francs, he could have walked out of the Casino, his wager won. But now he was intoxicated, not only from the champagne, which had begun to affect him more than he knew, after months in captivity, but from the atmosphere of the huge gaming room. He should have called it a day, but he could see an empty seat at the main chemin de fer table in a corner, under a long picture called La Nuit. He sat down and waited patiently for the game to start, watching the cards being shuffled. The table was familiar; he had played at it before the war, and remembered that it was reserved for the highest stakes. He was offered another glass of champagne and time began to tick away for Danny Morgan.

Chemin de fer is a game of nerve. For those who play it well, the game is simple.

Six packs of cards are shuffled and cut at the table, then put into a mahogany shoe or sabot. The players are offered this one by one. If they accept then they are the bank and play against a single opponent, seated at the table, who either matches the bank's wager individually or, if the sums of money reach extraordinary amounts, represents a group.

Two players are dealt two cards and a third card can be dealt if asked for. Aces score one, court cards count as ten, only the last digit of the total sum has value. The nearest to nine wins – simple.

The banker must continue to win to retain the shoe, doubling each time to increase the risk and the reward.

Three croupiers oversee the game. One, sitting in the centre of the kidney-shaped table, passes the cards on a long-handled spatulate palette, working around the table, but taking five per cent for the house from each hand dealt to the bank.

The rules of chemin de fer seem complicated to the inexperienced onlooker, but mathematically the odds very marginally favour the bank.

Danny Morgan, familiar with the game from years of play, had long been acknowledged by his friends as exceptionally good. Even his enemies conceded that he was lucky.

The croupier at the chemin de fer table spoke clearly.

'Sept à la banque.'

Danny looked at his cards and smiled. With a ten and an eight, he had a total of eighteen: discounting the ten his score was eight. He declared *La petite*.

A good beginning. The croupier scooped up the chips and passed them over. Danny had won eighty thousand francs more. The plump man opposite Danny shrugged and passed the mahogany sabot which held the cards. Two people refused the bank, then an Asian woman, decked in pearls, sitting two seats from Danny Morgan, accepted. She started with twenty thousand and won four coups against four different players. Then she came to Danny. The pot was standing at three hundred and twenty thousand francs. Danny accepted the whole bet with the word *'Banco'*. The croupier pushed his chips forward, making a total of six hundred and forty thousand.

The woman dealt. Danny glanced at his cards and immediately turned them up. A jack and an eight. *La petite* again. The woman glared at him

163

as if he had insulted her. He smiled. Now he felt lucky, and for a gambler that was everything.

The game finished. The six decks of cards were reshuffled, cut, and replaced in the sabot by the croupier. He disposed of the first five cards in a slot beside him at the table, then the sabot was offered to the large man, now perspiring noticeably, sitting on the croupier's right. He accepted it and became the first banker of the new game.

Danny counted his winnings while waiting for his turn. It came, and he was dealt a card. Then one to the bank, one more apiece, and each had two cards lying face-down. Danny asked for another. It was dealt face-up – the queen of spades. Danny remained impassive. The bank took a nine, then turned over the unseen cards. A four and a jack of diamonds. Nine plus four, discounting the court card, made thirteen. Only the last digit mattered so he had a total of three.

'*Trois à la banque,*' said the croupier.

Danny was holding a king and a five. The king did not count so he doubled his money on the five. His large opponent, who appeared to be German, scowled and passed on the sabot, and with it the bank, which was refused by a nervous Italian woman and then offered to Danny. He had been waiting for the moment for almost half an hour, so he nodded and accepted. He knew that he should have gone to the Fontvielle beach already, but champagne had made him reckless. Every minute he stayed in the Casino increased the danger, but Danny had gambling in his blood, and now *he* had the bank.

Nine people were seated round the table for the game and others beside or behind them were there to watch and place side bets if they felt like it.

A small audience had begun to build up, attracted by the big stakes at the table in the corner of the huge, crowded room. Roulette wheels spun in the distance and balls clicked into place. Baroque decorations in silver, gold and enamel glittered and shone.

The croupier at the chemin de fer table had already recognized Danny and greeted him with a discreet nod. On leaning over to pass Danny his first winnings he had whispered: '*Vive l'Angleterre.*'

Danny had known many of the staff for years, ever since his father, a regular gambler, had brought him into this inner sanctum of the Casino. So even his gaunt appearance and broken nose had not disguised an old friend, but the staff would do nothing to give him away. Danny felt safe and lucky as the croupier passed the cards on his palette.

The plump man at the opposite side of the table accepted the whole bet of ten thousand francs for the coup. Danny looked round at the piles of chips and plaques in front of his opponents. It was big money.

The man shook his head. No card. Danny watched him turn his cards face-up. A six and a queen, total sixteen, score six. Danny took a three. Then he turned up his other cards.

164

A four of clubs, and a jack of spades, total seven.

'*Sept à la banque.*'

The croupier tore the ticket that represented each coup from a small book that kept a house check on the game, then took the Casino's percentage from Danny.

'*Vingt mille francs,*' he stated. Twenty thousand francs for the next hand.

'*Banco,*' said the small Asian woman with the perfect pearls. She pushed a twenty-thousand-franc plaque into the pot and turned her face to Danny, who dealt the cards as the others looked on intently.

The Asian woman nodded for a card. Danny slid out a six of diamonds face-up. He held a five and a king. Dangerous – the bank was obliged to draw. Danny took a seven of clubs. The woman flipped her cards over. A king and a four. With the six, her total was nothing – zero. Danny showed his cards. Five and seven and the court card added up to twenty-two and counted as two.

'*Deux à la banque,*' said the croupier and tore the ticket slowly as several people in the crowd remarked on Danny's luck.

'*Suivi,*' said the Asian woman, accepting the now doubled pot. Forty thousand for the coup. Danny again paid the five per cent to the house as the croupier moved the woman's two twenty-thousand-franc plaques to the centre of he table and said:

'*Quarante mille, Mesdames et Messieurs.*'

Danny dealt. The Asian woman asked for a third card. He gave out a four of hearts, looked into her eyes for a moment and then shook his head. As banker he had no choice. He could not take a card. Immediately the woman showed a ten of diamonds and a queen. Neither counted, so her total was four. Danny turned up his cards. A five of spades and the ace of hearts.

'*Six à la banque.*'

The croupier rearranged the pot as the growing audience started whispering in several languages. Danny threw across the house commission and politely asked for the time. It was 10.36.

'*Quatre-vingt mille,*' said the croupier, raised his palette and waited. Eighty thousand for the hand.

'*Banco,*' said an Italian, who was middle-aged, well-dressed, and had the fixed stare of the dedicated gambler. Danny dealt. He gave a third card to the Italian, face-up. It was the queen of hearts. The man showed a seven of clubs and an eight of diamonds for a total of five. Danny breathed deeply: as banker he had again been unable to draw, and his upturned cards showed why. A king of spades and a seven of diamonds gave him seven.

'*Sept à la banque.*'

'*Suivi,*' said the Italian softly.

165

There was a gasp from the crowd, and the croupier tore up the ticket and glanced at Danny, who threw over four thousand-franc chips for the house percentage.

'Cent soixante mille.' One hundred and sixty thousand.

Danny dealt. The Italian smiled, refused a third card, and immediately flipped over his hand. Two nines made eighteen, so his total was eight.

'La petite,' he said.

Danny turned over his own cards and won. A jack and a nine of spades made the maximum possible score.

'La grande,' he said and smiled.

'Neuf à la banque.' There were exclamations from the crowd.

'The big one,' murmured Danny in English and received a warning frown from the croupier. He was in the Casino as Monsieur Brizard, after all.

The table was becoming the focus of attention in the Salle Privée. Drinks were brought. The plump German who had gone out briefly returned with more plaques and joined a large woman who might have been his wife or sister. The croupier took the house percentage from Danny, who nodded.

'Trois cent vingt mille.' said the croupier.

'Three hundred and twenty thousand for one hand!' exclaimed an American voice in the crowd.

The croupier glanced again at Danny Morgan, and raised an eyebrow. There was a moment's hesitation at the table.

'Banco,' said the German and, in an attempt at intimidation, he began to stack up hundred-thousand-franc chips in front of him on the green baize.

Danny slipped the cards out of the sabot, to be passed across on the palette. Only the distant noises from the roulette tables interrupted the concentrated silence at the table.

The German took a third card, a seven of spades and turned over a jack and a five; with the seven he had a total of twelve, which counted as two.

Danny took a nine of diamonds, then showed his other cards. A three and a two. With the nine his total was fourteen. Score four.

'Quatre à la banque.'

There was a gasp. Someone clapped and a slight argument began in the crowd. The croupier tore up the ticket, took the sixteen thousand francs Danny offered and waited until he nodded yet again.

'Six cent quarante mille,' said the flat French voice.

Someone brought Danny a glass of champagne. He sipped it and

166

accepted a second cigarette. He was into a run of luck, and although naturally buoyant, the knowledge of his danger had begun to make him uneasy. He was attracting too much attention and it was getting late – but he was feeling the familiar thrill of the successful gambler. He sipped the champagne then asked the time again. It was 10.45.

'Six cent quarante mille,' repeated the croupier. Six hundred and forty thousand. The German woman pushed her plaques towards the pot and looked at her companion triumphantly. The decision had been made.

'Suivi,' said the fat German nervously, and lit a cigarette. He was now gambling with twice his original stake. If he won it would only be a profit of a quarter of the pot, which was the bank's previous stake against him. Playing with his opponents' money, Danny reflected, was good value for the bank. He dealt the cards. The German quickly took a third. A five of hearts. 'Ha!' he said, and glanced at the matronly woman beside him, who smiled arrogantly across the table. Danny Morgan paused, waiting for the murmuring at the table to cease. When there was silence, he smiled and turned over his cards. The German flipped over his own confidently. A three of diamonds and a queen of clubs, with the five showing made a total of eight. He stared at Danny, who had a five of clubs and jack of hearts and had to draw. He reached for the shoe and turned over a four of spades.

'Neuf à la banque.'

There was an explosion of noise at the table. The croupier stared at Danny, who licked his lips and nodded. The fat German was purple in the face and sweating. The others still in the game were a middle-aged Frenchwoman wearing a sable coat over her shoulders and enough diamonds round her neck to buy the Casino, and a slim grey-haired man who might have been an Italian industralist, surrounded by a group of tough-looking young men. 'If they are Mafia, and I win, I'll be lucky to get out of the place alive,' thought Danny.

'Un million, deux cent quatre-vingt mille, Mesdames et Messieurs.' The Croupier spoke the figure clearly and calmly. There was a hush at the table.

'Banco,' said the Italian quietly. Danny nodded. Whispers circulated behind him. Plaques representing one million, two hundred and eighty thousand francs were piled in the centre of the table. Danny stared at his opponent, formidable behind his calm expression and elegant appearance. For a moment he felt dizzy. He reached for the champagne then stopped himself – only now did he realize how much it was going to his head. He tried to collect his thoughts.

The surrounding audience pressed silently closer.

Danny slid the cards deftly from the shoe. The croupier's palette carried them across the table. The two men glanced at their hands. The Italian nodded. Danny dealt him the third card face-up. A two of clubs. Murmuring began, then died in anticipation. The Italian showed his hand. A nine of hearts and ace of spades, ten, but the two of clubs added up to a total of two. Danny flipped his own cards. Two queens. He was obliged to draw a third card, which was a three of diamonds and gave him the edge with a total of three.

'*Trois à la banque.*'

The audience was stunned. In that moment's silence, the Italian spoke softly again.

'*Suivi,*' he said.

A babble of excited chatter broke out as Danny and the croupier looked at each other. The rules allowed Danny to 'garage' if he wished. He could drop the pot to about half a million and continue less dangerously, or he could take his winnings and walk out of the Casino with two million francs. But that was not Danny Morgan's style. He had survived too much to get to the Casino that evening, and he was already risking more than anyone knew. Around him were the enemy: Italians, Germans, French collaborators and all the other opportunist refugees who fed from the victor of the moment, the Axis powers. This made him all the more determined . . .

Danny's thoughts were interrupted.

'*Monsieur?*' asked the croupier, prompting discretely.

Danny looked at the familiar face, at the crowds surrounding the table, then at the impassive features of the Italian. It was men like this he had come here to kill months before. He smiled and decided to risk everything. There were gasps from the crowd as he nodded.

'*Deux millions,*' began the croupier slowly, '*cinq cent soixante mille, Mesdames et Messieurs.*'

Danny nodded to the Italian and swallowed. Two million, five hundred and sixty thousand. The man's face remained immobile; only his eyes fractionally changed expression as Danny dealt the cards. The Italian accepted a third card. A four of hearts. Danny had drawn a two of clubs and a three of spades for a total of five. Having dealt his opponent a four, Danny now had the option of sticking on five or drawing another card. For the first time in the game, he was indecisive. He had won on a low card before, but . . . He looked up at the Italian, who, seeing his hesitation, smirked at him.

The Italian's expression made up Danny's mind for him. He would stand on five.

The Italian turned up his cards, a king of clubs and an ace. With the four he had a total of five. When Danny turned up his cards there was a moment of total silence before the croupier said:

'*Egalité.*'

As Danny and the Italian had equal scores the hand had to be played again.

Danny dealt the cards once more. The Italian's hands on the green baize table were relaxed. He seemed unconcerned as he moved a finger for a third card.

Danny dealt him a three of diamonds, but was unable to draw himself. The Italian registered this, smiled and showed his hand. Ace, two, and a three for a total of six. Danny turned his hand to show a ten of diamonds and a seven of hearts.

'*Sept à la banque,*' said the croupier.

The audience began babbling. The Italian's lips tightened as he bowed to his right at the German, then to his left at the Frenchwoman in the sable coat. Under cover of the noise Danny leaned towards the croupier.

'Time?' he asked.

'Ten to eleven,' answered the man. The croupier began to rake the plaques together as the Italian spoke.

'*Suivi,*' he said quietly. There was the faintest hint of perspiration on his forehead, and Danny thought he could detect anger in his eyes.

He himself was fighting to control his nerves. As banker he had won nine times in a row. Even with one *égalité*, that was exceptionally lucky. The croupier glanced across at a Casino inspector who had arrived at the table. The man nodded.

'*C'est la limite, Monsieur.*'

The stake had reached the table limit.

The menacing young men behind the Italian had grouped together and were looking at Danny. They stared at the croupier, who swallowed nervously.

'*Tout seul, Monsieur?*'

The Italian shook his head. '*Avec la table,*' he said, and glanced at the German and the Frenchwoman, who both nodded. The German loosened his tie as the plump woman beside him wiped his forehead with a white silk handkerchief from his breast pocket. The crowds round the table pressed closer. The three were going to pool their resources to beat Danny Morgan, a procedure known as fading the bank.

The croupier looked at his palette poised above the pile of plaques – green twenty thousands and red and white one hundred thousands.

'*C'est la limite, Monsieur,*' repeated the croupier.

Having reached the limit, this would be the last draw. Danny gritted his teeth, ground out his cigarette and then nodded.

'*Mesdames et Messieurs,*' said the croupier, '*s'il vous plaît.*' He waited for the people round his table to stop talking, then spoke. '*Cinq millions, cent vingt mille francs, pour la banque.*'

For a moment no one moved.

'*Mesdames et Messieurs,*' said the croupier softly.

The plaques in front of the Germans were pushed towards the pot, leaving them only a single one-hundred-thousand piece. The Italian pushed what was remaining before him towards the centre of the table. The Frenchwoman, fingering her diamonds, stared at the Asian woman with her pearls, then joined the opposition to Danny Morgan. Male companions behind the two women pushed forward the chips and plaques, which were immediately thrust into the pile. The bank's stake was fully covered. Five million, one hundred and twenty thousand francs.

'*Cinq millions, cent vingt mille francs,*' repeated the croupier.

Danny remained outwardly cool. Someone offered him another cigarette and he inhaled deeply, then looked up to see Hugh Sullivan.

The Irishman appeared to have sobered. He stared at Danny Morgan with hate in his eyes.

'*Monsieur, s'il vous plaît?*' prompted the croupier gently.

Danny concentrated once more. His run of luck had been spectacular, and he hoped Sullivan was not the jinx which would turn the cards against him.

He dealt to the Italian, who represented the rest of the table.

'*Monsieur,*' said the croupier in a whisper. The Italian called for a third card from the sabot. He was passed a six of spades. He grinned and immediately turned up the cards, the king of spades and two of clubs. With the six the table had a total of eight.

Danny glanced at Sullivan's white face. He turned his cards face-up. Two aces. There was a gasp from the crowd. Danny's mind raced as he found himself staring once more at Sullivan.

The bank had to draw. Danny reached for a card as the crowd held its breath and his opponents round the table stared. When he slid the seven of hearts out of the sabot there was so much noise that the croupier had to stand and shout.

'*Mesdames et Messieurs! S'il vous plaît! Neuf à la banque.*'

Danny looked up from his cards into the deathly pale face of Sullivan, full of anger and the desire for revenge. The sabot was almost empty to the red marker, and the cards would have to be reshuffled. He knew there would be a pause in the game and knew he had had enough; moreover it was just after 11 o'clock. He said quietly to the croupier:

'*J'ai besoin d'un petit sac.*'

'*Mais oui.*' The man snapped his fingers and an attendant came over bringing a bag made of pigskin, and big enough to take Danny's winnings. They were scooped in and the neck of the bag was pulled tight with a drawstring.

Even after he had paid the Casino's five per cent, Danny had won close to ten million francs.

He stood up and gave a hundred-thousand-franc chip to the table. The croupier bowed his thanks, as Danny bowed courteously to his opponents.

It was his intention to go to the bar for a quick drink before leaving, but out of the corner of his eye he caught sight of a horrifyingly familiar face. Ten yards away, pushing urgently through the crowd, accompanied by several men who stood head and shoulders above the throng, was Gestapo Major Jürgen Pabst.

Chapter 22

The yellow and black Rolls Royce turned off the Boulevard des Moulins, down the curving road of the Avenue de la Madonne, took the short slope at the top of Avenue des Spelugues and came gliding into the Casino Square minutes before 11 o'clock.

Harry and Vondrakova had crossed the old border at Ventimiglia soon after 10 o'clock, but showing their passes and official documents had delayed them outside the Principality. Though it had been a long day for them, both were determined to reach Monaco and the comparative sanity of neutrality before midnight.

Harry pulled up in front of the Hotel de Paris just as a large black Mercedes came roaring into the square from the direction of the harbour. The car slewed round and screeched to a standstill. Harry recognized several of the men who leapt out, and he glanced at Vondrakova. She was slumped into her furs in the front seat, lying with her head back, eyes closed and almost asleep.

Harry looked again at the men in long black leather coats as they ran across the square to take the steps of the Casino two at a time. They were led by Gestapo Major Jürgen Pabst. Harry fought to remain calm and touched Irelena's face gently.

'Darling,' he said, 'we've arrived.'

She opened her eyes and stared vacantly for a moment, looking at Harry as if he were a stranger.

'Darling, we're back.' He kissed her lightly on the cheek.

In the distance, Harry could see an argument raging with the doorman of the Casino. Michel tapped on the windscreen and Harry stepped out of the car.

171

Michel saw the bruises on Harry's face but only smiled discreetly and said: 'Welcome back, M'sieur.'

Harry pointed to the Casino steps. 'What's going on?'

'Trouble, M'sieur, I think.'

'You know those men are German?' said Harry.

'Oui, M'sieur, it is not a secret.'

Irelena Vondrakova was now standing beside the car. 'Darling, Michel will take you to my suite. Lock the door and wait until I come up.' Vondrakova leaned her head slowly against his shoulder. He hugged her briefly, gave instructions to Michel, and was starting towards the Casino when Michel's urgent whisper halted him.

'Attention, M'sieur Harry, I think they go for Monsieur Morgan, the RAF flyer who was shot down!' Harry looked incredulous, so Michel had to continue. 'Yes, I saw him tonight with my own eyes. He has escaped. Please, M'sieur, take care!'

Harry was already running. He could see the Mercedes driver backing up fast in front of the Casino. Held, the tall German who admired Vondrakova, was standing at the top of the steps, no longer concealing the submachine gun, whose metal gleamed in the light under the canopy. Harry slowed, realizing that the Casino doors were barred.

Held stared belligerently about him, alert, suspicious. Harry turned. He could have rejoined Vondrakova and gone with her up the steps of the Hotel de Paris, through the revolving doors, to safety. Why should he get involved? Morgan was an acquaintance from a world long gone. Harry was in a neutral country. He was a citizen of the United States, a country with sympathies but no direct involvement in the European war. In good conscience he could declare that none of this demanded any action from him and just walk away.

He began moving quickly towards the side entrance of the Opera, remembering that there was a way into the Casino through the foyer, and if that too was blocked, then through the auditorium itself. The horrific events at the Furkahaus were seared into his mind. Harry Pilikian was no longer a man of peace.

Trapped in the Salle Privée, Danny Morgan realized that in a matter of seconds he would be recaptured by the Gestapo. Fear and anger exploded in him.

'No!' he bellowed, and grasped the bag containing his winnings and swung it with all his force at the first Gestapo man, who was nearly upon him. He ducked a punch from the first German then dodged to one side and ran towards the open doors leading to the white salon. The French guard, who had recognized Danny's face, hesitated for a moment as the tall German beside him began pulling at his pistol. There were screams from women in the crowd as Danny swung the weighty pigskin bag with all his might. It connected with a crack against the German's head. The man fell to his knees stunned, and Danny was through into the next room.

He guessed that the entrance would be guarded and the exits sealed. He had been betrayed by Sullivan and would not get out by going down – the slow lift would be a deathtrap and the huge stairway led nowhere but to the Cabaret. He would have to go up.

Danny smashed through the swinging doors into the packed kitchen where gamblers played for small stakes. The tables were arranged to form an oval in the centre of the room around a security area patrolled by Casino inspectors. There was no choice: he leapt on to the first table, where the dealer was about to draw twenty-one, jumped on to the green baize of the next table, slipped on a pile of chips which scattered into the players, regained his footing and sprang for an adjoining table. Immediately it began to totter, and he almost lost his balance when he jumped across a roulette table, swinging the sack wildly as hands reached out to grasp him. In front of him, blocking the door, stood a group of old women with gaping mouths. Danny swore, leapt over their heads and landed in a forward roll which took him right through the swing doors, sprawling onto a marble floor.

He was in a huge rectangular foyer with pillars, a balcony above and a stairway going up. As a boy, Danny had explored the Casino, despite the pleas of his parents and the protests of the staff. He was desperately trying to remember . . .

He skidded across the marble, slowing himself to get his bearings. From the corner of his eye he saw an armed German pulling at the barred outer doors amongst a group of Casino employees. Danny reached the stairway exactly as Harry Pilikian ran out of the cloakroom area at the other end of the marble hall. The doors of the kitchen were opening; everyone from the packed room seemed to be trying to get out at the same time.

Harry struggled in the seething throng, and began pushing towards the stairway, but Morgan was gone.

Danny Morgan ran through several empty offices till he found the narrow corridor and small door which had been his goal. It was locked, but he leaned against the opposite wall, cantilevered himself up with his feet resting on the door handle then, with a quick movement, smashed it open.

Before him was a metal stairway which he climbed quickly, unbolted a trapdoor and reached the roof. In darkness, the whole area became a maze, and for a time Danny Morgan's childhood memories faltered. Already below he could hear running feet. He threaded his way round ventilation ducts, pipes, drains, chimneys and gutters, making for the centre section above the white salon where the huge circular glass clere-story, almost sixty feet across, glowed with light from the four chandeliers suspended beneath its shallow convex fish-eye, veined with metal supports.

Danny began to make his way around it, climbing up on to the narrow ledge to bypass several obstacles. Behind him, on the roof, there was the sound of guttural voices. The Germans had seen his silhouette. He ducked low, breathing hard. If he could make it to the twin towers at the back of the building, he knew how he could climb down to where a small pathway led to the railway station. If he crossed the tracks and managed to get on to the Tir aux Pigeons he had a chance. It was a huge semicircle surfaced with gravel and red clay, jutting out into the sea, which had been especially constructed on the rocks for trap-shooting clay pigeons. The sea, no matter how cold, meant freedom.

But the ledge was slimy with bird droppings, and Danny was in a hurry. One foot skidded from under him, and he slipped. He fell, throwing his weight hard to one side away from the clere-story glass through which he had been able to make out the blurred images of the gaming tables more than fifty feet below.

'Get up!' said a voice directly behind him. He turned his head and saw a German breathing heavily, his face glowing in the light from below. Danny stood up slowly. *'Ich habe den Pilot!'* shouted the man. 'I have him!'

There were answering shouts from different parts of the roof and Danny heard the sound of men beginning to make their way towards him. The German's Luger was aimed directly at his heart. In the next few seconds he would be in Gestapo hands again. He remembered his wife's letter about a child he would never see, and gritted his teeth. Danny was a gambler after all, and, against all odds, he moved.

The German's bullet entered Danny Morgan's body between the third and fourth ribs of his left side, but not before it had passed through nearly ten million francs' worth of Casino plaques and chips. The impact was less-ened and the penetration not so deep, but all the same Danny staggered as his body lunged past the pointed gun. The German, taken by surprise, fell back, arms flailing, and broke with a scream through the clere-story roof above the white salon. Amidst cascading slivers of glass and broken metal struts, he fell headlong for thirty feet, smashing into a hanging chandelier, which exploded into a thousand pieces of crystal, then he plummeted a further twenty feet into the packed crowds below, breaking his back across a roulette table that had just stopped on zero.

Bent double by the pain of his wound, Danny Morgan made his way across the roof to one of the twin towers facing onto the Mediterranean. Below, in the distance, he could see flecks of foam on the choppy sea.

What little light there was from the Casino and the stars above allowed him to find a foothold on the ornate architrave. The ledge was very narrow, so he took his bag of plaques and chips, threaded his belt through the drawstring and re-buckled it tight. He allowed himself to slide from the architrave, fingers biting into the powdery stone. His body dropped to full stretch, but the pain was so intense that he almost let go. Then his feet found the first moulding above one of the triple windows that looked into the Casino's great room. Agony caused sweat to course down his face, drenching his body. The tight leather-soled shoes slipped as his feet sought the Corinthian capital below. The beak-like shape of the ornamentation provided a moment's rest.

The next few seconds would be the most difficult. As a boy he had climbed halfway up this façade before being caught by the guards. That bet lost with the gypsies had meant only a day's humiliation. This time it would mean death.

He swung his body once, twice, then leapt across to a stone carving in the shape of an eagle. He seized it with his arms as his body slammed against the stone, and fought for air. Harsh, urgent voices sounded from above: hunters after their prey. His feet sought the shallow ornamentation beneath, then slipped, and his arms could hold him no longer. Grasping vainly at the stone, he fell heavily on to the balcony ten feet below. He was badly winded, and lay for a moment straining to fill his lungs till he could reach for the balustrade and pull himself up. Then he stepped over and jumped the last twenty feet.

Danny hit the pathway hard, rolled over and lay still. His hand found the wound where the German's bullet had penetrated and warm blood flowed stickily between his fingers. He was losing his resolve, and was not sure that he could even stand or walk. It would be easier just to drift into unconsciousness . . .

'Get up!' said a voice urgently. 'Get up, you damn fool!' Two hands pulled Danny Morgan to his feet. He winced and bent over again. 'God dammit, they've hit you!' said the voice and Danny's eyes focused.

'I know you,' said Danny Morgan.

'Pilikian,' said the man, 'Harry Pilikian.' Shouts came from above on the roof of the Casino. 'Can you walk?' Harry lifted Danny to his feet.

'I don't think so,' came the reply, 'but I can bloody well swim.'

Harry stared for a moment at the airman's haggard face, then ducked his head beneath Danny's arm so that he lay across his shoulders. He began walking, as quickly as his burden would allow, along the pathway through the thick shrubbery towards the road at the entrance of the Opera.

'How did you find me?' mumbled Danny Morgan.

'I remembered that crazy story you told us before the war about some bet you had made climbing the Casino. I knew if you went up to the roof there was no way down for you on the inside.'

'I've got to get to the Fontvielle beach,' said Danny Morgan. 'A fishing boat is picking me up at midnight.'

'We'll make it,' said Harry Pilikian grimly. 'You'll get there!' It was seventeen minutes past eleven.

The two men, one supported by the other, reached the edge of the palms and bushes growing over the pathway. Harry staggered out on to the pavement towards his car, which would take them to the beach. He let Danny Morgan down gently. 'I'll get the car.' Then he saw the blood. 'You OK?' he asked.

'Shaky.'

'What the hell have you got round your waist?' asked Harry. Danny was beginning to answer when a shout went up, headlights snapped on and with the sound of an engine being revved, the Gestapo Mercedes appeared. Harry spun round: there was nowhere to go but back.

'Come on!' he shouted to Danny Morgan.

Summoning energy from his last reserves, Danny followed Harry Pilikian back along the path, turned off towards the station and took the steep slope down to the employees' entrance of the railway station, where Harry broke open the door. The platform was deserted. They jumped on to the tracks and crossed them, Harry helping Danny up on to the far platform and into the facing waiting room. At the back they saw an archway which gave access to the Tir aux Pigeons.

The sound of their pursuers was closer. Harry ran across the red clay and gravel keeping behind Danny Morgan, who fell several times but immediately pulled himself to his feet. Danny stopped at the edge of the sheer drop with Harry still two paces behind. They were sixty feet above the sea with nowhere to go.

Harry looked about wildly. Danny was sucking air into his lungs. Shouts from the Germans came to them loudly as their hunters crossed the railway lines. Danny peered below at waves foaming on the rocks.

'It's very deep you know. We used to dive off the harbour wall as kids. I once saw Buster Keaton do this in a movie,' Danny shouted, and jumped.

'*Achtung!*' came a voice from the distance. 'Halt!'

Harry Pilikian braced himself, and leapt out into the black void.

The Mediterranean in March is not warm. Few people care to swim and only the hardy enjoy it. To survive in a foam-flecked chilling sea for more than half an hour is a feat of endurance.

Without Harry Pilikian, Danny Morgan would have drowned. He did not fall straight and the impact on his spine half-stunned him. Pilikian entered the water vertically with his chin in the air, so that the mass of his body protected his head from concussion. He sank more than twenty feet, fought his way to the surface, found the limp body of Danny

176

Morgan, then, amidst buffeting waves, began to swim out past the mouth of the harbour towards the Rock and beyond.

Within minutes the two men were no longer targets, but lost in the darkness of the night sea.

Pabst and the other Germans, breathing heavily, peered down from the edge of the Tir aux Pigeons. They could see nothing.

'Bring the car!' breathed the Gestapo major. 'We will go around the Rock. He has help. We must find them both!'

'But . . .' began one of the men, gesturing into the night.

'I want them!' bellowed Pabst.

In the cold water of the Mediterranean, which had been a shock on impact and after thirty minutes was now numbing and sapping them both, Danny Morgan croaked instructions to Harry Pilikian. They were beyond the Rock now, and swimming directly out to sea. Danny was attempting to guide Pilikian to the fishing boat, which he knew would wait only for a few minutes after midnight. When the moon had risen it would be too dangerous to linger.

Morgan sank beneath the waves and Harry swallowed water. He was losing energy, fighting the sea. Some of their clothing had been torn off when they hit the surface, and both men were losing circulation. Harry had no idea of the time and was coughing the salt water out of his throat, clinging desperately to Morgan's heavy body.

As the moon rose the Mediterranean became a glittering sheen. Ahead, amidst the foam and waves, Harry could see nothing. He turned his head, desperately seeking the boat, and there to his right, not a hundred yards away, was the black welcoming silhouette of a fishing vessel. Beside it, rising and falling, he could make out a dinghy and the outlines of four men sitting in it. Harry emerged from a wave and summoned his last energies. 'Here!' he shouted and was again engulfed by the sea.

He turned on his back and with renewed strength began pushing with his legs, hampered by the struggling Morgan. Exhausted, Harry heard English voices.

'Two men in the water, sir!'

'Pull 'em in.'

'Grab 'im by the collar!'

'Who's the other geezer?'

'The bugger looks drowned.'

'Hang on to him then!'

'They're secured, sir.'

'Well, pull 'em up here but keep your eyes on the Frenchies in the dinghy. Harbottle, Gurney, let's get weaving!'

'Yes, sir!'

Moments later, wrapped in a blanket, Harry Pilikian found himself standing shakily on the deck of a fishing boat unofficially commissioned by the British Navy. Two seamen held him as he watched three men from the dinghy being taken below.

'What's your name, mate?' somebody asked.

'Pilikian.'

'Looks like you saved this cove good and proper,' said a young man dressed in dark oilskins.

'Morgan,' whispered Danny.

'It's the squadron leader, sir!' somebody shouted.

'He's wounded,' said Harry.

Although Danny was exhausted and barely conscious, he reached out and grasped Harry by the shoulders. For a moment they said nothing, then, touching the bag that hung from Morgan's waist, Harry asked with a grin:

'What's this?'

'Winnings, Harry, Just winnings,' said Danny hoarsely and began fumbling with the buckle of his belt.

Harry was urged to the gunwale and helped into the dinghy while the single oarsman steadied it, and then pushed off. For a moment the men on the fishing vessel were silhouetted by the surging, moonlit water.

'Harry!' cried Danny Morgan. 'Take it!' One of the sailors flung the bag towards the dinghy. Harry reached up and caught it, almost falling into the sea until the oarsman, swearing in French, hauled him back. Harry began to wave as the powerful engines of the fishing boat were started up.

'Let me know next time you're coming!' he shouted into the darkness.

'Gamble with it, Harry!' came Danny's voice, almost lost on the night wind. 'And win!'

The large fishing vessel turned, propellers churning the water, and within a minute had begun to plough into the foaming sea, her course set southwest, her destination Gibraltar.

On the flat roof of Agatha Parry's house, Ben Harrison crouched behind the shallow parapet and squinted through his binoculars. He watched the silhouette of the fishing boat disappear until there was only the heaving moonlit sea and a dinghy being rowed to the beach.

'Two men?' he muttered, perplexed. The plan was that only one would return. Tomorrow he would see Eva Trenchard to discover what had happened.

But now Malta would be waiting for his call sign. He had delayed the transmission by an hour. Losing sight of the dinghy in the dark water, he climbed through the skylight and crept into Agatha Parry's bedroom, thinking her asleep, but her eyes were wide open.

'They're away,' he whispered.

Agatha smiled. 'Thank God,' she said and lay back against the soft pillows. Ben kissed her gently and went out, closing the door behind him.

In the secret radio room, seated at the now familiar equipment, he began to transmit his code name – King's Cross.

Harry Pilikian and the Resistance man in the dinghy were lucky. Six minutes after they had beached and driven away in an old Peugeot, which dropped Harry at the back of the Hotel de Paris, the Gestapo men led by Pabst found the dinghy, ripped it apart, and cursed the night with all the German profanity at their disposal.

After Harry had taken a long hot bath, he crept into bed with Irelena Vondrakova, and fell asleep quickly in her arms. He dreamed of a soft summer sea lapping against a deserted shore, and in the morning, before he woke, there was a smile on his lips.

Chapter 23

The sleek white hull, more than eighty metres from stem to stern, nosed into the deep harbour of Monte Carlo. The motor yacht *Maracaibo*, churning the Mediterranean with her huge propellers, manoeuvred for almost ten minutes before she berthed at the foot of Monaco's rock. The boom and anti-torpedo net were pulled back across the harbour mouth and resecured below the south tower. With the ship tied up, crewmen let down a gangway for passengers to disembark into the spring weather of a brilliant May morning on the Riviera.

Doctor Solomon threaded his way through a small crowd gathered on the dockside, and was escorted on board by one of the ship's officers. The two men were swallowed by the shadows of the superstructure. Several figures lounged on the sundeck but no one came ashore, so the crowd eventually lost interest and dispersed.

Christopher Quinn stepped back from his balcony overlooking the harbour and sat down to a late breakfast of coffee and croissants.

He had returned to Monte Carlo from Amsterdam, where he had travelled in a last attempt to save his diamond transaction. He had located the source of each cache which had been signed away and legally accepted by Jan Van der Voors, but the owners, mostly Jews, were no longer in German-occupied Holland. Some had been interned, others killed, but the majority were untraceable.

Quinn adjusted his dark glasses, closed his eyes and felt the sun on his face. Pabst had stipulated, as the Swiss insisted, that the diamond transfer must be legal, but officially the diamonds still belonged to a dead Dutchman called Van der Voors, who had left no instructions for their disposal. As they belonged to his company, they should have been passed to its other three directors, but they too were Jewish and had fled abroad. It was not a quandary, it was an impasse.

The telephone rang. Quinn picked it up and heard Maggie Lawrence wishing him good morning.

'You sound in fine fettle,' he told her.

'How about lunch?' she asked him. 'Twelve thirty, in the Grill?'

Quinn smiled. 'Are you buying?'

'Why Mr Quinn,' said Maggie in her Scarlett O'Hara voice, 'it would be my pleasure to shell out fo' a gentleman.'

'I'll meet you in the upstairs bar,' said Quinn, and replaced the receiver.

He lit a cigarette and inhaled deeply, then picked up the phone again and began to dial the Gestapo number. He would begin with congratulations and condolences, all Irish charm. Pabst's father had been killed in a British bombing raid, and his son had inherited the family estates. He had also been told of his promotion to lieutenant-colonel.

A German voice came on the line.

'Is Colonel Pabst there?'

'Speaking.'

Quinn swallowed. The conversation was not going to be easy.

Ben Harrison stretched, feeling the sun on his body. He coughed, as he always did when his lungs expanded. The morning constitutional which he took every day round the Rock had been interrupted by the sight of a beautiful private yacht as it berthed in the harbour.

It was almost a year since he had arrived in Monte Carlo. Normally he would have been all around the Mediterranean and back. It was remarkable that he did not feel restless. He had moved from the Hotel de Paris and settled happily into Agatha Parry's villa.

'Bloody lovely yacht,' he said to himself, took out an oval cigarette, one of the last of his cherished hoard of Passing Clouds, lit up, coughed again and decided that he would go down later in the day to examine the *Maracaibo* more carefully. From a distance she looked even bigger than the yacht belonging to Prince Andrew of Greece, who had recently made a run for the port as the Mediterranean war hotted up. The only other difference Ben noticed, as he turned away to walk the hundred yards to the villa, was that this new arrival, ocean-going obviously, superbly kept, with spanking mahogany decks, cream superstructure, twin masts, a single funnel, and that long glistening white hull, was flying an American flag.

'Before the war it was all different,' said Ben. He had returned from his morning walk and was describing the yacht in the harbour. Agatha Parry sat in an armchair beside a fire; despite the pleasant weather, she had a rug wrapped around her legs. Recovery from her accident was proving difficult and she was still weak six weeks after she had left hospital. Ben had been looked after by the maid, Emma, until Agatha's return. Now both of them cared for Agatha.

He often found himself in the kitchen, wearing an apron and whistling merrily. A year before, he would not have thought this possible. The environment offered him the first stability for many years, and after more than a decade the gypsy in his soul had begun to settle down. The truth was that he had actually begun to enjoy himself with Agatha Parry.

The only substantial things in Ben's life, after his wife's death, had been a Swiss bank account, a futile affair with a diplomat's spinster daughter whenever he was in Cairo, and his flat in Jermyn Street. He had successfully lost himself in the big world, indulging his appreciation of valuable objects and collecting them – even if the price was merely a passing friendship. Older women had always found him charming until the day he moved on and they discovered they had mislaid their most valuable trinkets. Ben showed as much concern as they did if confronted, and had mastered just the right degree of horror to allay suspicion.

He was never short of cash, neither was he ostentatious. His years had given him dignity, and somehow he managed to avoid pomposity. This was why, with his tall lithe figure, open smile and clear eyes glittering their special message of trust, he remained a very attractive scoundrel.

Ben joined Agatha beside the fire. Emma brought them coffee, complained about the market prices now that vegetables had become scarce, then went to answer a knock at the front door.

'We have a lot to do together now, you and I,' said Agatha, and looked at Ben with eyes that failed to hide her feelings.

Ben smiled at Agatha. Since he had gently lifted her broken body from the roadway into the ambulance and cared for her each day at the hospital, he had come to love not only what he saw but equally the memory of her youth and beauty for which he had fallen once before.

And now they shared secrets. She had revealed to him that she worked

181

for the British government, which had prompted him to tell her everything about his former life. He had promised to reform and meant it.

Ben knelt beside Agatha, seizing her hand. She gazed kindly at his bronzed, lined face.

He had taken her head between his hands to kiss her, when the door opened and Gestapo Colonel Pabst stepped into the room. Ben stood up slowly. Pabst smiled and with sharp eyes quickly examined the décor. His gaze came to rest on Agatha.

'What a lovely room.'

Two men appeared behind him, then Emma pushed past them. 'They just walked in Ma'am. I told . . .' she stopped. 'Shall I call the police?'

'Yes,' said Agatha. 'Get Gerard!'

The quiet voice of the colonel stopped further action.

'The chief of police is seated outside in his car, Madame,' he smiled.

The colour drained from Agatha's face.

'What do you want?' snapped Ben.

'We wish to ask Miss Parry some questions.'

'On what authority?' asked Agatha.

'The Third Reich's,' he replied quietly. 'Can you walk?' Agatha shook her head. Pabst waved to his men as Ben stepped forward.

'You have no right to ask questions . . .'

'Ben!' shouted Agatha fearfully.

Pabst lost his patience and seized the Englishman by his shirt and tie, thrusting him against the door jamb. The German was strong and the older man's protests were cut short. Pabst whispered his words, anger accentuating the German voice.

'Do not worry, Mr Harrison,' he hissed. 'My questions will not harm Miss Parry . . . but her *answers* might!'

Maggie Lawrence was late. She had been shopping that morning, and when she arrived in the lobby of the Hotel de Paris, the bell boy who was with her suggested that they wait for the lift to come down again as it was more than half-full of people already. So they watched the doors close and waited.

The lift finally arrived and Maggie tipped the helpful bell boy then asked the lift attendant for the top floor and the Grill. As they went up, her eyes began to cloud with tears, but she stopped herself from crying. She wanted to be presentable for the man she was meeting for lunch.

The lift arrived and the attendant opened the gates.

'Could you get Mr Quinn?' she asked. 'He'll be at the bar, just around the corner.'

'*Oui, Madame,*' said the man and disappeared for a moment. Someone, seven floors below in the lobby, pressed for the lift, and there was a slight movement until Maggie reached up and pressed the 'stop' button.

Christopher Quinn arrived at the lift and greeted her with a smile. 'Welcome back to the real world. You look wonderful.'

Maggie knew what he was looking at.

'It's only for convenience, darling,' she said. 'Help me out.'

The dark Irishman and the beautiful blond in her wheelchair began lunch together in the top floor Grill at the Hotel de Paris.

At 1.30 Jürgen Pabst and Guy de Salis wandered through the bar and were shown to a window table, overlooking the harbour, in the crowded restaurant. News had just been released that the Deputy Führer, Rudolf Hess, had defected to Great Britain. Guy de Salis made a point of mentioning it.

'There is so much news in wartime,' said Pabst, shrugging off the disturbing implications. 'Who can tell what is fact or fiction? Propaganda is a great weapon.'

Claret was poured out and two steaks arrived. Mustard was offered and green vegetables served. The two men began to eat.

'I gather the war is going well?' de Salis began again. 'Now it seems Germany wants Greece.'

'We are helping the Italians, that is all.'

'And clearing the British occupation forces from the very seat of European civilization,' said de Salis.

Pabst smiled expansively. 'But we Germans revere Greece. The Führer is giving us a whole new world of art and architecture, so do not think that culture is not important to the Third Reich. Our military machine is only the might which gains us respect. It is our enemies that force us to ruthless measures.'

The two men finished their steaks, then ordered cheese and coffee. Rolls were brought and the last of the wine poured out.

'So!' said Pabst. 'There is a complication with the merchandise from Amsterdam?'

'The transaction is no longer possible.'

'Unfortunate.'

'For ourselves also,' said de Salis. 'There was a certain interest from a connection of ours in South America . . .' He looked across the dining room and spotted Christopher Quinn lunching with a blonde woman whose back was towards him.

De Salis continued. '. . . after all, the deal is worth many, many millions of francs, dollars, reichmarks – whatever currency you wish.' The Swiss banker's gaze wandered through the window to the vista over the harbour and Rock of Monaco. Beyond, across the Mediterranean, was North Africa.

Pabst smiled and looked into de Salis's eyes.

'The Dutchman was a Jew.'

'So I understood,' said de Salis. There was a harshness in his voice. He coughed to conceal it and sipped more wine.

'What is the Swiss attitude to Jews?' asked Pabst, finishing his claret.

'What is yours towards the wine, Herr Pabst? It is Jewish.'

'What is Jewish?'

'The wine,' said de Salis. 'The Rothschilds, who own the vineyard, came from the slums of Frankfurt.'

Pabst's smile contained no humour. 'But the grapes are French, Monsieur de Salis. That is the abomination of the Jews, that they are parasites. They infiltrate a healthy people and feed off them for their own gain. They have no allegiance but to themselves, acquisition and greed.' Although Pabst's eyes were blazing, his voice was low. 'It is our intention to eradicate the problem for the future.'

'Where there is money,' Pabst went on, inhaling the bouquet of a very special brandy, 'there you will find the Jew. But surely you know that?' He paused for a moment. De Salis sipped his cognac and said nothing. 'After all,' said Pabst in a genial voice, 'you must have many customers who are Jews. Jews with large, numbered accounts, shares, bonds, stocks . . . I am naive in such matters, but even as a boy I imagined those huge, mysterious underground vaults that make Switzerland almost . . . I was about to say "exotic".' His smile broadened. 'Walls, from floor to ceiling full of safe deposit boxes, each with a key, each with a number, a long number peculiar to the owner, and I remember asking myself, as many of us did after the National Socialist Party was founded on such meagre finances, how many of the owners of such boxes in Switzerland were Jewish.'

The banker was squeezing his brandy glass very hard. His knuckles showed white.

'Many of them are Jewish,' said de Salis quietly.

Pabst leaned across the table and whispered: 'And do these owners come often to open their boxes?'

De Salis was slow in answering. 'This is privileged information, you must understand.'

'The Swiss, Herr de Salis, are neutral. And all around is Germany.' Pabst's hand made a gesture circling his brandy glass on the table.

De Salis breathed deeply. 'The Jews do not come as often as before the war.'

Pabst reached out and seized the Swiss banker as if taking the hand of a comrade in arms. 'After the war, Herr de Salis, they may not come at all!'

De Salis leaned back in his chair, away from the German. 'What are you suggesting?' he asked quietly.

'I am waiting *for* suggestions.'

The men continued to look at each other, and nothing was said for a full minute.

Christopher Quinn, pushing Maggie Lawrence, passed by without a word to either of them. Pabst ordered two more cognacs.

'What is to become of the Irishman, Quinn?' asked de Salis.

'It depends upon the diamonds,' Pabst answered slowly.

'Without the necessary papers, any transaction would be illegal.' De Salis's voice was definite.

'You can see no solution?'

De Salis remained aggressive, mocking. 'You could steal them,' he said.

'An interesting thought,' said the German, appreciating the change in his companion's attitude. Both of them looked towards the lift, to watch Christopher Quinn push Maggie through the metal gates and out of sight.

'Herr Quinn knows a good deal about both of us. I ask your opinion only.' Pabst paused. 'Would you say that Herr Quinn was expendable?'

'More,' said the Swiss banker, his face hardening. 'I would advise it.' He sipped his cognac. 'Quinn has become a liability, and there are so many more important things to discuss, now.'

Jürgen Pabst had begun to see numbers, long numbers, and Jews, and a box in the wall of a huge vault: the very bowels of Switzerland opening, a single hand reaching out to reveal the contents, the untold treasure within. His imagination raced. There were *hundreds* of deposit boxes, *thousands* of hands, *millions* of Jews. If each had a number . . . Digits became imprinted in that German mind – as they would be tattooed into Jewish skin.

On the second floor of the Hotel de Paris, the telephone rang in the Blue Suite: Harry picked it up.

'Who is it?'

'Ben Harrison,' came the reply.

'Come up,' said Harry and replaced the receiver.

Vondrakova was away in Paris with Ludovic. She had been gone two weeks, and although she telephoned regularly, Harry was missing her badly. Since their return from Austria she had been different. She had withdrawn into herself, her humour was gone and with it the wonderful sparkle in her eyes; where once there had been mischief, there was now a challenging hardness.

Violence had penetrated her delicate defences. An innocence had been destroyed, her gentle heart irreparably damaged. Clinically she had not been raped, but physically the attempt had been enough. She had lost her vulnerability.

When Ben Harrison arrived, he was smoking nervously.

'The Gestapo have taken Agatha,' he said.

'Did they search the house?'

'Not yet. And I told Emma to keep the door locked and bolted.'
Harry poured two stiff whiskies.
'Sit down,' he said, 'you don't look well.'

Ben Harrison's enquiries, conducted the morning after Danny Morgan's escape, had unearthed some interesting facts. The gossip from the Casino had become public knowledge, but the exact method of the RAF pilot's departure remained a mystery. Then the Resistance man from the dinghy gave him the details.

Harry Pilikian had been approached several days later and agreed to meet the Englishman. Ben Harrison explained that he had certain contacts and indicated quite clearly that he was actively anti-Nazi. It was precisely what Harry Pilikian wanted to hear. Since his experience on the Brenner Pass, he felt himself to be at war.

A further meeting with Agatha Parry and Eva Trenchard showed that they had already discovered a great deal about Mr Pilikian before approaching him for help. At the end of the meeting Harry had agreed to do what he could. His last picture of Agatha was of a tenacious little Englishwoman, seated in an armchair by the fire, smiling goodbye with Ben stretched out beside her. Harry shook his head, wondering privately how the English thought they were going to win the war with such warriors. Aloud he said: 'Thank you for the tea.'

Ben Harrison was allowed to see Agatha Parry on the fifth day of her detention, in Pabst's basement cell.

When they were alone, Agatha put a finger to her lips, but Ben would not be silenced.

'I've spoken to Gerard and I'm going to the Palace again tomorrow. You needn't worry, we're going to get you out.'

'Talk to me about the old days, Ben, please,' said Agatha, with eyes urging caution.

Ben paused, recalling images of England and his wife Margaret, so long ago and so far away that it might have been another world. He coughed, and used a handkerchief to wipe tears from his eyes. What did it matter if Pabst heard? What did any of it matter? He had learnt already, to his cost, that what is given is eventually taken away. His mind filled with the past, and he told Agatha stories until she laughed.

'We all have our time, Ben,' said Agatha softly. 'Our only responsibility is to those who come after. I know you understand that.' She squeezed his hand. 'Please Ben, remember . . .' her voice lost its firmness, 'remember me kindly.'

The cell door swung open.

'*Raus!*' said a German voice. 'Outside!'

Slowly Ben got to his feet. 'I'll come again,' he said. Agatha just stared at him. 'Tomorrow,' said Ben, 'I'll come again.'

The cell door clanged shut.

Diplomacy at the Palace and legal pleas at the police station failed. The world situation was described as too delicate, as was the Englishwoman's presence and suspicions of her activities in Monte Carlo. The Germans had been victorious throughout the Balkans. They had won the battle for Greece and taken the island of Crete by storm. The police in Monaco therefore were constrained by forces greater than justice. Ben was not allowed into the prison the following day or any other. Unable to help, he could only pray.

On the twelfth day of her detention, under torture, Agatha admitted to her connection with the British Secret Service. Pabst now had every reason to take her to the Third Reich and Berlin for questioning. This Agatha knew she could not survive without betraying everything she had sworn to protect. Pabst wanted everything, and would get it if she lived. She began to make plans accordingly.

Chapter 24

The day of 31 May began badly. The weather remained warm but by the late morning it was pouring with rain. The atmosphere was heavy and the sound of thunder came from far out at sea.

Vondrakova had returned to Monaco and was staying with Harry at the Hotel de Paris. The tone of voice she had used with Ludovic on the telephone link with Berlin the previous day had persuaded him to return in order to emphasize the importance of the Moscow concert to his Leibchen. He hoped to allay her fears and ask Mr Pilikian to give up his single-minded battle to wrest his Vondrakova from her vocation. All the necessary papers had been arranged, granted in Berlin by the cultural attaché at the Russian embassy. Many of the communist hierarchy were to be present at the concert which was planned for the night of Saturday, 21 June. It would be an important evening.

When Ludovic arrived, Vondrakova and Harry had taken him directly to Cartier's where they bought each other presents, identical inscribed cigarette cases. The three of them sat down to lunch together. The meal started well enough, and they were all in good humour until coffee, dessert, and more conversation about Moscow. Ludovic and Harry began to argue.

'Please,' Vondrakova interrupted. People were looking at their table. 'I would like a cigarette.' Both men snapped open their new gold Cartier cases. They were empty. Together they pressed them shut, and with much laughter made a series of toasts designed to alleviate all the problems of a troubled world.

Vondrakova smiled generously. 'We are,' she began, trying to recall an expression of Harry's, '. . . lock, stock and barrel.'

'Hook, line and sinker,' countered Harry. They made a rendezvous, 7 that evening in the American Bar prior to Ludovic's 8 o'clock railway departure via Milan, Vienna and Prague for his destination, Moscow. Then Harry and Vondrakova went upstairs for a siesta.

By 6 in the evening it had become unusually dark, and the security they had found in each other's arms had turned to love. Throughout the late afternoon the rumbling thunder and occasional flashes of lightning in the sombre sky had disturbed everyone trying to snatch some hours of peace and sleep in the lowering Mediterranean weather.

Rumours of deteriorating relations between Russia and Germany had been growing for some time, and Harry was determined that Vondrakova should not go to Moscow. They had argued about it several times, then agreed not to mention the subject again. It was a promise he could not keep.

The two of them awoke, warm bodies entwined between cool sheets. Harry Pilikian, his head on the pillows, gazed at Vondrakova, who lay beside him propped on her elbows. Her blonde hair wafted against his face, borne by an early evening breeze. The long windows leading on to the balcony were open. Thunder rumbled again, louder. The Mediterranean summer storm which had been moving around the Principality was coming back.

'I *am* going, Harry. You must know that. I have to.'

Harry eased himself up in the bed, leaning against the headboard. His eyes were staring through the curtains out to sea, into the fading day, into the past.

'Harry, what is it?' she asked softly. Harry shivered.

'Nothing,' he answered. Vondrakova kissed him tenderly on the lips, slid from the sheets, turned on a low lamp, lit a cigarette from the now filled gold case on the bedside table then walked slowly to the windows opening on to the overcast sky of early evening.

She appeared to Harry, who watched her every move, like a vision from a dream. He climbed slowly from the bed and joined her by the open windows where she fell into his embrace.

'God I love you,' he whispered.

Vondrakova shook her head slowly.

'No, Harry, it is only passion.'

'It is more than that,' he murmured.

Vondrakova sighed, staring at him. 'I have seen those eyes before,' she sighed tenderly, and touched Harry's cheek.

'When?' he asked softly. Vondrakova's smile died.

'He no longer exists,' she said, and looked away. Outside, beyond the horizon, thunder rumbled.

'I love you,' Harry repeated softly.

'A moment,' she said, turning to him. 'We are a moment in time. That is all they will ever say of us.'

'And what will we say?' he asked.

Vondrakova leaned against him. 'Words?' she whispered.

'Yes.'

'They are only for songs, Harry.'

'And stories,' he said gently. 'I know.'

'Then hold me tight now,' she whispered. 'There is nothing else but now . . . .'

Their lips met. Only when their mouths had parted and she lay against him, head upon his chest, did she murmur the single word, 'Moscow.' But it was lost to Harry's ears in the sound of distant thunder.

In the bar of the Hotel de Paris, at 7 o'clock that evening in May 1941, all the tables were full. Despite the war there was no lack of finery. The older women wore furs, the younger revealing *décolleté* dresses, and all wore jewellery. Most of the husbands and companions or lovers were elegantly turned out in dinner jackets.

Ludovic beamed at Harry and Vondrakova, beckoning from across the room, where he had champagne waiting.

At ten minutes to eight, Ludovic, Vondrakova and Pilikian were on the station platform. There were hugs and kisses and tears from Vondrakova as the old Hungarian in his long black coat and Homburg climbed into his compartment, waved goodbye yet again as the train moved out, and amidst steam and smoke disappeared into the wet night.

When they came out of the station onto the pathway beneath the Casino, the rain had stopped temporarily. Harry closed the umbrella and hugged Vondrakova.

'We'll have dinner at the Café Vistaero in France. I know the guards, they'll let us across the border.'

Harry Pilikian drove the Rolls Royce along the glistening road towards Menton. Recently imposed restrictions meant that his sheaf of papers now allowed him only into Vichy France. They climbed the road leading high into the hills and mountains and eventually reached

189

the small restaurant above Roquebrune. They were seated at a window and to their right was Monte Carlo, partly lit, where no other lights showed along the entire coastline.

'One day,' said Harry, 'we will come back here together, after the war!'

'And there will be lights,' breathed Vondrakova excitedly squeezing his hand. 'Oh so many lights.' They kissed in the candlelight, ordered what dinner was available and reflected, yet again, on how lucky they were to be together.

In the cell occupied by Agatha Parry there was no sound but the hollow booming of the sea. Then she heard footsteps which came closer and stopped. She opened her eyes.

Colonel Jürgen Pabst was standing in the doorway looking up at the single electric light bulb in the cell.

'I hope you are comfortable, Miss Parry?' he asked.

'It's damp,' she said.

'I am sorry, we must move you to more elegant surroundings.' He smiled. 'Neumann, Koch!' Two men appeared in the doorway. Pabst's eyes were cruel. 'You have been lucky. You have seen a friend and had people plead for you in the Principality. But now you belong to Germany; to us!'

'What more do you want?'

'The right answers,' said Pabst. 'Your friend has seen you for the last time here in Monaco. I thought we might talk tonight before you go to Berlin tomorrow.' Pabst watched Agatha's face turn white. 'We have searched your house.' Agatha stopped breathing. Pabst smiled. 'And we found a British flag flying on the roof.'

'I have always flown that flag. Did you take it down?'

Pabst made an expansive gesture. 'This is a neutral country.'

'I can tell you nothing,' said Agatha. 'You know that.'

Pabst leaned on the table. 'I have a dinner party in an hour,' he said, 'in the restaurant of the Salle Privée at the Casino. Do you know it? Pleasant food. Bland, like the English.'

Agatha said nothing. The two Germans shifted their feet.

'Now, are you going to cooperate?' Pabst's eyes were vicious.

'I want to know who the others are?'

'No,' said Agatha softly.

Pabst's eyes narrowed. 'Neumann, Koch,' he rapped. 'Carry her!'

In the semi-darkness, Agatha Parry was taken down stone steps into the basement where a solitary cell had been carved out of the rock. No sound came but the heavy booming of the waves breaking against the cliffs outside. There was moisture on the walls and two dim electric light bulbs, one hooded, the other naked, dangled from the high ceiling, where there were also iron hooks embedded in the stone, a legacy of Napoleonic times. Several chairs were placed round a table at the centre on which stood bottles and scientific-looking equipment. Agatha Parry was lowered into a chair. Pabst seated himself opposite, across the table. The two men, Neumann and Koch, stepped outside but left the door ajar. Agatha Parry surveyed the cell cautiously. Pabst watched, amused.

'Imagine the souls who have been here, languishing in the bowels of this fairy-tale Principality.'

Agatha said nothing, already counting the minutes. She had recognized the bottles on the table and what they contained.

Waves crashed outside, moisture dripped from the walls, one of the light bulbs flickered. Pabst reached for a bottle, put it down closer on the table, then methodically lined up two more – playing with them as he was playing with Agatha's life.

'Sulphuric. Nitric. Hydrochloric.' He glanced at his watch. 'I do not have much time, Miss Parry.' Agatha remained silent. 'I wish to know precisely what is your connection with the British Secret Service.' He took the top from the thick glass bottle of nitric acid. 'Please Miss Parry, no games. I can save you a great deal of pain if you will answer simple questions.'

Agatha faked a smile: it was not easy. Pabst stared at the Englishwoman for a long time. 'Can you stand?' he asked eventually. She nodded.

The Gestapo colonel's eyes strayed to the ceiling with the hooks embedded in the stone. He took out a leather cigarette case, offered a cigarette to Agatha, who refused, lit one himself, inhaled and blew smoke into the cold atmosphere of the cell.

'Neumann!' he said. 'Koch!' The two Germans appeared in the cell doorway. 'Bring some rope,' said Pabst. 'I do not want to be late for dinner.'

In the villa overlooking the Mediterranean which Agatha Parry's family had owned for several generations, Ben Harrison sat in front of the communications equipment behind the concealed door in the library and tapped out his call sign once more. Even in the basement of the house, he could hear the approaching storm rumbling. He could get no reply. Tonight Malta seemed far away, and the bastion of England even further than it had ever been.

Ben turned to the small window of the ventilation shaft, hearing the falling rain, heavy, almost tropical, and imagined the despair of so many people listening to that same sound in occupied Europe. He remembered times on board ships, when he had been on deck during sleepless nights, watching the shifting ocean swell and feeling that same despondent hopelessness.

He tapped out his call sign yet again, but the great storm between Europe and Africa had enveloped the small island of Malta and created such atmospheric disturbance that there was no reply. He was sure that he could not be heard.

The screaming lasted for half a minute. It came from the very centre of the woman's body, a helpless expression of pure fear, the cry of a trapped animal, years of control failing against welling panic and intense pain. It was a sound not unfamiliar to the Gestapo.

In the deep cell, cut from the Rock, the naked electric light bulb shone on to the anguished face of Agatha Parry, tied to a heavy wooden chair, sweat breaking out over delicate skin. Pabst, smoking a cigarette, apparently unmoved, released a pipette of alkaline solution along a three-inch line on the woman's bare arm. The solution neutralized the burning acid on the white flesh of the upturned arm. The woman began sobbing and her head fell forward.

'It hurts, doesn't it?' said the German softly.

'How would *you* know?' spat Agatha Parry. She threw back her head, perspiration running from her brow.

'I watch,' said Pabst. He leaned forward with a cloth and began to wipe the sweat from Agatha's forehead. She shook her head from side to side.

Pabst smiled at her defiance. It was not unusual at this stage. He had only just begun. She had refused to answer simple questions for more than twenty-five minutes. Time was pressing and he did not want to be late for dinner. There were a number of Italians from military intelligence and the secret service coming to dine and gamble in Monte Carlo. At this very moment, they were doing him a service on the border at Ventimiglia.

'Neumann,' he ordered, 'check the open line to Italian headquarters.'

Neumann stepped into the corridor. Koch remained seated in the corner, impassive, watching, waiting to be of assistance.

The Gestapo Colonel again withdrew nitric acid from the bottle. The pipette hovered over Agatha's forearm. For a moment she stared at it, then turned her head, her eyes boring into Pabst's. He waited.

'All I wish to know is your function in the organization.'

Agatha said nothing. Pabst released the acid, drawing a careful line along the woman's arm. Agatha's screams came in spasms as she gasped for air. Pabst watched vapour rise, as he applied the alkaline solution. Again the woman's head bowed.

'Miss Parry, you must understand that this is merely improvisation. Here in Monte Carlo what else can I do? In Berlin you will be less comfortable, I assure you. It would be better to tell me everything, now.'

He looked at Agatha expectantly. 'You will,' he said. 'Everyone does eventually.'

For a full minute they were eye to eye. Pabst detected a glint in the woman's gaze which he could not identify. He hoped that it was cooperation, then recognized that it was not and lashed out, backhanding Agatha across the face, whipping her head to one side. He stood up, eyes blazing, staring at the hooks in the ceiling.

'Koch, untie her!'

From the corridor outside, there were footsteps. Neumann snapped to attention. 'The man has been taken from the train at Ventimiglia, sir.'

'Good,' said Colonel Pabst absently.

'Already they have discovered information in Russian.'

Pabst watched Koch untying Agatha Parry. 'Thank you Neumann,' he said. 'I will deal with that later.'

'They said you were to dine . . .'

'Yes, yes, I will. Neumann,' said Pabst. 'Get the ropes!'

The two Germans threw both lengths of rope over the two hooks in the ceiling. Pabst took one last look at the Englishwoman staring up at the two nooses now hanging over the table. 'As you find it so difficult to support yourself, we will do it for you'. He smiled, 'A bientôt Miss Parry.' He stepped out of the cell followed by his men. 'Suspend the woman from her arms' he ordered quietly, 'then tie both hands behind her back.'

'Yes sir,' replied Koch and snapped to attention.

'And be sure she is conscious when I return,' he murmured to Neumann who nodded. 'I am already late.'

The two Germans had barely reached the end of the corridor when there was a crashing sound from the cell, a scream cut short and a shout from Koch. Pabst spun around and ran back to the open cell. The table was overturned. Agatha Parry, her head to one side, was dangling like a limp puppet from one of the nooses. Already her eyes were dead.

'She jumped sir!' said Koch.

'How?' snapped Neumann. 'She had no strength.'

The Englishwoman began to swing more slowly.

'She found strength from somewhere,' hissed the Gestapo Colonel. He was breathing heavily, his anger barely controlled.

'Cut the bitch down!'

Chapter 25

In high spirits, Irelena Vondrakova and Harry Pilikian ran from the Café Vistaero out into the darkness and torrential rain. They were in France, high on the coastal bluffs above Monte Carlo, and they laughed with the pleasure of being together, stimulated by each other's company, good wine and, despite wartime privations, an excellent meal.

The Rolls Royce was parked under a canopy next to an old Citroën belonging to the chef. They climbed in, shaking the rain from their coats. Checking that the hood was secure, Harry started the engine and backed out into the downpour.

The night was almost impenetrable, but the road was familiar. He negotiated the descent carefully. At the intersection, he turned sharply on to the coast road and drove back in the direction of Monte Carlo. The dimmed headlights of the Rolls Royce finally picked out the border post, where Harry showed papers, first to the Italians, then to the Vichy French and finally to the Monégasque police. They passed through the barbed-wire border and began to see lights.

Moments later, the car was in the Boulevard des Moulins, passing down the Boulingrin Gardens and into the Place du Casino. Harry pulled up in front of the Hotel de Paris. Vondrakova encircled Harry's neck, clasping him with her arms. She rubbed her nose against his and presented her soft lips to be kissed. Then Michel was at the door with a great black umbrella, and the three of them, jumping over the rushing water in the gutter, ran towards the hotel, took the steps two at a time and pushed through the revolving door. Rain dripped from Harry's dark felt hat and sparkled on the scarf thrown over Vondrakova's blonde hair; her eyes were full of anticipation. Harry kissed her.

'What shall we do?'

The sound of a piano came from the crowded bar. Across the huge lobby behind them, telephones rang at the reception desk. Outside there was a crack of thunder.

'Gamble for Ludovic,' said Vondrakova, laughing.

They crossed to the cloakroom, where Harry left his hat and dark topcoat. Vondrakova took off her furs. She was wearing the gold dress which clung to her figure. It was the way Harry had first seen her and he was enchanted as she shook her hair free of the scarf.

'There, you see, I am ready!' She brushed some strands of Harry's dark hair from his forehead and wiped away raindrops as he kissed several that were on her cheek.

'Wait one moment,' he said, strode to the stairs and ran up them two at a time until he reached the second floor. In his rooms he unlocked a drawer, opened the pigskin bag inside, and took a 20,000-franc plaque from what remained of Danny Morgan's winnings.

Moments later he and Vondrakova, arm in arm, went back to the private lift just inside the entrance and down to the corridor which led directly to the Monte Carlo Casino. They took the steps up into the pillared foyer and made their way across the marble floor into the kitchen, which was full and noisy. The two of them threaded their way through the various groups and different nationalities thronging the tables, passed into the outer room of the white salon, and, with a nod of recognition from the guards, entered the Salle Privée. In the distance beyond the gaming rooms was the restaurant, where those who came to dine could watch the gambling and, as the evening developed, join the play.

Harry and Vondrakova went directly to the crowded tables and found a space at a roulette wheel, where Harry changed the large plaque he had brought with him for smaller chips. He watched Vondrakova play seven, eleven and seventeen. She lost three times and pouted like a child.

'I am not lucky tonight,' she said.

'Bet with the house, they always win in the end,' he whispered and put a large stake on zero. The wheel spun and the ball found its place.

'Zéro,' declared the croupier. Vondrakova laughed, Harry shrugged, they collected the winnings and moved on.

At the entrance to the restaurant the head waiter recognized Harry and bowed.

'C'est l'invasion,' said Maurice confidentially. 'We have the world here tonight.'

Shouts went up from some Italians at the roulette table nearby, and the host of a large party in the restaurant began complaining loudly to one of the waiters. A tall man, he stood up, arguing, then tore the bill to pieces. The head waiter bowed quickly and went to mediate.

'This is madness!' laughed Vondrakova in Harry's ear.

'Courtesy of Hitler,' whispered Harry in reply.

Vondrakova looked into his eyes. 'It gives them pleasure, Harry. Let them enjoy it. Do not be critical.' Her lips found his and lingered a moment.

'Herr Pilikian.'

Harry turned his head. Pabst was standing beside the balustrade above them. He smiled at Vondrakova.

195

'You look so beautiful, Fraulein. Perhaps you would both like to join us?'

Harry's face became a mask of distaste as he shook his head.

Pabst, in a dinner jacket, looked dangerously elegant. 'I had not expected to see you here.' He spoke to Vondrakova, although his eyes were on Harry.

A ball fell into place at a roulette wheel and there were screams of joy from women at the table, as their escorts finally won.

'We dined earlier,' said Harry.

Pabst reached into his jacket pocket and took out a cigarette case. He pressed it open. 'Can I offer you one of these?' The case was gold. 'Handsome, isn't it?' he said. 'Cartier.'

Vondrakova's face drained of blood. Harry felt her sagging on his arm. There was no need to read the inscription: it was Ludovic's.

'Where is he?' whispered Vondrakova.

'Who?' asked Pabst deliberately.

Vondrakova exploded. 'Where is he?!' In the immediate area around them the crowds were silenced.

'You will see him eventually,' said Pabst quietly. 'Do not make a spectacle of yourself. Go to the bar and wait. Do not attempt to leave here.' Someone at Pabst's table made a remark that set off roars of laughter. The Gestapo colonel snapped his heels, turned back and sat down.

Harry took Vondrakova quickly across the crowded room to a corner table at the bar and ordered brandy.

'They have taken him,' she said softly, staring but seeing nothing.

'Is it Moscow?' asked Harry, whispering. Vondrakova nodded her head. Tears filled her eyes. 'Tell me!' said Harry, seizing her. She turned her face to his.

'I am dangerous, Harry. Dangerous for you.'

'Why?'

'Because he works for the Russians.'

'What are you saying?'

Vondrakova gasped for air and when she spoke the words were almost inaudible.

'We both work for them.'

Vondrakova was on her feet and stepping through the curtains into the Salle Privée before he could move. For a moment he lost her, then glimpsed the golden dress and began to push roughly through the crowds. He saw her reach the Caisse and exit, which was barred by several men. She hesitated, then turned and plunged towards the huge, mirrored double doors, thrusting them wide on to the long staircase leading down to the Cabaret.

Pabst and another German had already jumped the steps from the

196

restaurant and were racing between the gaming tables. Harry lunged through the crowd, reaching the doors at the same time as Pabst's man. His momentum thrust the German into the mirrors, forcing wide the doors, which slammed closed behind them. He kicked out at Pilikian, who rolled over, then grabbed the man's foot and pulled hard. The German fell heavily, cracking his head on the brass balustrade, and began to slide down the stairs, one hand still thrust into his coat pocket, reaching for a gun. Harry seized the man at the throat, smashed two blows into his face, and he was still.

Above Harry, the double doors burst open and there was another pursuer. Harry glanced below. Vondrakova had hitched up her gold dress, kicked off her shoes and was running down the long stairway.

'Don't run!' he shouted.

She had reached the bottom and pushed through the exit doors, out into the rain, where the pathway led up beside the Casino to the square. 'Don't!' screamed Harry. But she had gone.

In the Salle Privée, Pabst forced a passage through the packed crowds and into the white salon. He ran through the reception and adjoining room to the kitchen. His men could follow her down, but if she got out of the Casino he wanted to cut her off. He was shouting commands to the two other Germans following close behind.

'I want that Russian bitch dead or alive!' he bellowed.

In the pouring rain, sobbing, Vondrakova ran barefoot up the slope towards the Casino Square. Behind her, Harry Pilikian was gaining fast.

'Wait!' he shouted. 'Don't run. Wait!' She was making for the steps of the Hotel de Paris. Harry Pilikian, already drenched, pounded past the front of the Casino and seized Vondrakova beside the Rolls Royce, which Michel had parked in front of the hotel.

'Leave me!' she screamed. 'Leave me, Harry!' Thunder cracked over-head. 'They have taken Ludovic! It is finished!' She pulled from his grasp and began to take the steps in front of the hotel. Halfway up she faltered and turned, her eyes imploring. 'Leave me, Harry, please! I am too dangerous for you!'

Thirty yards away, Pabst burst through the Casino doors. The first person he saw was one of his own men, Erich Held.

'Stop her!'

As a reflex to the command, Held pointed his gun.

'Fire!' ordered Pabst.

Across the square, through the pouring rain, lit by the dim lights of the Hotel de Paris entrance, the golden figure of Vondrakova was three steps away from the revolving doors.

'Fire!' commanded Pabst.

Held had recognized his target with horror. The woman who had found a special place in his heart – *his* Irelena Vondrakova. But he was a member of the Gestapo and had been given an order. He pulled the trigger of the 9 mm. Schmeisser machine pistol.

Bullets ripped through the revolving doors of the Hotel de Paris, smashing glass, ripping at wood. He had fired high. Deliberately.

Vondrakova froze in fear. Harry Pilikian leapt up the steps and seized her in his arms.

'Dushinka,' she whispered, 'it is over.'

On the Casino steps, Pabst had now pulled out his Walther pistol, extended his arm and squinted along the sights, aiming at the centre of Harry Pilikian's back. A flash of lightning filled the square.

Vondrakova saw the Gestapo officer beneath the canopy of the Casino, and knew that his target was in her arms. She spun Pilikian off-balance. 'No, dushinka,' she said, 'not you.'

Pabst fired twice. Both bullets found their mark, penetrating the gold dress, tearing into the soft flesh and sinking deep into Vondrakova's body. She arched backwards, her face raised to the night sky, rain washing hair from her forehead, sweeping away tears.

She was already fading, her eyes staring. Harry held her in his arms.

'There are no stars,' she whispered.

Pabst reached Harry first, dragging him from Vondrakova's body, then Held came through the pouring rain, dropped his gun and lifted the dying singer in his arms. Pilikian, on his knees, reached out for Pabst, who slammed the Walther's butt against Harry's temple, knocking him down the steps. Two more Germans ran through the rain across to the hotel entrance.

As Pilikian got to his feet, Pabst hit him again with a brutal crack on the skull. Harry began to collapse, but found Pabst's legs and hung on. Pabst hit him yet again with the gun butt, but Harry ignored his pain, sobbing with helpless anger. First one, then the other German began to pull at Pilikian. One of them kicked him, another punched the side of his face.

Held had found shelter beneath the hotel canopy and was oblivious of everything but the blond woman in his arms. As her blood flowed down his wet black leather coat, he began crying like a young boy, holding Vondrakova tight, whispering endearments to her in German.

Harry ignored the beating he was getting and reached towards Pabst's face, but one of the Germans picked up Held's machine pistol, raised it high above his head and brought the butt down heavily on the back of Pilikian's neck.

At that moment Gerard, the Monégasque chief of police, arrived with six of his men. They ran up the steps of the Hotel de Paris and roughly separated the Armenian-American's limp body from Pabst and the other Germans. Only that saved Harry Pilikian.

On 4 June 1941, Irelena Vondrakova was buried in the cemetery of Monte Carlo, overlooking the Mediterranean. The sombre weather continued and there was a fine rain throughout the service.

The story put out by the Germans was that Ludovic was a spy for Russia, and had been arrested at Ventimiglia carrying incriminating evidence. The Gestapo had been gathering information about his activities for some time. Only when they had discovered conclusively that the lovely Russian-born singer, Irelena Vondrakova, was also working against the Reich, had the order gone out to arrest them both.

When the funeral service finished, everyone filed slowly to the gate except for Harry Pilikian and a single German. Together they watched the gravediggers pile dirt on the coffin. Thick mud, falling in lumps. Harry looked at the German, tears showing on an impassive face.

'Held means hero in German,' Vondrakova had said.

'It is over,' murmured Erich Held.

Harry's eyes blazed through his own tears. 'Not yet,' he said between gritted teeth. 'It isn't over yet.'

When the small tombstone had been placed at the head of the grave, the two men left separately.

Chapter 26

Summer came; real summer. Cloudless days, hot sun and record temperatures at the beach. Harry had started drinking heavily and getting regularly drunk. From being amusing he tended to turn aggressive, much to Louis' concern. On 21 June, a Saturday, Louis had to help him upstairs and put him to bed. The following day, at lunchtime, Harry, wearing dark glasses, walked into a bar full of people babbling about Russia and the great invasion Hitler had launched on a two-thousand-mile front between the White Sea and the Black. The newspaper and wire service correspondents in the bar were having a field day, taking turns on the telephone and drinking copiously.

Harry wandered out of the bar and the hotel. He made his way slowly down the Avenue Monte Carlo to the harbour and walked all round La Condamine, feeling the sun on his face and the emptiness in his heart.

Having climbed the steps to one of the breakwaters that enclosed the calm harbour, Harry smoked three cigarettes in the course of an hour, staring out towards the distant, softly moulded coastline of Italy. His wounds were healing, but he felt his heart was broken.

The first breeze of late afternoon lifted his hair gently as he turned his back on the Ligurian coast. He stepped down on to the harbour wall, where so many beautiful boats were moored, and saw the *Maracaibo*. Her polished white hull was spotlessly clean, the raked superstructure gleaming where there was mahogany and shining where there was brass. He paused, reading the name etched in golden letters. From the stern flagpole, an American flag flapped gently in the soft wind.

A small face appeared at the railing. It was a little girl with blue eyes and dark hair in pigtails. She peered down at him curiously. Harry summoned a grin and waved. Her big eyes stared at Harry as he made a long face. She screwed up her nose.

'Why are you wearing a red tie?'

Harry looked down, it was an old one; he hadn't really thought about it.

'Because it's summer.'

She paused and cocked her head.

'What's your name?'

'Mr Red Tie,' he said.

'That's silly,' she said. 'Mine's Lisa. Lisa Lieberman.'

'Is your mother as pretty as you?' asked Harry, and drew deeply on his cigarette.

'Yes,' she said. 'Why do you smoke, Mr Red Tie?'

'I don't know, nerves probably,' he said.

The girl moved over to the top of the gangway and stood there. She was wearing a pink print smock.

Harry smiled. 'How old are you Lisa?'

'Six and three-quarters,' she said.

'Do you go to school?'

'Yes.'

'I bet you speak French.'

'Well, of course I do,' replied the little girl. 'The nuns teach me.'

Someone shouted for her. 'I've got to go now,' she said.

'Well, you tell your daddy that he's a lucky man,' said Harry.

The little girl smiled.

'Goodbye Lisa.'

'Goodbye Mr Red Tie.' She waved once and turned away.

Harry threw his half-finished cigarette into the harbour, took a last look at the *Maracaibo* and with a lighter heart strolled back along the harbour wall.

As June became July, Harry Pilikian stopped drinking almost completely, apart from the occasional glass of champagne in the American Bar, which seemed to be the entrance fee to joining the international group always assembled there to discuss the incredible German successes in the USSR.

Harry had nearly completed the first draft of his musical when news came in mid-July that Stalin's son Jacob had been captured near Vitebsk. Hitler was blasting his way into the heart of Russia, rolling back all before him on the road to Moscow. Even the Vichy French lost their scepticism in the euphoria of the destruction of communism. Hitler had declared that the world would hold its breath when it learned of the enormous undertaking to which he had committed the German people, and so it did – but life went on.

In America Di Maggio continued hitting his way into history; cattle were rounded up, branded, bought and sold on the sweltering plains of Texas; gangsters shot each other in seamy Chicago clubs, and more families moved to the orange grove promise of California. Three thousand Atlantic miles were a strong argument for Roosevelt's isolationist politics. For the United States, the war was far away.

Even to Harry Pilikian in Monaco, the radio bulletins of the Nazi propaganda machine, talking of distant victories, gave the impression more of a big budget Hollywood movie being shot and publicized each day by frantic producers than of a struggle for survival between two totalitarian giants. The horror of the facts seemed to sink home only when neutral sources, either from Switzerland, Spain, Portugal or the United States itself, confirmed that the Nazis were indeed at the brink of the most astonishing conquest in modern history.

The Mediterranean continued to lap softly on its shores. The sun shone and summer meandered towards its last month, before the gentle winds of autumn brought a cooling respite for the crowds basking on the southern beaches of the Riviera.

The Principality was booming. Jews had found sanctuary, refugees with money and possessions a second home. Good food could still be bought at a price. Alcohol, wine and cigarettes were plentiful. Entertainment at Le Sporting, the Cabaret and other clubs was continuous, and the Casino offered its choice of cards or roulette until the early hours of the morning, closing only to allow cleaners to sweep away the residue of the night as the accountants of the Société des Bains de Mer, the company which owned much of Monte Carlo, added up the profits.

Harry Pilikian received word from Evelyn Martineye that she was not coming back, but urging Harry to return to the United States immediately. The letter came via an eager American journalist working for *Life* magazine, who seemed to think he had the right official documents to join the German and Italian forces in Libya.

The days passed and the journalist remained in the American Bar. After a week, the prospect of the desert seemed to have palled and he joined the other reporters, who were setting records on their expense accounts and buying second-hand information which was conflicting and unreliable.

A train arrived from Milan with a number of high-ranking German officers who had been wounded in Russia. They had been granted the privilege of convalescing in the Principality. From several of these men Harry began to piece together the truth. Astonishingly it corroborated what had once been regarded as fiction. He realized that only one country in the world could now stop Hitler's Nazis, and, when the US did become embroiled, he was determined to take part.

He saw Ben Harrison regularly. They often visited Eva Trenchard, and Harry learnt that Danny Morgan had arrived safely back in England and that, since his successful escape, other RAF pilots had managed to get out of La Turbie.

Pabst had been denied further access to the Englishwoman's villa on the Rock. This was made clear to him with charm by the Palace but in blunt French by Gerard, the chief of police. If the Gestapo wished to maintain the privileged position they enjoyed they must behave themselves. The mystery of Agatha Parry's fate was explained away by the Gestapo, who said she was in Berlin and, as a self-confessed spy, of no further concern to the Monte Carlo authorities.

For the first time, Harry's monthly bill included a message asking him to see the hotel manager. Immediately he gave Morgan's remaining winnings to Eva Trenchard. She changed the plaques and chips in the following week, and when he saw Cornwallis it was with enough cash to solve the problem of the worst a man could be suspected of in Monte Carlo – poverty. So Harry began to relax and enjoy what time he had left in the Principality. Each afternoon, when he had worked from dawn to midday, collating information gathered from conversations and gossip into reports for Ben and for himself as the basis of future stories, he swam at the rebuilt Beach Club, ran the length of the Principality and worked out in the gymnasium behind the port. Around 4 o'clock, if he had skipped lunch, he would have tea beside the harbour and watch the schoolchildren swarm down to the quayside to examine the boats.

He often saw the little girl called Lisa with her friends wandering towards her floating home, the *Maracaibo*. 'This is my friend, Mr Red Tie,' she would say seriously to a giggling schoolgirl, and Harry would bow gravely and shake hands. When Ben was with him Lisa would introduce 'Monsieur Harrison', and the child would primly shake hands again.

Harry gleaned snippets of information from Lisa about the motor yacht's owner, a Mr Wilson, who was apparently not well. Lisa's mother had taken Mr Wilson to Rome to see specialists and had been gone for almost a month, Lisa explained. Then the summer holidays came and the children disappeared until the beginning of September, when school began again.

Autumn arrived early that year and the balmy weather turned suddenly sour.

Chapter 27

HMS *Sea Venturer*, an 'S' class submarine of the British Navy, broke the surface of the Mediterranean shortly before dawn, to recharge her batteries. Her young captain, Lieutenant Commander Nigel Haworth, climbed into the conning tower and began searching the horizon with powerful binoculars. Of welded construction, *Sea Venturer*, built by Scotts of Greenock, was highly manoeuvrable and in emergencies could dive in only thirty seconds. During the night she had been engaged in a running battle with Italian destroyers and a small convoy they were protecting. The convoy had scattered when the first torpedo blew the side out of a 20,000-ton freighter, heavily loaded and with ammunition on board.

'Quite some fireworks, sir,' said the second in command, Lieutenant Drummond, standing beside the captain.

'But we've lost the others.' Haworth could see nothing but the grey ocean and gloom as first light showed through heavy cloud cover.

The destroyers had made things hot for the submarine. One salvo of depth charges had come very close, and sailors were now examining the entire length of their vessel. Nigel Haworth had developed great respect for his forty-man crew, and at times like this, after the excitement of the night, he felt the weight of responsibility for their lives and families back home.

Still he saw nothing with the binoculars.

'It'll be sunrise soon, sir,' said Lieutenant Drummond.

'All right, Number One, I appreciate the danger.'

'And we're very low on fuel, sir. Shouldn't we start the run back to Malta?'

Haworth stared silently at his first officer, thinking. In the light of the explosion before they crash-dived to escape an Italian destroyer churning towards them, he had seen another freighter through the periscope. It was smaller, but had tanks on deck obviously destined for Rommel's Afrika Korps, which was creating so much strife for the British Army in North Africa.

'I want that other freighter, Number One,' said Haworth, remembering how close he had come. 'I thought we'd hit the damned thing!'

'We must have overshot, sir, because the second explosion was from the small tanker.'

They had done well. Both the first freighter and the tanker had gone to the bottom and so far they had escaped detection by the Italian navy.

'What's the damage, Bo'sun?' shouted Haworth.

His chief petty officer looked up to the conning tower from the bow. 'Only a few dents, sir, nothing to worry about.'

'Good,' said Haworth to himself. 'Is Sparks in communication with Malta?'

'I think so, sir,' replied his Number One.

'Have we fixed our exact position?'

'Yes, sir,' Drummond grinned. 'We're just south of the Riviera.'

'Where exactly?' asked Haworth, seriously.

'Well, I estimate that Monte Carlo is thirty miles due north.'

Haworth turned and looked in that direction, and there, in the growing light, he could make out the coastline. Peering through the binoculars, he suddenly tensed.

'By God, Number One, there she is!' And there, more than eight miles to the north, was the enemy freighter.

'She's running for Monaco.'

'But it's neutral, sir, isn't it?'

'There's no big sea,' said Haworth, 'and she's listing! By God, Number One, we've got her!'

'Not yet, sir,' said the young lieutenant soberly.

Haworth turned to his Number One, and for the first time he smiled. 'Send a signal.' He peered again towards land. 'Tell Sparks I'll give him fifteen minutes and that's all. It'll be dawn soon, and those destroyers are around here somewhere.'

The submarine rose and fell in a slight swell that began to pick up with the pre-dawn light. After ten minutes, the young lieutenant was back on the conning tower, peering down at the men who were still standing by at the guns, the 3-inch up front, mounted in the casing, and the .303 machinegun aft.

'Message reads, sir, from the Admiral: "Good luck, but leave Casino intact."'

Haworth grinned. 'Right, Number One, take her down and we'll have a look-see!'

Orders were given, the decks cleared quickly, the engines started, ballast tanks filled and hatches secured. *Sea Venturer* submerged to thirty fathoms, her speed seven knots, her course set due north.

By midday, the submarine was within three miles of the Principality. A slight wind had picked up, flecking the waves with foam, so Lieutenant Commander Haworth felt confident enough to raise the periscope and make a thorough scan. In the cramped quarters of what he still called 'the bridge', having originally served in cruisers, he peered into the periscope while around him men checked instruments. They were on alert, but not at action stations.

'Looks bloody lovely, Number One. Take a gander.'

The first lieutenant pushed back his cap and peered into the periscope. He could see the ship lying at the back of Monte Carlo's deep harbour, where it looked as if work was being done on her damaged hull.

'I can only think, sir, either that we bounced a torpedo right off her side, or she was hit by a blast from the other tanker exploding,' said Drummond.

'Maybe they're just scared stiff,' said Haworth.

The throbbing of the engines maintaining dead slow ahead became the only noise in the submarine as the crew waited for the commander's decision. He took up the periscope again. The silence continued.

'There's a bloody boom!' he exclaimed, and could just make out the floats supporting what looked like a torpedo net. If that was the case, they were done. He began to turn the periscope, and saw two Italian destroyers moving into a position which would put them just off Monaco's Rock. He snapped back the arms of the periscope and let it sink to the deck on its hydraulics.

'Dammit, the Eyeties have found her too!' he told his Number One, and thought for a moment. 'How much sea do we have?'

'Not more than thirty fathoms here sir, but further over, nearer in, there's a small shelf and then it drops steeply. It's very deep below the cliffs.'

'How close in could we get?'

'Close,' said Drummond.

Haworth turned to his petty officer. 'Let's go to the bottom, Bo'sun. Slowly.'

'Yes, sir,' said the man and began issuing instructions.

'And quietly,' said Haworth. 'We've a brace of Eyeties up there waiting to hear if we even cough.'

'But they're not to know we're here, sir,' said the petty officer.

'They will,' said the young captain. 'Come with me, Number One, let's look at the charts.'

Heads bent, the two men made their way down the narrow corridor, stepped into the small cabin and squeezed around a fold-down table. Haworth studied the large chart showing Monte Carlo and traced a course with his index finger.

'If we can move in this close, we'll be within half a mile of the harbour mouth. The freighter's at the very back, lying along the quayside and a perfect target for a broadside shot. If she's got any ammunition aboard, we can send those tanks to the bottom of the harbour.'

'It's getting away, sir, that's going to be the difficulty.'

'Well,' began Haworth, 'if we turn hard to port, we can dive into deeper water, because I'm damn sure those destroyers will have us on that asdic of theirs, however primitive.'

Drummond put his finger on a point just off the Principality. 'That's as near as we can risk, sir.'

Haworth stared at the chart. 'Ever been to Monte Carlo, Number One?'

'Yes, sir, once for the day, as a boy.'

'What's it like?' asked Haworth.

'Pretty, sir. A bit Ritzy for my parents as I remember.'

'Why?'

'Well, they're more county, and country, sir. Preferred Menton.'

'Beaches?'

'A club.' Drummond wrinkled his nose. 'Chi-chi, like the rest of it.'

'Girls?' asked Nigel Haworth.

'Good Lord, sir, I'm a married man!'

'That's right,' said the young captain absently, 'I keep forgetting.' He had already begun to work out their attack.

'Couldn't we wait for her to come out?' asked Drummond eventually.

'If she does,' answered Haworth, 'she'll come out at night, and with those two destroyers – well, we were lucky last time. If the whole Italian navy was as good as those two, we'd have an even bigger problem in the Med.'

A shudder went through the submarine as she touched bottom.

'What's the legal position?'

'What's that, sir?' asked Drummond.

'I mean, what's the position if we hit an Italian boat in a neutral port?'

'Pretty awkward, I'd say, sir.'

'But we've been told repeatedly that the Italians have occupied the damned place.'

'I think it's one of those difficult situations, sir. The facts are, they're sheltering an enemy vessel.'

'Hmm,' murmured Haworth. He was slumped back on his chair in the small cabin, cap on the back of his head, short-sleeved white shirt stained with sweat. The metal of the cabin wall felt cool on his back. Drummond stared at his captain with a twinkle in his eye, remembering the message.

'I think the Admiral is going for the Nelson touch.' Haworth squinted at his Number One and winked.

Harry Pilikian, in old running clothes washed so many times they were faded to an indeterminate colour between grey-green and brown, had turned at the Beach Club and was running along the sea road. He paused at the border post, where the barbed wire was pulled back during the day – an Italian concession to Monaco residents. Identified, Harry was allowed to continue on into the Principality. As he took the pathway behind the station and in front of the Casino which led on to the prom-enade, he glanced towards the sea. Laden cumulus clouds, threatening rain, moved across a sky that showed only patches of blue. Two des-troyers flying Italian flags were standing off the Rock, riding at anchor in the swell and white-capped waves. The wind had freshened and Harry was beginning to enjoy himself.

As he ran down the Avenue de Monte Carlo, there was a wonderful view of the harbour and the new arrival, a medium-sized freighter, low in the water, whose decks were crammed with what looked like machinery, covered in tarpaulins. A lot of activity appeared to be going on at the stern, where several small boats filled with seamen were churning the harbour, looking for damage below the ship's waterline.

Harry reached the quayside, sprinted the last two hundred yards, and entered the gymnasium shortly after 1 o'clock. He exercised for an hour, showered and decided to take a walk before meeting Ben Harrison at the small café on the quayside. With luck, if it didn't rain, they would be able to sit outside.

Ben Harrison, who had decided to walk from the villa on the Rock, arrived early for his meeting with Pilikian. He surveyed the scudding clouds, then sat at an outside table with his back against the wall. Behind him was the road which led down to the quay. The Principality was already running short of real coffee, so he ordered China tea for two.

When Harry arrived, Ben began talking about Agatha immediately. It was rumoured that she was in Berlin in protective custody. This was the hope he clung to. The villa was still under surveillance, which brought the conversation to Pabst and de Salis. Since the Banker had returned to the Principality his behaviour had aroused Ben's suspicions. He had investigated through his own bank, and discovered that several holding companies had been set up by the Germans, who seemed to be preparing to do business directly with Geneva.

At twelve minutes before the hour, the small cutter, part of the Italian navy, made ready to put out, as it did every day at 4 o'clock, to chug around the Principality, examining the coast from the sea, looking for signs of the extensive smuggling which had begun. Although everyone used the black market, which had become almost accepted, it was not officially condoned, and the Italians had become very sensitive to this abuse of their authority and the privileges they had granted to Monaco.

'I wonder what she's carrying,' said Ben. He squinted in the direction of the Italian freighter. 'What's she called?'

'*Salvatore*,' said Harry. 'And those are Nazi tanks.'

'How do you know?'

'The tarpaulins are all stencilled in German.'

The cutter cast off and moved slowly to the centre of the harbour. There were impatient shouts from the crew on deck and much gesticulating. Between the twin towers of the harbour mouth the boom was locked into place on the right-hand side. Some Italians let go the lines so as to allow the cutter passage.

'They make so much noise, you'd think we were fighting a war here,' said Ben. 'Just pray for the time when they can all go back to being waiters.' He grunted and glanced at Pilikian. 'Why do you keep wearing that bloody silly red tie?'

'Because Lisa likes it,' Harry answered, and checked his watch.

A shrill siren began to hoot across the harbour water. The captain of the small cutter steered his craft slowly through the narrow gap between the towers. It was two minutes to four.

Action stations were declared swiftly throughout HMS *Sea Venturer* as Lieutenant Commander Nigel Haworth, eyes locked to the periscope, issued fast orders through his Number One. The crew began running to their positions as the submarine slowly gathered way.

Haworth had taken his submarine up to periscope depth at 3.45, and spotted the cutter preparing to leave. His only chance of hitting the Italian freighter was if the boom remained swinging free.

'We'll take one shot, Number One, then make ourselves scarce.'

'Yes, sir.'

Nigel Haworth stared into the periscope, his eyes fixed on the target. It was 3.59 as the cutter cleared the harbour mouth. Activity on the quayside stopped and the boom was left unsecured.

'They're leaving it open, Number One! By God, we've got them!' exclaimed Haworth. 'Are we fully loaded?'

'Only two fish left, sir.'

The submarine continued to move slowly forward, all the crew in position. Haworth was calculating every second. He had to put a torpedo through a sixty-foot gap from nearly half a mile away. His face pressed against the rubber protection on the metal periscope.

'Time, Drummond?'

'4 o'clock, sir.'

All over Monaco, school bells rang. From the Lycée Albert Premier, Ecole Pigier, Ecole St Charles, Ecole de St Maur, on the Rue Princesse Marie de Lorraine, and the Ecole des Carmélites, just above the Condamine harbour, they sounded loud and long. Young children slammed down their desk tops, stuffed exercise books into their small satchels, tramped along corridors, ran down steps and began to race each other to the port, where the subject of their day's conversation, the Italian freighter *Salvatore*, was moored.

Lisa Lieberman was tall for her age, and long-legged. With two of her friends behind her, she headed the group that ran down the Rue Princesse Antoinette, all of them screaming with laughter. Lisa careered round a corner to catch her first sight of the quay. There before her, outside the little café, she saw Mr Harrison and her Mr Red Tie. She waved gaily. The two men saw her and waved back, then Lisa and her friends began running towards the freighter.

When Louis the barman started work at 4 o'clock in the afternoon, he walked from his small flat, up the Avenue de Monte Carlo, paused before the Casino Square beside the Opera entrance overlooking the harbour, smoked a cigarette, then went into the hotel to change. That day at two minutes past four he was peering over the marble balustrade, at the spectacular view of the little Principality, sighing with pleasure, appreciating that life was good.

As he stared at the foam-flecked waves, something caught his attention – something moving quickly below the surface, leaving a bubbling wake. It was much too fast to be a diver, and the long shadow was too big for a fish. He stared, perplexed for a moment, then realized that it was travelling too smoothly to be anything other than some kind of machine.

'Torpedo!' he whispered in horror.

It was six hundred yards out from the harbour mouth, but there was no doubt as to its target. Louis had just come that way, had even seen Harry down at the quay and waved to him. Now he began to run. The torpedo was five hundred yards out from the twin towers. Louis was already shouting:

'Harry, Harry!'

Harry heard his name called somewhere in the distance and looked up. There was Louis, running down the hill towards him, screaming like a madman. Harry waved back hesitantly, trying to make out what Louis was saying. He was pointing towards the sea.

'Torpedo!' screamed Louis.

Harry was baffled. He glanced at Harrison, but he had not heard the word and was frowning, shaking his head.

'Torpedo?' said Harry tentatively, his mind racing. Suddenly the word made sense. Italian freighter . . . Harbour . . . Torpedo . . . War . . .

He stared towards the twin towers at the harbour mouth and saw the floats of the boom. There was a definite gap between the boom, its underwater net and the harbour wall. 'Jesus Christ!' he hissed and spun round to Ben Harrison. 'Torpedo!' he yelled, then glanced across at the *Maracaibo*, moored in the distance. If they could get to the American yacht they would be safe, but it was too far away. Then he remembered the girl and was already running, bellowing:

'Lisa, Lisa!'

The little girl, almost a hundred yards away, slowed down and turned her head to see Mr Red Tie running flat-out towards her. She was so surprised that she stopped in her tracks.

The torpedo was three hundred yards out from the twin towers of the harbour. On the quay, Harry was fifty yards from Lisa, beckoning urgently and shouting: 'This way! This way!'

Louis, breathing heavily reached Ben Harrison. 'Behind the wall, M'sieur, quickly!' and he dragged him up at the same time screaming a warning into the café.

The torpedo was one hundred yards out from the harbour mouth as Harry reached Lisa. He scooped her up in his arms, pulled one of her friends by the hand, shouted at the other and began running back towards the thick wall directly behind the café. It stood three hundred yards from the freighter moored at the quayside of La Condamine harbour.

The wake of the torpedo passed right through the sixty-foot gap between the floating boom and the right-hand tower of the breakwater, travelling quickly into the calm harbour. Harry had almost reached the café when one of the children fell. He snatched her to her feet, set Lisa back on the ground, then they were all running together.

The torpedo was now eighty yards out . . . then seventy . . . and sixty . . . Harry threw the first child at Louis, who was standing behind the thick concrete wall.

Fifty yards from the freighter the Italian sailors on board saw the torpedo's wake and began to panic . . . Forty yards . . . thirty . . . twenty . . . The second little girl was over the wall, caught by Ben. Harry grabbed Lisa and jumped for the wall.

The torpedo hit. There was one second of absolute silence, then an explosion so massive that it lifted everything movable within half a mile; huge, deafening, horrifying and mightily destructive.

A roar from the crew sounded throughout the submarine as the unmistakable noise came to them, even below the surface, a dull 'whump'. Haworth, peering through the periscope, confirmed the strike.

'We've got her!' he shouted, watching flame and black smoke carry far into the sky. He turned the periscope to see the two destroyers. He had about three minutes, he calculated, when the advantage would be with *Sea Venturer*, then the destroyers would be moving in. If they backed the British submarine on to the underwater shelf, she would be trapped.

'Let's get cracking, Number One!' he shouted.

'Yes, sir!'

'Hard to port and full ahead!'

The submarine turned south towards the open sea, picking up speed with each minute. Haworth kept his eyes glued on the two destroyers. There was already movement on their decks. Only when he was absolutely sure that they would pass a mere two hundred yards to starboard did he lower the periscope.

'And take her down, Number One. We're moving into deep water, but we're going to pass bloody close. Let's hope the Eyeties are taking a siesta or whatever the hell they call it in Italy.'

But they were not. Already Haworth could hear the rumbling engines above.

'Take her down to eighty fathoms and don't spare the horses,' he grinned.

'Course set, sir?' asked Lieutenant Drummond.

'Malta, Number One, and home.'

Drummond laughed in relief. 'Three cheers!' he shouted, 'Hip, hip, hip . . .'

'Hooray! came the crew's answer, again and again as HMS *Sea Venturer* plunged deeper, passing below the two Italian destroyers. Throughout both warships emergency stations sounded and they began making steam, swinging around, engines boiling water, throbbing with power. Their asdic picked up the intruder, diving towards the open sea. Haworth's audacity had given him the advantage of surprise.

The first of the two destroyers crossed the wake of the submarine several minutes later, already travelling at more than fifteen knots. Depth charges were set and fired. Vast columns of white water followed the great shock waves, rising majestically then cascading back to the surface of the Mediterranean. Battle was joined.

A split second after the impact of the torpedo, its high explosive detonated and tore open the side of the *Salvatore*. The first explosion merged with an even greater noise, which seemed to take all other sound out of the air. Ammunition in the hold had gone up. Debris, limbs, whole bodies were thrown far into the sky. Reliable witnesses reported some falling as far away as the Casino Square, which even those who knew Monte Carlo well found hard to believe. But the indisputable fact was that a large part of the Post Office at the rear of La Condamine, across The Rue Albert Premier, had disappeared.

Everywhere people were screaming with shock. It was as if a vacuum had been created, oxygen sucked out of the atmosphere, and where the freighter once lay moored there was only wreckage and a dreadful silence beneath a huge pall of black smoke.

The three small girls were crying. Huddled in the arms of Harry Pilikian, Ben Harrison and Louis, they still pressed against the thick wall which had protected them from the blast as debris continued to fall out of the sky. No one moved, until everything had stopped, even the last crackling of what sounded like bullets going off. Harry was the first to look over the wall. Already he could hear the clanging bell of the fire engines coming from the station above the harbour. They were going to be badly needed.

There were a number of civilian casualties, but in the main it appeared that only the Italian crewmen of the freighter had lost their lives, which was as lucky for Monaco as it was unfortunate for Italy.

Louis took the other two little girls home. Ben followed Harry as he carried Lisa along the quayside to the stern of the *Maracaibo*. He handed her over to two of the sailors on deck, and watched them take her below.

Harry and Ben remained silent for several minutes, looking beyond the sleek white hull of the *Maracaibo* towards the settling hulk and the chaos across the harbour.

'War,' said Harry.

Chapter 28

The two men left the harbour with its sounds of sirens, bells, vehicles and rushing men in uniform. They walked quickly up the Avenue de Monte Carlo and pushed through crowds staring towards the horizon as booming noises came from several miles out to sea, where the Italian destroyers were searching for their elusive prey. They made for the Casino Square, the Hotel de Paris and the American Bar.

'Whiskies,' said Harry.

'Very large,' said Ben.

Hugh Sullivan was leaning on the bar. 'Bloody British,' he said, leprechaun eyes clouded by several hours of drinking.

'Well, what do you think they ought to have done?' snapped Ben.

'You are English,' said Sullivan pointedly. 'I was born in America . . .' He paused, searching for words.

'But your heart's in Ireland,' said Ben stonily. 'Is that what you want to say?'

'No,' grinned Sullivan wickedly. 'My heart's in America.' He pointed a finger. 'It's my soul that's in Ireland.' He focused on Ben Harrison. 'The Irish have only ever had one common enemy, past or present, Mr Harrison.' Hate seemed to clear the Irish-American's eyes. 'Not each other, but . . . the English . . . attitude.'

'I was there,' said Ben quietly, becoming dangerous. 'I know the problems.'

'The troubles are made only in London,' whispered Sullivan.

Harry Pilikian was drinking, saying nothing. His gaze wandered through the large glass windows to see a tall man – who would have been willowy had he not moved so confidently – run up the steps outside, push open the Opera door to the bar, enter quickly and stride across the room towards them.

Harry absorbed first impressions: greying hair, striped open-neck shirt, loose trousers, good shoulders, very little waist. The man's face was firm although his nose had been broken. Harry could see that he was solid, perhaps once an athlete.

'You're too bitter,' Ben was saying gently, remembering the effect of Bobby Avery's death on Sullivan.

His betrayal of Danny Morgan to the Gestapo had been gossip for months throughout the Principality. Only when the excuse of passion was found and accepted for what had been described as a crime was he forgiven. After all, Danny had escaped and Bobby was dead.

The man Harry had been watching arrived and grinned.

'Bitter and bent,' he interrupted, taking a cigarette from a packet and lighting it with the affectation of a woman under scrutiny from possible suitors.

'We don't need the blue blood of divine right in our veins,' mumbled Sullivan. 'In the Emerald Isle, it runs ordinary and red – in the streets.'

'You're an American, Sullivan,' said Harry softly, trying to cool the man down.

'You're drunk,' said Ben.

'All we want, Englishman, is our freedom.' Sullivan paused. 'Do you have another word for *that*?'

'My God,' said the tall new arrival, 'I thought this was a neutral country.'

'This is Ben Harrison,' said Sullivan, almost spitting out the words. 'He's English.'

213

'Howard Maitland,' said the man, extending a hand. The handshake was surprisingly firm.

Harry had turned towards the group, nodding to the barman for more drinks, when Sullivan introduced him.

'This is Harry Pilikian.'

'What a mess!' said the man. There was a challenge in his eyes. Harry extended a hand as Howard Maitland made a fuss of replacing the cigarette between his generous lips before shaking. 'The explosion, I mean. It looks awful. Did you see it?'

'We were down there,' said Harry.

'Well I hope they didn't hit our boat,' said Maitland. 'I'll have nowhere to sleep.'

'Howard lives on a yacht,' said Sullivan flatly.

'Very boring,' said Maitland, then grinned. 'Was it exciting down there?'

'I don't understand you,' said Harrison. 'That's not the word I would use.'

'Oh, that's right, the English are so good at words,' said Maitland. 'I'm American.' He inhaled deeply on his cigarette, which he then held between fingers set at an exaggerated angle. 'But I thought *you* would understand?'

'I said I didn't.'

Maitland accepted whisky, sipped it and peered coquettishly over the glass at Ben Harrison. 'You mean you don't,' he said.

Ben became irritated. 'Don't what?'

'Understand – excitement?'

The atmosphere was becoming tense. Maitland grinned wickedly, winked and spun round on his heels.

'Play us a song, Sullivan, if you're still capable,' he said.

'I'm capable,' said Sullivan with assumed dignity.

'We know that, but I'm talking about music,' replied Maitland.

'What do you want?'

'"A Good Man",' he answered, and glanced at Ben Harrison. 'But they're so hard to find, aren't they, Hugh? You know how true that is don't you? Play it.' Maitland ran a hand along the pianist's shoulder. 'You always get the other kind,' he said softly, then began clapping wildly, which started off most of the bar.

Sullivan crossed to the piano and sat down to play. Maitland started jumping up and down on his stool, waving his arms about. He fluttered his eyes at Ben.

'Just when you think you've found a pal,' he sang, extending a hand to within a hair's breadth of Ben's face, 'you find him foolin' round with some other gal. Then you rave, you even crave to see that good man,' he spread out the note, 'down in his grave.' People in the bar began staring at the

214

man's antics. 'So if your man is nice, take my advice,' he slipped from the stool and began to wiggle his hips, 'and hug him in the morning. Kiss him every night. Give him plenty lovin', treat him right. For a good man nowadays is hard to find!' The last note was drawn out to laughter and applause.

The telephone rang in the background.

'Monsieur Harrison,' said Jean-Pierre. 'There is a message for you at the desk.'

'Thank God,' he said.

Ben crossed the lobby to the message desk and was handed an envelope by a uniformed sailor. He opened it and read:

I am told by my daughter that you were responsible for saving her from what I feel would have been certain death. I would very much like to meet you and to thank you. I gather another man, Monsieur Louis, of the Hotel de Paris, saved one of the other girls. He is, in fact, coming to help with cocktails for the dinner party we had planned aboard the *Maracaibo*. We have decided not to cancel and I would feel honoured if you would accept an invitation for this evening. I do appreciate, Mr Harrison, that it is short notice, but do please try to come. I believe your friend, whom my daughter knows only as Mr Red Tie, was also, certainly from the description (you must understand my daughter is still upset), quite heroic. Do please try and contact this gentleman, as Mr Wilson agrees with me that it would be our privilege to meet you both. Please come at seven.

The letter was signed something Lieberman, Mrs – Ben could not make out the first name. The seaman was waiting at the desk. Ben folded the letter and put it in his pocket, feeling a little embarrassed.

'*Vous parlez français?*' he began.

'No, sir,' said the young seaman, 'at least not well. I'm American.'

'Oh,' said Ben. 'Well, please thank Mrs Lieberman and tell her we'll be there.'

'Yes, sir!'

Ben made his way back to the bar. He had nothing to do and hoped Harry would be free. It would be interesting to look over that beautiful motor yacht.

In the bar, Harry slid from his stool, nodding his thanks to Jean-Pierre, exactly as Maitland made a big finish of 'That Old Black Magic'. He had thrust both his arms wide, and a split second later would have connected heavily with Harry's head, but he ducked and caught the man's wrist firmly. Immediately Maitland was off his stool, eyes wild.

'Don't touch me!' he hissed vehemently.

Harry was surprised but dropped the arm roughly. 'Then take more care in public places,' he said.

For a moment they were toe to toe and eye to eye. Howard Maitland said nothing, for the first time unusually silent.

'Fools rush in,' sang Sullivan, 'where angels fear to tread.'

Ben Harrison entered the bar and beckoned. Harry waved back and began to move off, but not before Maitland slid back on his stool, leaned on the bar and blew him a wet kiss.

'Au revoir, angel,' he whispered.

It was unfortunate that the four men reached the lift at the same time, but Ben was explaining the invitation to Harry and both were pre-occupied until they stepped through the gates. The operator asked which floor.

'*Deux*,' said Ben.

'*Six*,' said Christopher Quinn.

The gates were closed and the lift moved up. Then Harry turned around and saw Pabst. For a moment he thought he would kill him there and then, in the lift, but Pabst, although his gaze was fixed on Pilikian, seemed not to notice him: his eyes were dead. Harry had promised Gerard, the chief of police, to do nothing, under any circumstances.

'*Deux, Monsieur*,' said the attendant and opened the gates. Ben and Harry stepped out. Only after the lift continued its ascent did Harry speak.

'I'd better change.'

In the privacy of Christopher Quinn's rooms on the seventh floor, just below the Grill, Jürgen Pabst felt free to talk.

'It would be a pity to have problems at this late stage.'

'No problems,' said Quinn. He had delivered a sheaf of papers several days before to Pabst's headquarters at the Prison. It had taken time, but Quinn had spent substantial sums of money to buy legal cooperation in Amsterdam. The Van der Voors documents had been reassigned to him.

'Has de Salis seen the copies?' asked Pabst.

Quinn hesitated for a fraction of a second. 'Not yet,' he said.

'Will he agree?'

'The papers have been reassigned,' said Quinn. 'It is quite simple.'

'Is it also official and legal?'

'Yes.'

'At what cost to you?'

'That is my business.'

'So you are now entitled to sell them for us?'

Quinn nodded.

'Then the deal will go through,' said Pabst and stepped towards the open windows. 'The diamonds are being shipped at this moment, I understand?'

'That's right,' said Quinn quickly. 'The time and date are in the papers I gave you.'

'Ah yes,' said Pabst. 'Those papers. So many names.' He affected surprise. 'So many Jews.'

Quinn shrugged. 'They are astute. Diamonds, gold. You should feel lucky. As a German you won't have any conscience that we acquired them for almost nothing.' He paused. 'I wonder how many of them actually bought their freedom with those diamonds?'

Pabst's gaze was unsettling. 'Very few,' he said. 'And those diamonds certainly did not buy Mynheer Van der Voors his freedom.'

Pabst stepped out on to the balcony and, head back, closed his eyes. He felt the pleasant sensation of a fresh evening breeze on his face, detected the smell of salt and ozone, heard the sound of the sea . . .

'They were loaded in Amsterdam this afternoon, I understand?' he said slowly.

'If your people have waived all the formalities as I asked.'

'Your requests were granted.'

'Then they will be in Geneva tomorrow morning, as I arranged.'

'Who owns the shipment at the moment – officially?' asked Pabst.

'A company, here in Monaco.'

'So then, they are already almost ours?'

'When they are delivered it will be official.'

'Good,' said Pabst. 'The Swiss will be pleased.' He turned to Quinn. 'I hope.'

'Why should they not be?' Quinn's voice was plaintive. 'I have done everything de Salis required.'

Pabst stared at Quinn. 'You two are no longer friends?'

'We never were.'

The expression in Pabst's eyes hardened. 'That is a pity. Business is such a whore, isn't it?' He watched the Irishman swallow hard as colour came into his cheeks at the obvious reference to Bonnie Lawrence. Pabst became expansive. 'I wanted to invite you for dinner, in the Grill. De Salis and I are going to play a little in the Casino first.'

'I have my own plans, in the Salle Empire,' said Quinn.

'Ah,' said the German, 'then at least we will both be here at the hotel. At 11 o'clock I will have news for you. If the diamonds have crossed the Belgian border, they will be already in Paris, en route for Switzerland.' Pabst smiled. 'There are still certain regulations.' He paused, as if the idea was spontaneous. 'We will telephone from here.'

'I shall be downstairs,' said Quinn.

'And I shall be up . . . stairs,' said Pabst. 'It will be a simple thing to meet for five minutes.'

Quinn nodded. 'At eleven, then,' he said.

Chapter 29

In black ties and dinner jackets, Ben Harrison and Harry Pilikian walked down to the harbour and along the quayside to the gangway of the *Maracaibo*. Ben gave his name and they were escorted on board by one of the crew.

The stern of the motor yacht was large and already crowded, the deck illuminated by a series of lights hanging above their heads beneath canvas awnings that spread the width of the boat. In the soft warm evening, diamonds sparkled and pearls shone, mink and sable were draped over naked shoulders, evening dresses flattered sun-tanned skins and carefully preserved features. The rich at play were flaunting all that was fashionable, even in wartime – indeed, most of the guests regarded the war as an awkward interruption to their otherwise perfectly sophisticated lives.

'If only this man Hitler would win,' an ageing White Russian prince was saying to an equally elderly princess, who claimed to have attended the Russian court. 'Then we could return and Leningrad would again be called St Petersburg.' Droll conversation. Monte Carlo chat.

A waiter offered them a drink. Ben tapped Harry on the shoulder.

'I'll try to find this Mrs Lieberman.'

Harry turned around, leaning over the stern rail. A full moon was rising beyond the fading coastline of Italy, far across the water. He lit a cigarette, watching new arrivals come on board and swell the babble of conversation.

Overhead, swirling masses of birds rose and fell on a light breeze, soaring and plunging, interlacing the brightness of the stars with their rushing silhouettes.

Something began licking Harry's hand. He glanced down and saw a beautiful chestnut springer spaniel, perhaps two years old.

'His name's Scottie,' said a small voice.

Harry turned around and saw Lisa. He took the dog by its forepaws. 'Hello, Scottie,' he said. The dog smelled smoke from the cigarette in Harry's mouth and barked twice.

'Scottie!' Lisa commanded. The dog immediately stood still wagging it's tail.

'Why aren't you wearing your tie?' she asked.

Harry smiled, reached into his pocket and showed Lisa the red tie he had brought with him.

'I've got something to tell you, Mr Red Tie.'

'What is it?' Harry asked.

She pulled him down to her, then put her lips to his ear. 'No, it's a secret,' she whispered, but kissed him on the cheek.

'Goodnight,' he said. Scottie barked and escorted his young mistress back through the crowd.

Harry stood up and leaned again on the rail of the yacht to watch the rising moon. For the first time in many months he found himself gazing into the future.

'There you are,' came Ben's voice behind him.

Harry turned around.

'Mrs Lieberman,' said Ben, 'I'd like you to meet . . .'

'We've met, haven't we?' said Mrs Lieberman quietly.

Harry was unable to speak.

'Need any help?' she asked softly.

It took several seconds for Harry to answer. Before him he saw not the beautiful, sophisticated woman staring at him with a secret expression in her eyes, but a girl standing on a New York pavement with her life in a heavy suitcase, poetry in her pockets and a devastating smile on her lips.

'No,' he whispered, 'I'm just doing this for exercise.'

He was looking into the face of Alexandra Cunningham.

Mrs Lieberman did as she had been instructed and took Harry Pilikian directly across the deck, to meet Mr Bradford Arnett Wilson.

The man was large and corpulent and, although not obliged to, used a wheelchair most of the time, so there were lifts on board the *Maracaibo* to give him access to the greater part of his ship. He had brilliant blue eyes, set wide and slightly protruding; they were his best feature. His grey hair was thin and his broad face merged baldness with swollen cheeks and a sagging neck. His lips, which were pinched, seemed always wet. His nose had enlarged nostrils into which, Harry later discovered, he alternately took oxygen for his emphysema and cocaine to provide him with sufficient enthusiasm to continue his luxurious life. Wilson's tailor had done an exceptional job in fitting his client's ample body into a midnight-blue dinner jacket with satin lapels. A plain white shirt, the starched collar and small bow tie almost lost in the folds of flesh beneath his chin, emphasized his formal dress, obligatory for every male present.

Wilson scrutinized Pilikian and forced a smile.

'Style is a luxury of life I insist upon. Heroism is a luxury I can only admire.' His smile faded. 'Mrs Lieberman tells me we must thank you for Lisa's life.' He held up a hand. 'It's her child, you understand, not mine.'

Harry said nothing.

'But I'm very fond of her,' Wilson conceded. 'Our ship has survived well enough, as you can see.' He waved. 'Some broken glass, fallen debris, but nothing that has not been repaired aboard. Life goes on.' He waved a hand again. 'And so will dinner.' He stared at Harry. 'You live here I am led to believe, Mr . . . ?'

'Pilikian,' Harry said.

Wilson's eyes narrowed. 'Armenian?'

Harry nodded, and the large man moistened his lips. 'That would account for your fine features.' He stared at Harry's face. 'Well, we're glad you could come. Summer seems to be over, where do you go in winter?'

Harry, who had barely been able to take his eyes off Mrs Lieberman, said: 'To the mountains.'

'You like snow?' Harry was interrupted before he could answer. 'So do I,' grinned Wilson. A tongue ran over his moist lips. 'You'll stay to dinner, sir?' Harry glanced again at the woman beside Wilson. 'My amanuensis tells me you have accepted our invitation.'

'It will be my pleasure,' answered Harry, and smiled.

The cocktail party finished promptly at 8.30, and twenty guests sat down in the oak-panelled, candlelit dining room. Eurasian waiters, dressed in sharply creased tropical whites with pink silk embroidery, began to serve. Fresh flowers and fine antique silver pheasants surrounded elegant Georgian candelabra. The menu had been specially printed, each with a guest's name in gold on the cover.

As the guests settled, Harry leaned forward and glanced at Ben Harrison, who whistled noiselessly. Everyone dining on board the *Maracaibo* that night was used to luxury, but this was more like the ostentation of an Eastern potentate from another century. Ben had already identified Persian wall hangings, jade ornaments, Renaissance figurines and several huge Ming vases, topped with dragon sculptures. Even the table itself was antique, and if it truly matched the chairs, it was as Georgian as the silverware. This was an astonishing display of wealth, and therefore power.

Harry recognized several faces, including the man seated beside Alexandra, who in turn was next to Wilson. It was Sullivan's friend from the bar, Howard Maitland. In evening dress he looked elegant, and was as animated as before. Alexandra appeared to be the perfect hostess. Her lightly tanned skin showed to advantage against a grey-green dress that seemed to shimmer in the candlelight. Her dark Titian hair was swept up, shaped to enhance her beautiful face and the perfect line of her neck.

The Eurasian waiters moved like phantoms on the thick carpet and Harry constantly had to remind himself that he was on board a yacht.

220

The windows of the large room were square, the curtains drawn, and only the ceiling, which was lower than it would have been in a French château, indicated that they were afloat. As the first course finished, a moment of awe silenced the babble and chatter of the table.

Those who were not already tipsy from cocktails had become inebriated by the time the superb food was placed before them. Friendships had been cemented, enmities reaffirmed, and strangers had made the usual exchanges of falsified facts and exaggerated truths.

By the time Lafite claret had been poured into yet another glass, wine had provided the excuse for veneers to slip, opinions to harden and personalities to illustrate their vices or virtues. The talk had grown louder, people were more preoccupied with one another than with their host, but Alex, whenever she caught Harry's eye, held it and stared at him across the table. Once they had not needed words.

Pabst had gambled and lost. De Salis, ever the Swiss banker, had played with patience and won. Leaving the roulette tables in the Salle Privée, after champagne in the bar, they strolled across the Casino Square to the Hotel de Paris and took the lift from the bustling lobby to the top floor. By 10 o'clock, while violins played discreetly, they were ordering dinner at a window table of the Grill. Below was the harbour, with several ships showing lights on their decks. The *Maracaibo* glowed especially bright, with her strings of illuminations reflected in the water. Only around the hulk of the destroyed freighter was there complete darkness.

The two men ordered and were served. Wine came. Pabst smiled – again it was Mouton Rothschild. The *sommelier* poured and the two men touched glasses.

'How long will it take?' asked Pabst.

De Salis hesitated. 'Two months, perhaps a little more.'

'Good,' said Pabst.

'I have with me the first names,' began de Salis.

'Then, to the Jews,' the Gestapo man said, and tilted his glass. He finished his *foie gras* and took out a cigarette from his newly acquired Cartier gold case.

'What is the price?' he asked.

'A percentage,' said de Salis eventually.

'Namely?'

'Half.'

'How will you take it?'

'At source,' said de Salis, 'as each box is opened and evaluated. There will be no problems. We will be scrupulous – I think that is the word. We have that reputation.'

The Gestapo officer surveyed the crowded restaurant. 'If this were known,' he said wickedly, 'you would gain another reputation.'

221

'It is merely . . . business,' said the Swiss.

Chateaubriand for two arrived.

'What are your requirements?' Pabst asked.

'Proof of ownership, a copy of the will, a legal letter . . . and . . .' he paused.

'What else?' asked Pabst patiently.

'A death certificate,' answered de Salis.

Pabst said nothing as his knife cut into the rare steak. He liked to see blood when he ate meat. He tasted a morsel.

'Excellent,' he said, chewing. 'I think we can provide everything you want. How many deposit boxes are we discussing?'

De Salis ran his tongue over dry lips. 'My initial enquiries lead me to estimate that between fifteen to twenty per cent of all ownership is Jewish. How many will you . . .?' he began, then stopped.

Pabst chewed his meat for a moment, swallowed, and smiled. 'Who knows . . . ?' he answered.

The two violinists and a bass player now began to play a request, for a large table surrounded by a wedding party. 'Oh How We Danced on the Night We Were Wed . . .' The plaintive melody quietened the restaurant. Pabst studied the faces of the guests of the bride and groom, some happy, others with sad expressions caught in the low lights. His eyes found the gleam of gold around the bride's neck and he recognized a Star of David. The melody faded away into silence.

'Do not worry,' Pabst said in a whisper, 'what we must do . . . will be done. I guarantee it.'

Christopher Quinn, seated amidst the plush baroque splendour of the Salle Empire on the ground floor of the Hotel de Paris, glanced at his watch and caught the eye of Maggie Lawrence. Other guests at the table were occupied with each other.

'What is it?' she asked.

'It's almost eleven,' said Quinn. 'I'll have to leave for a few minutes.'

'Where are you going?' asked Maggie, concerned at his serious expression.

'I have a meeting, but it won't be long,' he told her softly.

Maggie looked at the man with affection. 'I'll be right here,' she smiled, and kissed him quickly.

Quinn stood up and walked out to the lobby and the waiting lift. There was no one on duty, so he closed the gates and pressed the button for seven. It was just before 11 o'clock as the lift moved up.

Jürgen Pabst and the Swiss banker, Guy de Salis, had almost finished their dinner.

'Appetite,' de Salis was saying, 'is a gift from God.'

Pabst was suddenly interested. Wine was loosening his companion's tongue. 'We are talking about women?' asked Pabst. 'Or food?' His eyes became mischievous. They were cold eyes, pale and clear, always hovering on the brink of an expression which some saw as malicious, others as heartless or ruthless, and a few recognized for what it was – deadly.

De Salis leaned across the table. 'I hope we are talking about women.'

'And sex.' Pabst's voice was almost vicious.

De Salis leaned back in his chair again. 'That too, of course.'

Pabst placed a cigarette between his lips. 'Sex, like anything else, must be developed and refined,' he said, lighting the cigarette, smoke curling from his lips. 'There is an art in pleasure, a joy in possession, a power in dominance, whether it be with a woman or a man.'

De Salis actually grinned. 'That is the weakness in German philosophy,' he said. 'This need for dominance.'

Pabst's eyes became dangerous. 'And the Swiss,' he asked, 'what is their weakness? Diamonds?' He stared at the banker steadily.

'As for those, I have made the situation clear.'

'You have seen the papers?'

De Salis nodded and fixed Pabst with a vacant stare. 'I will not deal with those diamonds under any circumstances.'

'Why not?' asked Pabst.

'It is obvious that they are tainted.'

Pabst looked at the guarded expression in the Swiss eyes. 'No deal?'

De Salis shook his head. 'Too risky,' he answered. 'It is good business to eliminate risks.'

'And is that possible?'

De Salis shrugged.

Pabst stood up slowly and checked his watch. It was two minutes past eleven.

'Do excuse me for a moment.'

'Shall I order for you?' asked de Salis. 'Would you like cheese or some special dessert?'

'The special,' smiled Pabst.

Christopher Quinn leaped up from his seat as he heard a light knock on his door. Pabst entered and could see immediately that the Irishman had become agitated. The telephone was still on the balcony, so Pabst stepped through the open french windows, picked up the receiver and handed it to Quinn.

'Ring my headquarters,' he said.

The operator came on the line, Quinn spoke and replaced the receiver. Both men waited in silence. Thirty seconds later the phone rang and Quinn handed it to Pabst.

'Koch,' said the Gestapo colonel, and listened, staring at Quinn.

'Has the consignment arrived in Paris?' asked the Irishman nervously. Pabst held the receiver to his ear. 'The diamonds have not arrived.'

Quinn reached clumsily for the telephone but Pabst withheld it. 'Thank you, Koch,' he said. Taking a handkerchief from his top pocket he replaced the receiver and wiped it carefully. 'Greasy hands,' he remarked.

'Well?' asked Quinn, exasperated.

'There is a slight problem, Mr Quinn. The train arrived in Paris, but the diamonds did not.'

'What!' exclaimed the Irishman.

'They were taken by some men, apparently with proper authorization.' Pabst paused.

'But that's not possible,' said Quinn. 'Your own men were guarding them.'

'These others were in German army uniform,' said Pabst, and shrugged. 'What could my men do? Their papers seemed to be in order.' Quinn sat down heavily. Pabst's voice became harsh. 'You understood this to be a dangerous game, Mr Quinn. Now it is your responsibility.'

'It is *our* responsibility,' said Quinn weakly. 'We both . . .'

'No, Mr Quinn, *we* have no wish to accept any such responsibility. Had the diamonds arrived . . .' Pabst was expansive, but his voice remained hard.

Quinn was desperately seeking an explanation. 'But they have only been lost temporarily, surely your men could find . . . ?'

'They have been *stolen*.' Pabst emphasized the word.

'I don't understand,' said Quinn desperately.

'Mr Quinn, logic dictates that you understand. I will put it simply. I do not have the diamonds here, they are not legally negotiable, nor are they in your possession. Our transaction is cancelled.'

There were two lamps in the room, so Pabst turned away from Quinn, stepped out onto the balcony and began to pull on a pair of thin surgical gloves. Quinn started to shake his head in bewilderment and panic. 'Then I will go to the commanding officer myself!' he shouted angrily. 'To Müller, Himmler, Hitler if necessary! This has been my life. You don't understand!'

'I do understand,' said Pabst softly. 'And it is finished.' He slid his hand into a pocket, took out a narrow case and opened it, confident of his reflexes and sure that the Irishman could not see what he held.

'What are you doing?' asked Quinn, looking out to the balcony.

'Thinking . . . how unfortunate it is,' said Pabst. He held a hypodermic syringe in his gloved fingers. Inserting the needle into a phial, he drew out the contents. 'You know too much about us. That is the first problem . . . and there can only be one solution.'

The phial was now empty, the hypodermic full of nitric acid. Pabst stepped back into the room and stood absolutely still.

224

'What are you doing?' asked Quinn in a frightened voice. Then he saw the hypodermic in Pabst's hand. 'My God . . . You took the diamonds! You took them!' he repeated softly.

'Yes,' said Pabst quietly. 'And now they must be hidden until this war is over, when we will *make* them negotiable, legally and officially.'

'But you've stolen them!' shouted Quinn.

Pabst smiled. 'Only you know that.'

Quinn screamed and lunged forward, kicking out. Pabst sidestepped, protecting the delicate medical instrument. The needle was long, and although the eighteen gauge steel was tough it would snap like a rapier if bent too far.

Quinn turned the handle of the door, pulled it open, jumped into the corridor and began to run. Pabst was a few paces behind him. Quinn reached the lift and pressed the button wildly. Pabst was almost on him. Quinn kicked out again and caught Pabst squarely on the thigh. The German fell to his knees, allowing Quinn to pull back both gates of the lift and stumble in, but the Gestapo officer was on his feet, pushing at the gates. Quinn's breathing was shallow as he pressed with all his might to get the gates closed. Pabst placed his back against the wall and pushed with his free arm. His other hand protected what was now a deadly weapon, and there was nothing Quinn could do as he watched the lift gates open an inch at a time. Then Pabst leaped in after him. The gates crashed shut. The Irishman screamed and pressed the button for the ground floor.

Pabst's forearm smashed into the neck of Christopher Quinn, slamming him against the damask wall of the descending lift. The German had to be quick, very quick. Quinn's arms flailed against Pabst and found a grip, but too late. Pabst thrust hard with the hypodermic needle, piercing the Irishman's shirt, penetrating the skin, the fine steel plunging upwards through soft tissue, into the body, until it reached the man's heart, entering directly above the left ventricle. Quinn convulsed with shock, but Pabst's weight pinioned him against the side of the lift. They were now passing the fourth floor and still going down.

Pabst pressed the plunger, and twenty cc. of nitric acid flooded into the centre of the Irishman's heart. The German was hissing words of anger as the Irishman fought for his life, clawing at Pabst's arm. The horror of what was happening to him hit the Irishman's brain. He was dying in agony. The pain was so intense that his face went chalk-white. His eyes began to protrude and his mouth opened and closed soundlessly, like a dying fish sinking into the depths. The nitric acid was spreading fast, searing into his heart, burning, eating away the muscle from within.

As the third floor level passed, Pabst began to sweat. If the lift reached the ground floor, where the lobby bustled with night life, he would be

225

caught. Suddenly, the Irishman's body arched and became rigid, his eyes bulging. Pabst's hand shot out and a finger pressed the 'stop' button. Quinn was sucking for air, but found none, and like a tired child reaching for the protecting arms of his father, he fell into Pabst's embrace. The German pulled quickly at the needle, which came out cleanly, and let down the body against the bench so that Quinn's head faced upwards, his already sightless eyes staring at the small chandelier above.

Pabst pressed the button for the seventh floor. Slowly the lift began to rise. He laid the hypodermic syringe in Quinn's left hand, placing the depressed plunger against his thumb, and lodged it between the dead man's fingers. Dropping the small case open on the floor beneath the body, he peeled off the thin surgical gloves and slipped them into his pocket. He looked up, determined that if anyone was waiting on the seventh floor, he would kill them too.

The lift continued upwards, both men inside staring at the ceiling as if in a hurry to arrive, the one straining to hear a voice, even a footfall from above, the other no longer aware of anything mortal.

The lift stopped. Pabst dragged back the gates and found the corridor empty. He took a last look at the body of Christopher Quinn, unmarked but for a pinprick through his shirt.

'Clean,' he said, and closed the gates. Immediately the lift began moving down as impatient guests pressed the button in the lobby.

Pabst took a deep breath, walked along the corridor to the stairs, ran up them two at a time, strolled through the crowded Grill and sat down opposite his dinner companion.

'The strawberries are excellent,' said de Salis. 'A little acid, but superb with sugar.'

'Good,' breathed Pabst, 'then I'll have some sugar.'

The lift stopped on the ground floor of the Hotel de Paris and someone reached for the gates and pulled them back. There was a gasp from the small crowd waiting to go up. People stepped away from the horror of a body lodged against the seat, staring at the small chandelier.

Maggie Lawrence, who had wheeled herself to the ladies' room, pushed slowly towards the group and saw Christopher Quinn, his eyes opaque, arm hanging, clutching the hypodermic syringe. The shock silenced her, but there was no need to ask: she could see that he was dead.

Chapter 30

The body of a large man, bent over, naked, arms spread, hands apparently grasping a bench in what seemed to be a park, was complemented by another sylph-like young man whose hands grasped the wide hips before him. His slim, erect penis was poised, about to enter from behind. Perched on the bench above the head of the first man, who was apparently bald, a cupid-like figure held a powder puff. The young man was smiling; his partner had a straining expression of expectation and his eyes were closed. The drawing was graphic and beautifully executed.

'I was never thin,' said Bradford Arnett Wilson, 'as you can see, Mr Pilikian.'

The ladies on board the *Maracaibo* had retired to the outer cabin. The men remained in the dining room smoking cigars, but Harry Pilikian had been invited into Wilson's large private study. On one wall there were a number of black and white drawings.

'I knew Aubrey Beardsley,' said Wilson, 'just before the turn of the century – can you imagine that, looking at me now? He said he would draw me as I would become, and he was right.' Wilson smiled. 'Pour us both a brandy.'

Harry found the decanter, poured and brought a glass to the man in the wheelchair. The study confirmed what he had already seen. Wilson had taste as well as money. Rosewood panelling, green leather-topped English Regency tables and a large captain's desk made of yew, old brass navigational instruments and Fabergé ornaments set off a huge Gobelin tapestry hanging against one wall. The lighting was low from green-shaded lamps and the effect reminded Harry of prints he had seen of San Francisco houses in the heyday of the previous century.

'Beardsley came here to die in '98, much as I am doing now. We were friends.' Wilson paused.

'I'm sure that . . .' began Harry.

'Mr Pilikian,' interrupted Wilson, 'at my age I need no flattery. I have the facts. I have created my own world here on my ship, and I have limited expectations.'

'It's very impressive,' said Harry, sipping his brandy.

'Is it really?' asked Wilson.

'You know it is.' Harry perched himself against the desk.

'To others,' smiled Wilson. '*I* am no longer impressed by anything other than the hereafter.'

'That impresses us all.'

'More so, when you yourself are on its brink.' Wilson coughed. 'I gather you knew Mrs Lieberman in . . . another life?'

'We have met before,' said Harry.

'How did you meet?'

'On a street, in a city.'

'New York?'

'Yes.'

The two men sipped their brandy.

'I am very fond of her,' said Wilson.

'So was I,' said Harry.

'And I am a jealous man, Pilikian.'

'You have a right to be.'

Wilson stared at the young man. 'You're very handsome,' he said. 'I can see that you've begun to age, but I can also see that you are still very attractive.'

'Thank you,' said Harry. 'When a woman tells me that, I am flattered.'

'And when I say it?' questioned Wilson.

Harry's eyes narrowed. 'I am wary,' he said with a forced smile.

There was silence between the two men as laughter, music and conversation came to them from the other rooms. Outside there was a rumble of thunder. Harry turned his head as if the noise heralded an intruder.

'Marching to a distant drum,' said Wilson. 'Don't worry, the storm was expected, it will pass beyond the horizon. Distant thunder, like the First War, it affects none of us here – yet.'

Harry sipped some more brandy.

'Would you like a cigar?' asked Wilson, pointing to a large humidor.

'No thanks.'

Wilson put out a hand and lifted the top of a second box, smaller and made of silver, full of white powder. 'Cocaine?' His eyes twinkled.

Harry shook his head.

Wilson stared at his guest, lowering the silver lid slowly. 'There are many men, Mr Pilikian, who would give up a great deal for some of this.'

'I'm not one of them,' said Harry.

'I have cruised the Mediterranean many times, Mr Pilikian. I was very young when I inherited money. My father developed railroads, my grandfather traded not only with the Far East but with Africa and the Hanseatic merchants of northern Europe.' He stopped himself. 'And you are Armenian?' Harry nodded. 'Then you would have appreciated Nijinsky. He was a phantom, Mr Pilikian.'

228

Harry wandered to the wall and saw a beautiful watercolour costume design by Bakst, one of many from several ballets.

'Did you ever see him dance?'

'No,' said Harry, 'I never had the opportunity.'

Wilson's voice became louder. 'Chaliapin would have coffee across the Casino Square. Caruso, after a triumph at the Opera, would drink champagne in the bar of the Salle Privée. Can you believe any of this was real, Mr Pilikian? It is already another world, which perhaps only ever existed in the imaginations of those who have survived.'

'People will say the same thing about us one day, I am sure.' Harry finished his brandy.

'I am homosexual, Mr Pilikian. Does that mean anything to you?'

'No,' said Harry.

Wilson smiled. 'I can see that,' he said. 'You have something in your eyes which I admire.'

'What?' asked Harry.

'Masculinity,' said Wilson softly. 'You know, if I had had a daughter I could only have wished that she would be like Mrs Lieberman.'

'Alex,' said Harry.

'Alex,' repeated Wilson.

'And who is Howard Maitland?' asked Harry.

'*What* is he, don't you mean, Mr Pilikian? We have been lovers; is that what you want me to say to you?' Wilson stood up awkwardly, swaying to find his balance. 'Do you know, Mr Pilikian, what it is like to have *everything*? And to be unable to expect *anything*, but the hope that you might wake in the morning?'

'No,' said Harry quietly.

'Then think!' said Wilson, almost shouting. 'Look around you. I am the residue of several generations of wealth and look at me. A plantation slave I could snuff out in a gesture, a buck nigger in the fields, a fifty-cent whore *breathes* without trouble, without pain, and I cannot buy what they do not even think about!' Wilson was so close that Harry could smell the man's breath; the brandy masked a terrible smell of decay.

'Think, Pilikian, what it means. Even a bootblack is not required to understand the process of absorbing oxygen. Even a plant finds it quite natural!' Wilson was staring into Harry's eyes. He pressed his lips tight and drew air heavily through his nostrils. He clung to the desk and swayed a moment, then slammed a fist on the green leather surface.

Someone was knocking. The door opened and Alex came in quickly.

'Sullivan is ready, Bradford.' She looked at Harry. 'They're going to dance.'

Bradford Arnett Wilson began gasping, obviously in distress. Immediately Alex helped him to his wheelchair, where he sat down heavily. Beneath the seat was an oxygen supply, which she gave him

229

through a mouthpiece until his breathing became regular. Outside, the quartet which Sullivan had organized began to play the first dance tune. Alex felt Wilson's pulse: it had slowed down.

Grasping the oxygen mask, his eyes protruding above the dark rubber, Wilson waved the two of them out. 'Go!' he mumbled. 'Both of you.' Alex was hesitant. He took off the mask. 'On deck! Leave me!' He looked into Alex's eyes, sucked more oxygen and spoke again: 'Get out . . . and dance!'

Harry and Alexandra walked out onto the stern, under the awning, moved round the dancers and leaned against the rail. They gazed at the moon hanging above the coast of Italy, and stood silent for several minutes, listening to giggling from women in the saloon and roars of laughter from the men beyond, in the dining room.

'Where do we begin?' asked Harry.

'Let's dance,' said Alex. There was a moment of hesitancy before they touched, then Harry took her firmly in his arms and they waltzed slowly into the group on the improvised dance floor, surrounded by tables and chairs. The Eurasian waiters were in attendance as if it were a small private nightclub. Harry felt Alex's body pressed against his; it was not difficult to recall.

'How did all this happen?' Harry said, trying to encompass the ship in one small movement of the hand.

'He was a friend of my father. He remembered me when we met at a party in Hollywood.'

'So you didn't become a star?'

'No,' she said, smiling. 'I didn't . . .' The distant storm rumbled beyond the horizon, its noise competing with the group as they started up another melody.

'The weather's changing,' Harry said softly.

Alex looked into his eyes. 'It always does this time of the year,' she said.

'You've been here before?'

Alex nodded. 'Monte Carlo seems to be a place where everyone comes eventually.'

'Everyone who's anyone,' said Harry cynically.

Alex's eyes recognized the young man she had once known. 'Everyone is someone Harry, to someone else.'

He smiled. 'Harry,' he said.

'What?' whispered Alex.

'You said Harry. It's been a long time.'

They danced well together, gliding between the others. Harry smiled into her eyes with obvious pleasure, and Alex touched her cheek. 'I think I'm blushing.'

Harry felt her vulnerability, and immediately spoke his mind harshly. 'Where is dear John?' he asked. 'The man you spent so much time writing to me about from California.'

'He was my husband,' said Alex.

'Lieberman?'

Alex nodded. Harry began to laugh with relief at the tense Alex had used. 'Was?' he asked.

'We're divorced.'

'Why did you marry in the first place?' asked Harry bluntly.

'Because I wanted . . . my baby,' she said.

'Lisa,' said Harry. They looked into each other's eyes. There was a pause in the music, and Harry eased Alex to the ship's rail. 'This is terribly romantic,' he said.

'So was Hollywood,' said Alex. 'At first.'

'Who's Wilson?'

'One of his companies bought the studio from John,' Alex told him.

'You mean Mr Lieberman?'

'Yes,' she smiled. 'John described the assets and represented the board at a dinner party we gave. That was when Bradford remembered me as a girl.'

'A friend of your father's, you said.'

'He is a kind and loving man,' Alex insisted, looking towards the moon. 'I have done what I can to organize his life.'

'Private life?' asked Harry.

'*Personal*,' she said.

Laughter came from the dining room as a door opened and closed with a slam. Several women seated at the tables round the dance floor had begun to gossip. Harry could hear their high-pitched giggles rising above the music. 'Do you really belong here?' he asked quietly.

Alexandra stared into Harry's steady eyes. 'You tell me,' she said. 'Why not? What else did I have?'

They were silent for a moment, unearthing the clues to love.

'We had each other – once,' said Harry.

Her eyes hardened. 'That once happened a long time ago Harry, to different people.'

Voices sounded from the quay. A young man in a Hotel de Paris uniform was arguing with a sailor as the two of them made their way up the gangway to the *Maracaibo*.

'Mrs Lieberman.' The sailor hurried up to Alex. 'There is an emergency at the hotel. Somebody has died and they want Doctor Solomon.'

'I think he's still in the dining room. I'll get him,' she said, and began to move.

'I'll come with you,' said Harry. They made their way through the

231

dancers, into the saloon and across to the large dining table. Alex tapped Solomon on the shoulder and whispered in his ear.

'Please make my apologies to Mr Wilson, Madame, and thank him for a wonderful evening,' said the doctor.

She glanced towards the study. 'I'd better go in and tell him.'

Alex opened the study door, and Harry followed her. She had actually composed the words 'Doctor Solomon' on her lips, but they were never spoken.

Harry saw two men standing near the table beside Wilson. The silver box full of cocaine was open. When the Italian Colonel Navara turned from Maitland to stare wide-eyed towards the two figures in the doorway, there was fine white powder on his nose.

It was too late for Harry to move. He could already see trouble in Howard Maitland's eyes.

'You miserable little bitch!' he hissed at Alex. 'I've told you before that when I want privacy' – his voice became shrill – 'you stay out.' Maitland had already taken too much cocaine to be stable.

Wilson's eyes darted towards Harry. Alex had begun to back out of the door.

'Stay where you are!' screamed Maitland. He moved quickly across Wilson's study, wearing only shining patent leather shoes and dark trousers, his white shirt unbuttoned to the waist. He was exploding with anger, and, as Harry could see, his tanned, muscular body looked dangerous.

'Howard,' said Wilson, 'you are a guest on board. That's enough.'

'I'm sorry,' said Alex, 'I didn't mean . . . to intrude.'

Maitland slapped her across the face, so hard that she fell against the door and on to her knees. Harry did not even stop to think – it was all instinct. He threw his best punch, but it only clipped Maitland's chin as he stepped backwards.

'Pilikian, you're a dead man!' he said.

Alex was sobbing on the floor. In the dining room and on deck, Maitland's voice had stopped the conversation. He stepped towards Harry Pilikian and started a left-hand punch. Harry ducked, to be caught immediately by an explosion on his jaw. The move had been a feint. Maitland had connected with a right cross and half his body weight. Harry staggered back, shaking his head, but Maitland was already on to him. A second blow caught Harry squarely on the cheek, whipping his head to one side. He fell, and knew that he must get up quickly or be finished.

Harry's face was turning as a third blow arrived, a perfect left cross to his chin. He staggered behind a table beneath the Gobelin tapestry on the wall, breathing heavily, blood running down his face. He heard Alex's sobs and shouts from the other room. He was dazed and trying to

232

clear his vision. The punches had been incredibly accurate and hard. He saw Wilson across the room, watching with more than curiosity – his eyes held vicarious pleasure.

'Maitland was a middleweight contender, Pilikian. He hasn't forgotten much!'

Harry's adversary was already halfway round the table. At arm's length from Pilikian he stopped, squaring himself, feinted one way and threw a punch the other. Harry thrust out a straight right centred on Maitland's face, but the man was already under the fist and coming up fast with a right upper cut. Harry barely managed to avoid the blow then countered with a left hook, blocking the other man's arm. Then he felt a body blow in the belly, pushing his diaphragm flat. He gasped and another blow caught him on the chin, snapping his head back. Harry put up his hands, fists together, elbows pressed tight, his head seeking sanctuary between his arms. A left hook, then a right cross caught both his ears, and they started burning. A fist buried itself again in his belly and another smacked into his forehead, knocking him against the panelling of the study. Now he could not hear Alexandra's screams or the shouts from the dining room: only the hurricane roaring in his head made any sense. There was a flash of light, an intense pain under his right eye, and he found himself grovelling on the carpet of the study. He had yet to land a punch.

'I'm being taken apart!' he thought to himself, barely controlling panic.

What changed everything was the patent-leather shoe that Harry saw a split second before it would have landed. He dropped his head, and Maitland's foot smashed into the table, knocking it over along with twenty-two ounces of cocaine from the open silver box. The Italian colonel, cowering in a corner, shouted loudly.

The noise seared into Harry's brain and distracted Maitland momentarily, which was all that Harry needed. He was halfway to his feet and saw the body of the middle-aged homosexual poised before him. Harry's fist was destined for a target below Maitland's waist. Queensberry rules no longer applied. He was fighting for survival.

Harry landed his first blow and it sank deep. Maitland screamed wildly. For Harry this was only the beginning of revenge. Wherever he could feel, he hurt. He could barely breathe. Blood was running from his nose and ears. His aggressor was swaying, features taut with the pain between his legs. Harry prised himself from the floor, focused, then hit out with a straight right and straight left that landed in the centre of Maitland's face. The ex-boxer staggered but remained on his feet. Harry stepped forward and again a straight right and a straight left smacked sickeningly into Maitland's face, then a right upper cut snapped his head back, arching his body. A left cross sank into his stomach. Harry pushed the man away and watched him sink to his knees. Out of the corner of his eye, he saw Alex, her face red, tears streaming down her cheeks, and behind her a crowd at the door.

Harry stepped back, then kicked the man in the face. His shoe caught Maitland beneath the chin. The man seemed to leap backwards across the room, sprawling at Bradford Arnett Wilson's feet. Harry bent double, suddenly feeling the pain; he was breathing heavily and thought it was over, but cocaine and a background of thirty-seven fights and twenty-three knockouts had given Maitland astonishing resilience. His body curled from the floor. He was sucking his lips, tongue exploring cracked teeth, but his eyes were unmistakably fixed on Harry Pilikian.

Harry swore to himself.

Maitland ran screaming at Pilikian. He caught him by the throat and propelled him through the crowd gathered at the doorway until both bodies fell against the huge dining table full of precious objects.

The silver pheasants were the first to fall, then the candelabra, the china, Georgian cutlery, beautiful vases and sprays of flowers on the pale pink tablecloth. Coffee cups and brandy glasses fell next, as the weight of the two men upended the table and they, along with everything else, slid onto the carpeted floor.

Harry was lucky. Coffee from a large silver pot splashed across Maitland's face, and the man screamed in pain from the scalding brew. Harry forced him away then drove a left hook hard into his throat. In the next moment Harry found himself on top. Maitland instinctively brought up his right knee between Harry's legs, but they were too close and the blow had no force. Now Harry went to work not as a boxer but as a man who had grown up in the streets. His was the resilience of a child who had survived a holocaust in a far-away country.

If Maitland got up, Harry knew he was finished – but there was no way the man could rise again. Every blow Harry landed was into Maitland's face, and every blow began at Harry's waist and landed with the jolting strength of a man demented.

Somewhere Harry heard a voice screaming, shouting, and only when he realized it was his own did he stop. Hands pulled him from the inert body and he looked up to see Ben Harrison.

'Steady,' said Ben quietly. 'Steady!' Then he whispered to the others: 'He's all right now. He's all right.'

Harry found himself swaying in Ben Harrison's firm grip. Around them was total silence.

Chapter 31

Harry felt cold water on his face, and opened his eyes. Alexandra had taken him below to a private cabin.

'How does it look?' he asked, and saw that there was still a red weal on her face.

'You'll pull through,' she said, leaning close to wipe his brow. He could smell her scent and reached towards her, but she caught the hand and placed it on his chest, continuing to dab his forehead with the cold, wet flannel.

'Have you always been as wild as this, Harry?'

'Tough childhood,' he replied, trying to grin. 'I was a very disturbed youth, you know that.'

'How could I forget?' she said softly.

Harry gazed into the cool dark depths of Alex's eyes, and winced as she touched a bruised and delicate area beneath his lip.

'Does that hurt?' she asked.

'Not when I'm looking at you.'

'You haven't changed much, Harry.'

'I've changed completely,' he said.

'Not to me,' she replied. Her slender fingers moved down the man's inflamed cheek, gently exploring the bones beneath the flesh. 'You could have come to California,' she murmured.

'Three thousand miles is a big argument,' said Harry.

'Later,' she said.

'You were already someone else.'

'I was *with* someone else.'

'You married him.' Harry stared at her for a long time.

'You weren't there.' Alex smiled slowly. 'And Lisa was on the way.'

'Yes, she's beautiful. She's got your nose and hair,' said Harry, reaching up to touch strands of the dark hair that had fallen either side of her face. 'And mouth.'

Alex smiled, her lips parting over perfect teeth. 'She has your eyes, Harry.' Her caress strayed from Harry's jaw and found his hand, to touch it gently. 'And your fingers,' she said. Her head was on one side, scrutinizing his face. 'She's capricious too.'

'So were you.'

'So is her father.'

Harry's eyes, which had been warm, hardened. 'I never met him, remember.'

'You've known him all your life.' She was like a child with a secret. There was a silence between them as his eyes searched her face. 'I don't believe you,' he said.

'Watch her. Look at her eyes when she smiles.'

'I don't believe you,' he repeated.

'See how she moves.' Alex's voice was distant and there were tears in her eyes. 'She has sensitive fingers, they describe everything she says.'

'She plays?' asked Harry.

'Very well.'

'So did I, at her age,' he smiled proudly.

'You told me,' said Alex.

He stared in silence. 'She's mine?'

'Ours.'

'You should have told me.'

'How could I?'

He stared at her and took his time – it was a big question. 'What do we do now?'

Alex shivered. 'Kiss me,' she whispered.

There was no scandal. Gossip, of course, but no scandal. In Monte Carlo there has always been a way of dealing with difficulties. Reputations are made and broken in private, and that privacy extends as far as the last person of any consequence who will listen to a whispered version of the facts in the corner of some public place.

Christopher Quinn's death was hushed up to avoid unfavourable publicity. After an autopsy, the authorities declared it to have been a very inventive suicide, and the body was buried. Gerard, the chief of police, was unhappy about the inconclusive evidence, but the coroner's report was made official. Gestapo Colonel Pabst had been unusually cooperative and expressed concern and regret at the death of the man who had been a valued acquaintance. The Swiss banker, de Salis, had been cold and correct. Only the beautiful Miss Lawrence, whose profession Gerard knew quite well, showed any real emotion and refused to accept that Christopher Quinn had not been murdered.

The police harboured justifiable suspicions. Quinn was right-handed, and the needle had been found between the fingers of his left hand. And why should anyone choose such an agonizing death? Surely no suicide would plan to die in a lift – but was it planned? The body had been buried, but in the mind of the chief of police, the case was not.

As to the gossip about the *Maracaibo* and the fight that had taken place that same night, rumour was rife for almost a month as the yacht remained berthed and a source of speculation. Jokes were cracked and stories embellished until even Louis the barman refused to answer questions.

But one thing was certain: Harry Pilikian had changed. Louis could vouch for that. Suddenly there was something mysterious about him. Perhaps it was only the weather, thought Louis gloomily, looking out through the large glass windows towards the leaden Mediterranean. It had begun to rain heavily, day after day.

In the lounge of the Blue Suite, Harry Pilikian sat at his piano, a cigarette hanging from his lips, white shirt sleeves rolled up. He stared out through open french windows at the bucketing downpour of an already darkening day, and began to play a melody that he felt was almost appropriate. It contained many of the elements he had enjoyed, observed and endured in Monte Carlo.

So many people came to the Principality to be part of the glamour, to mingle with the rich and famous, hoping that the spin of a wheel could change their fortune or alter their destiny, but reality is patient and waits for everyone.

Harry played the last note, ground out his cigarette and looked once more at the sheets of paper beside the typewriter on his desk. Only then did he stand, hands in pockets, lost in thought.

Alex had come to see him often, and it was becoming more difficult for him not to be with her every day. He had not been back to the *Maracaibo*, so he had caught only glimpses of Lisa. She was now being driven to and from school each day by taxi, accompanied by a sailor. He disagreed with so much cosseting, so he and Alex had had their first argument as parents.

Harry lit another cigarette. So many years not dead but reborn.

'Nineteen thirty-three,' he murmured aloud, and blew smoke through the open windows into the rain.

Alex had discovered that she was pregnant soon after her arrival in California. She had been afraid to tell anyone, and her panic had increased when she realized that Harry was unable to join her because of the trial. John Lieberman, her aunt's friend, had made the transition from Samaritan to husband with Hollywood charm, and at least partly because he believed she would become a star. Possession of a beautiful wife palled, but did provide the boardroom vice-president with enough confidence to go on to other things, leaving Alex comfortable in a lovely house with a child, a nanny, two servants and a career that had never really started. Then Mr Wilson had appeared, naively curious about the film world and delighted to find that John's wife was the daughter of his old friend George Leonard Cunningham.

Alex had believed in the sometime friendship that Mr Wilson claimed with her father, and had never since had cause to doubt the sincerity of the man who became known to her as 'Bradford'. She had accepted his invitation to Palm Beach that first winter, and their relationship had developed during a Caribbean cruise on the *Maracaibo*. The motor yacht was Wilson's latest acquisition, and he wanted Alex to go with it, and what remained of his life.

So she had become the personal assistant and hostess to a man with diverse interests both in business and the arts. Consequently she grew to admire many things in Wilson – his education, his knowledge both studied and acquired, and his experience of people and places in most parts of the world. Above all, his kindness and generosity to both herself and her child.

Throughout the late thirties, they had travelled with the seasons. From California to the Hamptons; from Florida to the Far East. But always they found themselves in Europe, where Alex's benefactor was fascinated with the historical glories and physical decadence of so many cultures bordering the Mediterranean. Finally, the war had forced even Wilson into the neutral port of Monte Carlo.

Harry pieced together this picture of Alex's attitude to the man, his life and background from the stories she had begun to tell him during long afternoons spent quietly talking in the lounge of Harry's Blue Suite. 'Renaissance'. Wilson had spoken the word to Alex in Rome, at sunset overlooking the Colosseum. 'It is a magnificent word, Renaissance. A rebirth, an exhumation of the great ideals, lost to mankind. If only we could all have a Renaissance instead of death.' He had gazed a long time at the shell of the amphitheatre, until twilight had fallen. Alex described the scene with emotion, and Harry listened patiently. They were slowly rediscovering each other. It took time before Harry asked the important question. 'When do we tell Lisa . . .' They finally agreed, on her birthday.

On that day, in the Salle Empire of the Hotel de Paris, violins were playing, tea was being served, and the chandeliers were already lit. Lisa looked about her in wonder.

'Hello,' said Harry quietly. Lisa grinned with delight.

'Hello, Mr Red Tie,' she said. 'Are you having tea with us too?' Harry smiled nervously and sat down. Alex was reminded of the gauche young man with whom she had drunk tea in New York's Plaza Hotel.

'Happy birthday,' he said, and took out a small present.

Lisa discovered a red box and opened it. Inside was a gold heart-shaped locket and chain. On the back was inscribed 'To Lisa with Love'.

Each half revealed a small portrait – on one side Alex Cunningham, on the other Harry Pilikian.

Lisa jumped up, threw her arms around Harry's neck and kissed him. There was an awkward pause. Lisa, wondering what was about to happen, looked at her mother and then at Harry.

'How are we going to do this?' he asked.

Alex shrugged, her eyes wide, knowing in that moment that she loved this man as if nothing had changed.

Lisa smiled, 'Are you going to be my daddy now?' she asked.

'I am,' he answered.

It was almost 6 o'clock and already dusk before they left the Salle Empire for the lobby.

The man, woman and child, for the first time a family, stepped out of the Hotel de Paris and paused at the top of the steps.

'Look up,' Harry said. The three of them stared into infinity. 'What do you see?' he whispered.

'Stars,' said Lisa softly.

Heavy rain began later that evening. Harry picked up Alex from the *Maracaibo* at 9, as they had agreed, and drove slowly up the Avenue de Monte Carlo back to the Hotel de Paris, he in a dinner jacket, she in a long grey silk dress and sequined jacket. They entered the Salle Empire for the second time that day, but now it was beautifully laid out for dining. This was not the first time, nor would it be the last, that the two of them had gazed into each other's eyes over dinner, but it was different that night.

Once young lovers, they had become friends. There was trust between them, based not only on rekindled memories or gratitude to fate and the pleasures of coincidence, but upon the astonishment at discovering that each had felt the same sense of loss during their years apart. What was between them now had nothing to do with the past, but everything to do with the future.

The waiter had to cough several times to draw Harry's attention to the bill, which needed his signature.

After the meal, Alex and Harry went directly upstairs to the Blue Suite, where the maid was told she would not be required, then the outer door was shut firmly – and locked.

They were hesitant at first. Two people attracted to one another but reluctant to make the initial move.

They began by taking off each other's clothes, until both were naked.

In the background the radio played dance tunes.

'We were children,' whispered Alex.

'And now?' asked Harry.

'We will be lovers,' she answered softly.

Harry ran his hands down her back, finding the narrow waist, slowly pulling her closer. He stepped forward pressing himself against her body. Alex closed her eyes and her mouth widened. Harry held her firmly.

She slid her legs around his hips, clasping him tight, her arms locked round his neck. Then she felt his erection pushing against her. She gasped and her head fell back.

He kissed her neck and she started to moan with pleasure. Harry carried her to the bed and then they were falling slowly, he onto the softness of her body, she into the sheets and covers, where their bodies' familiarity returned with the rapture of urgent, passionate love.

Chapter 32

Winter came early that year. Trees shed their leaves quickly as if in preparation for what they knew was inevitable. Bright days were few. Autumn disappeared in Monte Carlo, in Europe and in Russia.

On the huge battle front in the heartland of the USSR, the Wehrmacht began to succumb to the first of nature's obstacles – rain. Such roads as existed turned to thick mire, and with the fields impassable the thrusting attack on Moscow bogged down, then came to a halt. The Germans hoped to enjoy a well-earned rest. After all, it was only rain, and it affected the Russians equally – it would stop eventually. By the time the really cold weather arrived the Wehrmacht would be in Moscow, the Russians beaten. The war would be over by Christmas. Everyone said so. Russia was just a rotten door to be kicked in, as the Führer had predicted, and he had been right so far. Everything had gone just as he had promised.

Soon, after the victory, half the army would be able to return home to Germany, or to her new territories, the occupied countries. The lucky ones might even go south to the sun. The Mediterranean. Anywhere away from winter, away from the war. Surely not much to ask for a fighting soldier of the Master Race?

Ben Harrison watched the Italian engine, billowing smoke, pull in to Monte Carlo's Casino station in the late morning of a Tuesday at the end of October. The rain was teeming down.

'Bloody cats and dogs!' he muttered solemnly, then stepped aside to allow an old woman with several children access to the approaching carriages and found himself directly beneath a hole in the iron lattice canopy. Rainwater poured on to his hat and the shoulders of his trench coat, and immediately extinguished his cigarette.

'Damn!' he bellowed. He lit another cigarette as the train stopped, hissing and steaming. The carriages were full. The uniforms were German: army officers from Russia, most of them wounded.

Harry Pilikian pushed through the crowd on the platform and tapped Ben's shoulder. He grunted acknowledgement. 'Look,' he said sarcastically, 'the Boches have come for their hols.'

Harry accepted a cigarette from Ben, remembering that the Englishman was a veteran of another war, and blew blue-grey smoke into the air above grey-blue uniforms. Wounded German officers were nothing new – they had been arriving for months – but somehow these men looked different. These soldiers of the Wehrmacht, their generals, even the Führer, had only just realized that the war might not be over by Christmas. And those who had actually fought the Red Army already knew in their hearts that the Third Reich had taken on more than it had bargained for in Russia. Behind the confident official bulletins, it was becoming a gamble. These officers were unsettled, their boisterous behaviour was camouflage.

'Look at their eyes,' whispered Harry.

Despite the dirty weather and his filthy mood, Ben smiled. These supermen were really shaken, which gave strength to his resolve that if he could do nothing else, he would contribute to the Nazi downfall.

Harry nudged Ben, and both of them watched Guy de Salis step from the train to be met by tall men in long black coats and dark hats.

'Pabst's goons,' muttered Ben.

Harry nodded. 'Something is definitely up.'

They lost the Swiss banker in the crowd.

Ben and Harry had come to meet Alexandra, who had taken Bradford Arnett Wilson to see a specialist in Milan. Without her, it had been a long week for Harry, although he had managed to see Lisa most days at the hotel, and had begun to cement a real relationship.

'Where the devil are they?' asked Ben Harrison. Then he saw two sailors from the *Maracaibo* carrying the wheelchair, and two others lifting Bradford Arnett Wilson from his first class compartment. The nurse was fussing over Wilson as they walked up. The old man looked older. His face was grey, his eyes frightened.

When Harry saw Alex, his heart leapt. She kissed him quickly. 'He's had a bad attack,' she whispered. 'They could do nothing for him.'

Harry heard the old man wheezing. Wilson looked him up and down, then turned his head towards Alex.

'Don't be jealous, young man, we've only been a week without you.'

Harry's eyes narrowed, but Wilson's were actually twinkling. He had baited Harry successfully. 'And how are you going to keep your two beautiful girls in the manner to which they've become accustomed?' he asked.

A French voice was shouting for everyone to clear the platform. The train was about to pull away.

'I'll provide for them, if that's what you mean.'

'How?' snapped Wilson.

'I'll find a way.'

'Like love, eh?' suggested Wilson harshly.

'God damn you!' shouted Harry. He had been touched where he was most vulnerable. 'If you could even stand, I'd knock you down!' Two of the sailors closed in.

A whistle blew; the locomotive in front let out smoke and steam. The long line of carriages began to move out.

Awkwardly, painfully, the rug falling from his knees, Bradford Arnett Wilson stood up in front of Harry Pilikian. The effort was immense, and he could barely control his breathing, but he swayed there, defiance sparkling in his eyes. For a moment Harry had forgotten that Alexandra was the only woman in Wilson's life and he was fighting to keep her.

The old man swung his arm with surprising speed and slapped Harry hard across the face. There was a gasp from Alex and the nurse. 'Is that your answer to everything, Pilikian?' he rasped.

Harry was white with anger, knowing that he could not retaliate.

'You meet an obstacle in life and you just knock it down?' – Wilson wafted a hand. 'Like these Germans?'

The carriages picked up speed and began rattling noisily out of the station as Harry tried desperately to control his rage.

'Pilikian, you and I come from different worlds, and yet here we are, in the same one for a moment. Isn't that curious?' Wilson lost some of his strength and began to sway, but pushed at the hands that reached out for him.

'She is precious to me now, Pilikian,' hissed Wilson. 'I can't let you take her away from me yet.' The man's voice became weaker. 'I won't let you!' he said, raising his chin.

His body began to slump, then he fell, but Harry's strong arms caught him. His breathing was erratic and he could no longer speak, but his eyes continued to stare into Harry's as if he were pleading with a lover.

Harry set Wilson gently back into the wheelchair. The nurse quickly wrapped the old man in blankets and clapped an oxygen mask to his face as the sailors pushed the wheelchair along the platform. Alex glanced at Harry, tears in her eyes. He was about to speak but she turned from him and joined the group which went down the platform, out of the station, and into the rain.

Harry was unable to move. He was still white-faced from anger and shame, fearful that he had lost more than his temper. Ben touched his arm gently.

'Fancy a drink?' he asked.

The two men went directly to the American Bar, where Harry got drunk and argued with some newly arrived German officers until the situation became dangerous. Louis suggested that Ben should remove Harry to maintain peace between Germany and America.

At the news of his rapid promotion to full colonel, Pabst had been congratulated throughout the morning by the men under his command.

There was a jubilant atmosphere in his prison headquarters on the Rock of Monaco. The reports that came to them daily, directly from Gestapo headquarters on the Prinz Albrechtstrasse in Berlin, confirmed their hopes and often even exceeded their expectations. Everyone agreed that in a month, Russia would be beaten.

In the afternoon, Pabst called his men together to address them. Several had asked for transfers to the Russian front to take part in the great crusade against communism before it was all over. Having toasted the Führer and Himmler with schnapps, Pabst began his first speech as a colonel.

'We are as important to the success of the Third Reich as the leader of a Panzer tank regiment. Under the guidance of those who command, it is our job to ensure the ultimate victory of National Socialism. We are the guardians of its foundation, we provide the stability not only in the Reich but in all our territories. We are feared because we are powerful and we must be vigilant to protect that power as we protect so many others, to secure their peace.'

Pabst paused, his eyes bright.

'When the enemy is cunning, we are ruthless. When the enemy is weak, we are strong. When the enemy shows cowardice, we take our revenge. When the enemy falters, we seize our opportunities. Gentlemen, to National Socialism!'

He raised his glass. His men sprang to attention.

'The Führer!'

'Final victory!' said Pabst, and they all drank together.

'It was a good speech,' Pabst mused an hour later. Now he had to make a decision, the first in his new rank. He had asked for certain sophisticated equipment, as it appeared that they would be occupying their temporary headquarters in the prison for some time to come.

A young officer had arrived with an ingenious monitoring system which worked in conjunction with their radio, and they had discovered that regular transmissions were being made from the Principality, although so far it had proved impossible to decipher the messages. 'It is a one-time code sir,' the young man called Obermeyer had told Pabst. Now the signal had been monitored again.

Pabst sat down and looked at Obermeyer's notes. The room was small and damp but full of equipment. A bare bulb hung from the ceiling and a table lamp illuminated Obermeyer's calculations, the light glinting off his wire-rimmed spectacles.

'The signal is very strong, sir,' he said.

'On the Rock itself?' asked Pabst.

'Yes, sir.'

'Have you plotted the source?'

Obermeyer bent over the map spread across the table, and his finger traced a street and stopped at a villa. He drew a circle. Pabst smiled slowly. Moments later he had issued his orders, and the Gestapo made ready to do what they did best.

Ben Harrison could hardly believe the message he had received. It took more than an hour to decode. Harry Pilikian raised his eyebrows curiously.

'Can I see it?' he asked. Ben handed over the message he had written out in capitals. Harry read it slowly, then put the message on the small desk beside the transmitter. The two men looked at each other in silence.

'They expect you to kill him?' Harry asked.

Ben inhaled deeply, then coughed, nodding. 'Who else?'

'Eva Trenchard?' suggested Harry.

Ben shook his head. 'Too risky for her.'

'One of her men, surely?'

'They've never done it,' said Ben, who was now afraid and on edge.

'Have you?' asked Harry.

'In another time and another war!' said Ben coldly. He coughed again. 'Let's have a whisky.'

They turned out the lights, went through the panelled door and sprawled in the library. Harry poured.

'How did they find out?'

Ben shrugged. 'We must have people in Switzerland.'

They both drank whisky.

'Jews,' said Harry.

'De Salis,' said Ben and there was no time for anything else.

The banging on the front door was so loud that it sounded as if it was

244

coming from the next room. Their alarm turned to panic, as even in the bowels of the house they heard the outside door being split open.

Ben was on his feet. 'Jesus Christ!' he exclaimed.

'How the hell do we get out of here?' snapped Harry.

The downstairs library was built in what had once been a storeroom. The panelling along one wall matched the laden bookshelves. It was always cool and peaceful, and offered a womb-like security, but for anyone suffering from claustrophobia it was a nightmare. There were air ducts and false curtains, but no windows.

On one wall of the panelling a concealed door opened on to a small room where Agatha Parry had installed her equipment. Here, at the rear of the house, where it was embedded in the rock, the builders had left a ventilation shaft for the basement. The only real window in the lower part of the house was in the hidden room.

Running feet on the stairs outside the library galvanized the two men into action. Ben pushed Harry through the panelled door and closed it as the Gestapo burst into the library.

'The lights are still on, sir,' murmured Erich Held. Pabst examined the room quickly. He crossed to one wall, noticing that most of the books were English classics. Held sniffed the whisky in the two glasses. It was newly poured and there were several drops still moist on the glass table. He pointed. Pabst nodded.

'Good, so where are they?'

Beneath Held's long coat was his Schmeisser submachine gun. He gripped its butt then put a finger to his lips. Intrigued, Pabst took out his Walther pistol and watched Held.

The man crossed to the panelling, examined the square moulding pattern and began moving down the wall, tapping with his fingertips.

Ben Harrison and Harry Pilikian held their breath as the voices stopped.

'Are they going?' asked Ben.

Harry shook his head. He was already unfastening the catch of the one window, which he opened as wide as it would go. He should be able to squeeze through into the narrow space outside. The noise of tapping came from the library. Harry pointed at the window. 'Come on!'

'You go first,' Ben hissed, and reached for the drawer beneath the radio equipment where Agatha had kept a pistol. The tapping stopped.

'Stay away from the door and keep low,' whispered Harry. Ben nodded urgently. Harry stepped onto a chair and like a contortionist eased himself quickly out of the window.

The tapping started again, reached the door and stopped. Ben began to breathe heavily as Harry dropped outside, falling against the rock several feet below. He pressed his back against the cold slippery granite, bent his knees and with his feet against the house wall locked his body across the shaft. He looked up and estimated the height to be about eighteen feet. Painfully he began to push himself up, using his shoulders and feet. Then he heard Ben's racking cough.

In the library, Pabst pointed. Held fired a burst at the hollow panelling and bullets whistled over Ben's head, smacking into the wall, several shattering the glass of the window. Held kicked at the panelling until his heavy boot broke the lock and the concealed door swung open. Immediately he and Pabst pressed themselves on either side of the door jamb. From within Ben fired wildly, and Held raised the Schmeisser, but Pabst shook his head – he wanted the man alive.

'Enough!' he screamed as if Ben were under his orders. Ben fired again and swore.

Pabst did not lack courage: he timed his move perfectly. As Ben fired a fifth shot, splintering the door jamb, Pabst ducked, spun into the opening and fired a bullet into Ben's leg, just above the kneecap. The Englishman fell as Held leapt into the room, kicking the gun from his hand.

'The window!' barked Pabst. Held reached it, and knocked out the remaining glass.

'What is outside?' Pabst snapped at Harrison. Ben's grimace at his pain turned to a wicked grin. Held leaned cautiously through the window, his eyes adjusting to the semi-darkness.

By now, Harry Pilikian was almost at the top of the shaft.

'Hurry!' screamed Ben, propping himself against the desk. Pabst hit Ben across the cheek with the muzzle of his pistol.

'Get the other man!' shouted Pabst.

Erich Held thrust the machine pistol through the window and looked up. 'Too late, sir,' he said. Pabst pushed Held away and by the time his eyes adjusted, Harry had gone.

The rain had stopped, but the ground was still wet. Harry climbed into a small overgrown garden to one side of the house. He reached a low wall, pulled himself over and ran off down the street. A shout from behind spurred him on as he raced through the deserted streets of the old town, into the Place de la Visitation, along the Avenue des Pins and came out at the top of the Avenue de la Porte Neuve. He sprinted down towards the harbour of La Condamine, taking a small road leading to the Avenue de la Quarantine and the quayside.

Harry slowed to a walk. At the port there might be police, but he saw none. Then he spun round, hearing the noise of the Gestapo Mercedes in the Rue du Port, approaching the Boulevard Albert at speed. As it screeched to a halt he took a deep breath, dived into the dark water of the harbour and began swimming beneath the surface in the direction of his only possible refuge, the *Maracaibo*.

Chapter 33

Gasping for air, Harry rose to the surface of the harbour beside the dark silhouette of the American yacht *Maracaibo*. He swam the eighty metres of her length to the stern, pulled himself up on a slack mooring rope, scrambled onto the quayside, staggered to his feet and reached the gangway.

'Hold it,' said an American voice above him, and Harry heard the sound of a bullet loaded into the breech of a rifle.

'It's Harry Pilikian,' he said.

'Halt!' came a shout from behind him. The Gestapo men were already running along the quay. On the gangway Harry was halfway to safety, seconds from capture, and not yet recognizable.

'Please!' he said, and looked up.

Standing beside a sailor carrying a Winchester was Howard Maitland, smoking a cigarette. Harry's expression changed as he saw the man he had knocked senseless.

'What is it?' Maitland asked.

'It's a man calling himself Pilikian.'

The Gestapo men came to a halt in the darkness behind Harry. 'This is not your business,' shouted Pabst, his breath rasping. 'That man is definitely ours.'

Maitland looked directly into Harry's eyes.

'Let him come on board, Henry,' he said.

'I repeat . . .' said Pabst.

'If they try to board, Henry,' said Maitland, 'shoot them.' Two other sailors had arrived at the stern, then a fourth and a fifth. All were armed.

Harry clambered up the gangway and fell on to the deck. Seven armed Germans were now standing beside Pabst, looking to him for orders.

'This will cause serious complications,' said Pabst icily. The American sailors levelled their rifles at the Gestapo men, light glinting on the steel barrels of their Winchesters. For a moment Pabst hesitated, then he snapped his fingers and the Germans moved away into the darkness.

'Well, well,' said Maitland and lit another cigarette. 'What do we have here?'

Harry, lying against the rails at the stern, reached up and took a cigarette.

Harry Pilikian was taken below, and Maitland found him a change of clothes. He had just put on a crewman's baggy trousers when Alex knocked.

'What's happened?' she asked.

'The Gestapo have taken Ben.' He pulled a shirt over his head.

'Here?' Alex was incredulous. 'But why?' she whispered.

Harry took her gently by the shoulders and looked into her eyes. 'Because . . .' he began.

There was a cursory knock on the half-open cabin door and the sailor called Henry appeared.

'Mr Wilson would like to see you, sir.'

Harry squeezed Alex affectionately and nodded to the sailor. The three of them walked down to the end of the corridor, where a door was ajar. Henry opened it cautiously and a nurse beckoned them in.

The master bedroom was as large as a state room on an ocean liner, with low, subtle lighting. Cylinders of oxygen lined one wall and there was some machinery hooked up to the large fourposter bed, which stood out as a legacy from another era, in contrast to the modern equipment surrounding it. Bradford Arnett Wilson was propped against pillows, and black rubber tubing connected to the oxygen led to nasal cannulae set behind his ears, across his cheeks and into his nostrils.

'Come in,' he said irritably, his chest heaving. 'Sit here, on the bed. Well, Mr Pilikian.' He paused. 'I think an explanation is called for.'

'Why?' asked Harry, and remained standing.

Wilson watched Alex, then as she sat on the covers he looked more kindly at the younger man. '*I* baited *you*, Mr Pilikian. *I* apologize.' Wilson's chest heaved again. Harry glanced round the room before speaking.

'I have no real possessions I do not carry with me. You, as you said, have everything.' Wilson attempted a smile as Harry went on. 'But they are only things – tapestries, paintings, possessions from other eras which have had many owners before you, and will belong to others after . . .' he paused.

'My death,' said Wilson, 'it is a word more familiar to me than to you. Go on.'

Harry looked at Alex. 'Even the most delicate treasures can endure a thousand years. People don't. That is what makes them so much more precious. We should be grateful to find real feeling, not for things but for each other. This is the *most* valuable possession.'

Wilson stared at Harry with bright eyes that clouded with tears. Only the machinery of the ship hummed in the silence between them. He took several deep breaths, labouring, and made a small gesture.

'For my possessions I require this entire yacht.' He stopped abruptly sucking in air. 'You need only . . .' he held up Alex's hand, 'I envy you Mr Pilikian, and I want to help.'

'You have already,' said Harry.

'Thank you,' said Wilson, and actually managed a smile that pleased him.

With a brisk knock on the door, Howard Maitland stepped into the bedroom to see Wilson's hands holding, on the one side Alex, on the other, Harry Pilikian's.

'The doctor's here,' he said.

'Thank God,' muttered the nurse.

'And the chief of police, Pilikian,' Maitland added.

Alex and Harry stood up. Wilson made a grimace at the sight of Dr Solomon, who nodded curtly to everyone and immediately began to examine his patient. Maitland looked his former adversary up and down and smiled.

'We're just different, that's all.' The two men shook hands.

Alex and Harry hurried upstairs into the main saloon, where Gerard, the chief of police, was waiting. He stood immediately, as did his uniformed men. He nodded to Alex, then stared at Pilikian with the steady eyes of a policeman. He hardly knew where to begin. He had a job to do in a neutral country but had his own loyalties.

'Have you joined the navy?'

'This is a private uniform,' Harry replied.

'Then it is appropriate, because you appear to be fighting a very private war.'

'Go to the prison and speak to your Nazi friends,' Harry snapped back, his voice harsh. 'They've taken Harrison out of the villa.'

Gerard seized Harry's arm and led him out of earshot.

'You must leave Monaco, Pilikian. I can no longer guarantee your protection. If you stay, Pabst will kill you.'

'Then I shall leave.'

'Good,' said Gerard.

'But not without Ben Harrison,' he said.

Gerard became exasperated. 'What can I do?' he said. 'The power of Germany is growing. I'm fifty-eight years old. I had my adventures in another war. When it was over I expected sense and peace.'

Harry grasped Gerard's shoulders. 'If you want to keep what others are prepared to take away from you, even if you are a man of peace, Gerard, there comes a time when you must fight! Or give up.'

Gerard passed a hand across his face. 'I am what you call on the fence or in the middle.'

'You'll have to climb down one day.'

Gerard began to walk away.

'And be careful you don't do it at night.'

The chief of police stopped.

'Why not?' he asked.

'You might find yourself on the wrong side.'

A Doctor Fouquet, who had strong Vichy sympathies, was summoned to Monaco's prison with a nurse, to take care of Ben Harrison's wound. The patient was unconscious when the doctor arrived. After he left, Ben slowly began to stir. He opened his eyes to find Pabst looking down at him.
'Good day, Mr Harrison. You feel better, I hope?' He reached out and touched the bandages wrapped around Ben's thigh where the trouser leg had been cut away.
'The doctor has done a good job.' Ben swallowed as Pabst's fingers straddled the wound. 'He seems to have relieved you of any pain,' said Pabst, in a genial manner, and suddenly squeezed hard.
The agony was too much. Ben thrust out a hand to pull Pabst's arm away, but the Gestapo colonel stepped back.
'You bastard!' said Ben, through gritted teeth. The pain began to subside.
'Life is not all pleasure, Mr Harrison, we Germans understand that. There must be pain for some to safeguard the pleasures of others.'
Ben was sweating; he sank back onto the couch. Pabst, with his dark suit, tie, white shirt and well-groomed appearance, gave the impression that he had just come back from some formal occasion. Ben said nothing, but his eyes followed the German's every move.
'How were you going to kill De Salis?' asked Pabst softly.
'Who?' asked Ben.
'The code has been broken. We found your message written in its original English capitals.'
'What is it you expect me to tell you?' asked Ben.
'Everything,' smiled Pabst.
He was almost considerate at first. After several hours had passed, Obermeyer was brought in to ask questions about the code. Ben was given water, then taken below, to the small cell where Agatha Parry had once languished alone. With the doors closed, in darkness, a sense of despair flooded Ben, but the tears that came into his eyes were not of self-pity. They came in memory of Agatha who, on the same bunk bed, had fought her captors to the end. The thought engendered anger, then hatred and finally a resolve that he too would fight. Eventually, with the taste of fear in his mouth, Ben sank into a troubled sleep.

Gerard, the chief of police, went to the prison on the following day. He was not allowed to see Ben Harrison. Instead he was taken to the Englishwoman's villa and shown the transmitting equipment. Pabst even insisted that Gerard should step on to the roof and examine the flagpole where the aerial had been concealed; then he showed him the decoded message.

The policeman climbed the steps from the prison to the Oceano-graphical Museum with a heavy heart. He stood at the top to regain his breath and gaze out over the Mediterranean at a sombre grey sky, low clouds scudding in a wind that whipped at his hair. He checked his watch – he had an appointment with his Prince at 11.

The Grimaldis had fought against all comers to establish themselves upon the Rock of Monaco. When the odds were too great they had resorted to brilliant diplomacy and survived. Turbulent centuries passed before a Casino and several grand hotels brought fame to their Principality, providing a reason for so many rich foreigners to come on visits and for some to settle. The Rock itself jutted like a flying buttress out of the huge bluffs behind and into the sea, so it was not unusual that this royal family should be interested in what lay beneath the waves. As they had understood politicians over the years, seeing beneath veneers and using their knowledge and experience to keep their small country secure, so the Princes found fascination in oceanography and built a museum to house the results of their explorations.

Gerard went in and walked through the high, bright rooms. At the end of a long corridor, silhouetted against a large window, surrounded by glass cases, was the old Prince, bent over examining a specimen. It was quiet in the room, with only the muted sounds of the sea crashing against the rocks below.

Gerard stopped and coughed politely. He had made a decision. He could not continue to cooperate with Colonel Pabst. 'My Prince . . .' he said.

Prince Louis slowly stood up and turned to the chief of police, whom he had known for many years. A tall man, the Prince had great presence and dignity. He smiled. 'Yes, my friend?'

Gerard swallowed – resignation would not be easy.

Chapter 34

The meeting between the Gestapo colonel and the Swiss banker, in the half-empty bar of the Hotel de Paris, started at 11 and finished thirty minutes later. After Pabst left, de Salis was visibly shaken and drank several whiskies, glancing now and then across the room, to where another man was quietly sitting. He had been introduced as Erich Held, assigned for protection duty. Pabst had told the banker that London had

251

uncovered his activities and there was some danger for him in the Principality. He had also reminded de Salis of the infinite rewards to be gained by taking risks.

Guy de Salis represented a Swiss consortium, so his responsibility had been to conclude the deal with the Gestapo. He had compiled a second list of Jewish depositors in Geneva, and the black attaché case containing the information had been deposited in the safe of the Hotel de Paris. After this, he was determined not to leave Switzerland again. Travel was becoming increasingly dangerous. The RAF were bombing not only Germany, but selected targets throughout occupied Europe. This new threat was something he had not bargained for.

De Salis caught himself staring at his bodyguard, Held, as the barman served yet another whisky. Only now did he realize that he was committed to something from which he could not escape.

Louis was clearing empty glasses when he noticed the frightened look in the man's eyes change to relief. De Salis stood up and pointed. Louis turned round and there was Maggie Lawrence, dressed superbly, walking into the bar and looking magnificent.

'Louis, please ask her to join me,' whispered de Salis.

Louis moved quickly towards Maggie, took her hand and kissed it.

'It is a miracle, Mademoiselle.'

'They said I could try it slowly at first.' Maggie's eyes twinkled.

Louis leaned closer to her: 'There is a gentleman who wishes you to have a drink with him. He is an acquaintance, I think.' In the distance, de Salis stepped forward and smiled. 'I think he needs company,' said Louis softly, and helped Maggie to perch on a bar stool.

Maggie looked de Salis directly in the eye.

'Change of heart, cowboy?'

'I am surprised and pleased to see you walking,' said de Salis. 'Congratulations.'

'Champagne,' said Maggie.

'I remember that you like Krug.' He was trying to be ingratiating.

'Well, that's a start,' she said. Louis produced a bottle. 'Could we have lunch?' asked de Salis tentatively.

'Sure,' said Maggie.

'You don't have to like me,' de Salis whispered. 'I'll pay you. I need . . . someone . . .'

'I'm a nun,' said Maggie, grinning wickedly, 'but large contributions are always welcome.'

De Salis's eyes flashed for a second, his ego hurt. He gulped champagne and glanced at Held, sitting in a corner of the bar, his face impassive. Then he leaned towards Maggie.

'Can we go upstairs, for old times?' he asked.

'Before lunch?'

'Why not?'

Maggie slid from her stool, smoothed down her cream silk dress and gave the Swiss banker a professional smile. 'The rates are double,' she said.

Afterwards de Salis began to talk too much. For the first time a combination of drink, anxiety and sex had loosened his tongue. He told Maggie about Switzerland, banks, boxes and Jews, and described the profits and hazards of good business, before the two of them dressed and returned to the bar. They finished the rest of their champagne, and only then did they go to lunch, followed at a discreet distance by Erich Held, who unknown to them both had waited patiently outside Maggie's rooms.

The Salle Empire was full of officers in uniform from various armies: German, Italian, Hungarian, Romanian, even some colonels from Spain. Maggie and de Salis were seated near the long windows, which were closed, as it was too windy for the terrace. There was no sun and an atmosphere of winter gloom had enveloped the resort. By the time they had eaten *hors d'oeuvres* they had succumbed to this mood, and to counteract it were halfway through a second bottle of champagne. Waiters bustled efficiently and the volume of noise in the restaurant seemed to increase.

'You asked why *I've* stayed on, but why do *you* keep coming back?' asked Maggie.

'I do not intend to come back again.' De Salis paused. 'It is becoming too dangerous to travel.' He looked towards the entrance where Erich Held stood watching customers come and go.

'You want to get stuck in Switzerland?' asked Maggie, giggling.

'It is my country, why should I not want to get stuck there?' De Salis repeated the words aggressively. He stared at the woman and the recollection of her sexual prowess was dispelled by a wave of self-disgust.

The conversation continued and they both became a little more tipsy. Across the room, Erich Held wondered when he would be allowed to eat. The colonel had promised to relieve him for a short time, saying that he wanted further words with the Swiss banker.

Maggie Lawrence cut into her meat with a sharp, pointed steak knife and put a morsel into her mouth. 'Isn't it delicious?' asked de Salis. She nodded. 'You see,' said the banker, 'the Swiss are not without taste.'

Maggie swallowed. 'Depends what you're chewing,' she said.

De Salis reached for his wine to cover a moment's embarrassment. A sip gave him courage. 'Was Quinn any different from all the other men in your life?' Maggie chewed her meat without answering. 'You have had so many, I am sure,' stated de Salis.

'*You* are different,' said Maggie.

253

'Why?' asked the Swiss banker as he cut a piece of meat and put it into his mouth.

'You are the worst.'

De Salis stopped chewing and swallowed. 'And you are a bitch.'

'No,' smiled Maggie, 'I am Jewish.'

De Salis stared long at Maggie, his eyes bright and cruel. When he spoke it was with contempt. 'Quinn was a nobody,' he said.

'He was a great fuck,' retorted Maggie.

De Salis's lips curled. 'He was a pawn, a fool, and worse – he was expendable!'

Maggie's knuckles showed white on her knife and fork.

'What do you mean?'

'I mean that he was incapable, incompetent, and the people with whom he was dealing were . . .' he checked himself, 'displeased.'

'What are you saying?' hissed Maggie.

'Nothing more, now that he is dead.'

'He was murdered, and you knew it!' cried Maggie harshly.

De Salis chewed his meat for thirty seconds, then swallowed and reached for his wine glass. He glanced across the restaurant to see Pabst and Koch talking to Held at the door. That gave him confidence. When he spoke, the words were soft, but he stared at Maggie cruelly.

'I advised it.'

To his credit, Erich Held began to run as soon as Maggie Lawrence pushed herself from her seat. Screaming like an animal, she lunged across the table and thrust her steak knife deep into de Salis's throat. His eyes widened with shock then squeezed tight with agony as Maggie twisted the knife.

A split second later Erich Held was on her, kicking the table aside, slamming her to the ground, pinioning the woman who, had already been knocked unconscious. Screams filled the restaurant as Pabst and Koch, only paces behind Held, stepped over the debris of the table, reaching out for de Salis. There was terror in the Swiss banker's eyes; he was clutching at his throat, trying to speak, but only the gurgle of blood emerged. He pressed himself backwards across the carpet, as if to escape the pain of the knife embedded in the soft flesh beneath his chin.

Pabst was swearing in disbelief. The banker's head became lost in the curtains, and with what strength he had left, de Salis began to pull himself up. His feet were slipping in his own blood, his knees no longer able to support a dying body. Pabst saw the man's knuckles straining as his hands gripped the curtain material. Then the fingers lost their tension and the body slid to the carpet and rolled from under the window, the steak knife protruding grotesquely from his throat.

The head waiter was shouting for a doctor, and Fouquet was found quickly, but he arrived too late. Pabst ground his teeth as the body was removed. De Salis meant nothing to him, but their plans . . . The Jewish names and numbers were secure in the hotel safe, but in order to make use of them he would be forced to seek some other Swiss banker's co-operation. That might be difficult, and it would certainly take time.

'*Scheisse!*' he hissed.

The chief of police had been totally disarmed by the Prince's blunt rejection of his resignation. He had been made to feel essential to the welfare of the Principality. He had also been reminded of his duty as a Monégasque, and his allegiance to the Grimaldi family. So it was a more resolute man that Colonel Pabst met in the lobby of the Hotel de Paris as his men were carrying the still unconscious body of Maggie Lawrence to a large black Mercedes.

'I understand there has been an incident.' Gerard's voice was harsh.

'We are dealing with it,' said Pabst.

'You are doing nothing of the kind.' Gerard snapped his fingers. He had arrived with four policemen. Two of them took the body of the blond American and gently carried her to a police car outside the hotel. The lobby was crowded so the moment was public.

'There has been a murder, don't you understand?' rasped Pabst.

'Then it is a police matter and no concern of yours.'

'He was . . .' Pabst hesitated, 'my friend.'

A glint came into Gerard's eyes. 'I had no idea you had friends,' he said.

Pabst's expression was venomous as he pushed past Monaco's chief of police and strode out of the hotel.

Chapter 35

'I came here to emphasize that you, too, are now in danger.' The notion seemed quite incongruous to Harry, as he stood at the window of Eva Trenchard's sitting room, drinking her best Darjeeling tea. From below came the babble of the tea rooms. Gossip and rumour. The prattle of middle-aged women who are no longer a part of the rush of life, for whom the world has turned one notch too far. There was no change in Eva's expression.

'Couldn't the Resistance get Ben out?' Harry pressed.

Miss Trenchard shook her head. 'If they were to take direct action in Monaco, the repercussions would be enormous. The Italians might move in, or the Germans take over. Our delicate neutrality is more important while it lasts. We must make the best use of it.'

'I'm American,' he reminded her, 'and we're neutral too, while it lasts.'

'Yes,' said Miss Trenchard.

'Agatha Parry, and now Ben Harrison,' said Harry. 'You have a lot of courage. How will you escape if he talks?'

'He hasn't yet, or I would not be here,' she replied quietly.

'What will happen to him?'

There was a silence between them as Miss Trenchard took up her cup and delicately sipped her tea. 'He has become a liability,' she said, and looked up. 'So are you, Harry.' Her gaze was unwavering. 'But you are American, and despite Pabst's suspicions his hands are tied here, for the moment.'

'What if they move Ben to Berlin?'

'I have spoken to the chief of police. It promises to be a most complicated procedure.'

'Will they torture him?' Harry asked.

Eva Trenchard smiled sadly. 'Don't be naive, Harry. They are Gestapo.'

Harry slumped in his chair and spoke almost to himself. 'So I must help.'

'Only if you want to,' said Eva softly.

'And if I don't?' he asked.

The Scotswoman's eyes were hard although her lips still smiled. She spoke quietly, her meaning clear. 'He will die eventually anyway, in the hands of the Gestapo.'

Harry was disbelieving, 'You would kill him?' he whispered.

'Someone would,' she replied. 'What alternative do we have?' Harry stared at her in silence. 'You have no obligations, Harry. This is war now. Duty is only for those involved.' His eyes remained fixed on Eva's pleasant face as she poured hot water into the teapot.

'Can you get me a revolver or automatic?'

'A revolver would be easier,' said Eva calmly. 'More tea?' Harry shook his head. She sipped from her cup again. 'You will also need a great deal of luck. I can get you an old plan of the prison, but I do not know how the Germans are using it or where they are keeping Ben.'

'Can you find out?'

'I'll try.' She put down her cup. Harry stood up then bent down and kissed her on both cheeks.

'How continental, Mr Pilikian,' said Eva, amused.

'I like it here,' said Harry.

'So do I,' she whispered. 'Just the way it used to be.'

'And will be again.'

Eva looked at the conviction in the young man's eyes, and remembered her brother and all those other young men in London ballrooms before they went to the front, during that first autumn of the Great War. The sin in heaven, she thought, if paradise admits such a possibility, is that during any conflict it is almost always the best that are taken.

The sun shone weakly through thin cloud, rising slowly above the still dark and forbidding landscape of distant Italy. The crippled Greek freighter *Ariadne*, packed with refugees, a tub of a boat by any standards, went to Slow Ahead then stopped completely on a shifting sea in the halflight of dawn on 3 December 1941. It was one mile off the Rock of Monaco. Communications with the harbour authorities began at once, and a cutter put out from the quayside with an Italian officer, the chief of police, a representative from the ministry of the interior and several armed guards.

The officials who went on board the freighter to examine its condition found filth everywhere, and an appalling stench, but the Alexandrian captain, who appeared to be permanently drunk, seemed unaware of the conditions. The ship wallowed in a grey sea which became rougher with the increasing light. Throughout the cabins and corridors was a pervading smell of sea-sickness.

The captain merely wanted to dump his load and get back to Alexandria. Forged papers had allowed him out of the port of Piraeus, now occupied by the Germans. Once into the Ligurian Sea, he had made a run for the Riviera, hoping to reach the neutrality of Spain several days later. At nightfall, an Italian corvette had ordered him to heave to, but the freighter's captain had a prison record and was still wanted in Italy. He could not afford to be taken. The Italian coastguard ship closed to several hundred metres and further demands sparked off an exchange of rifle fire from the freighter and machinegun bursts from the corvette.

In his desperation, the captain managed to shoot out both of the corvette's searchlights, and the two ships drifted apart in heavy seas during the night. But considerable damage had already been done to the freighter.

The squalid conditions were observed by the Monégasque authorities; so too was the fact that of the three or four hundred refugees on board, the majority were Sephardic Jews, fleeing from the Nazis. Some of the women began to wail at the sight of police uniforms. The Italian liaison officer attached to the port authority of La Condamine had just showered, shaved and cologned himself; he felt contaminated, and walked around holding a perfumed handkerchief under his nose.

Gerard could barely control his anger, and pity made it difficult to explain to these people that there was very little he could do for them. Monte Carlo was already full and the facts of life were simple. To live in the Principality cost money, and the refugees crammed into the large hold had nothing but their religious convictions and their hopes of survival. All of them had paid what little money they had to the captain. Gerard was only able to suggest that they try to repair the freighter so that it might at least reach the coast of Spain, where the captain said he had connections in Barcelona.

The Italian and the Monégasques left the freighter *Ariadne* and clambered aboard the cutter, which was rising and falling in the increasing swell. It churned back through the open boom, passed between the twin light towers and crossed the relatively calm water of La Condamine to dock not far from the yacht *Maracaibo*.

'What can we do?' shouted the Italian, as he jumped on to the quayside.

'Everything we can,' replied Gerard, and that was his intention.

When Pabst was informed later that morning that a freighter had appeared offshore, he was at first amused by the identity of its passengers. Then his mind began to apply itself to his own immediate security problems. His orders were to safeguard a major arms shipment that would travel along the Riviera in a week's time. Assembling in Milan, it was bound for Marseilles. Tanks from Germany, 88 mm. shells, wagonloads of rifle and machinegun ammunition, mortars and mines, destined for the Afrika Korps – munitions that would ensure Rommel's victory.

Pabst understood the importance of his task. November had been a catastrophic month for the Axis in the Mediterranean. More than sixty per cent of their supplies to North Africa had been sunk by British aircraft and submarines out of Malta and Egypt. Now new routes were being tried, in an effort to avoid the direct and, in practice, almost suicidal cargo route from southern Italy to Libya. A convoy from Vichy France to Vichy Tunisia had been assembled as a last resort. Without supplies, the German expeditionary force would perish in the desert.

Of course the shipment would be guarded – the Italians and the Vichy French would do all that they could – but that might not be enough. The strength of the Gestapo lay in vigilance unrestricted by conventional security measures. The Vichy French had assured Nazi Germany that they had internal terrorism under control, but sabotage was proving more effective than had been anticipated. The South of France was out of range for normal British bomber formations – with the vexing exception of the Beach Club incident – but French resistance was something new and dangerous. Pabst hoped the Gestapo would soon be able to operate openly without restrictions being imposed on them. Soon this fingernail on the European map, this tiny enclave of neutrality which was Monaco, would be occupied and officially recognized as part of Axis territory.

Pabst looked round the bare room, Apart from portraits of Hitler and Himmler, only filing cabinets broke up the drabness of the stone walls. In a way, he enjoyed the austerity of the prison. Nietzsche had said: 'Praise be to that which toughens.' It was an ethic he approved, and not a day went by when he did not put himself through a rigorous physical training routine. But he missed the mountains, and looked forward to Christmas at Kitzbühel, where he would be able to discuss the future with fellow officers of the Third Reich. They would ski all day and drink a little schnapps at night before . . . He put the cigarette in his mouth and sucked smoke into his lungs, thinking of beautiful Austrian mountains thrusting into a clear blue sky.

Harry Pilikian packed up everything he had accumulated since he came to Monte Carlo. By Saturday 6 December, he was ready to leave, impatient to be gone, but reluctant to move without Ben Harrison, who had been in the hands of the Gestapo for over a month. Pleas and protests from the Palace and the authorities had been of no avail. Pabst said the man was an enemy of the Third Reich, and declared that if there were complications about his extradition to Germany, he must remain under the protection of the Gestapo at the prison. The pro-Vichy doctor, Fouquet, was allowed to see the prisoner several times a week, but was unable to stifle the rumour that Harrison was being tortured.

Harry Pilikian's own position in the Principality was becoming increasingly dangerous. Gerard brought him to the police station and urged him to keep his head down until travel arrangements could be made for his departure. Maggie Lawrence had been charged with murder and was being held in custody awaiting trial. Raising an eyebrow, Gerard informed Harry that she had asked to see him. Harry only smiled wryly.

The decoded message Gerard had been shown in the villa on the Rock had contained orders for de Salis's death. He knew that it was from the British Secret Service. Harrison was obviously connected with the clandestine wireless, and his friend Pilikian was suspected by the Gestapo of aiding and abetting him. Gerard wondered whether the American woman, Maggie, was also a British agent. If she was not why had she killed the Swiss banker?

Harry shrugged. He knew nothing. Harrison was only a social friend. Gerard explained that Harry was only at liberty because he was American. He took him to see Maggie Lawrence and left him alone with her for half an hour. Harry emerged with a grim expression. Maggie had told him everything she had learned from de Salis: box numbers, Jews,

259

treasure, Gestapo and, once again, Pabst. The information she had pieced together confirmed the Swiss banker's part in Quinn's murder.

Harry told all of this to Gerard, who found it difficult to believe. 'I am only a policeman,' he said, shaking his head. 'Espionage is not my business.'

'What will happen to Maggie?' Harry asked him.

'Trial, prison, death, who knows?'

'Could she be allowed to escape?'

Gerard gestured helplessly. 'How? There is a law against murder in the Principality as well as in the rest of the world.' He escorted Harry to the door. 'The law, remember,' he said. 'I want you to keep it. Forget everything else or you too will be imprisoned or killed. I like you, Harry, and I want to see you live.'

So Harry had kept to himself, staying in his rooms, or in the bar of the Hotel de Paris. Only occasionally, at night, did he travel down to the *Maracaibo* to see Alex and Lisa. His musical, *Legal Tender*, was finished, and if he were forced to make a run for it that would be the only luggage he would take with him. The white suits and lavender shirts could stay behind. Looking at them, lined up in his wardrobe, Harry realized that he had become a different person. Through a newspaper correspondent he had yet again received a letter from Evelyn urging him to return to America, in the hope that they could take up together again. Harry knew that was now impossible.

That evening he went down to the bar, which was crowded as usual. Louis and his staff were rushed off their feet, and a lull developed only when Sullivan began to play. Louis winked at Harry and glanced around, indicating all the uniforms. Europe had fallen, but Russia had not, neither had the British in North Africa, and to prove it there were wounded German officers in the audience, a privileged few from the Wehrmacht.

Sitting on a bar stool, looking across the crowded room and seeing the gaudy women with these officers, it suddenly seemed bizarre to Harry that he should be in Monte Carlo. For the first time in more than a year Sullivan had begun to repeat himself and his music sounded tired. He 'Da-da'd' his way through half of the lyrics now, but no one seemed to care. Alcohol, expensive food, then the Casino or a cabaret at Le Sporting or elsewhere, followed by what sex was available, what sleep could be snatched and mornings at the Spa and Turkish Baths recuperating, which was how these people spent their days. It was no longer Harry's idea of life.

'Monsieur Harry,' said Louis, 'a gentleman wishes to buy you a drink.'

'Tell him . . .' began Harry.

'He knows you, Monsieur,' said Louis, and pointed.

260

Howard Maitland pushed through the crowd and sat on a stool beside Harry Pilikian. 'I'd like to introduce you to a friend.'

A well-built German officer snapped to attention, then shook hands with Harry. 'Major Heinz Rahdl.'

'He speaks English very well,' said Maitland.

'I was in the United States just before the war.' Rahdl's English was East Coast-accented.

'Did you like America?' asked Harry.

'It is very big.'

Harry noticed the way Rahdl was carrying his right arm and made a guess. 'So is Russia,' he said.

'You are right,' said Rahdl ruefully. 'I understand the American joke you make, but you are right.'

Harry immediately began to like the German. Honesty is valid currency in any language.

'We all thought we would be in Moscow by now, and I am in Monte Carlo. Life is funny, yes?' Rahdl laughed.

'No, it's become very serious,' said Harry. 'Where is your division?'

Rahdl grinned. 'On the outskirts of Moscow. With a few roubles they could take a tram to the Kremlin.'

'Soon you'll be drinking Russian champagne and gallivanting around Red Square,' said Maitland, lighting a cigarette and blowing out smoke ostentatiously.

'Soon,' nodded Rahdl.

Harry regularly drank morning coffee or cocktails with the few correspondents who remained in the Principality. Many of them had been recalled, travelling to the small airport at Nice where an American military aircraft was allowed in once a week bringing updated instructions and fresh gossip. That very morning, Harry had been told of a huge Russian counter-attack, on the outskirts of Moscow. Ten winter-equipped armies, one hundred divisions, brought from the depths of Siberia, had, as the temperature fell to thirty below zero, smashed into the exhausted Wehrmacht freezing in their summer uniforms. They had torn a two-hundred-mile hole in the front, hurling themselves against the invader, and had already penetrated many miles behind the lines.

Harry conveyed the news to Rahdl and watched the man's face turn white. He stayed talking for a few minutes, for the sake of appearances, and then excused himself. This was Louis' cue to lean across the bar and tap Harry on the shoulder.

'There is a package for you at the desk, M'sieur Harry.'

Harry slid off his stool, said goodbye to Maitland, and stepped out into the lobby. He crossed to the message desk, and Gastaut passed over a heavy parcel, which Harry took up to his rooms. It was certain to be the gun which Eva Trenchard had promised him.

Later that night, Harry drove down to La Condamine and the *Maracaibo*. He said goodnight to Lisa, who was still half-awake, then went into Alex's cabin.

'I'm going to leave,' he said.

'When?' asked Alex.

'In a few days.' There was a pause between them. 'And I want you and Lisa to come with me.'

'Where?'

'To Nice. The authorities allow an American military plane to land occasionally, taking correspondents in or out. I have already asked . . .'

Alex interrupted. 'The *Maracaibo* is also leaving in a few days, Harry.'

'I want you to come with *me*,' he said.

'And Bradford wants me to go with him.'

'Do you really have a choice?' Harry's tone was almost casual.

'I don't know,' said Alex, lowering her head. Harry had burst into her life again, and at the beginning everything had seemed clear. Now her years of security with Wilson were urging her to think beyond passion. 'I have a daughter,' she said.

'*We* have a daughter,' said Harry.

'Where will we go?'

'Lisbon,' said Harry. 'Then take the Clipper to America.'

'And then?' said Alex quietly, looking Harry in the eye. He grinned. 'We'll be married and live happily ever after.'

Alex smiled slowly. 'That's a late proposal, isn't it?'

Harry stood up and reached out a hand. She took it and moved into his embrace.

'Let's get it right this time,' he whispered, and kissed her tenderly.

Sunday started strangely. The weather was heavy, clouds lowering over the sea. Most of Monte Carlo's big gamblers were recovering from the night before in the Casino. Of those who had played, few had won. The profits of the gambling table were rising dramatically.

Harry Pilikian exercised in the gymnasium at the back of the harbour, then went for a run, showered and returned to the hotel. He was waiting for final instructions from Eva Trenchard.

In the early evening, the bar was almost empty, so he accepted an invitation from Maitland and the German major out of sheer curiosity. They wandered down to the Cabaret and watched the American chorus girls high-kick their way through the show.

Just before midnight, the three men wandered back to the bar of the Hotel de Paris.

'I hear you are leaving, Pilikian,' said Maitland.

'Yes,' answered Harry.

'Bradford told me to ask you to come with us.'

'I'll find my own way,' said Harry.

'Proud?' asked Maitland superciliously.

'Selfish,' Harry answered.

Sullivan had just finished playing 'Deep Purple'. The usual crowd at the tables were drinking and had already become raucous. It was several minutes before midnight when an American correspondent burst into the bar, flushed with excitement. His first shout silenced everyone, despite the rowdiness and noise. He began reading, his voice rising with each sentence:

'Shortly after dawn this morning, at Pearl Harbor naval base in Hawaii, the American fleet was attacked by a large force of carrier-based Japanese military aircraft. Casualties and damage are classified but we must understand that from this moment the United States of America considers itself at war with Japan.'

There was absolute silence in the bar. The newspaperman again referred to the communiqué:

'The Tripartite Pact immediately brings into question the position of both Germany and Italy. We must await further developments and seek the fullest information from all sources.'

The man lowered the paper. Everyone stared at him.

'Ladies and gentlemen, America finally got itself a shooting war!' he said, grinning like a schoolboy.

Sullivan broke the silence, playing with gusto, his voice tremulous:

'Oh say can you see, by the dawn's early light,
What so proudly we hailed at the twilight's last gleaming?
Whose broad stripes and bright stars thru the perilous fight,
O'er the ramparts we watched were so gallantly streaming?
And the rocket's red glare, the bombs bursting in air,
Gave proof through the night that our flag was still there,
Oh say does that star-spangled banner yet wave,
O'er the land of the free and the home of the brave?'

Voices joined in the singing and, despite the gravity of the situation, the atmosphere was one of exhilaration. By the time Sullivan had finished, there was laughter throughout the bar. Conflict between Nazis and communists ,the continuing imbroglio of the Japanese in China, had already created a war that absorbed half the earth. Now, with the Americans finally involved in battle, the war was worldwide.

'To survival!' said Maitland, and lifted a glass. 'Come on, Pilikian, and you, Rahdl. God knows when we'll meet again!' The three men clinked glasses, as did many others that night, out of sheer bravado.

'Now we'll *have* to leave,' said Maitland, '*I* certainly don't want to get stuck in this cesspool!'

Harry looked at the German major. 'Will you go back to Russia?'

The eyes of the Wehrmacht officer narrowed. 'If I'm lucky,' said Rahdl. 'Where will you go, Herr Pilikian?'

Harry looked the German in the eyes. 'Depends who we're fighting,' he answered.

'The Japs, didn't you hear, Pilikian?' said Maitland.

Harry looked at him, then at the German major. 'Hawaii for a start,' he said.

'Have you ever been there?' asked Maitland.

'Not yet,' said Harry. 'Beautiful sea, wonderful palm trees. Always an ocean breeze.'

'Sounds like paradise,' said Rahdl.

'It is, sweetheart, but I hope *you* like snow.'

Maitland raised his glass again. 'To destiny!'

Rahdl snapped his heels together and lifted his glass. Maitland grinned.

'I'll drink to that,' said Harry, and even Louis leaned across the bar and joined in the toast as Sunday night 7 December 1941 became Monday morning. An end of the old world and the beginning of a new.

Chapter 36

Jürgen Pabst, smoking a cigarette, stared at the inert body of Ben Harrison, sprawled on the bunk bed in his cell. Erich Held remained by the open door, watching. Both Ben's hands were bandaged and bloody.

'Harrison,' said Pabst patiently.

The body stirred. Ben began coughing and rolled over. He had lost weight, his skin was sallow and his face sunken. When he opened his eyes and saw Pabst, he tried to speak, but the coughing would not stop. The Gestapo colonel waited and finally spoke.

'You may be interested to know that our Japanese allies are even now moving down the Malay peninsula towards Singapore. Soon there will be no more Far Eastern empire for the British. As a nation you are finished.' He shook his head. 'You should have listened to the Führer's proposals after the fall of France – he offered you peace with honour.'

Ben managed several deep breaths. Pabst smiled. 'As I explained to

264

you, resistance is useless. Shortly we will take you to Berlin, where others will examine you with less concern.' Ben's mouth opened and he coughed again. 'Bring him some whisky,' said Pabst.

Held left the cell.

'A new epoch has begun,' Pabst stated. 'The English have never known when they were beaten. It has proved an unfortunate lesson for you, but there is no longer any doubt. Your own stupidity has ensured that your centuries of pre-eminence are over.' The last words were said with satisfaction.

Ben began to raise himself on his elbows. Despite his haggard appearance, his clear eyes gazed steadily at the Nazi colonel.

'We, too, have allies, Pabst.'

The German nodded. 'And they, too, are now in trouble,' he said.

'America, in trouble?' Ben tried to laugh, then began coughing once more.

'They have entered the war,' said Pabst.

The words seemed to provide Ben Harrison with energy. He stifled his coughing. 'You are fighting the United States?' His voice was hoarse, but excited.

'Soon,' nodded Pabst, inhaling smoke. 'It must come soon.'

At midday that Monday 8 December 1941, Jürgen Pabst, accompanied by Neumann and Koch, climbed the steps from the prison and walked around the Rock of Monaco until they had a perfect view below. One mile out to sea the Greek freighter *Ariadne* was rising and falling in the winter swell of the Mediterranean. The Englishman was no longer Pabst's main preoccupation: now he had other problems on his mind. The entire campaign in North Africa might depend on his ingenuity.

'I have an idea,' he said softly. Koch and Neumann remained respectfully silent. Pabst pursed his lips as he watched several small boats attempting to repair the old freighter. Waves foamed against her stern.

'We are going to liberate those Jews.' He enunciated every word clearly, as if speaking for posterity.

By 11 o'clock on the morning of 10 December, the American Bar of the Hotel de Paris was already crowded. Louis had again brought in a wireless set, and with Jean-Pierre he monitored every possible radio station that could give them news of the changing course of history.

Hitler's navy had been ordered to sink American ships on sight, but there was still no open declaration of war. In the late afternoon, news crackled from the radio: the Japanese had sunk first the British battleship *Prince of Wales*, then the battle cruiser *Repulse* off the Malayan town of Kuantan. It had also now been confirmed that five

American battleships were at the bottom of Pearl Harbor, with three more badly damaged. The Japanese were victorious everywhere and both the Americans and British were falling back on all fronts.

That night, Harry went down to the *Maracaibo* for what he thought might be the last time. Looking at Lisa, curled up, already asleep, he realized that no matter what, they must leave together – he, Alex and their daughter. He went up on deck and waited for Alex under the awning, out of the rain.

Wilson's condition was worsening and the captain of the *Maracaibo* had been persuaded to try and make the run to Casablanca. The Vichy authorities there might at least allow them to refuel: if not, they could put themselves under British protection at Gibraltar. There were already rumours of their proposed departure, and the Italian authorities outside the Principality were urging the harbour officials to impound the yacht for the duration.

Alex arrived on deck and stood beside Harry Pilikian, who was unshaven, wearing a dark felt hat and dirty trenchcoat.

'Not at all the elegant Mr Pilikian,' said Alex.

'This ain't a time for elegance, kid,' said Harry out of the corner of his mouth. Laughing, they descended to the quay, drove up to the Casino square and went on to the Cabaret for one of their last dinners together in the Principality.

Later, upstairs in Harry's rooms, they made love as if it might also be the last time. Only afterwards, when Alex went to look for a brush in one of the dressing table drawers, did things change between them. What she found was the Smith and Wesson .38 revolver which Eva Trenchard had sent Harry. She closed the drawer, walked back to the foot of the bed, and gazed in the low light of the single lamp at the naked body lying on the bed half asleep.

'What are you looking at?' he murmured.

'You,' said Alex simply.

'Which part?'

'All of you.' Her voice was barely louder than the falling rain.

'You'll have plenty of time to do that,' said Harry, smiling. 'If I drive fast it will take just over an hour.'

'To where?'

'The airport. It's outside Nice, just before Antibes.'

Alex stared at Harry for a moment longer. 'I've got to go back to the *Maracaibo*,' she said. 'Lisa misses me if she wakes and I'm not there.' She began to dress.

'And do you think she misses me?' asked Harry.

Alex fastened each of her stockings and began pulling on a skirt. 'We both miss you, Harry,' she said. 'We always have.'

Harry watched Alex finish dressing, step into her high heels and put on the fur coat she had worn that night.

'If you'll wait,' he said, 'I'll take you.'

Alex turned to him. 'Thank you. I'd like that.'

At 2.15 on 11 December 1941, the news broke from Berlin. Ribbentrop had informed the American chargé d'affaires that President Roosevelt would be given what he had sought for so long. The Third Reich made it official. They declared war on the United States.

The bar of the Hotel de Paris was thrown into an uproar of both panic and celebration. By 6 o'clock in the evening, most of the Americans who were leaving were being fed black coffee by hotel staff, in the hope that they would at least know where they were going.

Harry wandered through his suite. The rooms were full of ghosts waiting for the next occupant, but looked neat and empty without the chaos his work had created. He opened the french windows. Outside it was dark, raining and bleak – suddenly he felt cold. Now America and the Axis were officially at war, God knew what would happen when they ventured outside Monte Carlo.

The bedroom mirror had shown him a man wearing an old trenchcoat, dark felt hat, creased white shirt, crumpled suit and a black tie, loose at the collar. Harry Pilikian. He rubbed his beard, which was already growing back after the hasty shave he had given himself that morning. He shook his head.

'What you need,' he said, 'is a good woman.'

He could feel the gun shoved into his waistband. In the pocket of his trenchcoat were two boxes of ammunition. If it did nothing else, Eva Trenchard's gift made him feel more confident and less vulnerable. Harry knew he could not leave without Harrison, and the odds began to turn his blood cold.

Touching the crucifix around his neck, he remembered his father and said a short, silent prayer. Then it was time to leave. Carrying only the small case, which contained the drafts of his manuscripts, he stepped out of the Blue Suite, walked along the corridor, took the wide marble stairway two steps at a time, and crossed the lobby to present his attaché case at the cashier's desk.

'Manuscripts,' he said. 'Very valuable.'

'I am sure, Monsieur Pilikian,' said the cashier, 'but we have no more room.'

'Only for a few hours,' said Harry. 'I'll be back for it, I promise.' He watched the cashier step to the safe, open it, spin the dial deftly and place the case inside, beside two others. He wrote the name Pilikian on a piece of paper, fixed it to the case, then slammed the huge door shut and wrote out a receipt for Harry.

'For a few hours only, Monsieur Pilikian.'

'A favour,' said Harry, offering one hundred francs.

'*Oui,*' said the dour-faced French cashier as he accepted the money. 'It is a favour, Monsieur.'

Eva Trenchard seldom came into the Hotel de Paris alone, so her hesitation at the entrance was natural. Harry crossed the lobby and found a quiet corner near the revolving doors where he listened to her whispered instructions.

'Everything has been arranged,' she said. 'At midnight, an American military plane will take out those US citizens who wish to leave, and journalists who have been instructed to return to America. It is a final concession granted by the Vichy government, so the plane will be able to land at Nice. I do assure you, Harry, this will be the last chance you will have to leave until the war is over.'

He was about to speak, but she interrupted him: 'You must be on that plane, Harry, even if Ben Harrison remains in prison. The plane will fly directly to Lisbon. From there you can take the regular Flying Boat to America.'

The little woman was wrapped in a dark blue gabardine raincoat, a grey beret over her white hair. She wore no makeup, but her firm features, clear skin and bright eyes seemed to suggest that the war had brought her to life.

'Remember, Harry,' she said, 'you can take only what you carry. There is no room for anything else.'

'Except Alex and Lisa,' said Harry.

'And Ben . . .' said Miss Trenchard. For a moment she stared out into the pouring rain of the Casino Square, then she touched Harry's face.

'Courage will not be enough,' she said, 'and I cannot say be careful, so be lucky.' Harry tried to speak but no words came. Eva Trenchard kissed him on both cheeks. 'Come back,' she said, then was gone.

Harry looked about him at the people preparing for another evening of pleasure and entertainment. He pulled the belt of his trenchcoat tight and stepped out into the rain and darkness. His business that night was altogether different.

It was shortly before 9 o'clock when Harry ran down the steps of the Hotel de Paris, and climbed into the yellow and black Rolls Royce. The engine was already running and Michel slammed the door.

Harry drove down to the harbour and turned the car on the Quai de Plaisance, so that it was facing the way it had come. He stepped out, crossed to the gangway of the *Maracaibo*, waved to a sailor on watch and ran up to the deck. Alex was waiting below.

'Well?' he asked.

'I don't know, Harry.'

He took her in his arms. 'I do,' he said. 'You belong with me.' She stared at him. 'I never expected to meet you again,' he said quietly.

'Something else decided for us,' said Alex. 'The child we made.' She paused. 'Destiny, remember?'

Harry kissed her tenderly.

'Well, well,' came the voice of Maitland. 'The love birds!' They turned to the open door of the cabin. 'I came to inform Mrs Lieberman that we're leaving at eleven.'

'Pack,' said Harry softly. 'Be quick.'

Alex kissed Harry quickly and felt the gun at his waist. Her eyes widened. 'Harry! What are you going to do?'

He ignored the question. 'Be ready,' he said.

'You're going for Ben, aren't you?' whispered Alex.

He nodded. 'But Harry, you can't.' Her pleading eyes filled with tears. 'Please. Not now.'

'I'll be back. I promise.' Harry reached out for her, but she turned away from him. He seized her firmly. She lifted her head and stared at him.

'You're a fool,' she breathed. 'You are prepared to throw away everything.'

Harry looked into the face of this beautiful woman. 'I love you,' he said.

'Love is a bitter memory, Harry.'

'Could I leave Ben?' he asked quietly.

Alex pulled away. 'Then go,' she said coldly.

Maitland flicked his hand impatiently. 'As you're here, Pilikian, Bradford would like to see you before his place turns into Noah's Ark.' He looked Harry up and down. 'You're beginning to look a real mess. If you're not coming with us, where are you going?'

Harry's eyes were following Alex as she walked away down the corridor. He answered absently.

'Where angels fear to tread.'

Maitland's eyes glinted. 'Can I come?' he asked. 'It sounds exciting.'

In that moment Harry saw the strength of his former opponent, which it had been so difficult to defeat. He said nothing, and accompanied Maitland down the corridor to Wilson's door. Harry pushed hard and stepped into the large bedroom. Dimly lit, it was oppressive.

'You wanted to see me,' he snapped. Wilson, lying against his pillows, with the cannulae over his ears, strapped to his nose, sat up awkwardly. His breathing was more laboured than Harry had remembered. He motioned Harry to approach and the nurse moved away from the bed. The large, protruding eyes stared at the young man and Wilson began to laugh.

'Goodbye, Pilikian,' he said hoarsely. 'Remember me.'

'I will,' said Harry.

Wilson sank back onto his pillows and closed his eyes. Harry looked down at him for a moment, then turned towards the door, where Maitland was waiting.

'You're coming back, I hear?' Maitland said.

'For Alex and Lisa.'

'Where are you going now?'

Harry stared at him before answering. 'The Rock,' he said. 'For Harrison.'

Maitland smiled. 'And you have a gun, she tells me.'

'I have a gun,' said Harry.

'Then you need help,' said Maitland softly, and opened his jacket to reveal a .45 automatic in his waistband.

It had taken Pabst only an hour to ferry every single Jew from the Greek freighter *Ariadne*. They had been put in seven Italian army trucks which waited, without lights, for the prearranged signal. Shortly before 8 o'clock a large Mercedes arrived and a number of Germans in black leather coats issued instructions to the Italian soldiers. In teeming rain, the trucks had turned on their lights and driven slowly up to the Casino station, where two cattle wagons were waiting. The women began wailing immediately.

Almost two hundred of the Jewish refugees were counted and put into the wagons. One hundred and ninety-seven exactly, including the children, Pabst was told. The sliding doors were closed and locked, and the Jews waited under Italian guard for the train that would take them out of the Principality.

When the ammunition shipment from Milan arrived at 11 o'clock, the cattle wagons were to be connected to the rear locomotive. The train would then continue to Marseilles with both explosive and human cargo. There were enough of the railway staff on duty to see what happened, and Pabst knew that the news was sure to spread quickly. The French Resistance would think hard before they made an attempt to blow up the train. If the inconceivable happened, and they did manage to breach the extensive security already protecting the munitions, they would have to sacrifice the Jews.

As he was driven back to his headquarters at the prison, Pabst smiled with satisfaction. He was learning, as everyone must, to wage total war. Perhaps it was time to take out the black uniform of the Gestapo, the mere sight of which now generated so much fear throughout the territories of the Third Reich. 'Yes,' mused Pabst. 'It will soon be time . . .'

The news from the station threw Eva Trenchard into a panic. Everything had been set up and the explosives were already laid. The rails, somewhere along the route, had been heavily mined to destroy the shipment of German arms. The Resistance felt confident that it could be done, and she had left them to their own devices, but that meant that she had no idea where the attempt would take place. It had been difficult enough to establish contact many days before, when she had first had reliable information about the munitions train. Now, she was afraid, it would be almost impossible to alter the arrangements. She reached for the telephone – she must at least try to warn the saboteurs . . .

Chapter 37

Harry Pilikian turned the Rolls Royce in front of the Oceanographical Museum, backed the car into its shadow and switched off the engine. For a moment, he could see nothing. He heard Maitland inhale, two long deliberate breaths.

'What are you doing?' he asked.

'Sniffing cocaine,' answered Maitland. 'Do you want some?'

'No,' said Harry, 'I'll do this straight.' He took a deep breath.

The two men stepped out of the car. It was difficult to see in the pouring rain with the headlights turned off. Only a dim glow from the windows of some of the houses on the Rock gave them an idea of the way down.

Slowly their eyes grew accustomed to the darkness.

'We may have to carry him,' Harry whispered.

'Then we'll do it together.'

'Are you sure you're up to this?'

Maitland's teeth flashed. 'Are you?'

Harry reached beneath his trenchcoat and pulled out the Smith and Wesson.

They made their way to the top of the steps leading down to the prison. There they discovered the large Gestapo Mercedes pulled up against the kerb. It was locked but unguarded. Monaco, after all, was neutral.

'Wait!' hissed Maitland, and took a clasp knife out of his pocket. In thirty seconds he had slit open all four tyres. 'Used to be a novelty when I was a kid,' he murmured. Both men were already soaking wet and their

271

shoes squelched with water, so they moved cautiously down the steps of the prison, where only a single light showed.

Again there were no guards outside and they reached the outer door of Gestapo headquarters undetected. Harry sighed nervously and his fingers found the gold crucifix around his neck. 'Good luck!' he whispered.

Maitland grinned. 'I'd have beaten you in the ring, Pilikian.'

With that Harry opened the door. A stone corridor about sixty feet long was lit by naked bulbs hanging from the ceiling two yards apart. Doors led off one side, and halfway along there was a staircase leading below. No one was in sight, but they could hear German voices.

Maitland pulled out his automatic and Harry stepped lightly towards the first door. The rooms were old cells, each with bolts on the outside. Several of the doors were half open, and stronger light shone out into the corridor.

Through the first doorway Harry could see several Germans, lounging on frayed sofas, relaxed and unsuspecting. He seized an iron handle and in one movement slammed the door closed and slid home first the top and then the bottom bolt. Immediately there were shouts from the cell. Harry and Maitland began running.

The second cell was dark, with no one inside. In the third, several Germans were already moving, having heard the shouts of their comrades. A tall Gestapo man loomed up in front of them, but was taken by surprise as Harry hit him with a perfect straight left. He fell back with a cry, and Harry pulled the cell door closed and again slammed both bolts into place. Behind him he heard Maitland fire twice, then a third time. At the end of the corridor, beyond the staircase, he saw two Germans. One was falling. Maitland had missed the second, who was raising a submachine gun.

Harry and Maitland fired together. The Gestapo man was knocked off his feet, smacked against the wall and fell in a heap, his limbs jerking.

At the fourth door a young man stepped out, an expression of shock on his face. Maitland fired twice and the German spun half round before collapsing on to the corridor floor, moaning. Harry grasped the cell door and slammed it shut, again throwing the bolts. Someone inside pressed a gun through the two small bars in the cell door and fired wildly out into the corridor. With an upward sweep, Maitland knocked the Luger out of the hand, then put his own automatic between the bars and fired four shots into the room. He crouched and reached into his right-hand pocket for a second magazine to reload. Harry ran on past the central staircase leading below. He was heading for the other cell doors.

They both knew that they could not risk going below until they had secured this first floor. As Harry approached the end of the corridor, two Germans leapt out. Maitland shot the first, the second seized Harry by the throat and started to choke him. Harry rammed the muzzle of his revolver against the man's chest and fired. The body sprang away from him as if hit by a steam shovel.

Harry slammed the cell door and bolted it. Three more to go. Suddenly it seemed as though the end of the corridor was full of men. Maitland shouted, 'Four!' Two were levelling guns already. All of them were dressed in dark suits. Harry quelled his panic and remembered his father's advice from childhood: 'Stay calm and shoot straight.'

He stood as if shooting at targets. Two of the Germans fell, the third fired, and Harry felt searing heat, then warm blood on his cheek. He aimed again, pulled the trigger, and heard only a heart-stopping 'click'.

'Down!' screamed Maitland. Harry threw himself flat and four rapid shots passed over his head. Another bullet from the German's pistol sent stone chippings flying into his face. He rolled on to his back, emptied spent shells from the chamber of his revolver and as fast as his fingers would allow, pressed in six more rounds.

Maitland jumped over Harry and ran to the end of the corridor. There was no light from the first cell and the second was empty. Light shone out on to the bodies in the corridor from the last cell where one man remained inside, his face white with fear. Maitland grinned at him and pointed his automatic.

'Goodbye, darling,' he said, and shot him through the head. He turned to see Harry on his feet again, breathing heavily. Maitland had thrust his left hand into his coat pocket. Harry could see that his arm was bleeding.

'Are you hit?' he shouted.

'Don't feel a thing!' said Maitland and pointed the muzzle of his gun at Harry's face. 'You don't look so pretty yourself, sweetheart.' Harry heard noises from below. 'Let's get this over,' said Maitland. He put the automatic into his left-hand pocket and with his good arm leaned down to pick up the Schmeisser machine pistol still grasped by one of the dead Germans.

Harry leapt the first flight of stone steps and braced himself at the turn. He pushed himself off the wall and jumped down into the lower corridor, looking to his left and right. It was the same layout as above. Electric lights burned, but there was no one to be seen. All the doors were closed, and there were no lights within the cells, which were all bolted. He ran first to one end of the corridor. As he turned Maitland leapt down the last steps. He was grinding his teeth, showing pain in his face.

'Where the fuck is he?' he growled.

'There's one more floor below,' shouted Harry, pointing to a smaller staircase they had not noticed.

'Then get him!' hissed Maitland. 'I'll cover you.'

Harry ran down the steps and found a single cell at the bottom. He drew the bolts and pushed open the door. Ben Harrison had heard the noise and was already on his feet. He swayed towards Harry.

'Can you walk? asked Harry.

'I think so.'

'Then hold on to me!'

'I can't,' whispered Ben. 'They've broken all my fingers.'

As he stepped into the light, Harry saw the bloody bandages on his hands.

'Come on!' Harry began to drag him up the steps. Harrison stumbled at first, wheezing and coughing, then the urgency of the situation gave him the strength to reach the corridor, where Maitland thrust the sub-machine gun at him.

'I can't . . .' began Harrison.

'Halt!' screamed a voice.

The three men looked towards the other end of the corridor. Pabst, in the black dress uniform of the Gestapo, stood between Koch and Neumann. All of them held automatic pistols aimed at the intruders.

Harry, Maitland and Ben were frozen in surprise. 'The guns,' said Pabst, ignoring the sound of his men above, trying to break free from the bolted cells. His eyes were unwaveringly focused on the two Americans and Ben Harrison.

The Englishman dropped the submachine gun and Harry let his Smith and Wesson fall to the stone floor. 'Thank you,' said Pabst grimly. He stared at Maitland's wounded left arm, with the hand still thrust into the pocket. 'And you are wounded,' he said, with genuine pleasure.

Maitland grinned dangerously. 'And you are dead,' he answered quietly.

Pabst's face hardened. Harry was counting seconds.

'Koch!' snapped the colonel. The man moved forward to take the guns. Harry glanced at Maitland, whose body was contracting, like a big cat about to spring.

'Maitland,' whispered Harry in warning.

'What do you suggest, sweetheart?' said Maitland, still grinning at Pabst.

'Don't,' said Harry. Koch leaned down for the guns, cautiously, knowing he was covered but sensing danger.

'Goodbye, darling,' said Maitland and moved . . .

The .45 automatic in his pocket roared a split second before Pabst fired, and the colonel would have been dead but for the reflexes of Koch. Seeing the American move, he had leapt up with a cry, cut short as the heavy calibre bullet, fired at close range, tore into his face and took off the back of his head. Pabst's shot hit Maitland in the centre of his chest, breaking bone and knocking the American back against the wall, where Neumann's bullet missed him and ricocheted across the corridor.

Harry grasped the butt of the Smith and Wesson and fired from his knees. Pabst had begun to turn away, but Neumann was hit and thrust off his feet. With a shout he fell sprawling on to the floor. Still holding his gun, Neumann fired along the length of his body, aiming for Pilikian. Harry was already running and loosed off a shot at Pabst, who leapt back through the doorway into the last cell. Neumann's bullet was low and actually passed between Harry's legs, then somehow Ben Harrison managed to pull the trigger of the machine pistol. The two-second burst ripped clothes and flesh off the fallen Gestapo man; his body convulsed and then was still.

Harry, pressing himself against the cold stone of the stairwell, was distracted by Maitland behind him. He turned his head to see the American sliding down the corridor wall, coughing blood and swearing. 'Oh fuck!' he was moaning.

Anger and hate exploded in Harry and he forgot all else but Pabst. He sprinted to the end of the corridor and, panting heavily, lay against the wall outside the last door. There were noises from above, but nothing from inside the cell.

Harry gritted his teeth, took a deep breath and jumped into the open doorway, crouching low. Two bullets passed straight over his head but he was already firing, shouting wildly, aiming at the snarling black figure . . . He hit him twice, and the force of the .38 calibre impacts hurled Pabst backwards into a corner, knocking him against the thick glass bottles lined up on a row of shelves. Some of the bottles fell and were smashed as his body collapsed in a heap, his mouth gasping for air. Those bottles which had only tipped over began to pour their contents on to the man beneath.

Pabst started screaming in agony. The single electric light bulb swinging from the ceiling cast grotesque shadows. Harry stepped around the desk, arm extended, gun pointed, watching the German's limbs flail helplessly as blood stained the black tunic and clear liquid seared through its cloth on to naked flesh.

Only then did Harry realize that the bottles contained acid. For a moment he absorbed the terror of the Nazi colonel, his shrieks drowning all other noise, until Harry heard the banging upstairs where the trapped Gestapo men were attempting to break out. There was no time to watch Pabst's death throes. He ran from the cell and back along the corridor, where Maitland was sprawled against the wall, bleeding badly. Together with Ben, Harry lifted Maitland to his feet. The wounded man immediately bent double with pain but somehow managed to stagger up the first flight of steps.

'Get on with it!' he was growling. 'Get on with it, Pilikian!' His face had lost all its colour and he was sweating, but there was fight in him yet and they reached the first corridor where the cell doors had been bolted. Ben Harrison was wheezing with the effort.

275

'Come on!' shouted Harry.

Below, blood-curdling screams still echoed down the corridor from Pabst's office cell. Around them, the trapped Germans were hurling themselves against the cell doors. Soon their combined strength would break the rusty bolts. There were too many of them for the doors to hold.

Supporting Maitland and dragging Harrison, Harry reached the outer door.

'Leave me!' said Maitland.

Harry's pity turned to anger. He hit Maitland in the face with the back of his hand. 'Move, you bastard!' he shouted.

Spirit came into the ex-boxer's eyes and he actually grinned. 'Then open the door, sweetheart!' he hissed.

The three men stepped out into the pouring rain and darkness. How they made it to the top of the steps, Harry never knew. Lights came on in the houses near the prison as people began to peer out, to see the men clambering into a black and yellow car. Harry started up the engine and pulled away, his headlamps cutting into the night.

The car raced down to the harbour and screeched around the Boulevard Albert and along the Quai de Plaisance, where it slithered to a halt on the wet stone. Harry shouted up to the deck of the *Maracaibo*. Several American sailors in oilskins ran down the gangway. It was difficult to get Maitland out of the car, so Harry unclipped the hood and pulled it down. The sailors lifted him gently and carried him on board.

Ben sprawled in the back seat.

'Wait!' shouted Harry. He ran up the gangway onto the stern and strode through the main rooms. The *Maracaibo*'s engines had been started and he could feel rumbling throughout the ship. Harry watched Maitland as he was laid carefully on a divan in the saloon. The man's head had begun to loll and one of the sailors placed a pillow under it. Harry looked around and saw Alex beside him. She buried herself in his rain-soaked trenchcoat. He kissed her hair then lifted her face.

'Oh Harry,' she said. She stared at the limp body sprawled on the divan. 'What's happened?'

'Maitland's been shot badly.'

'Doctor Solomon is below with Bradford . . .' she began.

'Then get him up here fast,' said Harry. He could see Lisa coming towards them, her eyes wide.

'You're hurt,' said Alex, seeing blood on his cheek where the bullet had gouged into his flesh. He wiped it quickly and shook his head, then Lisa was standing before him. He picked her up in one movement and spun her around, blocking her view of the wounded man.

'It's all right, Lisa,' he said. 'We're going to be all right.' Alex was frozen at the sight of the blood all over Maitland's chest. Harry gave Lisa to her.

'Take her out,' he said urgently. 'Be ready to leave in five minutes and get Solomon now!'

'But Harry . . .' began Alex. He interrupted,

'If Wilson ever gets to Morocco he'll be lucky. The Vichy French are Germany's allies and America is no longer neutral. Even if the *Maracaibo* arrives . . .'

'Harry,' interrupted Alex, 'Bradford says . . .'

Harry stopped her. 'The plane's a risk, I know, but it's a fact not a gamble.' He touched Alex's cheek. 'Five minutes!' he repeated, and turned to make his way out of the saloon. He stopped beside Howard Maitland. The man opened his eyes and Harry forced a reassuring smile.

'Fools rush in, eh, Pilikian?' he whispered, holding up a hand. Harry shook it.

'Thank you,' he said.

Maitland winced with pain, then grinned.

When Harry ran down the gangway, there were sailors on deck, all armed with rifles.

'Five minutes, Henry!' he shouted. The sailor nodded.

Harry jumped into the car. 'You all right, Ben?' he yelled.

'Just drive!' said the Englishman sprawled in the rear. He had pulled a blanket over him against the rain. Harry started up, drove back along the quay then turned sharp right up the Avenue de Monte Carlo, leading directly to the Casino Square and the entrance of the Hotel de Paris. Michel, holding an umbrella, was astonished as Harry leapt out and seized his hand.

'Turn the Rolls round!' he ordered, then ran up the steps into the crowded lobby.

Sullivan, a coat about his shoulders and dressed for travel, was standing with a troupe of tall dancing girls in feathered plumes and stage makeup, holding furs and gabardines to their bodies.

'Pilikian!' exclaimed Sullivan.

'What's happening?' asked Harry.

'We're getting out, on the *Maracaibo*. It's war!'

'Then hurry!' shouted Harry. 'She's leaving now!'

Immediately there were screams from the girls.

'You're hurt!' exclaimed Sullivan.

Harry put a hand to his face where the blood was still wet. 'Go now!' he shouted.

Louis came to the entrance of the bar and saw his friend.

'Harry, what is it?'

'I came to say goodbye, Louis.' He was already running to the cashier's desk beside the Reception. 'Open it up!' he shouted. The cashier's mouth fell open as Harry sprang around the counter. 'I want my case!'

The cashier hesitated, and Harry pulled out his revolver. 'Open it up!'

277

'*Oui, M'sieur,* immediately!' said the cashier and spun the dial several times. The door swung open. Harry could hear shouts of alarm from behind as the cashier took out the attaché case containing Harry's manuscripts and removed the 'Pilikian' name tag.

'And the others!' said Harry. The cashier hesitated again but Harry prodded him with the muzzle of his gun. Immediately the cashier pulled out the two other attaché cases, one full of diamonds brought to the Principality, and labelled 'Van der Voors', the other containing the list of names from Geneva which had belonged to de Salis, its tag hanging from the handle.

'Harry!' shouted Louis. 'What are you doing?'

Harry paused, staring at the two cases. 'Only room for one, Louis.' He took off one of the labels and tied it to his own manuscript case. 'Merci,' he said to the cashier, seizing one of the three cases. 'Take care of the others!' Harry stepped back around the counter.

'But, M'sieur . . .!' began the cashier, 'that does not belong to you!' Harry was already striding across the lobby.

Sullivan and the chorus girls from the Cabaret had gone from the entrance as Harry plunged through the revolving doors, down the steps to the waiting car. Michel was trying to secure the hood of the Rolls Royce, but the catches would not fasten. Harry threw the attaché case into the rear seat beside Ben Harrison, engaged the gear lever, and the car began to move away.

Louis burst out of the revolving doors, followed by some of the hotel staff and Robert Cornwallis.

'Harry!' he shouted.

'We'll be back after the war!' Harry waved once and was on his way.

Ben, slumped in the rear, stared at the attaché case as the open Rolls turned fast at the bottom of the Avenue de Monte Carlo.

'What's in the case?' he asked.

Harry glanced at him. 'Jews' names, at a guess,' he said. The car raced along the quay and braked beside the *Maracaibo*. 'Are you all right?' Harry asked Ben Harrison.

'The hell I am,' he answered. 'Just let's get out of here!'

'We're going,' said Harry. He left the car ticking over and ran to the gangway of the motor yacht.

Chapter 38

The stern of the ship was crowded with refugees from the Principality. Sullivan and the chorus girls had just been taken aboard. Sailors had begun to let go the moorings and there amidst the confusion, dressed and ready, sheltering from the pouring rain under an awning, were Alex and Lisa. Harry held out a hand. Alex picked up her daughter and ran towards him. Lisa turned her head over her mother's shoulder.

'Scottie,' she said. 'I want Scottie!' Harry seized Alex's hand and took them down the gangway. 'I want Scottie!' shouted Lisa again. Alex put her down beside the car as Harry opened the door for them to get in.

'Oh Harry, this is crazy,' she said.

Harry kissed her. 'We'll do it.' His eyes were on a car which was making its way fast along the Quai de Plaisance. 'Quickly now!' he said.

The Citroën turned onto the harbour breakwater and stopped beside the Rolls Royce. The chief of police and several of his men stepped out and stared at Harry. Gerard snapped his fingers. 'Take Mademoiselle aboard!' he said. From the back of the Citroën, two policemen helped Maggie Lawrence to her feet.

Gerard answered Harry's questioning look: 'Miss Trenchard confirmed certain information about de Salis and his connections.' He paused. 'After all, Miss Lawrence is an American citizen in – what is the word you use – jeopardy?' He took a step towards Harry and noticed the wound on his cheek. Then Gerard saw Ben Harrison lying in the back of the car. He shook his head. 'I won't ask how,' he murmured, 'but don't miss that plane, Harry.' His voice contained a warning but he held out a hand. 'Go now.'

Harry smiled as the rain poured from the brim of his hat, 'I'm glad you got off the fence.' The two men shook hands.

'Go!' shouted Gerard.

Harry jumped into the car, next to Alex, and Lisa clambered into the back with Ben Harrison. The car began to move forward, then Harry accelerated along the Quai de Plaisance towards the Boulevard Albert and the Rue du Port – the way out.

Everyone on the quay and aboard the *Maracaibo* could hear her great engines churning in the harbour, but above them came the sound of barking. Scottie was at the head of the gangway on the stern of the ship. Lisa turned her head and began to wave wildly. The dog jumped on to the quay a moment before the gangway was pulled aboard the *Maracaibo* and the last moorings let go.

Harry was driving from the quay, turning on to the road at the back of La Condamine, when he saw the twin headlights of what looked like the black Mercedes racing down from the Avenue de la Porte Neuve to the harbour. The Germans had finally broken out of the prison, been delayed by the ripped tyres and were now trying to cut off his escape. Harry spun the wheel sharply to his right towards the Rue Antoinette. His rear-view mirror was blocked by Lisa, who was leaning out and shouting.

'Get her down!' said Harry urgently to Alex.

'It's Scottie!' shouted Lisa, and there, perhaps two hundred yards behind, running along the quay towards them, was Lisa's dog.

'Stop, stop!' Lisa shouted to Harry.

He glanced over his shoulder. 'Get her down!' he bellowed again, and stepped on the accelerator. Alex screamed as she saw a lorry directly in front, pulling slowly across the narrow street. With a shout of alarm Harry turned the wheel hard over, pressing his foot flat on the brakes. The car slewed to a stop. Immediately the little girl jumped out.

'Lisa!' screamed Alex. She was running towards her dog, shouting: 'Scottie, Scottie!'

Harry swore, fumbling with the gears to find reverse and back up fast. Ben swung himself over the side of the Rolls and began stumbling after the little girl.

'Lisa! Come back!' he shouted. The dog bounded towards Lisa but Ben had reached her. Ignoring the pain of his damaged hands, he lifted her up in his arms exactly as the Gestapo Mercedes rounded the corner in front of them.

'Oh my God!' said Harry to himself. Ben was twenty yards behind the Rolls, Lisa clasped to him, the dog jumping around his feet. In the German headlights he was a perfect target. Several shots rang out. Ben staggered and Alex screamed. Harry raised himself in his seat, turned around and fired just above the beams of light where he knew the driver would be. Another shot came from the Mercedes as Harry aimed again. Ben fell against the Rolls, hoisting Lisa into the back seat.

'Get in!' said Harry. He fired twice more at the Mercedes, which immediately reversed round the corner, out of sight as Ben hauled himself into the car, then Scottie leaped in. Harry slammed the gears into first, drove onto the pavement and threaded the narrow space behind the lorry. He changed up quickly and the car roared away westwards.

In the wheelhouse of the *Maracaibo*, the captain ordered a searchlight to be pointed directly at the port beacon at the mouth of La Condamine. He had brought the yacht round and was waiting for the boom to be opened.

Bradford Arnett Wilson had insisted on being transferred to his wheelchair and taken up to join the officer on the bridge. He was wrapped in blankets and the nurse fed him oxygen from the cylinder beneath the wheelchair. They had just come from the saloon, where Doctor Solomon, despite volatile protestations that he was being kidnapped, continued to treat the wounds of the now unconscious Howard Maitland.

'Consider it piracy for which you will be well paid,' Wilson had said. Now on the bridge, Bradford Arnett Wilson glanced at the green glow of the ship's clock, set amidst the mahogany fascia framing the instruments. It was several minutes before 11.

'Why aren't we moving?' he snapped.

'They refuse to release the boom, sir,' replied the captain.

'We have a steel hull, have we not?'

'Yes sir,' the captain began, 'but . . .'

'And the keel provides protection for the propellers and rudder?'

'Yes sir.'

'Then ram the damned thing at the centre where it's weakest!' said Wilson.

'Sir, I don't advise it!'

'I'll take responsibility!' snapped Wilson. The excitement caused his pulse to race and his breathing to labour.

'Is that an order, sir?'

'Yes, Captain, it is. Full ahead!'

'Full ahead both,' ordered the captain and the *Maracaibo* surged forward.

The power behind the weight of her steel hull immediately lifted the bow across the boom, then the steel hawsers, pushed below the surface, dragged their way towards the stern. In seconds the *Maracaibo* had successfully cleared the harbour entrance and within minutes she had turned south, then southwest. Extinguishing all her exterior lights, and running on instruments alone, the American motor yacht *Maracaibo* set out from southern Europe into the rain and darkness, her course set for the night, bound for the Pillars of Hercules.

Two huge Italian locomotives, smoking and steaming, pulled a long, heavily guarded ammunition train through Monte Carlo's Casino station. As instructed, the train was brought to a halt beyond some points, which were immediately changed. The two cattle wagons were shunted quickly onto the main line and their couplings secured to a third locomotive which was pushing the train from behind. Those who witnessed the event heard wailing and shouting from the wagons.

Once the human cargo had been attached, a signal was given by an Italian army officer temporarily in charge of the station. Slowly, the three locomotives began to move their load, gathering momentum towards the west. Everyone on the train was aware that they carried dangerous cargo, and the nervousness of the engineers was reflected in the speed which they forced from the great boilers. Pistons ground wheels against the steel rails, faster and faster. Speed was their best defence against potential enemies.

All along the Riviera, the line had been cleared for this shipment. The train carried blood for Rommel's arteries. Without these armaments the winter campaign of the Afrika Korps would be crippled.

As the last locomotive, pulling the two cattle wagons, crossed the limits of the Principality, heading for Marseilles, only a single red light could be seen disappearing into the wet night.

Rain lashed at the Rolls Royce as Harry took the familiar coast road, fighting to keep his car from skidding on the corners. They had passed on to the Basse Corniche directly through the border posts, which were kept open to allow access only to vehicles bound for the small airport outside Nice. This was the agreed exit for American nationals, which was why the Stars and Stripes flag was once again prominently displayed on Harry's windscreen.

When a first, then a second Mercedes, following several minutes behind, passed through the same border post from Monaco to Vichy France, the authorities were alarmed. The cars belonged to the Gestapo and the leading Mercedes had several bullet holes splintering its windows.

Erich Held and the others who had broken out of the upper cells of the prison were in hot pursuit. It had taken some time to change the tyres on the big Mercedes, which proved to be sluggish on corners. The most frustrating thing for the Gestapo men was that they could see the lights of the Rolls Royce far ahead, carving a path at the base of the sheer cliffs which soared into the night. Every turn revealed to the Nazis that their quarry was slightly further away.

Next to the Mercedes was the long snaking train, roaring along beside the road, lost as it entered a tunnel, then found again as it emerged, stoked fires glowing at the locomotives' footplates, sparks carried high into the darkness. The Mercedes slewed round every bend, at maximum speed – but it was not fast enough. After several miles, the train passed the Gestapo car, then in the long curving bay beyond Cap Estel it began to gain on the Rolls Royce. Just before Beaulieu the locomotives were parallel with the road, running neck and neck with them.

Harry could see the lights of the Mercedes in his mirror and knew that their pursuers were not far behind. He was using full headlights on the Rolls, despite the wartime restrictions. Speed was vital.

'I'd say it's the train we heard about,' Ben shouted above the wind. Squinting into the driving rain, he caught Harry's eyes in the mirror. 'And I'll lay odds that the Resistance want to blow it up!'

'Terrific!' said Harry.

In spite of her thick coat, Alex was shivering. Harry glanced quickly at her and grinned encouragement.

'Will it help if I apologize?'

'For what?' retorted Alex, wiping her wet face.

'I don't know. If it's important to you, for everything.'

'We're going home, and we're together again,' shouted Alex. 'That's all that matters!'

Harry attempted a smile. 'I've not much to offer you.'

'What did you ever?' shouted Alex. 'A dirty raincoat and a four-day beard.'

'I'm a responsibility,' he said.

'I accept it.'

'Louder!'

'I accept!' she yelled.

Harry accelerated on the straight. 'You'll marry me?' he shouted.

'Why not?' replied Alex.

'Because every other guy's called Harry,' he said, 'but who wants to be called Pilikian?'

'I do,' Alex said.

Beside them the train curved away into the town as the Rolls descended the long hill to Nice harbour. Harry quickly dimmed his lights then turned sharply to drive beside the quay. They saw the barrier across the road just in time. The car stopped and Vichy French police surrounded them, demanding their papers.

'We are citizens of America, booked on the military plane at the airport,' said Harry, first in English, then in French. Shining torches into the car, with their submachine guns slung carelessly, the Vichy police in their small peaked caps and black oilskins looked dangerously alert. Harry was desperate, knowing that the Gestapo Mercedes was approaching fast. He pointed to the American flag on the windscreen. The Frenchmen were surprised that the car was open on such a wet night, so Harry explained that the hood was stuck. The Vichy police laughed, ridiculing the English Rolls Royce, lifted the barrier and waved the car through.

When they reached the long straight Promenade des Anglais, Harry accelerated but could now see the lights of the first Mercedes behind them. As the Negresco Hotel flashed by on his right, Harry glanced in his mirror and noticed Ben's head beginning to loll back.

'Are you OK Ben, answer me!' he shouted.

The Englishman opened his eyes. 'I'm fine,' he mouthed.

Lisa poked her head from beneath the blanket and immediately her face became wet. She reached up to wipe away the rain, letting go of Ben, and saw that her hands were covered in blood.

'He's hurt!' she wailed. 'Mr Harrison's hurt!'

'Ben!' shouted Harry.

'I said I'm fine, Pilikian, just get there!' Alex leaned back towards the Englishman but he waved her away. 'I'll be all right!' he said, but Lisa began to cry. 'Shush, little girl,' said Ben and began coughing again. Blood trickled from his mouth. Seeing the anguish in Alex's face, he tried to smile it away, but tears came into her eyes.

The distant headlights of the Mercedes behind them lit up the long straight road. Harry glanced at his watch. It was ten minutes to midnight. He looked at the fuel gauge and saw that the tank was almost empty. There was no time for mistakes.

Suddenly to their right once again were the huge twin locomotives, travelling as fast as the car, and for two miles they raced side by side. Harry could clearly see firemen shovelling coal into the furnaces; sparks flew and smoke streamed the length of the train. It lasted less than two minutes, but the enveloping roar created a nightmare. Then the locomotives began to curve away inland, where the train would travel beyond Cannes, and into the hill country past Fréjus, on its way to Marseilles.

Harry spotted the first signs to the small airport and braked hard, skidded, then turned sharply through an open gate towards the first barrier. Ahead was a collection of small buildings, but on the runway, with an American star painted on its fuselage, was the Douglas Dakota, their passport out of occupied Europe. As the car slowed, the French authorities stepped forward.

'C'est trop tard, Monsieur,' said a long-faced French policeman. 'Ce n'est pas possible.' He waved a submachine gun. 'Not possible,' he said in English. 'Too late.'

Harry turned to Ben Harrison, only half conscious of Lisa trying to wipe blood from his mouth with the sleeve of her dress. From the runway, Harry heard first one, then the second engine of the aeroplane start up.

'I have the papers,' said Harry urgently. 'We're American, and we're leaving.' The Frenchman shook his head, but looking into the car he noticed a little girl with big eyes staring at him. 'Please,' pleaded Lisa. For a moment there was compassion in his heart. He shrugged. 'Bonne chance, Monsieur!' he said, and gave orders for the barrier to be raised.

Harry drove a hundred yards to the Customs office but a wide metal gate blocked his access to the grass and tarmac strip. Through the rain on the windows of the building, Harry could see the Customs men waving their arms and shaking their heads at the car.

There was a screeching sound behind as the first Mercedes turned off the main road, its powerful headlights illuminating them like trapped prey. Harry gritted his teeth, gunned the engine and whispered: 'Come on, old girl!' At first the wheels would not grip on the wet road and spun wildly, then the yellow and black Rolls Royce seemed to leap at the gate, smashing through, swinging it wide open. Alex and Lisa screamed, Scottie began barking uncontrollably and Ben was flung backwards, groaning. Harry skidded in a semicircle and drove flat-out towards the Dakota. The passenger door was still open, but the steps were being pulled up from inside. He flashed his headlights.

'Hold on!' he shouted, and braked hard. Someone who had stepped from the two-storey control tower fired a Very pistol into the night. The flare exploded high in the air, casting an eerie red glow over the whole airfield. Then a searchlight was switched on, cutting a path through the night rain, holding the American plane in its beam.

'Out, out!' commanded Harry.

Alex was already pulling Lisa away from Ben, sprawled in the car. 'He's hurt, Mummy, he's hurt!' she was crying.

Scottie needed no urging and jumped out at once. Harry leaned into the back and picked up the black attaché case once owned by Guy de Salis. It was full of deposit box numbers and the names of Jewish owners which the Swiss banker had collected for the Gestapo.

He thrust the case at Alex. 'Go!' he said, pointing to the plane. 'Go!'

She hesitated. 'Harry . . .' she began, tears welling in her eyes.

'Run, damn you woman! Run!' he shouted.

Alex seized Lisa's hand and they started running.

'Daddy, daddy, he's hurt, he's hurt!' cried Lisa, trying to twist her head back to see Ben.

Behind the control tower Harry saw the Mercedes headlights swinging round, then lost them for a moment behind the buildings.

'Come on, old man,' he said. 'Let's go!'

Ben shook his head, 'I can't,' he said and coughed blood.

Harry took Ben's head in his hands, staring into his eyes.

'It's only a hundred yards. I'll carry you!'

'I can't move,' Ben hissed, in pain.

'You must!' pleaded Harry.

Ben's head lolled back and there was a sad smile on his face.

'Do you think she's still alive somewhere, Harry?'

'Who?'

'Agatha,' whispered Ben. 'I like to think so . . .'

285

Harry tried to speak, but his voice broke. Ben's expression contorted with pain. 'Get out, Harry. Go!'

Harry glanced towards the airport buildings, where the Mercedes headlights had reappeared, turning through the broken gate. Pity became anger.

'Goddamn you!' he exploded, and seizing Ben Harrison, he pulled him bodily from the car. The Englishman groaned in agony, but Harry ignored him. He could see Alex and Lisa climbing into the American plane and a man silhouetted in the doorway by the steps and shouting at him.

He bent beneath Ben's chest and lifted him onto his shoulders.

'No, Harry!' coughed the Englishman. 'No. Save yourself.' But the Armenian-American was already running. Despite Ben's weight, fear gave him strength.

They were fifty yards from the plane when the first Mercedes came to a halt beside the Rolls, spewing out Gestapo men. In the forefront was Erich Held, who immediately began to run round the English car to get a clear shot.

Forty yards, thirty, twenty. Harry and Ben were almost there. The searchlight from the control tower picked them out clearly. The American voice in the Dakota's open doorway came to Harry clearly even above the bellowing engines of the plane. He forced his head up. Five paces to freedom.

Beside the English car, Erich Held knelt down quickly, unslung his Schmeisser machine pistol and levelled the barrel to aim. He squinted against the rain to make out the man called Pilikian bundling the Englishman's body into the open doorway of the plane. His target was reaching up to willing hands when Erich Held, a Gestapo officer of the Third Reich, now at war with the United States, pulled the trigger to fire a three-second burst of 9 mm bullets. His aim was perfect. The bullets ripped up the tarmac exactly where Harry had stood a second before.

Everyone in that small airport of Nice saw the passenger door slammed shut, heard the aircraft engines roar to maximum pitch, and, as the searchlight followed, watched that last American plane become airborne into the night.

Just beyond La Napoule, emergency charges on the railway line were set off to stop the ammunition train. Several miles further on, red lights flashed and the locomotives came to a halt. The Italian military and Vichy French guards immediately protested loudly at the dangerous delay, and one minute later the train started up again, on its final run to Marseilles.

In the hill country, three tunnels before the junction at Fréjus, the French Resistance detonated the carefully laid British cyclonite. The explosion could be heard for miles around, even by the one hundred and ninety-seven Jews who were at that very moment being taken down from the cattle trucks the Resistance had disconnected from the train fifteen minutes earlier.

In the darkness high above the Côte d'Azur, as the pilot circled beneath the clouds to swing on to his westward bearing, everyone on board the American plane had a spectacular view of the massive explosion, its smoke lit from beneath, glowing orange as more and more ammunition ignited. But to the passengers there was only the deafening noise of the twin Pratt and Whitney engines that were carrying them towards Lisbon.

Harry Pilikian looked away from Ben Harrison, who lay in the narrow aisle being tended by an American doctor and a nurse from Nice hospital, to see the wet but shining face of his daughter Lisa, as she peered in wonder through the window of the plane. Then he saw the lips of her mother – his wife to be – his Alex, as she leaned towards him. He closed his eyes gratefully, and as he felt her kiss, he realized that now, after all, perhaps they'd made it.

If fate has a face, it must smile often. If fate has a voice, it would say:
'You might get lucky if you're careful.'